Finding

Persephone

Copyright © 2022 PJ Braley

Cover Design by Cherie Fox

Liminal Books
Between the Lines Publishing
1769 Lexington Ave North #286
Roseville MN 55113
btwnthelines.com

First Published: June 2022

Liminal Books is an imprint of Between the Lines Publishing.
The Liminal Books name and logo are trademarks of Between the Lines Publishing.

ISBN: (paperback) 978-1-950502-73-8
ISBN: (eBook) 978-1-950502-74-5

Finding Persephone

PJ Braley

Finding
Persephone

Assignment: GatesWay

It was Timaeus's proposal of having the women come to them that the Lyostian collective found so remarkable. Not only would the clinics attract a large selection of women, but their continuing presence would be ensured through the honey produced in caverns throughout the world. Once only psychologically addictive, his recommendation of adding certain chemicals to make it physically addictive would be put into action before he boarded the plane for Boston.

Sitting alone at the table in the Sidereal Chamber, located in the fifth room of the fifth tunnel on the fifth level of the underground Lyostian colony in Casablanca, Timaeus felt his heart race as the sandstone walls dissolved, and he was once again suspended in an ancient universe. Folding his hands over the large envelope, he composed himself and waited for the voice of the elders to fill his mind.

Timaeus.

Yes.

You have your travel plans?

I do.

Before you leave, we would like to review the details of your North American assignment for the archives.

Of course.

From the beginning.

As he opened the envelope labeled NAFTRAM: *New Agenda for the Retribution Against Mankind,* several sets of documents and drawings spilled onto the table. Lifting them one by one so he could mentally transmit their contents, he scanned them in meticulous detail.

His eyes recorded sketches of building plans, marketing designs, and the rules by which every colony in the North American Sectors would be governed. He created backstories for the resident brothers and prepared confrontation scenarios and client discussion scripts to minimize possible exposure through unexpected inquiries. To provide the broadest base for testing the hybrid serum, he included a list of certain criteria for their preferred clientele.

When he finished scanning the documents, he returned them to the envelope. The starscape did not change, and he knew the collective was not finished with him. He closed his eyes and waited.

An undertaking such as this will require that you be within a ten-hour traveling distance from any North American colony for disciplinary purposes. Therefore, we are assigning you to the Midwestern sector for our initial four-year mission. Your assignment is our primary settlement in North America to be known as NAS-M1: GatesWay.

I appreciate this opportunity to be a small part of the collective's success.

Yes. And we thank you for your diligence…Grant Gates.

He raised his head from the documents and stared into the cosmos around him.

Grant Gates?

Yes. As a reward for your innovative planning initiatives and invaluable assistance to the collective in meeting its preliminary goals, we have decided not to contradict the assumption that all the fire slayers of the last Tuzurias generation have been destroyed. You may leave your post in Casablanca and go to North America as our representative with your assigned identity as your archive name.

Grant reached his arms to the ends of the table and grabbed the edges with all his strength. The Fire Slayer Timaeus Tuzurias—hated, despised, and feared—was dead. His nefarious past as an assassin and the hell of the last five years of his life were forever buried in the desert sand. Touching his forehead to the hard surface in gratitude and relief, he humbly promised to serve the governing hierarchy and protect the secrets of the Lyostian collective with his life.

Just as they knew he would.

Grant Gates

Grant stood lookout on the embankment above the river. Cresting high because of the early spring rains, he was confident no one would find the car or the girl for months. By that time, he estimated, the remnants of the embroidered logo of her flight attendant uniform would be the only clue to her identity.

To rest his eyes from the continual glare of headlights on the road, he looked down at the car perched on the edge of the river. The driver's door was propped open, and all the windows were rolled down. After calculating the angle of the bank and the depth of the river, he glanced up at the starless sky. *It will storm soon*, he thought, nodding in satisfaction. The rain would wash away the tire tracks as well as any bits or pieces that might be overlooked after they buckled what remained of her body in the front seat and drove the car deep into the water.

It wasn't the way he wanted to begin his work in North America, but it had been a long flight, and his brothers were hungry. The sounds of their feast drifted up to him as he tracked the cars speeding toward Boston. Standing too high for casual observance, he was almost invisible in the darkness. Rubbing more mud onto his glasses to shade his eyes against the flashing lights, Grant mentally prepared for his first meeting with the members of his new colony.

It kept his mind off the fact that he was hungry, too, but he would not join them.

Removing the muddied black leather gloves, he glanced down at his hands and remembered the fleeting look of surprise on the young woman's face when he snapped her neck. She thought he was going to kiss her.

It was impossible for her to know that the handsome doctor who so kindly insisted that he walk her to her car had never kissed anyone.

Shoving the gloves into the pocket of his coat, Grant lifted his head and stared at the road.

First Impressions

Beneath the tall glass building encased in a granite façade, six Lyostian brothers came together for the first time. Since arriving at NAS-M1, the Lyostians knew they resembled each other, but there were differences in dress, mannerisms, preferred spoken language, and other individual characteristics that set them apart. Sitting at the table in the underground conference room dressed in identical lab coats and wearing the same tinted eyeglasses, each thought he was looking into five different mirrors. Some reflections were slightly broader, taller, faces narrower, hair and skin a shade or two lighter or darker, but these distinctions were minor. No human would question their assertion of a sibling relationship.

Grant waited until everyone was seated before removing a small stationery box and five file folders from the case beside his chair. He opened the box and took out six business cards. Placing the top card upside down on the table, he passed the rest to his left.

Not yet ready to test their grasp of the English language, Grant utilized their powers of telepathy.

Please place the top card face down in front of you.

When they each had a card, Grant turned his over. Engraved below the embossed GatesWay logo was *Grant Gates, Ph.D., M.D.*

"Greetings, my brothers," he said in English. "My name is Dr. Grant Gates. Please introduce yourselves…and remember…these are our names for the duration of our assignment at this facility. Our *only* names."

Before Grant could turn to the brother on his left, the one across from him addressed him in Lyostian.

"Can we trade?"

Grant's eyes moved in the direction of the voice.

"Excuse me?" he answered in English.

"Can we trade? You know, if I like your name better than mine, can we trade? Or are we stuck with the card in front of us for the next, what? Three to four years?"

There was much to cover at this meeting, and Grant was not going to argue every point. Deciding to begin with a level of congeniality, he promised himself that if they made this meeting difficult for him, he would not suffer alone.

"As I am the collective's appointed representative, my name has already been recorded in our archives, so no, you may not have my name. However, I will give you one minute to turn the cards over, and if you do not like your name and someone wishes to trade, you will have that one minute to do so. One minute."

Grant leaned back into his chair and closed his eyes.

Everyone quickly turned his card over. Gabriel loved his name and hoped no one else wanted it; Grayson hated his, but no one would trade with him; Gregory, the one who raised the question of trading, was immensely satisfied, and immediately envisioned himself as Gregory Peck in *Roman Holiday* and the *Guns of Navarone*. For reasons they kept to themselves, only Garrett and Gordon exchanged names.

Exactly one minute later, Grant opened his eyes and looked at the names. He knew the card each brother received and was gratified that most kept the names they were given. Looking at his brothers, he said, "We will talk out loud and in English. If you are unsure of the correct word, we will help each other. We may transmit our thoughts in Lyostian, but we will always speak English."

He took a deep breath and repeated his carefully rehearsed introduction. "My name is Dr. Grant Gates. I have recently arrived from Boston, and I am pleased to meet all of you."

He looked at the brother on his left and smiled expectantly.

"Oh, my turn. Um."

Glancing quickly at the card, he said, "I am Dr. Gabriel…Gates. I have just arrived from Los Angeles, and I am happy to be here."

The introductions went around the table. Garrett had traveled from Vancouver; Gordon and Gregory, twins, had "blown in" from Chicago; Grayson, on Grant's right, was from Philadelphia.

Satisfied that they all spoke English quite well, Grant continued, "There is much work to do, and to assist us, six interns will be arriving in two weeks. Before then, however, we will establish a routine so their only function will be to support the colony's structure and objective. Because they will be completing their medical studies, they will have little direct input into the facility's operations. That is our responsibility, and those roles will be determined today."

Without giving them time to respond, Grant distributed the five files. "This is our backstory. You will not deviate from what is written here when speaking to clients or staff. A misspoken phrase can lead to questions that may result in the exposure of the colony." He looked at each one slowly. "I assume you know the penalty for any brother who puts the colony at risk, so I will not go into those details."

The room became quiet. Even the brothers' thoughts were silent as they contemplated the "details" Grant omitted. He knew their imaginations would fill in the blanks better than his words, but not nearly as well as his memories. He decided to spare them that misery…*for now.*

Taking the remaining cards from the box, he said, "In addition to our duties as client consultants, obstetricians, and medical researchers, each of us will have one or two additional responsibilities that are listed on these cards. I am the facility's director, systems designer, and architect. I will be available to meet with you as questions arise regarding your specific assignments. I hope it will not be too often."

Anticipating his question, he looked at Gregory. "You may have one minute to trade, but keep in mind that these responsibilities were assigned to you based on your expertise and experience."

This time, Grant did not close his eyes. Instead, he watched their expressions and scanned their thoughts. It was critical to discover who was dissatisfied with his position within the colony's structure.

Gabriel smiled; his assignment as human resources director and accountant was a good fit. Garrett was pleased as well; building security and manager of the physical plant of the facility was perfect for him, having assisted in that position at their North American Headquarters in Vancouver. Gordon looked up at Grant and nodded. As the facility's chief chemist, it was precisely what he would have chosen. When Gregory read that he was to supervise all underground excavations and assist Garrett with the utility systems, he looked at Gordon. Gordon laughed and shook his head. Grayson was momentarily vindicated with his assignment as their corporate representative. It only took a few minutes for it to occur to him that he would be responsible to the collective for any failures within the overall operations. Being little more than the colony's mechanic—charged with keeping the engine running while Grant steered—wasn't nearly good enough.

Grant noted the change in Grayson's mood and Gregory's disenchantment. "Once the facility is fully functional, there will be other assigned responsibilities, and remember, we will each have an intern to assist in these duties, so they should not be too arduous. Are there any questions?"

In a toneless voice that Grant was soon to despise, Grayson asked, "When do we choose the colony leader?"

Gregory looked from Grayson to Grant.

"You are not the colony leader?"

"No. I am the collective's appointed representative in this region and, as such, may be asked to temporarily relocate from time to time. Therefore, I may not be elected to lead any one colony." There were other reasons, of course, but this one would do. It was a matter of structure, actually; one could not be the judge, jury, *and* executioner.

"And, before you ask, Gregory, nor do I vote." Adding telepathically, *so do not waste your smiles on me.*

He paused for a moment and looked at Grayson. "One week from today. It will give us time to settle into our responsibilities and become more acquainted as we work together. Until then, as the facility's director and NAFTRAM's regional representative, I will assist you with any questions or difficulties you may encounter. Are there any additional questions before we proceed?"

"Just one. What's NAFTRAM?" asked Gregory.

"The official corporate name for our North American facilities," he said. "This information was included in the initial assignment order, which, apparently, you have not yet had an opportunity to read."

Garrett suspected there was something Grant was not telling them. When he tried to scan Grant's thoughts, he found that he could not, and this made Grant unique among his brothers in the colony. Also, he was too formal, and his English pronunciation was too perfect. Even if he'd just arrived from Boston, he hadn't been there long. Garrett did not sense any change in the mood of the room, so no one else felt it, but he knew instinctively that Grant was a force separate and apart from the other members of the colony, and he didn't want to be the first to disappoint him.

"I would like to ask a question, if I may?"

"Of course."

"As the facility's director, what are your expectations?"

Grant smiled slowly. "As unrealistic as it may sound, I expect perfection. I expect that until we introduce the unpredictable human element into our midst, the collective's goals will be met with as little delay and discord as possible. In fact, there are only a few things I will not tolerate, now or ever, and I want to thank you, Garrett, for bringing these issues up for discussion so there will be no misunderstandings later."

Garrett was instantly bombarded by unfriendly thoughts from his brothers. Before he could defend himself, Grant resumed talking, and Garrett, more than anyone else sitting at the table, felt it was important to pay attention.

"The facility and the tunnels will be clean. I don't mean swept. I mean washed, dried, and polished. Our prospective mothers must see this facility as a utopia they *want* to inhabit. It will be beautiful. There will be fresh flowers delivered every other day and the entire building will be cleaned every evening: no spots, no dust, no marks on the walls. The facility will look as new from the moment we open until the moment it lies in ruins. Therefore, for our duration at this facility, Garrett and Gabriel will work together to maintain that standard. We will hire a janitorial crew for the building, and the interns will be responsible for our living quarters in the tunnels.

"We will wear clean clothes every day: white shirts, dark slacks, ties, and lab coats. We are doctors. It is the expected uniform and will inspire trust. As our assistants, the interns will wear white knit shirts and tan slacks. Slovenliness on the part of *anyone* in the facility is a dismissible—or punishable—offense.

"Human women desire order and beauty, and we will present GatesWay in pristine condition as though they were discovering it for the first time every time they enter our building. The humans working for us will represent the goals we set for our clients: healthy and glowing."

He turned in Gabriel's direction.

"We must hire the very best who apply, and they must adhere to our rules. We cannot afford any mistakes or allow any legal investigation into our operations. Therefore, carelessness on anyone's part will be dealt with severely."

He looked back at the group. "There will be no dissension. We will work as one to make a success of our life together as we work to make a success of the facility. Rules will be made by all, agreed to by all, and obeyed by all for the benefit of the colony. This is not only my directive but the edict of the governing hierarchy of the collective.

"Finally, I expect perfection from each of you. I am not privy to where or how you have lived before, but you are here now and being given an opportunity to succeed at what you were created, educated, and trained to do. If I think you are not fulfilling your responsibilities to the utmost of your ability, I will want to know why. Specifically."

He looked down at the table and said softly, "I am not asking anything of you that I do not require of myself." Thinking to them, he added, *We are one.*

We are one, they echoed.

Even as their mental voices simultaneously repeated the words, Garrett was aware that two brothers believed Grant's expectations unreasonable, two were already planning to replace him, and he wasn't the only one who feared that Grant was not telling them everything. Expecting that level of cooperation and standard of efficiency was one thing, but getting and maintaining it was another. Looking at the resolute expression on Grant's face, Garrett wondered—not for the last time—whose *real* identity was concealed behind the unsophisticated and overly Americanized name of Grant Gates.

It was not long before everyone in the colony asked themselves and each other that question. Even Grayson, as he campaigned silently for the role of colony leader, and Gregory, who campaigned openly, marveled at Grant's quiet professionalism, his ability to get things done, and his absolute refusal to reconsider any of his expectations. Returning from individual meetings with him, each brother was impressed by the scope of Grant's knowledge. He seemed to have anticipated their concerns and questions by preparing workable solutions for them in advance. Only Garrett and Grayson noticed that he rarely smiled, seemed to go out of his way to avoid direct physical contact, and spent more time watching and listening than interacting when they were together in the dining room or watching the latest film Gregory procured—and only Garrett cared.

On the appointed day, Grayson was elected colony leader on the third vote. Grant was not surprised, but he was not happy. He had already calculated the obvious outcome, but he'd learned quite a bit about his brothers and preferred nearly anyone else. The time, however, was not wasted. During the week, he'd discovered and catalogued most of his brothers' flaws and weaknesses and devised several different ways to exploit Grayson's limitations.

His brothers had learned almost nothing about him.

When Grayson's election was approved and confirmed by the collective, he received permission to view the background of all the colony members. Although Grant's complete dossier was not made available to him, the collective allowed enough access into his past so that Grayson knew Grant could be counted on to enforce any punishments or other duties necessary to protect the safety and identity of the colony. It was made quite clear to Grayson that exposure was not an option and that Grant's skill in these matters should be kept confidential.

Whether deliberate or unintentional, Grayson did not keep his thoughts to himself, and the information gradually leaked out. His brothers did not know *who* Grant was; not even Grayson had that knowledge, but it was evident by the end of the first few months *what* Grant was before being assigned to their colony. Although he ate with them, slept with them, and was an integral part of the colony leadership and their lives, they could sense the hard edge that defined him.

Eventually, two of the interns had to be reprimanded for breaking the rules, and their tales of Grant's complete lack of hesitation, empathy, or mercy were recounted throughout the colony. Garrett was not the only one to discover that trying to read Grant's thoughts was like running into a brick wall. Whenever a brother tried to scan him, Grant calmly recalled the screams from the most recent punishment. Those were the only thoughts he allowed them to hear. By so harshly rejecting these first attempts, Grant made certain his brothers never scanned him again. Surrounded by brothers he could neither love nor trust, Grant knew most of them were only one punishment away from hating him.

He would have preferred a more lenient way, but as the finishing touches were put in place, it was imperative that the facility progress smoothly and efficiently under his direction. He could not afford any delays. GatesWay Fitness Clinic and Health Spa, scheduled to open three months in advance of the other facilities, was their corporate flagship. As concerns or difficulties developed, Grant modified the original design to resolve any issues prior to the collective's launch of their remaining one hundred and twenty-three facilities in North America.

With the wind at his back, the first phase of the Lyostian retribution had begun with Grant Gates—architect, physician, psychologist, and assassin—at the helm.

The Training Room

By staffing the NAFTRAM facilities based on the criteria Grant developed, the collective had to restructure many of their established colonies. As a result, friction developed as brothers who did not previously know each other competed for leadership positions within their new colonies. Not all of them were pleased with the outcome and tried to disrupt their facility's progress. Mutiny was a banishable, or worse, offense. Still, the Lyostians needed all their doctors, so the dissenting brothers were told they were being temporarily reassigned for additional training. If, after a lengthy training session with Grant, a brother was not fully persuaded as to the importance of total cooperation, he was prevented from returning to his colony.

Realizing Grant's time was too valuable to be spent traveling, the collective decided it was more efficient and less disruptive to send such miscreants to GatesWay for discipline. No doubt remained in anyone's mind as to Grant's true role as disobedient brothers began dropping out of the collective after their temporary relocation to the NAS-M1 colony. It was not long before the governing hierarchy realized that the mere threat of a "training" reassignment to Settlement-M1 was enough to ease any conflict within their North American facilities from Manhattan to Los Angeles and Vancouver to Miami.

Grant was relieved not to have to leave GatesWay. Remembering his reception as he moved from colony to colony during his first assignment, he did not miss the constant suspicion or unnecessary deaths instigated through fear. After GatesWay opened and the other facilities followed with their countless daily problems, he remained on-site in NAS-M1 for the duration of NAFTRAM's operations in North America as its first—and final—line of defense.

Grant did not disclose all his responsibilities as the collective's representative to Grayson or his brothers at their early meetings. Not wishing them to regard him primarily as a disciplinarian, it was his intention that they saw him first as a creative and resourceful colony member. However, the collective's decision to send the disobedient brothers to him changed all that.

Sooner than he expected, Grant had to give Gregory blueprints for a newly excavated room lined with steel plate. When Gregory went to Grayson for an explanation, Grayson went to Grant.

"Grant."

"Grayson."

"Gregory said you requested a room entirely lined in steel."

"Yes. Was there any part of that request Gregory did not understand?"

"Um, well, I guess he didn't understand why."

"As the director of this facility, must I give Gregory a reason for the requests I make of him?"

"No, of course not, but I would like one, Grant. That is, a reason for such an unusual request."

It was not going to be like this. He was not going to give Grayson an explanation—essentially asking his permission—every time he wanted something done.

"It will be so much easier to show you why the room is necessary, Grayson, than to tell you. I could just say that it is required to complete some work for the collective, but as colony leader, you *should* be included in the details. Could you please ask Gregory to proceed with my instructions as requested? Then, at the first opportunity, I will demonstrate its use. Thank you, Grayson, for bringing your concerns to my attention. In the future, I will be happy to relate to you all the details of these requests."

It was only after Grant walked away that Grayson realized he still didn't have a reason for Gregory, but as colony leader, he only needed to approve the request. He would tell Gregory…or not…as soon as he understood why Grant needed the room.

Once the excavation was completed to his specifications, Grant added a water cooler and bolted a table and two chairs to the floor. The room remained empty for the first several days. Then, one afternoon, Grayson was asked to bring his own chair into what Grant referred to as the new training room.

Training room?

Yes.

What kind of "training" requires a steel-lined room? I've already been to medical school, thank you.

As I mentioned when you first inquired, Grayson, it will be much simpler and less time-consuming to show you. So, please join us. We will wait for you.

Us, we?

Yes, Gerard from NAS-M34 has arrived.

Ah, our settlement in Atlanta, Georgia.

Seattle, Washington.

Oh, right.

We will wait for you.

Ever the politician, Grayson walked in with a chair from the conference room and a big smile for the visiting brother.

Not noticing the stern expression on Grant's face until after he closed the door, Grayson realized his hospitality might be misplaced.

"Gerard, this is Grayson, our colony leader."

"Really?" Gerard pivoted toward Grayson. "How did you manage that? Perhaps you can give me some pointers because I sure as hell need them. No one listens to a damn thing I say in that colony."

Bewildered at the vehemence of Gerard's verbal attack, Grayson looked at Grant.

"Gerard, we have discussed this. You were not elected the colony leader. You must listen and follow his direction. The same guidelines that are in place for your colony are in place for all the colonies—"

"Yes, but—"

"And, therefore, must be followed by everyone, including the colony leader."

"But they should have elected me! I was the leader in my last colony, and I don't even know who this brother is! My hierarchy is higher than his—"

"You do not know that absolutely."

"But I can feel it."

"Yes. Tell me, Gerard, can you feel this?"

Before Grayson could stop him, Grant climbed over the table, pulled Gerard out of the chair by his throat, and slammed his head against the steel wall.

Again, he asked, "Can you feel it?"

Gerard's hands covered his ears, and Grayson fell to his knees as the burning pain in Gerard's mind also echoed within his consciousness.

Grant saw Grayson fall and a tight feline smile crossed his face as he threw Gerard back into the chair. He went over and helped Grayson up.

"So sorry, Grayson, did you feel that, too?"

Grayson angrily pushed Grant's arm away. "What do you think? Is that why this room was built? To hurt our brothers? How can you possibly call that 'training?'"

"You may have a point. As English is somewhat new to me, perhaps training is not the proper term. Tell me, Grayson, what is the correct word when someone forgets who he is? Why would any of us stand in the way of the endeavor for which we were born? You are right. This is not a training room...it is a reminding room. Specifically built for reminding some brothers that if a Lyostian cannot cooperate with his colony to move our plans forward, we will move forward without him."

Grant turned toward Gerard.

"That is your only choice today, Gerard. You can either remember who you are and become an integral part of your current colony's success or…not."

"I prefer returning to my former colony."

Grant shook his head. "That is not part of your choice."

"Then what's my alternative? Because I will not work under that—"

Grayson backed slowly against the door as Gerard's tears, prayers, and promises turned to screams. It was only when he tried to slip out unnoticed that Grayson realized that there was no handle on the door. Unable to escape, he looked on with horrified eyes as Grant relentlessly pounded Gerard's skull against the metallic wall until it collapsed inward with a sickening thud.

Calmly brushing his hands together as he stepped over Gerard's limp body, Grant went to the water cooler, poured two cups of water, and handed one to Grayson.

"When you leave, please tell Gregory I will need a small burial room."

"I should think that everyone knows you will need a burial room!"

"No…no one knows yet, just you."

"I don't understand."

"The galvanized steel plate, Grayson, no one can hear beyond it. Gerard could scream all day and…no one…would…hear…him."

Grayson's heart beat like a drum in his chest. This wasn't a room; it was a torture chamber, and he was trapped in it alone—with Grant—and no one would hear him if he screamed.

"Yes. However, you asked for the reason, Grayson, and is this not simpler than explaining it to you? You may have missed my full meaning."

Grayson watched silently as Grant pulled a plastic sheet from a box in the corner and expertly wrapped Gerard's body. When he finished, he walked over to Grayson and pressed a hidden latch next to the door.

"Please also tell Gregory we will require a drain in here. Do I need to explain that, or any other request, Grayson?"

"No."

"Thank you."

Concerned it would get back to Grant, Grayson was disinclined to give anyone the details of his experience. Appreciating his reluctance, Grant established a routine wherein Grayson, without hesitation or further probing, would approve any of his requests to Gregory. Shortly afterward, a new brother would arrive for what Grayson referred to as an orientation visit. The brother would be gone a few days later, and the newly excavated room would either be empty or sealed.

The first time Gregory found it sealed, he thought it was a mistake and broke through the opening. Seeing the wrapped body of the latest arrival, Gregory backed out slowly and resealed the room. Leaving to find Grayson for an explanation, he ran into Grant.

"Gregory."

"Grant."

"Can I help you with something?"

"There is a brother's body in the new room."

"Yes."

"Do you know why?"

"Yes."

"Then why, Grant?"

"He asked too many questions."

"Oh."

At first, Gregory thought Grant was teasing and started to grin, but there was no answering humor on Grant's face, just a look of strained patience and studied indifference.

"Yes." Grant paused. "Do you have any more questions, Gregory?"

"Uh, no."

"Good."

Finding Grayson a few minutes later, Gregory posed the same questions to him. Grayson's response was one word.

"Grant."

"What? Why?"

"It is what he is."

Gregory grew quiet. He had heard of brothers whose sole purpose was to keep order within the collective. He knew Grant was not officially designated that position within their colony structure and now realized that any infraction would be addressed not by Grayson, but by Grant.

"You were elected colony leader."

"I know, but the collective assigned him to M1 for many different reasons. Discipline is only one of them."

"Why him?"

"He is the collective's regional representative and one of the most capable of his hierarchy."

"Which is...?"

"Like most of us, mid-range…nothing special, probably the higher end of his particular spectrum."

"What is his name?"

"Grant Gates."

"No, his name in the collective's archives."

"Gregory, I wouldn't tell anyone your or Gordon's names, and I certainly will not tell you anyone else's."

"Well," he laughed, "it was worth a try."

Wanting to change the subject, Grayson asked, "What's the movie tonight?"

Gregory was the film aficionado of the colony. He delighted in finding both obscure and popular movies and endlessly analyzing them.

"*Cyrano de Bergerac.*"

"Which one? Depardieu?"

"No, Steve Martin."

"Oh, *Roxanne*! Perfect. It's in English."

Gregory left laughing. He wasn't going to tell Grayson they were going to watch it with French subtitles.

Catching the edge of Gregory's thoughts, Grayson started to smile, but remembering the rest of their conversation, his smile faded. His unwillingness to reveal Grant's hierarchy was not to maintain any promise of confidentiality; he really didn't know. Reflecting on recent events,

Grayson wasn't sure he wanted to know. In a culture where worth was dictated by social structure, if Grant's level was much higher than his, it would make an already difficult relationship unbearable.

Show Time

Cinema and cable television were everything to the Lyostians in North America. Taking advantage of late twentieth-century entertainment technology, videocassette recorders and DVD players, together with large-screen televisions, were installed in every facility. Unable to venture beyond the range of their colony, movies and television shows were their primary resource as to how humans reacted in certain social situations. History had taught them that humans were unpredictable, and confronting—or even observing—them in person was too dangerous. The Lyostians had used popular books for hundreds of years to gauge human social expectations and motivations; however, they were always slightly behind the curve. The most current information, and their favorite medium for preparing for the onslaught of human women they would soon be encountering almost daily, was on screen.

Gregory, because he begged, was appointed movie critic. He took the designation seriously and only considered requests one night a week. Other than himself and Gordon, films were the only things Gregory loved, and he preferred movies to most of his brothers in the colony.

The colony's role in planning their eventual possession of the planet consumed nearly every moment of every day, requiring them to be in the building with lights that hurt their eyes. After a day of making constant small adjustments so the facility would run smoothly and spending hours talking with humans—both staff and clients—who were necessary to the success of their mission, the Lyostians yearned for nothing more than an evening spent in the quiet, peace, and shadowy darkness of their underground rooms. The only way most of them made it through each day, especially during the first hectic months of preparation, was by anticipating that night's movie experience.

To accommodate as many of their clients as possible, the Lyostians began the day before dawn. The double doors to the lobby were unlocked at six in the morning, six days a week, with exercise classes starting at six-thirty and running until seven in the evening. The administrative staff and salon professionals came in at eight-thirty and worked until five except for special events and holidays. Then the nightly cleaning crew arrived at exactly six forty-five and left promptly at eight forty-five. As soon as the last human exited the building, the interns bolted the doors and set the alarms. The facility was closed on Sundays but not out of any religious observance. On that day, the cleaning crew returned and shampooed each carpet, dusted and polished every surface, and reported any ripped or frayed fabric to Garrett for immediate replacement. As Grant demanded, every Monday morning the facility looked brand new.

Deliberately arranged so the building would be free of humans by nine each evening, Gregory's scheduled showtime was nine-thirty. At first, they watched movies in the conference room, but Gregory wanted something more authentic and was rather proud of the screening room he excavated. He had installed special speakers, inclined seating, and even ordered a popcorn machine to create the classic movie theatre ambiance knowing that none of them would, or could, eat the popcorn. To further create a professional mystique for their "cinematic experience," he imposed a restriction that excluded anyone not seated in the screening room by nine-thirty sharp.

It was a short-lived rule.

Arriving at nine thirty-five one evening, Garrett and Grant found the door locked.

Gregory.

Grant.

Unlock the door.

No, you are late. You will ruin it for everyone.

In keeping with that night's film, *High Noon*, Grant solved the problem by shooting the lock off the door with his pistol. After the door swung open, he and Garrett sat down, oblivious to the film's black and white images flickering on the stunned faces of their brothers. Unnerved by Grant's casual violence, being late didn't bother Gregory quite so much anymore.

The incident, however, bothered everyone. Grant was not the only brother with weapons training, but he was the only one with a gun at his fingertips—a reality none of them had experienced before. Immediately after the film, they brought their concerns to Grayson and left him, as colony leader, to confront Grant alone.

"Grant."

"Grayson."

"It wasn't necessary to ruin the door by shooting off the lock."

"I asked Howard to replace it. The door, not the lock."

"That is not the point."

"The point then, Grayson."

"There were other ways, better ways, I think, of handling that specific issue."

"Perhaps. However, one of our colony's rules states that no brother can exclude any other brother from attending a group meeting without cause. Five minutes late is not cause. Let us say it was my way of sparing Gregory any punishment for that particular infraction."

"Hmm, well, we don't need to use that kind of force, so I, ah, must ask you for the gun. I, um, will lock it up in the facility's safe."

"No."

Grayson was getting angry. He'd promised to take the gun away from Grant and was aware there was a small wager on whether or not he would succeed. There was also another, more personal reason he was determined to secure Grant's pistol. He was the colony leader and a brother with a weapon was a brother who could not be controlled and a direct affront to his leadership.

"Grant, as colony leader, I am afraid I must insist."

"What bothers my brothers—and you—most, Grayson? That I have a gun or that I am not afraid to use it?"

"That is irrelevant. If you don't have a gun, you can't use it…on door locks or anything else."

"Grayson, I did not purchase my weapon, nor was it issued to me at a former colony. The pistol I carry was delivered to me by the collective for use on its behalf. I cannot betray the trust of the collective and hand it over to you. Please remember that you and I have very different roles within the colony's structure. I am here to support your role and must ask that you do not seek to challenge mine."

Listening more to his tone than his actual words, it eventually dawned on Grayson that now would be a good time to cool down and compromise.

"I didn't know that, Grant. I, um, thought it might be something you picked up in, uh, Boston. I didn't realize the collective requires you to possess a weapon. So, of course, I will not ask you to relinquish it. Only that in the future, let's discuss rule infractions, rather than damage the colony's property to make a point."

"As you wish, Grayson."

"Um, yes. Thank you, Grant."

The brothers who bet on Grant demanded their money, but it was ultimately decided, in a gentlemen's agreement, to call it a draw. Only Grant and Grayson knew the truth.

Grant smiled when he heard the outcome of the bet. Surrendering his pistol to Grayson or anyone else was out of the question, but to protect the colony structure, he could not let Grayson lose face.

Grateful to Gregory for the opportunity to demonstrate that there were limits to his patience without having to hurt anyone, Grant was relieved not to have to carry his gun anymore. The next day he placed the gun and holster in the secret safe under the floor of his office. Now that they knew he had it and would use it, he didn't need it. His father's slender flashlight, however, was always in his pocket, and his mother's dagger never left his side.

Gregory's Girl

"You have to stop following me."

Jemma twirled around at the sound of irritation in Gregory's voice, but when she saw him smiling at her, a look of pure adoration shone from her pretty face.

"I can stop following you, but I can't stop my feelings, can you?"

Gregory looked at the young woman and thought how nice it would be to keep her. Jemma was petite with short blond hair and lovely blue eyes that sparkled whenever she saw him. Gregory thought she was the perfect foil to his tall, dark handsomeness, but he would have to be careful and not allow her infatuation to go too far. He knew the rules…*Grant's* rules…but she had just left her class and smelled divine, and he wondered how she would taste. He had been allowed to taste women at his former colony and remembered how intoxicating they could be.

Knowing that keeping her off balance was one way of directing her emotional response, he frowned at her.

"Yes, I can."

As if on cue, tears filled her eyes.

His glance traveled down her body, and he smiled as he whispered, "If I wanted to."

He backed her up against the wall. Leaning toward her, he heard Gordon coming out of his office and pulled back. *Soon,* he promised himself, *soon.*

Arranging a massage and meditation room for her a few days later, he found out exactly how she tasted. Jemma, however, lulled into a deep sleep by the massage was unaware of Gregory's mouth on her skin. Although he knew it was safer for him if she stayed asleep, Gregory was disappointed. Just once, he would like to hear a woman sigh his name, but she lay dreaming peacefully with a slight smile. Gregory was smiling, too, until he opened the door and found Grant leaning against the wall, arms crossed over his chest...waiting.

He called for Gordon, but Gordon wasn't fast enough. He was punished, of course. Clients and staff were more than off limits; they were untouchable, but he wanted more and redoubled his efforts to get her alone. Believing he had everything under control, Gregory continued to manipulate her emotions by teasing and flirting with her one day and then ignoring her the next time he saw her.

The worst morning of Gregory's life began like any other until five minutes past six when, bleary-eyed and disheveled, Jemma stormed into his office.

"You never leave the building," she accused.

"What?"

"You don't leave the building after work. I waited all night for you, but you didn't come out. What is going on? Do you live here or something?"

Alarm bells rang in Gregory's ears. How could he deny it? How much could he tell her? What if she wanted to see his room? This kind of confrontation wasn't covered in the backstory he'd only partially read. Not knowing what he was supposed to say, he telepathically screamed for Gordon.

A moment later, the door opened.

"Gregory, about these numbers..." Gordon said, walking in without knocking. Acting surprised to find Gregory with a client, he smiled at Jemma. Gordon lacked Gregory's boyish charm but not his talent for false sincerity.

"Good morning, Miss Barton. Lovely as always, I see, but maybe a little tired around the eyes. Shame on Gregory for making you get up so early for a consultation."

Quick to Gregory's defense, she smiled at Gordon and said, "Oh, he didn't—"

"No? Then you have an early class?"

"No, no class until four-thirty this afternoon."

"Well, I am sorry to interrupt, but I'm going to need my brother for more than just a few minutes." He turned toward Gregory. "Gregory, you're available to meet with Jemma after her class this evening, aren't you?"

"Ye…es."

"Well, that works out for everyone."

Walking Jemma to the door, Gordon added, "As I said, I'm sorry to interrupt, perhaps Gregory could arrange for a small supper for the two of you after your class. Would you like that?"

Jemma's smile brightened, and her eyes flashed at Gregory in anticipation.

"Seriously, Dr. Gregory?"

Speechless at this turn of events, Gregory could only smile and nod.

"Oh, Dr. Gordon, that, that would be great."

"Good. Will this evening around six be convenient? Here, in his office?"

"Absolutely," she said. Smiling broadly now, she blew a kiss to Gregory on her way out.

As soon as the door closed, Gregory glared at his brother. "Have you completely lost your mind? What am I supposed to do with her at six o'clock?"

"No, I haven't lost my mind, but apparently, you have lost yours. What were you thinking? I know what you've been up to, and I know why, and I hope you enjoyed directing this little romantic farce of yours, but there is a line we cannot cross, my brother, which you have defied, and it cannot be uncrossed…not for her."

"But why did you tell her to meet me here at six? Really, Gordon, supper? What is she supposed to eat?"

"What does that matter? She left, didn't she? And I am willing to bet she was smiling all the way out the front door. She didn't make a scene, didn't leave crying or accusing you of anything loud enough for the entire facility to hear, and that was what she was about two seconds away from doing."

"Is that what you think? She wouldn't have done that. I have this under control, Gordon. I can handle it."

"You can? Then whose voice was screaming in my head five minutes ago? You cannot handle someone who waits for you outside the building all night. That level of attachment is beyond your control."

"Can you do something?"

"I thought I just did. But, for what you mean, no. We have to talk to Grayson about this. Or Grant…you choose."

"Grayson."

Standing in front of Grayson's massive desk, Gregory tried to explain but faltered, and Gordon finished with his recital of the morning's events. He did not go into all Gregory had done to entice Jemma—only her confrontation. Any hope Gregory had of keeping this between the three of them ended when Grayson tilted his head.

Grant, will you please come to my office for a moment?

Busy, Grayson.

Yes, but we have a problem that requires your area of expertise.

Grant scanned the thoughts of his brothers in the building and found Gregory and Gordon in Grayson's office. Gregory's thoughts were a mad jumble, and Gordon's were angry. Wondering what Gregory had gotten them into this time, Grant was already walking out of the door when he responded, *On my way.*

Gordon was more than angry, he was furious. "You didn't have to call him!"

"Of course, I had to call him. How do you see this playing out, Gordon? Gregory cannot influence her. Any additional attention he gives her might be taken as encouragement. Even if he hands her over to one of us, she isn't going to go away, and we cannot risk her wanting to get more involved with him. What if she decides to sneak into the building and sets off the alarms?"

"We can discontinue her membership."

"Not without thirty days' notice, and if we discontinue her membership sooner than that, what's to keep her from suing us?"

"The fact that she would never win."

Grant's thoughts intruded into the room seconds before he entered. *Yes, but we cannot risk any legal investigation, no matter how spurious. This is far more serious than you realize.*

Entering the room, Grant pointed at Gregory. "You get me her file…and Gordon, look up her profile in the facility's records. Now. I'll wait here."

When they left the room, Grayson looked at Grant.

"What will you do?"

"Neutralize any danger to the colony."

"Does that include Gregory?"

"Are you asking me to neutralize Gregory? Unless it was intentional, I cannot do that without a direct request from the collective. It is within your discretion to inform them of his misconduct and request a final disposition."

"No. I prefer to keep this in-house and keep him alive. Of course, this matter will require disciplinary action."

"Yes."

"Not in the training room."

"If you insist."

"I do."

The slow smile that Grayson had learned to dread appeared for a moment on Grant's face. "I will take care of it, Grayson. Or rather, we will take care of it. I really see his punishment as a team effort."

Before Grayson could ask Grant what he had in mind, Gregory and Gordon entered the room. Walking in together, the first thing they noticed was the couch was upended, and Grant was sitting in the only other chair in the room. His eyes closed.

"Lock the door."

The deadbolt clicked into place.

"Now, Gregory, tell me everything from the first moment you saw her until she left this morning…and I mean everything. Gordon, when he is finished, I will talk to you."

Gregory was too terrified to lie. Afraid the last room he excavated would be his and Gordon's burial chamber, he told Grant everything. Through his tears, Gregory described the staged meetings, each practiced look, and the carefully manipulated dialogue in every scene of his romantic screenplay. Finally, he confessed how much he wanted her, how delicious she was, that he thought he could control her, and his surprise, fear, and confusion when she confronted him that morning.

"Gordon."

"Grant."

"What is he leaving out?"

"Nothing."

"Yes, I know. Now, what did you do this morning?"

Gordon telepathically sent Grant a replay of the morning's events.

"Anything else?"

"Yes, I invited her to meet Gregory for dinner at six o'clock this evening after her class."

Grant opened his eyes. "You did?"

"Yes."

"Did she accept?"

"Yes, with enthusiasm."

"What do we know about her family? Work? Friends? Who does she have that will come looking for her if something…unfortunate happens?"

Gregory sputtered, "What, what's going to happen to her? It's not her fault."

Grant stood and turned in his direction. Unable to escape the burning depths of Grant's eyes, Gregory knew what it was to look through the windows of hell.

"No, it is not her fault. It is yours. And you will pay as dearly as she will, just on a more metaphysical level. No one, Gregory, is allowed to put the colony in danger and go unpunished."

"Grant…" began Gordon. Grant turned his gaze to Gordon's angry face, and the room was immediately silent.

"Do not tell me, Gordon, that you were unaware of what your brother has been doing. You knew his actions could endanger the colony, yet you did nothing. However, your fast thinking this morning not only alleviated a potentially disastrous scene but set up a rendezvous in which she is a willing participant. You have saved me much trouble, and for that, and that alone, Gordon, I am prepared to forgive your lack of judgment."

Experience had taught Gordon that he could not help Gregory if he was being punished as well. "Thank you, Grant. How can I help you now?"

"You have looked at her computer records, and Gregory has looked at her file. What are her connections?"

"She's a junior at SLU. Usual roommates but no close friends here at the facility, and her parents live in Virginia. To accommodate her schedule, we have arranged her fitness classes around her part-time job at the mall."

"Does she move her car when she comes here from the mall?"

"Based on Andrea's notes, sometimes she walks here for the exercise, and sometimes she drives; it depends on the weather."

"And today the weather is…."

"Clear and cool."

"Excellent. Are there any nice restaurants near the mall, Gregory?"

"Yes."

"Supposing you ate restaurant food, and you were actually taking her out this evening, which one would you choose?"

"Café Remington, they're supposed to have the best— "

"Do not tell me. Tell Monique to order it and have it delivered at, say, twenty minutes past five. We want her to be comfortable."

"Grant, please—"

"Don't start, Gregory. Just tell Monique what to order. And bring it to my office at exactly five twenty-five. Do not make me look for you. It is my…goal, shall we say, for you to come out of this incident unbruised, but accidents happen."

"Grant, I just want to say I'm sorry. It wasn't supposed to be like this."

"Of course not, but rules are made for the benefit and protection of the colony. You have broken them before—and been punished for it. The rules have not changed, Gregory, but neither have you. Perhaps you will learn something this time."

"Grant, please…don't—"

"This discussion is over. Call Monique, Gregory. I will see you at five twenty-five. Do not be late."

Leaving Jemma's file on Grayson's desk, Gregory followed Gordon out of the office.

Grayson, who watched the entire exchange without interrupting, stared at Grant and silently wondered how he could harness that force for himself. He no longer wondered if Grant's hierarchy was higher than his; his main concern was how much higher. As the colony leader, he had the allegiance of the other four brothers as well as the six interns, but seeing what Gregory saw when he looked into Grant's face, Grayson felt he was a battalion short.

"Grant?"

"Grayson."

"Anything I can do?"

"Why yes. I would like to invite you and my brothers to join us this evening at twenty minutes past six."

"Where?"

"The dance studio on the sixth floor."

"That's all?"

"Yes. Oh, come hungry."

"Grant, we aren't going to eat anything Gregory orders."

"I know."

Jemma was late for class. She had intended to drive over, but her tire was flat. There was no time to call anyone about it, and she had to practically run to GatesWay. She planned to phone one of her roommates to pick her up as soon as dinner was over, but if everything went as she hoped, perhaps that wouldn't be necessary. Maybe Gregory would fix the tire—or better yet—take her home in his car.

For the hour she did stretches and lunges, she thought about Gregory. He was so handsome, funny, and sexy beyond belief. All she wanted was fifteen minutes alone with him. It wasn't much, was it? Only fifteen minutes and she knew he would love her forever. Having nearly half an hour to shower and reapply her makeup, she took her time. Looking radiantly happy, she put her workout clothes into the locker and slipped into the sapphire blue dress she'd bought that afternoon at the shop next to the food court. At five-fifty-nine, she rode the elevator to Gregory's office.

An envelope taped to his door had her name on it. Opening it with trembling fingers, she read, *Dear Jemma, We have the entire sixth floor to ourselves. Please join me there for dinner ... dancing ... and dessert. Yours, Gregory.*

Hers? He was hers? Jemma's heart skipped a beat as she quickly walked back into the elevator and pressed the button for the sixth floor.

So focused on Gregory's note, Jemma didn't notice that it was unusually quiet in the facility for a weeknight. There was no one to see Jemma Barton leave the shower, walk down the hall to Gregory's office, or board the elevator. The corridors were empty because Grant posted a notice on the lobby's double doors canceling all evening classes as soon as she walked into the building. Five minutes later, the staff, informed of an air conditioning problem, was happy to leave early. At four forty-five, Grant contacted the cleaning crew and dismissed them for the evening.

By six o'clock, Jemma Barton was the only human left in the building.

The elevator's doors opened. Beautifully decorated with clear twinkling lights and honey-scented candles softly illuminating the room, the dance studio had become a fairyland. Sheer white fabric suspended from the ceiling created a maze that gently swayed in the breeze from the ceiling fans. Jemma was enchanted. Catching sight of herself in one of the dance mirrors, she pirouetted and smiled as she watched the flared skirt of her dress ripple and wave. She hoped Gregory liked it; the color matched her eyes.

She immediately regretted that little bit of exertion. Despite the fans and her sleeveless dress, she was becoming uncomfortably warm and felt that all the heat in the building had collected on this floor. She heard the elevator doors close behind her with a soft chime, followed by footsteps. She turned.

"Gregory?" she said softly.

A man she did not recognize emerged from the other side of one of the white panels.

Smiling, he extended his hand. "No, Jemma, not Gregory. In fact, I do not believe we have met. I am Gregory's older brother, Grant. Gregory is trying to get the air conditioning fixed and asked me to meet you so you would not be angry with him for being late." He released her hand and added kindly, "You are not angry with him, are you, Jemma?"

"No," she said, trying not to appear disappointed. She glanced around for something else to say. "It's quite beautiful up here."

"I'm happy you like it. Gregory and I worked on it all afternoon."

"Well, thank you," she said, her eyes bright with happiness. "The food smells wonderful, too."

"Yes, Gregory ordered dinner from Café Remington to surprise you…and Jemma, Gregory has another surprise for you. He picked this up at the mall while he was ordering dinner and wanted to know if you would be so kind as to wear it this evening?"

"He bought something for me? Really?" she said excitedly. "What is it?"

Jemma watched as Grant removed something draped over his arm.

"This."

The long silk wrap was exquisite, sheer, and expensive. The knowledge that Gregory had chosen something beautiful made her happy, but it was so transparent she was embarrassed.

"Um…I don't think I would be comfortable wearing just this."

"Oh no, of course not, Jemma, but you could slip it on over your dress. The flowers match it perfectly."

Seeing her hesitation, he said softly, "I cannot remember the last time Gregory bought anyone so nice a gift. Don't you like it?"

Although she was already melting in her dress, Grant's words made her feel special, almost like family. Thinking that sometimes dreams really do come true, she stroked the delicate silk.

"Yes, yes I do, very much."

"Here," Grant said, holding it for her. "Let me help you. Gregory will be so pleased when he sees you already wearing it." Then, stepping back, he added, "Very nice. You look like a model."

She tried to smile, but she was so warm that she could barely breathe.

"It's really hot in here."

"I know…oh, what a poor substitute host I am! Gregory will be furious with me. Let me get you something to drink. Water or wine?"

"Just water, please, and thank you. Cool water would be wonderful right now."

"Well, then, follow me."

He led her through rows of silken corridors to the center of the room, where a small table was set with shining silver and delicate porcelain plates. Instead of chairs, there was a single low bench next to the table.

Jemma saw the bench and smiled. *The perfect size for two*, she thought.

The silk was already sticking to her skin. She didn't think it was possible, but it was even warmer in the center of the room. She was dying for some water.

Her eyes lit up when she saw an elegant side table with a crystal pitcher of water and ice, wine sweating in a silver bucket, and aromatic dishes covered with silver domes.

Jemma laughed and said, "This looks like a movie set."

"Well, that's our Gregory. He loves to make an impression."

Grant handed her a glass of water in a beautiful crystal goblet and checked his watch. "He should be here any minute. You know, I think the air feels fresher already."

Jemma didn't think so. She wanted nothing more than to rip off the wrap that felt more like a blanket than a beautiful shawl. She gratefully lifted the glass of water to her lips. The water was delightfully cool. It wasn't until she drank half of it that she noticed it had a slight flavor.

"Umm, this tastes good. What is it flavored with?"

"Berries."

"It's wonderful..." she barely finished saying the words before the goblet slipped from her hand.

Grant caught the glass—and Jemma—before they fell to the floor.

"Yes. Yes, it is," he said, placing her carefully on the bench. He checked his watch. Six-eighteen. His brothers would be arriving in a few minutes. He turned and removed the silk panels surrounding Gregory, who, gagged and bound to a support post, had heard every word.

"You have good taste, Gregory. Attractive, amiable, and ah, she does smell delicious. I can see why you were tempted, but there are reasons why we have rules, and there are always consequences for breaking those rules."

Grant, what are you going to do with her?

"Why, we're having dinner. Regrettably, however, you are not invited to join us this evening."

The elevator chimed.

With eyes brimming with tears of frustration and hopelessness, Gregory watched Grant walk back in Jemma's direction.

In the center of the room, Grant thought as he emptied the plates of food into a black plastic bag.

At first, all the brothers could smell was the human food. As they moved toward the center, they caught her scent and walked faster, ripping down the fabric walls and crushing the soft silk beneath their feet.

Setting out four jars of honey and four scalpels, Grant lifted Jemma onto the table, removed the silk wrap, and quietly disappeared behind the remaining panels. To keep Gregory's mind occupied, Grant sent him a lightning headache to accompany his unobstructed view of the tragic final scenes of Jemma's life.

Grant took a deep breath before closing the door. Yes, she smelled quite delectable.

He lingered on the landing for a moment. Like his brothers, he wanted to taste her, sip the sweetness of her, and ultimately eat honey from her warm flesh. He just didn't care for an audience and decided to wait and hope for better opportunities. Perhaps he could find a woman alone, quiet, and obedient, one he would not have to share. He glanced down at his hand on the door handle and knew it was too late for him. He would never possess a woman like that. Turning away, he stepped onto the catwalks and began the long descent to the tunnels.

If any of his brothers took note of his departure, it was only in gratitude.

The atropine killed Jemma slowly. While his brothers dined without him, Gregory watched in anguished fascination, desire, and guilt. He tried closing his eyes, but he could not escape the sounds of their enjoyment. Finally, when he thought he could endure it no longer, he got his wish. As Jemma's escalating temperature caused her to slip from unconscious to comatose, she sighed, "I love you, Gregory."

Although her pretty face was left untouched, no one, not even her mother, would have recognized Jemma the next morning.

Gregory did not say one word when Grant released him but went down into the tunnels to excavate a new room. Carrying what remained of Jemma and her blue dress out of the dance studio, Gregory vowed never to care about another one. Despite his expert direction, human women could not be trusted to understand their role and keep to his script.

Grant referred to the underground chamber where Jemma was placed as the "serai," an old Turkish word for a small resting room. Eventually, all the brothers adopted the name partly in jest and partly in respect, but mostly because Lyostians *never* let their women leave the colony regardless of why or how they died.

Meghan

As Grant expected, there was a police inquiry a few days later. The detective made a few notes and found two eyewitnesses who stated that Jemma had left the building with everyone else after her class. Measuring the time and distance from GatesWay to her car, the detective reported it was a reasonable walk on a nice day, especially for someone who exercised regularly. Despite their thoroughness, the police could not find any additional leads. When they impounded and searched her car, they found no evidence. The detective's report speculated that when she returned after her class and discovered the flat tire, she was abducted before finding someone to help. When the detective checked the mall's surveillance equipment, he discovered that only half of the exterior cameras were operational. Nothing from that section of the parking lot had been recorded for several months. After Jemma's mother finished with the mall's owners in court, however, there were new cameras covering every square inch of the mall's parking area.

Mrs. Barton did not stop there. She did not believe the detective's theory. She had her daughter's credit card bill, and the words, "Where's the dress?" became her battle cry. She had evidence showing her daughter bought a new dress that afternoon, and she wanted to know the whereabouts of the dress. Jemma's car was locked; she could not have worn her workout clothes *and* the dress. Mrs. Barton went to the store and bought an identical dress, snipped off a piece of the fabric for police records, and posted flyers of Jemma's face everywhere. She hired private detectives who meticulously trailed the authorities' steps. Creating a composite picture of Jemma wearing the dress, the investigators showed it to every store clerk in the mall and inquired at the surrounding restaurants, but they, like the police, did not find any trace of Jemma. Carol Barton's daughter had vanished, and after months without any new leads, the police and the private detectives closed her file.

With Garrett's assistance, Grant hacked into the police computer files and monitored their search for Jemma from his office. Only when he was able to report that the investigation had been suspended pending new evidence did the Lyostians allow themselves a moment of relief, but it was only temporary.

Jemma was the first GatesWay client to sleep in the serai. She was not the last.

No one, especially Garrett, suspected that he was being shadowed by a quiet young woman named Meghan Carter. Too shy to approach him directly, she blended into the background of all the other women Garrett saw every day. Since the breakup of her last romance, Meghan entertained herself with an active fantasy life featuring Dr. Garrett as her white knight. In her fantasy, she knew that if she was patient, one day he would turn his handsome face in her direction, their eyes would meet, and together they would live happily ever after.

Past mistakes had taught Meghan to keep her newest crush to herself—she knew her friends would tease her and tell her she was only rebounding—and watched Dr. Garrett at every opportunity. After a couple of weeks spent learning his routine, she began moving closer until she became extremely good at following him around the facility without being noticed. She became so adept at her stalking that one morning she followed him through the employees' exit on the exercise floor without being seen. She should have been less vigilant.

As soon as she hurried through the closing door, her wristband set off an electronic tone. At the sound of the alarm, Meghan's fantasy came true.

Garrett turned around, and as the narrowing shaft of light illuminated his face, their eyes met.

Following that single hoped-for moment, three things happened. The door lock clicked into place, Garrett tilted his head, and Meghan screamed.

Shoving the side of his left wrist into her mouth, he held her head against the door as he fumbled in his pocket for his glasses. Grant arrived less than a minute later.

Who is she?

Meghan, her name is Meghan.

Smiling gently, Grant took her left hand and, in his kindest voice, said, "Meghan, if I ask Dr. Garrett to release you, will you stop screaming, please?"

Grant's eyes never left her face as he caressed her palm and stealthily removed her wristband.

Her head nodded slightly.

"Good. Dr. Garrett, please let Meghan go. I am certain she is sorry she screamed."

Without looking away, Grant continued to stroke her wrist. "Aren't you, Meghan?"

She nodded again.

Lowering his arm, Garrett backed away. Meghan rubbed her jaw and punched him.

"That hurt, Dr. Garrett. It was your fault anyway. You scared me…and what's wrong with your eyes?"

Rubbing the shoulder where she'd hit him, Garrett had no idea what to say or expect next. He looked at Grant and tilted his head. *Um, Grant. Would you like to take over from here?*

Still holding her hand, Grant said, "The better question, Meghan, would be, what is wrong with your eyes? There is a large, a very large, very red 'Employees Only' sign on the door you just walked through."

"Um, yes, but—" Megan said. Disillusioned, she looked up at Garrett and shuddered. "I'm sorry. I don't know what I was thinking, Dr. Grant. Trust me, I'll never do that again."

"No, Meghan, I seriously doubt you will."

Garrett, what do you know about her?

Single, she's here because she recently broke up with her boyfriend and wanted, you know, to attract another one.

You?

Honest, Grant, I had no idea. I haven't said two words to her except during our consultations. I have seen her in the building a lot lately, but I thought it was her classes. I mean. look at her; she's not—

—Your type?

Well, no, she isn't.

Grant knew that was true. Garrett's tastes ran to buxom cheerleaders with long hair. Meghan did not fit that description. Tall, boyishly thin with short dark hair and glasses, she looked more like a stereotypical librarian or turn-of-the-century schoolteacher than a cheerleader.

Meghan turned to leave and put her hand on the door, only to realize it had no handle. She smiled up at Grant.

"So, how in the heck do I get out of here?"

"I am afraid there is no 'getting out of here,' Meghan."

"What? Wait! You can't keep me here."

"Why, yes, we can," Grant said.

Meghan jerked her hand out of Grant's grasp. Quickly looking around, she saw a flickering exit sign several floors below. She liked the odds. There were only two of them. She was fit, and she was fast.

Grant, seeing the direction of her eyes, scanned the tunnels and summoned the interns who were not in the facility. *Be quiet and come through the tunnel entrance to the catwalks. Howard, you stay in the shadows next to the service entrance. The rest of you will wait until she sees you before climbing the stairs. Move slowly. Let's see how long we can make this last and, to make it more interesting, whoever catches her gets the first five minutes. Alone.*

Smiling to himself, Grant took a quick step toward Meghan to set her off.

Crouching down, Meghan dove under the platform's railing to the metal stairs below. Garrett and Grant walked calmly across the platform and down the stairs, herding her toward the lower floors where the interns waited. It was not cat and mouse; it was live-action pinball. Meghan ran down the stairs of the catwalks. As soon as she saw the red exit light reflecting off the interns' white shirts, she started climbing back up only to see Grant or Garrett moving toward her. She jumped down again, but the interns began climbing up as Grant and Garrett moved inexorably downwards. Out of breath and sweating profusely, Meghan dashed across the platforms, leaping from one set of stairs to another. Now above the light, the interns were almost invisible in the shadows. Smiling in anticipation, they moved steadily upward, vying with each other to be the first to catch her and earn five delicious unshared minutes.

Even before Meghan knew what she was going to do, Grant alerted Howard that she was coming down. A moment later, her heart beating furiously, she jumped over the bottom railing. Landing feet first just inches from the exit door, she was in Howard's grasp before she could touch the release bar.

"Meghan, it is so nice to meet you," Howard said, crossing his arms over her body and pinning her against him. Holding her tightly, he lowered his face to her neck as she squirmed and kicked at him.

"Stop that!" she said, moving her head from side to side.

"No."

She slammed her head back against his. Howard was not hurt, but he only had five minutes, and her resistance was wasting them. Holding her to him with one arm, he pulled the leotard off her shoulder.

"You have two choices. Either let me…um, kiss you, or I will rip this off and let you stand here naked."

Meghan stopped struggling and tried to ignore Howard's "kisses."

Grant and Garrett quietly stood in front of her as the other interns returned to the ground floor. Grant checked his watch, and Meghan, looking from Grant's calm, resolute face to Dr. Garrett's contrite expression, realized there was no hope of escape. She wasn't sure what he was, but he was not her white knight. No one was going to ride in and rescue her.

With tears in her eyes, she looked at Grant and begged, "Please, Dr. Grant, please."

"I am truly sorry, Meghan, but rules are made for the benefit and safety of all. They are simple rules, but you disregarded them, so forgive me if I must disregard your regrets."

Grant rechecked his watch and tilted his head. As Howard straightened up, Grant removed a syringe from his pocket.

"What, what's that?" Meghan's voice escalated with panic as she leaned away from him.

"Shh, Meghan, it is just medicine. It will make you sleepy, and when you wake up, this will all seem like a dream to you."

"A nightmare in hell, you mean."

"As you wish," he said, pressing the needle into her bare shoulder.

Within moments, she was lying limp in Howard's arms, hot, sweaty, and still alive. Garrett and the other interns edged toward her.

"How long, Grant?" Garrett asked.

"About two hours."

"Who?"

"Everyone who helped, of course."

Remembering Gregory's punishment, Garrett wasn't sure what he was supposed to do. Would he be made to watch—or did Grant have something worse in mind for him? Fear colored his thoughts, but mostly he wanted to taste her while she was still breathing. Not wanting the interns to hear, he tilted his head.

Umm, did I help?

Is she finally your type, Garrett?

Garrett stared at the floor.

Yes, Garrett, you helped by not letting her escape and calling me immediately. Thank you.

"Moreover, I will still need your help." Grant looked at the wristband in his hand. "Invite Harris to join you. We will need him afterward. I want her purse and all her clothes—untorn—and I need to know which car is hers."

Garrett was becoming aware of every minute they spent talking. "Now, Grant?"

"No. Two hours. I must report this incident to Grayson. He'll be disappointed he missed all the fun. In fact, don't be surprised if he joins you...but I won't hurry."

"Aren't you going to join us?"

Grant lifted her arm and ran his tongue along the skin from her palm to her elbow. He shook his head.

"No. Do not forget to invite Harris. He will be very uncomfortable this afternoon, and I want him to have something in return."

Grant turned and began climbing the stairs. Behind him, running footsteps echoed in the hallway leading to the tunnels.

Grayson?

Grant.

We need to talk.

Two minutes.

By the time Grant got to Grayson's office, his client was already standing at the elevator.

"What is it?"

Grant smiled and looked at his watch.

"Well, I think Garrett, Howard, Harris, Hayden, and Hugo are calling it brunch. Or, rather, calling her brunch."

"What?!"

It had become Grant's custom not to let Grayson's outbursts bother him, but he had already killed one person that day and had no problem killing two.

"Yes." Grant briefly explained what had happened and how they would circumvent being involved in another investigation.

"But finding ways to elude inquiry by the authorities is only a containment problem. The main problem, Grayson, is preventing these regrettable incidents in the future. Eventually, someone will confide in their best friend, sister, or mother, and when something regrettable happens— like today—that person will be pointing a finger, and the police, in our direction. I cannot allow these infatuations to jeopardize our mission. They must stop. Now."

"So, Grant, tell me how we will manage that. I know you didn't come in here without already having a solution. You just want my approval, not my input."

Grant was constantly amazed at Grayson's grasp of the obvious. Of course, he had a plan. They didn't have two years to wait for Grayson to come up with an idea.

"Yes. It is my responsibility to have solutions, so this is what I propose," he said, smiling at the pun. "We are engaged—all of us. In certain human cultures, men are engaged to women of their own religion and background who are chosen by their families. Because it is part of our backstory, the staff believes we have lived abroad. It helps explain our accents. We will let it slip, once or twice, that our family has engaged us to women who are waiting for us to return and marry them at the end of our residency here. When the interns take over, they will also be expected to marry who is chosen for them."

"And the women will back off."

"No, not all of them, but it will discourage most, and if anyone gets too close, we have a ready excuse to refuse them. And we must refuse them. There *will not* be a next time, Grayson, without dire consequences. We will have a meeting tonight to discuss this, and then everyone will choose a name for his fiancé—or, to make Gregory happy, we could each pick a movie star. That process will allow us to know her name and what she looks like."

"That could take hours."

"Or I can throw six names in the middle of the table, and Gregory will want to trade."

"We'll pick our own."

"Yes."

Grant stood up to leave but hesitated a moment. He knew Grayson would ask.

"Um, Grant."

"Yes."

"How much longer until she...."

To keep Grayson waiting, Grant checked his watch. "About eighty-five minutes."

"Where?"

"In the main tunnel."

"Well, then, if you will excuse me."

"Of course, Grayson."

Grant smiled on his way back to his office as he amused himself with thoughts about his imaginary fiancé. *Julia...No. Beautiful, but too independent. Marilyn? No, too obvious.* Although he reflected on it from time to time, Grant never decided on a movie star fiancé, and no one ever asked her name.

Garrett escaped punishment, but it became his responsibility to monitor the frequency of their clients' visits and their duration. To help him, Grant redesigned the GatesWay wristbands from status identification bracelets to sophisticated tracking devices. A client who entered the facility more often than necessary or lingered outside the building was intercepted. If her reasons were evasive, she was assigned a different consultant. When her contract expired, it was—with Dr. Grant's deepest regrets—unable to be renewed.

That evening, Grant's proposal was accepted and implemented the following day. The rumor that the doctors were engaged circulated throughout the facility like wildfire. The doctors noticed a difference in their clients' attitudes almost immediately, and the staff treated them more professionally as well. Grant noted these results in his next report to the collective. Within two weeks, every Lyostian in North America was engaged...to a movie star.

Testing Phases—One...Two...Three

The preliminary tests were failing.

During his research in northern Africa, Grant perfected the Reconception procedure that prevented the embryo from attaching itself to the mother with an umbilical cord. This development kept the formic acid from leaking directly into her bloodstream or causing internal infections at the site of attachment. The collective was encouraged by this gestational breakthrough and pleased that everything was progressing on schedule. Eighteen months prior to the date the new generation of hybrids was to be born, Grant confidently outlined the Reconception protocols for the North American colonies so they could verify the serum's success in real time. Deciding to make these tests a full-scale rehearsal, each doctor followed Grant's detailed criteria by researching his consultant database and monitoring their clients for new pregnancies.

Timing meant everything in the selection process. In little more than a year, GatesWay needed to be prepared to reconceive twelve embryos a day for five straight days. However, for the preliminary analyses, Grant insisted on caution. He and his brothers knew their clients' bodies—inside and out—better than the clients themselves through observation and monitoring their metabolic pathways. This diligence allowed them to identify their pregnant clients, even at the earliest stages, without difficulty. With their future generations at stake, Grant deliberately staggered the procedures so the women could be observed in phases and adjustments made as the pregnancies progressed.

Protocol one was perfect; the reconceived cells did not form human embryonic sacs but soft, malleable shells that resembled a pale oval on the sonograms. Thin hair-like tentacles held it in place, enabling the fetus to absorb nutrients from the mother without transmitting any of the formic acid back to her. The entire colony experienced a heightened level of optimism. Grayson wanted to report their success right away, but Grant advised against it.

Grayson had not been with him during the fetal development trials to see the bodies of the women who died trying to give birth to their brothers. The hybrid serum was genetically perfect, and the Reconception procedure was working as expected, but Grant was aware that the most crucial element—how long the mothers would stay pregnant—was still unknown.

As the first two pregnancies entered their third week, everything started to go wrong, and Grayson appreciated Grant's foresight. When the prospective mothers came in complaining to their consulting doctor of unexpected bleeding, Grant and Grayson were alerted right away. The interns wheeled the sedated women into the underground operating room where Grant and Grayson performed emergency surgery. Both women survived and were told only that they had suffered a miscarriage.

The genetic analysis of the aborted embryos indicated they were not the anticipated human hybrids but the Lyostians' genetic equals. The serum did as it had always done. Instead of successfully combining with the human DNA within the rapidly dividing cell structure, it invaded and destroyed ninety-nine percent of the human genetic material. The women's bodies, sensing the alien DNA within the embryo, rejected it.

The serum was not compatible with the new conception procedure.

Declaring a one-week moratorium, Grant called Gordon into his laboratory.

"This is not a problem, Grant. We can go back to adding the serum with a needle."

"It will not work. Trust me. It has to be the serum—not the procedure."

"It's not the serum, and what if I don't want to 'trust' you?"

Grant understood Gordon's animosity. Although he had never punished Gordon, as Gregory's twin, he'd experienced all of Gregory's punishments. However, Grant did not think this unnecessarily unfair as Gordon was a witness, willing or unwilling, to all of Gregory's transgressions and had kept silent every time.

Therefore, Grant did not necessarily feel compelled to spare Gordon the more gruesome details of the results of his tests and experiments along the Mediterranean coast. Smiling grimly, he watched Gordon's face grow more and more ashen.

"Trust me now, Gordon?" he asked softly.

"Yes. Sorry, Grant."

"Yes."

"But Grant, the serum is genetically perfect. You know that. You've worked on it longer than anyone, and you have—you know you have—stood over me as it was adjusted and modified. It isn't the serum."

Grant closed his eyes. There were only so many variables. He checked each one in his mind looking for flaws, irregularities, or fluctuations within the prescribed protocols.

When he opened his eyes, Gordon knew he had solved it and looked at him expectantly.

"The timing."

"I don't understand. How long the women have been pregnant?"

"No. The timing of the serum bath. It is too long. That is why it is destroying the human DNA."

"So, it's not the serum."

"Not technically the serum."

"Thank you." It was the first time Gordon ever smiled at Grant.

Grant smiled back and thought if Gordon wasn't Gregory's twin, they might have been friends…for a while.

"We only have four women left…how are we going to test this?"

"We already know six minutes is too long, so five minutes probably is, too. Of the remaining four, we will bathe the embryo for one minute, then two, three, and four minutes."

Recalling the memories Grant showed him, Gordon shuddered. "If we are wrong, this will be a really big mess for the colony to clean up."

"Do you think it could be anything, absolutely anything, else?"

"No. It is the only item on the list of protocols that can be altered. It makes perfect sense. It has to be the timing of the serum bath."

"Yes." Grant tilted his head and told Grayson they needed to test a change in the protocols starting as soon as possible.

The Lyostians never intended to allow any of the embryos to mature to full term. The synthetic milk was not ready, and the nursery facilities were still under construction. The minimum infant survival threshold for their infant brothers was three months; based on his previous experiments, Grant theorized if they could keep a woman pregnant for eight weeks, they could keep her pregnant for thirteen. Every Lyostian on the planet held their collective breath for the next several weeks as they waited to see if GatesWay would be successful in keeping a prospective mother pregnant—and alive—long enough to validate the newly established protocols.

It wasn't an easy time for anyone, especially Grant. After assisting with three emergency surgeries, including one near fatality, they were running out of time...and prospective mothers. Leia, one of Gabriel's clients, was the only one who remained pregnant after four weeks. Grant haunted the halls and catwalks, watching her every moment she was in the facility. At seven weeks, he allowed Grayson to report to the collective to limit the serum bath to exactly sixty seconds. As the colony celebrated its success, Gabriel contacted Leia and scheduled a consultant appointment for the following Monday. One of his loveliest clients, he had not wanted to choose her, but she was pregnant at the right time. Gabriel was relieved that she would suffer nothing more than a "vitamin" shot to sedate her long enough to allow him to end her pregnancy.

Leia did not make it to Monday.

Friday morning, during her yoga class, she began singing and waving her hands around in time to the music. Gabriel, like Grant, watched Leia every spare minute he had and noticed it at once. He sent his intern in with a message devised to remove her from the class with as little attention as possible.

Grant. Grayson.

Gabriel.

Leia. Surgery. Now.

Grant was already running down the stairs. *On my way.*

Grayson followed slower, wondering what he was going to tell the collective if this was another protocol failure. After a moment, he smiled to himself. *He* would tell them nothing. Protocol reassessment was Grant's problem.

Hugo, charged with getting Leia from her class to the operating room, watched in horror as she began to cry and beat her head against the elevator wall. He had not yet completed his medical training and called Gabriel for help. When the elevator doors opened, the gurney and Gabriel were waiting.

Gabriel rushed in and swept Leia into his arms.

"Leia, hush now, everything will be all right. I'm here."

Even in her delirium, Leia recognized Gabriel and hugged him, sobbing, "Help me, Dr. Gabriel, they're after me!"

"Who, my dear, is after you?"

"Them," she said, pointing to the empty hall. Gabriel's heart sank. It had been going so well.

Hugo gently removed Leia's arms from Gabriel's neck and helped him settle her on the gurney. Talking softly, Gabriel, the kindest brother of all, slipped a hypodermic needle into her arm.

"Goodbye, Leia," he whispered, kissing her forehead.

"Where am I going…?" Her voice trailed off, and her eyes closed.

With a deep sigh, he motioned Hugo away and wheeled the gurney into the operating room by himself.

They could not wait for the abortion drugs to take effect. To prevent the toxins from further poisoning her blood, the fetal sac had to be removed immediately, and that required major surgery. Carefully removing her workout clothes, they gasped at the bruises on her arms, legs, and body. Fresh purpling across her abdomen competed with older, yellowed areas that spared only her face and neck.

The doctors in the room looked at her in stunned silence. Only one creature in the known universe would beat a woman like that: a contemptible human male.

When they removed the embryonic sac during surgery, they found it had ruptured, releasing formic acid into her bloodstream. The embryo, deprived of the liquid that kept him alive, was stillborn. Holding his small brother curled in the palm of his hand, Gabriel sang Anya's lament, and his lilting voice echoed throughout the tunnels.

Leia lived only because Gabriel would not let her die. This was not her fault; it was his. Unlike his brothers, Gabriel did not see her as an experiment. She was a prospective mother, blessed by Anya, and, as such, he loved her as his own mother. Regardless of Gabriel's feelings, it was not long before the entire colony realized it might have been more merciful to let her die.

Using the mall's new surveillance cameras to their advantage, Leia was seen getting into her car and driving away shortly after two in the afternoon. That was the time the sun's reflection from the NAFTRAM windows into the camera lens was the greatest, and driver identification could only be assumed, but it was enough to divert investigative interest from GatesWay.

Within twenty-four hours, a room was arranged for Leia next to the basement storage area. Having only the barest amenities, Gabriel did not think it was worthy of her, but Leia did not mind because she had no idea where she was. She lived perpetually suspended between two worlds: a beautiful drug-induced existence where there was no pain or fear and a dark world where large creatures pinched her with claw-shaped hands. At first, she would plead with them to go away, but as the sedation wore off, the fiends moved steadily closer, and when their pincers began tortuously opening and closing, she screamed.

Gabriel attended to her as kindly as any loving son. When he had to be above ground in the facility, Hugo monitored the IV drip that kept the painful dreams away. Regardless of how hard they tried to balance their two schedules, they could not be with her every moment of every day. One evening, shortly after the facility closed, her piteous begging became nonstop screaming that echoed throughout the tunnels—and the facility. Although the fearful sounds lasted only a few minutes, Grayson was afraid it would happen during the day and agreed to let Gabriel arrange for all the interns to alternate when he could not be there. Once the new routine was in place everyone, including Leia, slept easier.

Gabriel did not miss one day of the six weeks Leia lived underground. He liked to see her in the morning, bathe her beautiful face, and bring her fresh flowers. Although she never said anything to him, she smiled when she heard him sing Anya's song of protection, and her hands made graceful movements above the white coverlet as though she were playing a piano.

One morning, Gabriel specifically waited for the florist's delivery so he could bring daffodils to brighten her room. She seemed to respond to red and yellow, and Gabriel, believing them to be her favorite colors, brought her flowers in those shades whenever they were available. Approaching her room that morning, he knew something was not right. Despite the fragrance of the daffodils, Gabriel could detect an odor he did not like. He tilted his head and scanned the room looking for Hugo, who had the Sunday evening shift. When he received no answering echo from her room, Gabriel began to walk faster.

The smell in the hall became more unmistakable with every step.

The flowers slipped from his hand as he stood in the doorway. He would have thought Leia was sleeping except for the smear of blood across her face. Her graceful hands stilled forever above the red-soaked coverlet. Reluctantly, he walked to her bedside, lifted her arm, and saw where she chewed through the veins in her wrist to escape the dark monsters that hunted and hurt her. He gently placed her arm down on the blanket and, kneeling beside her bed, began singing Anya's prayer for forgiveness and then the lament.

When the prayers were finished, he stood and called for Grayson. Then he called for Grant. Never in his life had Gabriel deliberately hurt another living creature, but someone deserved to be punished for this level of neglect.

Grant arrived first and immediately sensed Gabriel's profound grief. Standing next to him, Grant put his hand on Gabriel's shoulder.

"I am so sorry, my brother. Please tell me what happened and how I can help you."

"I also called Grayson, and we will await his arrival to talk about what has happened here. But, Grant, I called you because I want whoever is responsible for this punished, and I don't know the procedure for that—or even if *I* should ask you to do it—or do it myself. However, if you are the right brother to ask, then I wanted to ask you myself rather than let it be delegated to you. I have other requests as well, but I will wait for Grayson."

Grant looked at Gabriel for a long moment. He was actually relieved that Leia was dead. Every moment she was alive was a moment someone looking for her could get a search warrant and find her. Now she could be buried where not even bloodhounds could track her. Despite his feelings, he was acutely aware of Gabriel's pain and anger that she was left alone long enough to slip into madness and kill herself. Grant did not share Gabriel's sorrow, but he was angry as well. This silent room screamed of disobedience and disrespect, two highly punishable offenses, and he would do whatever Gabriel wished.

"We will get to the bottom of this, my brother. I promise you—and Leia—that I will personally punish the responsible brother or brothers to the extent that you deem satisfactory."

"Thank you, Grant."

At that moment, Grayson entered Leia's room, and before considering the perspectives of the brothers already present, he said, "Thank you, Anya, mother of us all."

Not hearing their grateful agreement in response, he looked at Gabriel and Grant's faces and realized he'd spoken too soon.

"I mean, of course, that she is no longer in pain."

When they still didn't respond, he continued, "Ah, yes…hmmm, Gabriel, can you tell me what happened?"

"I don't know what happened, Grayson. I came in this morning, like I do every morning, and found her like this. The IV bag is empty, and she…," Gabriel paused a moment, "she had been conscious long enough to tear through the skin on her wrist and bleed to death. Our mother died neglected, alone, and in pain. Grayson, I request punishment and sanctions against those responsible."

Wondering if it was necessary, Grayson glanced at Grant and saw the flash in Grant's eyes. He would do whatever Gabriel wanted. Grayson hoped Gabriel's grief did not require a death for a death.

"What do we know? Who was supposed to be here?"

"Hugo."

Grayson glanced around the small room.

"We need to move this discussion to the conference room."

"No. Here is where she died, and here is where we will find the truth."

Grayson tilted his head and called Hugo.

Where?

Leia's room.

Be right there.

Recognizing the smell of death as soon as he stepped into the hall, Hugo ran toward the room. "Oh, Sweet Anya, what happened?" He fell to his knees, pressed his hands against his eyes, and sang Anya's lament.

When he finished, Gabriel began his interrogation.

"Why were you not here this morning?"

"I had to study. Three of us have exams this morning, so I traded nights with Harris. I waited here until he came, and then I left."

"What was her condition when you left her with Harris?"

"Stable and sleeping peacefully. I had just changed the IV bag and capped her feeding tube."

Gabriel raised his eyes to Grayson, who called Harris. There was no response. He called louder to both Harris and Gregory.

Gregory answered first. *What is it, Grayson?*

Where is Harris?

I sent him into the northeast tunnel system last night to check a water source. Why?

He was supposed to be in Leia's room.

Yeah, I know, but this was more important. I cannot have that section flooding, or we will have to divert to another level. I told him I would check on her.

And did you check on her?

Not yet, I was coming up in about an hour.

You need to come up now. Then, only to Gregory, he added, *and you better bring Gordon with you.*

Soon Leia's small bedroom was the site of a murder trial.

Although he did not say anything, Grant thought Gabriel would reconsider his request when he realized it was Gregory instead of an intern, but he did not.

There were few things Gabriel believed in, but the reverence that Lyostians owed to their mothers was at the heart of them all. He genuinely did not understand Gregory's lack of concern or Grayson's attitude that they were better off with her dead. She was gracious and lovely, and her death was their fault.

Gregory and Gordon entered a silent room. Leia's body spoke for her, but before Gregory could defend himself, Gordon argued that Leia's boyfriend was the guilty one. Gabriel agreed that was true, but it did not change the fact that she was once pregnant with their brother and was their mother, too, and Gregory's neglect had killed her.

During the trial, Grant sat in the small chair in the corner, listening to their spoken and unspoken arguments, and waited. It only took a few moments before he distilled several things. One, he was going to have to punish Gregory again. Two, Gabriel, as quiet and efficient as he was, was immovable when it came to Lyostian piety and devotion toward their mothers. Three, Gordon was correct; the human male who beat Leia—

killing both her and their unborn brother—needed to be punished. And lastly, Grayson, instead of leading or even mediating the discussion, was jumping from argument to argument without any resolution.

They did not have all day to deal with this tragedy. Sending them all a brief, sudden pain, he stood up.

"Grant, did you do that?" Grayson demanded.

"I do not know what you mean by *that*, Grayson. I just felt a stabbing pain behind my eyes. I hope I am not getting another damned lightning headache."

"Oh, okay." Grayson backed off accusing Grant. He had been getting lightning headaches himself off and on for the last couple of months and hoped he wasn't getting another one as well.

"However, while I have your attention...," Grant continued, "I have a few suggestions because as sad as I feel today that we have lost Leia, our mother, we must agree to a declaration of accountability for her death."

Um, Grant, I think that is my role in this matter, Grayson thought to Grant privately.

Grant had been working in his office since three o'clock that morning. There was still more to do, and he needed to bring this incident to a successful closure.

"Grayson, you have done an admirable job in calling everyone involved to discuss this tragedy, and the person responsible for Leia's death, thanks to you, has been determined. Gabriel has requested punishment, which is, regretfully, my role in this matter."

Nodding to Gabriel, Grant said, "Gregory, you and I will discuss this further tonight at nine in the training room. Gabriel, you may attend if you would like. Gordon, do not be there."

Gabriel spoke up. "No, Grant, I will not attend...I'll be here."

No one misunderstood what Gregory meant as he looked at her body with renewed interest. "Um, Gabriel, are you sure I can't meet you in here tonight instead?" he said, his eyes gleaming.

Before he could finish smirking at his own joke, Gabriel took two steps forward and savagely backhanded Gregory across the face, knocking him against the wall.

Gordon stepped in between them and shoved Gregory out the door. Turning back to the men in the room, he said, "I am sorry, Gabriel, for everything. I did not know." Nodding to Grant, he added, "He will be there…alone."

"Thank you, Gordon. It will be better if I do not have to find him."

Grant looked at Hugo, who had been trying to blend into the wall during the entire confrontation. "You can go, Hugo. I hope you do well on your exams. This was not your fault. Gabriel, please tell Hugo you do not blame him."

Gabriel walked over to Hugo and tilted his head. Hugo nodded and whispered, "I am so sorry, Gabriel." Taking one last look at Leia, he fled the room.

Staring after him, Grant wished he could leave as well. Human blood had an ugly, metallic odor, and he was actually getting a headache. Raising his hand to his eyes, his last thought reverberated in his mind.

Her blood.

Realizing they would have to act quickly, Grant turned to Grayson. "Do we still have the clothes she was wearing the day of her operation?"

"No, they were incinerated. Why?"

"I wish we had some of her clothes…for evidence."

"We do," said Gabriel.

Grayson and Grant turned toward Gabriel. "We do?"

"Yes. I cleaned out her locker after the operation…you know, just in case."

"And you kept them? Where are they?"

"Yes, I kept them. They were her things." He walked to Leia's side and pulled a small wooden box with brass latches from underneath the bed.

This had been a day of revelation for Grant into the mind of his brother Gabriel. He did not know Gabriel brought her flowers every morning, had not understood that this devotion was a tangible part of who he was, and when anyone else would have thrown her things into the incinerator, a shopping bag, or plastic tub, Gabriel put them in a beautiful wooden box. Grant knew that when it was opened, the clothes would be folded and her belongings organized in the hope that one morning when Gabriel walked into the room, she would be well and need them.

Grant knew firsthand the pain of living with that hope and secretly rejoiced that Leia was dead so Gabriel could forgive himself.

When Gabriel opened the box, Grant was not disappointed. Pulling the clothes out and crumbling the soft folds in his hands, he began to blot the blood on the bed. Gabriel looked at him aghast.

"Grant, Grant, please stop. What are you doing to her clothes?"

Without answering his question, Grant said, "Is there a comb or brush in her bag?"

"Yes, a small brush."

"Perfect, brush her hair if you don't mind, Gabriel…or, if you do, I will do it when I'm finished here."

"No, no. I would like to," he said. Moving toward the front of the bed, he gently brushed her short dark hair away from her face and tucked it behind her ears.

Grayson, silently watching the grisly pantomime, finally exploded. "Grant! Will you please tell me what is going on? Why are you doing that? Why is Gabriel brushing her hair?"

Looking at him, they tilted their heads. *We are avenging our mother*, they said simultaneously.

Grant thought it was going to take days to track down Leia's boyfriend, but she told them everything they needed to know. A freelance court reporter, Leia had her entire life in the small planner slipped neatly into the side pocket of her purse.

If it had been any other night, they would be watching a movie that Gregory selected, laughing uproariously at the human emotions and motivations they didn't share or understand, and thought were ultimately self-destructive. It would have been a more pleasant way to end the day.

Instead, Gabriel spent the evening in Leia's room. He put clean linens on the bed and, after he bathed her, dressed her in a beautiful red and yellow silk kimono. Gently placing her on the freshly made bed, he crossed her hands over her chest.

Bending down, he kissed her forehead for the last time.

"Goodbye, Leia," he said.

He threw the dirty clothes and soiled linens into the incinerator, removed the IV stand and monitors, and brought the chair into the hall. Closing and locking the door, he sat in the chair. He and Hugo would keep watch for the next three days. Gabriel was adamant that no one would disturb her, and after three days, no one would want to. She would be safe.

As Gabriel prepared Leia's crypt, he was also observing Gregory's punishment. Gregory's first defense was that thinking about it all day should be punishment enough, but Grant calmly looked at him and let him talk. Eventually, Gregory's words became sobs of fear and then howls of pain. Ignoring his pleas for mercy, Grant did not desist until Gabriel was satisfied.

Deciding to include Gregory in that conversation, Grant tilted his head.

Really, Gabriel? Already?

Gabriel, understanding what Grant was doing, stalled.

Yes, I think so. Don't you?

On the floor with his arms wrapped around his head, Gregory looked up hopefully through his tears.

Please, please, please, he thought to both of them. *I am so sorry.*

Yes, Gregory, I know. I've been listening to your litany of regrets for half an hour. The question, of course, is how much sorrier does Gabriel wish you to feel.

Please, Gabriel.

Thank you, Grant. There is much for you to do tonight, and so I am now willing to accept Gregory's apology on Leia's behalf. To Gregory alone, he continued, *Gregory, you are a bad son, and I warn you. Never neglect or disrespect one of our mothers again because I promise that Grant and I will both be in the training room next time, and you will need help to* crawl out.

I understand, Gabriel. Thank you. Almost afraid to look up, Gregory saw that Grant had already gone. Pushing away from the floor, he called Gordon to help him stand so he could walk out of the room.

Grant had the evidence ready. After getting the information he needed from her purse, he wiped it down and pressed her fingertips on everything she would have touched. Locating her boyfriend's house, Grant, Howard, and Hugo waited until all the windows were dark except for television shadows flickering in an upstairs room. Wearing black workout clothes and surgical gloves, they silently buried Leia's bloodied clothes next to the house. Placing her lingerie in her purse, Howard climbed through a broken garage window and hid it under the back seat of the car.

It stormed on the third day following Leia's death. That night, Gabriel went back to sleep in the dormitory. The following morning, an anonymous call was made from the mall to the county sheriff's office with a tip on one of their missing person cases.

Christopher Lorca was already a "person of interest" in Leia Sutton's disappearance, but even without an alibi, they could not arrest him. So far, they only had a missing girl and two past domestic abuse reports. Cadaver dogs found her buried clothes, and the resulting search warrant turned up her purse in his car with calendar entries placing them together on the day she disappeared. It would never be enough to convict him, but it was enough to hold him on suspicion of murder while they looked for further evidence.

No one knew exactly how it started, but shortly after his arrest, a rumor that the latest inmate had beaten a pregnant woman to death made the rounds of the detention facility. Without warning, Christopher found himself receiving daily "accidental" punches, kicks, and body slams against hard prison walls. Protesting his innocence, the inmates laughed at him; they were all "innocent," too. Four days before the district attorney scheduled his release for lack of evidence, Christopher Lorca was found hanging in his cell.

The prosecutor and criminal investigation team reported it as a confession by suicide and closed the case. When the coroner's analysis arrived with detailed photographs showing the gruesome condition of Christopher's naked body, it was filed away without comment.

Although still technically missing, the police no longer believed Leia Sutton was alive and, without any new leads, discontinued their search. They knew it was only a matter of time before her body was found in an abandoned building, a shallow grave, or a secluded cornfield.

Gabriel took the scrap of newsprint outlining Christopher Lorca's brief life and slid it under the door. They had avenged the death of their mother, and Leia would rest peacefully. His ethereal voice echoing in the hall, Gabriel sang as he sealed the door to Leia's crypt with concrete, blending it perfectly into the rest of the freshly plastered wall.

Their mother was safe. No one would ever hurt her again.

Introspection

Whenever Grant gazed into a mirror, he thought of his beautiful mother, but she was not in his face any longer. The honey he constantly consumed had darkened his eyes, leaving little of the original blue and green. No longer able to find her outside himself, he looked inward.

The memory of her touch, which enabled him to endure great amounts of pain, also left him with an equally great need for gentleness that had gone unanswered all his adult life. Only the faint remembrance of her love concealed the torment within him and kept it carefully under control. Not even the collective suspected the source of Grant's endurance and sacrifice were the few memories he kept of his human mother.

It was ironic to him that the touch he craved existed solely as a child's dream, but it sustained him. Sometimes, however, unbidden and unwanted, the brief memories of how it felt to be loved haunted him, and he speculated on the life he would have experienced if his mother had not been mistaken for a colony wife. He was quite young when he'd discovered the truth from an overheard conversation; that it was an accident he was a Lyostian fire slayer and not human. An accident that cost him everything except his life.

Grant knew that being human would not have saved his family or prevented what happened at the colony. In moments like these, Grant saw himself as a human son fighting alongside his father in their attempt to protect his mother and, when inevitably overpowered, the three of them dying together. Their bones, indistinguishable from each other, lying sun-bleached and partially buried in the sand.

Grant closed his eyes and mentally surrendered to his mother's memory. He could still see his parents as they existed during her few sane moments when love and light came together. Desperate to share that love and claim his rightful place beside them, Grant's mask of cold indifference disappeared as he told himself he was an artist, a talented surgeon, a brilliant geneticist, and pleaded with them…*Please, you must love me; I'm your son. I'm not…I'm not a monster.*

Looking down at his hands, capable of so much beauty and perfection, he remembered what else they were capable of and knew that yes. Yes, he was.

No one would ever love him again. The dream of his mother's touch was the only kindness he would ever know. Overcome by the loneliness of his life, Grant screamed inside with the same voice as his father, who shouted to a colorless sky one terrible afternoon twenty-eight years earlier, "WHY?!"

The same scorched silence answered them both.

Grant's hands slowly became fists, and he covered his eyes. He prayed for forgiveness for his only weakness: the unending desire to be Timaeus, the beloved human son of Destani and Venzel, whose blood mingled valiantly with theirs, forever staining the desert sand.

His anguish at the impossibility of ever having that life—or death—never left him, and the love he could not deny them twisted into something cruel, becoming one with the raging fires of the Tuzurias heritage that relentlessly clawed at his heart. The inferno grew hotter with each moment of regret, and he wondered how long it would be before the flames finally began consuming his mind.

Only these quiet intervals prevented Grant from acknowledging that they already had.

Finding Persephone

...and he knew, most importantly,
that he could have been held responsible for her death—
the death of a surviving and compliant human mother—
the one thing the collective, with all its accumulated wealth, could not buy.

Borrowing from Greek mythology, the Lyostians who lived near the
Mediterranean called such priceless women Persephone.
The bride of Hades, god of the underworld,
who was stolen from her world of light
and carried down into his kingdom of darkness
to rule beside him.
Forever.

Groundwork

It was almost self-serving, Grant thought, not to care too much about his brothers; he never knew when he would have to kill one of them. However, as the months grew into years, he fell into a congenial, if slightly apprehensive, relationship with Gabriel and Garrett. Gregory avoided him, and Gordon treated him with a level of suspicion that was not conducive to more than the briefest acknowledgment. Grayson, he loathed. Pompous, overbearing, and—Grant was sure of it—he occasionally used the threat of Grant's "training" sessions to get his way. When Grayson became too obnoxious, Grant sent lightning headaches to quiet him. Although his brothers didn't know Grant was responsible for the peace that reigned whenever Grayson retired to the darkness of their dormitory, he sensed their gratitude.

A more tangible vindication was the reaction of the collective's governing hierarchy. Initially believing his proposal was too complex, they were impressed to discover that once the facilities were operational, they functioned precisely as he predicted. Most of the clinics had waiting lists, and if they chose the younger, healthier women ahead of those less suitable as prospective mothers, few complained. To the collective's continued incredulity, the facilities were not only self-sustaining but also paid back the setup and building costs within the first year. With such success, the collective listened to every suggestion Grant made to improve NAFTRAM's North American Settlement phase and kept him fully involved during its implementation. With over one hundred and twenty thousand women enrolled in their program nationwide, the NAS operation was the most ambitious the Lyostians had ever attempted, but such ambitions were not without risks.

Although they had always chosen the loveliest mothers they could procure, the Lyostians in North America were surprised to discover how attractive they were to their clientele. The physicians at GatesWay were not the only brothers to experience unwanted attention, and Grant's suggestion of pretending they were all engaged worked amazingly well. Stricter dress and behavior codes were enforced throughout the colonies, and no further incidences were reported.

The doctors did not, however, wear large signs saying they were engaged, and the brothers were intrigued to find that nearly all of their new clients, both single and married, inquired of the staff if the doctors were "involved" with anyone. Since the Lyostians had access to the video cams installed in all the public areas of the facility and the microphones located in the more private sections, there was an ongoing competition to determine who received the most inquiries. Gregory was the most popular, but it was a secret source of pride to Gabriel that he came in second. Always interested in human psychology, Grant began breaking down the demographics. He discovered that Gregory, Gabriel, and Garrett were the most popular among single women; Gregory, Gordon, and Grayson were the most popular among married women. What surprised Grant was that he was number four in both categories. Finding the rankings interesting, he started to pay attention to his client's responses. He gave a list of films to Gregory for additional research and began adding certain mannerisms, broadening his vocabulary, and practicing expressions of empathy in front of the mirror he kept in his desk.

Within two weeks, he moved to number three on the singles' list, just edging out Garrett and, after thoroughly trouncing Grayson, tied for second among married women. Once he'd gathered the requisite information regarding the behaviors their clients responded to favorably, the challenge was met, and Grant went back to being himself.

Regardless of their relationship status, Grant was not unhappily surprised to find that most of their clients were still attracted to the Lyostian doctors they believed were human. The real challenge was attracting their ideal mother, Persephone. The kind, obedient woman who would love their children—children who were so obviously *not* human.

Grant scanned the details of hundreds of client applications on his computer in an attempt to isolate a single marker or find a consistent combination of variable traits that would guarantee success. He found nothing. Their mostly middle-class clientele was too independent. Coming of age in a feminist society, deferential compliance was out of the question. There had to be something, Grant thought, that would make them *want* to obey. The kind of grateful, unhesitating obedience one could expect from…

Love.

American women were fools for love. Half the movies Gregory chose were focused on classic or contemporary romance. What if, but no…it would be too complicated. American women might be fools for love, but all the films indicated that they liked to date, flirt, be held, and, he closed his eyes briefly, made love to. Additionally, he could not risk getting involved with anyone who might reveal their relationship or make a scene. Gregory's little escapade showed them the cost of that particular inevitability.

Then there were the odds. Out of the possible two hundred women who made up his personal clientele, what were the odds of choosing the precise two or three who would: 1) have a successful pregnancy; 2) survive both physically and mentally; 3) care for him or the child enough to submit to his control; and 4) trust and/or love him, or the child, enough to be nurturing, caring, accepting, and, most of all, willing to let the child go after one year?

Astronomical. Unless he waited and chose carefully.

For several days Grant considered the possibility from every angle. The most efficient way would be to treat all his suitable clients graciously. He would smile, pretend to listen to them, and empathize with their difficulties, thereby laying the initial groundwork, but without any spoken commitment or physical affection in the event of a miscalculation. When he chose the ten most likely to succeed, he would escalate his overtures to harmless flirting, innuendoes, and slight touches here and there. He knew their physiology more intimately than they did, and he could, through the honey they were eating, manipulate their desires to parallel his timetable. For prospective mothers who stayed pregnant, he would raise his level of involvement to a higher emotional commitment until they were infatuated with him and he was able to influence their actions.

To obtain the colony's cooperation, he would have to express it as a psychological and physiological experiment. Proper empirical research demanded establishing a baseline of identical stimuli to detect measurable similarities that could be exploited to the Lyostians' advantage. This method of data collection appealed to him on a scientific level, and the resulting report could lead to a human psychological blueprint for future generations to follow. During the next twenty-five years they were going to require nearly a million Persephones all over the world. Anything that would assist in identifying and persuading these women would be very useful.

Grant was determined to keep his hypothesis confidential until he decided to proceed with the data collection. It would not be easy. He was devoted to all the women in the facility; they were his species' only hope for survival. He loved them like he loved clean air, water, and, well, food. Regardless, he knew that listening to them and trying to please them would be difficult enough, but having to pretend an affection he did not feel would be the most challenging part of his experiment.

Caroline

It started with a kiss, as many life-changing events do…the casual love affair, a marriage, and long journeys. It ended with a promise to love unquestioningly and uncompromisingly, even beyond death. I didn't understand in the beginning, but I do now. We were like those stars that, from the first moment of creation, are set in motion by invisible forces to collide millions of years later. Nothing in the universe can alter their path, prevent the silent scream of stars crashing, or escape the resulting aftermath of destruction and debris.

Eric was one of those stars. I can't remember the weather, what I was wearing, or recall the exact date he walked into my office, but I remember how I felt the first time I saw him. Standing in my doorway, scruffy in a collared shirt and khakis, he was staring down at the folded paper in his hand unsure of where he was or where he needed to be. Looking up at me with desperation and hope in his dark blue eyes, my heart went out to him, and, for a while, I let him keep it.

Lives were destroyed in the fiery aftermath of our particular collision, but not mine. Salvaged from the glory and wreckage, a new star with a different source of light was set on another unalterable path.

Looking back for the last time, I wonder, *was it always inevitable? Was there any way we could have escaped?*

No.

We never had a chance in hell.

Eric

Eric started at the university in his sophomore year. Older than many of our new students, he wasn't arrogant the way many college athletes were, but he seemed so lost that I was extra patient as he asked the same questions I'd answered a zillion times. Bumping into Suzanne, my student assistant, on his way out was the first time I saw him smile.

It was a smile to steal your heart, and I tumbled like a smitten schoolgirl.

Suzanne hovered in the entryway and watched him leave. As soon as the hall door closed, she turned on me in a fury.

"Caroline! What was Creepy McCreeperson doing here?"

"Who? No, his name is Eric Harman."

"No, that is Creepy McCreeperson. I met him when I was in high school, and he tried to get me to go to his stupid minor-league baseball games. I thought he'd disappeared from the face of the earth, but I ran into him last year when he decided to go back to school. After that, it was like he'd stuck a GPS locator on my forehead. I would be somewhere, and then he'd show up. Downtown, in the library, the café, wherever. Totally creeped me out...and now he's here. Great."

"Not only here at the university, but also one of our new majors, so you'll be seeing him at least twice a year when he comes in for academic advising."

"Grr, please make his appointments when I'm not scheduled to work. It's just too weird being in the same room with him."

"I'll do what I can, but your classes are going to overlap once in a while."

"Yeah, probably, but if he asks, please don't tell him what my work schedule is."

"Of course not," I said. "Your secrets are safe with me."

I had a horrible thought. "Suzanne, do you think he's stalking you?"

"Oh no," she said, flashing a big smile. "Just one more guy hanging around that I wish was on the other side of the world. He's not the only one. There's lots more."

"Of course, there are," I said, laughing with her.

Eric's name was at the end of a long list of men she had mentioned in the last two years. She couldn't help it. Varying shades of cream and tan from the top of her head to the tips of her polished toenails, Suzanne's beauty was only surpassed by her intelligence and good nature.

After dismissing Eric's obvious admiration so abruptly, I scheduled his advising appointments when Suzanne wasn't working, but I couldn't stop him from occasionally dropping by the office on his way to class looking for her. They rarely connected, so I talked to him when she wasn't there. I tried not to anticipate his visits and believed Eric was another student who, as our conversations grew longer and less academically focused, I would eventually consider a friend.

It should have happened that way, but when Suzanne graduated a year ahead of him, the dynamics of our relationship changed. The academic assistance during his sophomore and junior years became banter that bordered on flirting in his senior year. I tried to resist, but he would show up with a problem that I would somehow miraculously resolve, and when his intense blue eyes looked into mine and he said I was "wonderful," my heart rate doubled. Even if he was teasing, after nearly twenty years of marriage, I felt breathless and excited that someone young and attractive thought I was wonderful.

Knowing the source of these feelings would disappear as soon as he graduated, I tried not to become dependent on Eric's smiles. All my students graduated eventually, continuing their lives in other places, while

I stayed and looked forward to the students returning in the fall who still needed me.

Eric, however, had other post-commencement plans.

May 1999

Graduation was over, and I could finally breathe. Senior GPA checks and recommendation letters for graduate schools had all been sent. The campus seemed unnaturally deserted, but I was looking forward to a little downtime to catch up with the backlog of emails, filing, and software updates.

I took the stairs to burn a few extra calories. Opening the hall door, I saw a dark silhouette outlined against sunlit walls. The shadow stepped into the hallway at the sound of my footsteps.

It was Eric.

Seeing him was a welcome surprise. I smiled at his gallantry as he took my keys, unlocked the door, and stepped aside as I walked into my office.

Turning to thank him, the smile left my face when he firmly closed the door.

As unmovable as a statue, he leaned against the doorframe and crossed his arms over his chest. The blue eyes I'd smiled into for the last three years belonged to a stranger. A tremor of fear touched my spine. Eric was not as tall as Dan, but he was an athlete. Constantly conditioning for baseball in the summer and coaching soccer in the fall made him strong enough to be dangerous.

I fought to remember that I was the adult, and he was the student. To maintain that balance, the first rule has always been "remain calm and show no fear."

"Please open the door, Eric," I said, using my professional voice.

He did not move.

"I'm not a student anymore, Carrie. You can stop pretending you're in charge."

"But I am in charge, Eric. This is my office."

"Is it? With the door closed, it's just another room." He looked down at my keys in his hand. "It's so convenient you come in early. I *like* morning people…and there are so few of them around in the summer."

Was he threatening me? My mind was a blur. *How did we go from harmless flirting to this?* I swallowed. *Show no fear.*

"Well, I'm glad that's convenient for you, Eric, but why are *you* up so early? Between all the graduation parties and training drills, you should be exhausted."

"I am. Very."

He closed his eyes.

"Why not go home and get some rest? Come back later, and we'll chat some more." *Finally*, I thought, *I'm gaining some control of this situation.*

His eyes flew open. "No."

It was the calm finality of the word that frightened me the most.

Crossing the room before I could reply, he pressed his mouth against mine. Hot, demanding, and, forgive me, *so sweet*. His hands threaded through my hair and held my face to his. Resolute with one hundred and seventy pounds of unyielding muscle, I found it impossible to push him away. Refusing to respond, I pressed my fists against his chest and waited for him to release me.

When he dropped his hands and stepped back, my knees buckled, and I fell into my chair.

Touching my bruised lips, my fearless façade crumbled, and I looked up at him.

"Why did you do that?" I whispered.

"How could I not do that?"

"What, what do you mean?"

"I have watched you for three years. I know when you're sad, and I know when you're happy—and you know when you're happy, Carrie? You are only happy when you are helping a student. Your eyes glow, your smile is unforced, and you are relaxed. Every other minute, you are like a woman on a tightrope."

"And that...that was your way of saying what? Thank you?"

"No, Carrie, that was my way of saying I'm tired of seeing you pretend that everything is okay and, well, I want to give you another reason to smile."

Was he right? Sure, Dan and I had problems. Climbing the corporate ladder had taken its toll on our marriage; the higher he went, the harder he worked, and the more he drank to cope with the stress. I couldn't even remember the last time he kissed me like that...certainly not in this decade. Usually, it was me trying to kiss him, but after a while it seemed like begging, so I stopped. It suddenly occurred to me that he probably never even noticed.

Tears of embarrassment and self-pity stung my eyes.

Seeing them, Eric was immediately penitent and knelt beside me.

"I'm sorry, Carrie, so sorry if I hurt you, but I've wanted to do that for so long. Sometimes, I would come in to talk to you just to watch your lips, and I thought, well, since I'm not a student anymore, maybe...you would...see me differently. I guess I was wrong. I'm sorry. I'll leave now. I won't bother you again."

Despite his words, he did not move. He seemed to be waiting for permission. Permission I was powerless to give.

"Oh, Eric, I have *always* seen you differently," I said. "But this, this is impossible."

He shook his head stubbornly and got to his feet. "No, not if you care. I won't believe that."

I sighed. He was so young.

"How then, Eric? How do you see this working for us?"

"One day at a time, Carrie. One glorious day at a time."

I shook my head. There were no "glorious days" left in my life. He had no idea who I was. Usually, we talked about him—not me.

"Eric, I'm, I'm married…I have a son going to college in the fall."

"I know. In fact, I know more about Brendan than I know about you." He looked down for a moment. "Oh, Carrie, couldn't you give me a chance to know you better?"

I could not misunderstand his meaning and felt my face burning.

"Eric, I'm too—" I was about to say *old for you*, but he stopped me.

"If you finish that sentence, I will prove how wrong you are right now, but I would prefer to wait until later…when we have more time. Wouldn't you?"

I needed to think.

"Later, then, Eric. Get some rest and come back this afternoon. We'll…talk some more."

"And you'll be here? You won't leave early or run away or anything?"

"No, I promise. I'll be here."

He turned to go.

"My keys, Eric."

Smiling, he gently set them on my desk and closed the door on his way out.

I stared at the back of the door.

What the hell had just happened?

My hand hovered above the phone to call campus security, but I pulled it back. What would I tell them? That a student kissed me? Assaulted me? I shook my head. It may not have been innocent, but it was not a crime to steal a kiss.

And it wasn't a crime to tell the truth. He was right about Brendan. Estranged from Dan's affection, I'd become my version of the perfect mother. My entire life revolved around Brendan, his health, his clothes, his school, haircuts, toys, games, movies, birthday parties, music, and sports. Sharing Brendan's social life was the only one I had. After all, he was the only one who never noticed the three pounds I'd put on every year for the last fifteen years. Of course, I adored Brendan; no one else loved the woman I saw in the mirror.

Yet, here was this boy. *Boy?* Panicking, I searched Eric's record in the advisor directory. He would be twenty-five on the thirteenth of August. *Would he wait that long?* I touched my still tender lips and did the math. Two pounds a week was almost thirty pounds. A little toning, a flatter tummy…yes, it could be done.

Recalling the pressure of his mouth, I wondered how it would feel on other parts of my body and gasped at the pleasure of the thought. *Perhaps he was right. It could be…it might be…glorious.* Somehow, Eric had seen past the weight and caught a glimpse of the girl I was before forty extra pounds made me invisible. Maybe he could help me find her again.

I didn't worry when Dr. Bennett's four-thirty appointment was canceled, but my heart skipped a beat when he closed his office early and said he was going home. The silence of the building after he left made it impossible to concentrate.

What if I was the only one still working?

It was too risky, and Eric's expectations seemed impossibly optimistic. Either he would find someone younger and leave me, or Dan would find out about Eric and leave me, or someone would mistake me for Eric's mother, and I would die of humiliation. Unable to find a good way out of any relationship with him, I decided it was better not to begin one at all.

At four-forty-five, I threw my keys into my purse and was ready to bolt at the five o'clock bell. At four-fifty-five, the clang of the hall door echoed in the corridor. My heart started beating so fast that I could scarcely breathe.

Once again, Eric closed the door to my office.

"So," he said, "what have *you* been thinking about all day?"

Taking the stairs again the following morning, I was grateful there was no one to witness my foolishly broad smiles. Shyer than I expected, Eric's gentle affection took me by surprise. I'd forgotten young men could be so charming.

I teased him a little bit and let him kiss me again, but when he wanted to take matters further, I stopped him. Despite his prediction, I knew there was nothing glorious about being out of breath on a faded carpet, especially being out of breath *and* out of shape. To distract him from his disappointment, I promised to spend his birthday with him and gave him every indication that his slightest wish that day would be my command.

Sharing his anticipation, I confidently marked Friday, the thirteenth of August, as a vacation day on the office calendar. There was time to join a gym, lose weight, and look well, maybe not eighteen or even twenty-eight again, but better…oh, so much better.

Then, it could *be glorious—for both of us.*

Every nerve in my body fairly hummed in the brightly washed world I now inhabited. Reliving the excitement and tender romance, I didn't care if I had to give up eating entirely…I would not disappoint him. It wasn't love, but in one giddy, reckless moment, I decided to have this young man and let the chips fall where they may. Knowing it would be such a delight to be happy with my body, I let my desire for him inspire me to do something I should have done years before.

Grabbing the phone book and turning to my computer, I searched for gyms close to the university or my house. I was going to make a different life for myself, and I couldn't wait to get started.

A flash of the diamond in my wedding ring brought memories of a honeymoon on a pink beach with a husband who held me close every night, and my optimism caught fire. *If I were really thin, would Dan notice? Would he want to kiss me again?* Happy thoughts continually percolated through my mind, and I knew that regardless of the eventual outcome, I was moving in the right direction.

In the one realistic moment I had that morning, I knew there was an entire summer until Eric's birthday and that many *young*, beautiful baseball fans crowded the players after every game. Despite the excitement of his declarations the night before, I knew it would not hurt me too much if his infatuation faded in the Florida sun.

Suzanne

Taking a moment from my internet search to check my email, I found a message from Suzanne asking if I would meet her for lunch. She wrote that she had a new job just for the summer and fall because she was leaving in mid-January to teach abroad. It had been weeks since I'd seen her, and dismayed at losing her for an entire year, I agreed to meet her at our favorite restaurant.

Suzanne was eager to talk about her news, but being polite, she asked first about the college and Dr. Bennett, and I gave her the brief update I gave to all the alumni when they asked the same questions.

She smiled at my short, rehearsed answers.

"And what about Brendan? How are you coping with that?"

The dark cloud that thoughts of Eric had kept at bay returned. My automatic responses eluded me, and my eyes filled with tears. I saw the concern on her face and admitted to her the fears I had hardly acknowledged to myself.

"He graduates in four weeks, Suzanne, and I am happy, proud, and devastated. No one ever tells you that the disadvantage of having one child is the first and last time for each milestone happens at the same time. You're never prepared for the emotional impact, good or bad, so everything hits hard. Brendan? In college? Who will wake him up, remind him to take his keys, or care for him if he gets sick? It's so hard to turn it off, Suzanne; I don't know how to stop being his mother."

I tried to smile through my tears. "You know, the wonderful part of my job is getting to mother all the children I never had."

"And we love you for it," she said softly.

"I know, and it's wonderful, really. But he has always been my only little one. Once, when he was five, we were at an amusement park, and he let go of my hand. For a few moments, he was lost. I couldn't find him."

"Was he hurt or scared when you found him?"

"No, he was fine. I was the one who was scared. Without his little hand in mine, it was as though I'd lost my place in the world." I looked into her soft brown eyes. "Suzanne, I keep feeling that panic over and over these days."

Seeing the worried look on her face, I said, "I'm sorry, dear. I know this isn't why you asked me to lunch. But you know, because I talked about him for the two years you worked with me, that nothing has made me happier than being Brendan's mother. I'm not sure who I am going to be when that's over."

Getting up from her chair, she gave me a hug. "Perhaps you will find a new place in the world and something else to fill your heart, Caroline. Or someone else. You just never know."

She smiled mischievously, and Eric's voice echoed in my mind, "*I want to give you another reason to smile.*"

Would I let him? Yes, I would.

I dried my eyes on the napkin and took a shuddering breath.

"Wow, I simply don't know where all that came from. So sorry, Suzanne, thank you for listening, and now, you must tell me about your new job. I'm really ready for some happy news."

"Well, if you're sure."

"Absolutely."

Suzanne stood up, and every man in the room watched her walk back to her chair.

"Caroline," she began diplomatically, "working with you was wonderful, but this new job…is…so…great. It's at GatesWay Fitness Clinic and Health Spa. The pay is way more than I've ever made, and the perks are fabulous! They've been around for about three years, have a huge clientele, *and* it's right behind the mall near your house! It's like ten minutes away from you. We could have dinner some nights, go shopping, or to the movies, or just whatever we want."

"You're working at a fitness clinic? Seriously? I've spent half the morning searching for a gym. I want to see how fit I can get in three and a half months. I'm not hoping for miracles, of course. I would just like to look, um, healthier." *Not true,* I smiled to myself, *I am hoping for miracles.*

"Caroline, it's practically fate!" she said, laughing. "But why three and a half months? Is it your high school reunion or something?"

Recalling her disdain for Eric's attentions, I knew I couldn't tell her the truth. Not only because it was Eric but because he was a student, even if he had graduated. I felt slightly foolish. *If I can't be honest, why am I doing this?* Remembering his whispers in my ear, a quick shiver of pleasure touched my spine, and I smiled at her.

"How did you guess?"

"Mom's reunion is this year, too, and she wants to join. Wouldn't it be great if we were all there?"

"It would be absolutely great. Where do I sign up?"

"Well, there's an interview process. They want to be sure GatesWay is the right place for you."

"I can handle that. What else do you know?"

"Well, like I said, the company is about three years old, and NAFTRAM—that's the corporate name—is national, like one in every major city in the US…sometimes more if the city is huge like LA, New York, or DC. There are rooms for dance, floor exercises, yoga, weight and aerobic machines, a whirlpool, and a sauna, and that's only the fitness side of it. The spa side does facials, massages, and manicures. They do everything, Caroline. 'Head-to-toe fitness and personal image enhancement' is their motto. Oh, and there's a reward system, too, so as you lose weight, you get spa treatments, and they are, like, for free. You'll love the instructors, and the floor supervisors are, you know, like me, and the doctors are so nice."

"Doctors?"

"Yes. It's run by six doctors who are brothers. The executive director is Dr. Grant, then there's Dr. Gabriel, who hired me, Dr. Gregory and Dr. Gordon, who are twins, and two more whose names I can't remember right now."

"If they're brothers, why do they have different last names?"

"Oh, Caroline," she laughed, "their last name is Gates, but if you called them all Dr. Gates, then no one would know which one you were talking about."

"I suppose everyone's name starts with G?"

"How did you know?"

"I'm a mom, I know how that works…but Suzanne, what gym needs *six* doctors?"

"It's a *fitness clinic* and *health* spa with nearly twelve hundred members. That's like two hundred per doctor, which is a lot, so six really isn't that many when you think about it. They specialize in nutrition, physical therapy, exercise, and motivation techniques, and there's probably a psychologist somewhere in the bunch. Oh, and they have an outstanding success rate, too. So, if you want to look great by the middle of August, this is the place to go. They won't let you be stupid and starve yourself until you start binge eating.

"So, what do you think? I think it will be perfect for you! My mom would so love it if you were there. She wouldn't feel like the only newbie. Please," she wheedled irresistibly, "as long as you were going to get skinny anyway, you might as well do it where I can encourage you and tell you how great you're looking."

"Okay, give me the number. When I get back to the office, I'll call to make an appointment for the interview. Is there anyone special I should ask for?"

"Well, they are all gorgeous, of course! And you can't pick. Interviews are scheduled on rotation, but if you get Dr. Gregory, don't get too close. I've heard he's handsome enough to make a woman hyperventilate."

"You haven't met them all?"

"Not yet. I've only been there a few days, and it's a big place, but I will eventually."

"No doubt, Suzanne, no doubt at all. Every male who has ever seen you wants to know who you are. Even Brendan and Dr. Bennett still ask me what you're up to."

Cheered by her optimism, our eyes met, and we laughed together. I felt so happy, so focused on the possibilities, so blissfully unaware that another star, brighter, hotter, faster, was moving on its own path toward me, and my lunch with Suzanne would cost me far more than the check. It was going to cost everything I had.

I called the number Suzanne gave me at my first opportunity.

"GatesWay Fitness Clinic and Health Spa, how may I help you?"

"Umm, a friend recommended your facility. I would like to lose weight and take some fitness classes."

"Of course. I will be happy to schedule an interview for you with one of our admission consultants and a program designer."

"Program designer?"

"Yes, ma'am. Each client has a personally designed exercise program. It's updated periodically as your body changes, so you won't get bored with repetitious exercise classes. We insist on helping you reach your goals as interestingly as possible."

"That sounds wonderful. How soon can I start?"

"The first available interview is Monday at noon. Will that be convenient?"

"Yes, that will be perfect. My name is Carrie...with a c...Taylor...with a y."

"Thank you, Ms. Taylor. When you arrive, please come into the lobby and give the receptionist your name."

"I will. Thank you."

"You're welcome. Thank you for calling GatesWay Fitness Clinic and Health Spa."

Taking Turns

Gabriel entered Grant's office.

"Yes?"

"GatesWay has two new clients to be interviewed on Monday, Grant, and it's your turn."

"I think, Gabriel, if you check your records, you will find I have a full complement of clients."

"Two emails received this morning indicate otherwise."

"Who and why?"

"No one to be overly concerned with losing. They are both moving—not together, of course—with the usual regrets. So, you're up."

"What time?"

"Noon and two-thirty."

Grant glanced at his monitor screen.

"I will accept one new client. At noon. It is the only time I have."

"But—"

"One."

GatesWay Fitness Clinic and Health Spa

I will never forget the first time I walked beneath GatesWay's blue and white awning. Stepping through the beautifully carved entrance doors, I was surrounded by candle-scented air as I entered a perfectly appointed drawing room of timeless elegance. Low tables adorned with shaded lamps and fresh flowers encircled by curved cushions created little islands of intimacy begging to be shared. Tugging at my memory like a forgotten dream, the faded familiarity of the room called to me as though I had rediscovered a home patiently awaiting my return.

The doors closed silently behind me. Embracing the ambiance as I would an old friend, a sense of serenity slowly drifted over me, and every reason I was there—Eric's stolen kiss, my promise to Suzanne, and my hope for a reconciliation with Dan—vanished. The only thing that mattered at that moment was that I was there.

The dark-haired receptionist, who appeared to have been chosen as carefully as everything else in the room, looked at me expectantly.

In a whispery voice that was not quite my own, I asked, "Is this…is this GatesWay?"

She smiled as though she shared my thoughts.

"Yes, it is. May I have your name, please?"

"I'm Carrie Taylor. I have an appointment at noon with an admissions consultant."

She glanced at her computer monitor. The briefest frown touched her forehead and disappeared.

"Yes, Ms. Taylor. Please be seated. I will call an escort for you."

Entranced by my surroundings, I did not notice the young man until he stood beside me.

"Ms. Taylor?"

"Yes."

"Please follow me."

We walked down a short hall that widened into a circular room. In the center was a double spiral staircase curving around a glass elevator.

"That's impossible," I said, walking closer to gaze upward into the nearly invisible coils of balusters and handrails.

My escort cleared his throat. "Um, not entirely impossible," he said, glancing at his watch. "Let's take the elevator today. We don't want to be late."

Standing behind him in the elevator, I couldn't help but notice how perfectly the white knit shirt clung to his broad shoulders and pressed khakis fit his trim waist. If not for his tinted glasses, I would have considered him exceptionally nice looking and wondered if *he'd* met Suzanne yet.

The elevator doors opened soundlessly to a long corridor. Fan-shaded sconces decorated the walls between the three offices on each side of the hall. My escort paused at the last door on the right.

Turning the knob, he pushed the door ajar and stood aside.

"Someone will be with you in a moment," he said. "I'll return after the interview."

Moving quickly toward the elevator, he left me alone in front of an unlocked door with no name or number. Not knowing who or what to expect, my hand shook slightly with anticipation as I pushed open the door and entered the room.

Meeting Caroline

Sensing his protégé's presence on the edge of his thoughts, Dr. Grant Gates tilted his head and acknowledged him telepathically.

What is it, Howard?

Sorry to interrupt you, Grant. I'm bringing up your noon appointment.

What are your impressions?

She is in her mid-thirties, wearing a wedding ring, and, typical for the Midwestern demographic, needs to lose about thirty–thirty-five pounds.

Attitude?

A little more overwhelmed than most. We are getting into your "impossible" elevator now.

My impossible elevator?

Yes, that is what she said when she saw it.

That's not *typical,* Grant thought to himself.

ETA, Howard?

Less than two minutes, Grant.

Thank you.

Grant's preliminary research wasn't going as well as he hoped. Cataloging Howard's description of his newest client, Grant knew that every client who did not meet his basic criteria would make it more difficult for him to choose…but that was months away, and the weather was getting warmer. He wasn't worried. There was always an influx of young single women who waited until the last minute to get in shape for summer vacations. He just needed to be patient. Checking the spelling of his client's name on his calendar, he pulled a new folder out of the drawer and wrote "Carrie Taylor" on the tab.

Rising from his desk, he began preparing the tea and crackers he offered every new client. He tried not to think of all the other things he could be doing that didn't involve listening to one more overweight married woman complain she couldn't lose any weight when she probably had two candy bars in her purse. He sighed. He'd promised himself to treat all his clients as though they were exactly what he was looking for so it would appear natural when Howard brought him someone he *could* use.

Regarding this interview as another dress rehearsal, Grant composed his face into its most congenial expression and returned to his desk to wait behind the partition that shielded his eyes from the lights in the outer office.

When he heard his office door close, he began counting to twenty-five. He liked to give his new clients a chance to know him from all the visual clues he left in the front room. However, most seemed not to notice. He kept waiting for some woman to comment on the color scheme, the architectural details, or the perfectly balanced arrangement, but so far, no one had said a word.

Gregory's clients were lavish with their admiration for his office. They did not realize that it was his intention to make them feel inferior by displaying paintings and sculptures of the idealized female body. Fortunately for Gregory, his clients believed the perfection surrounding them to be encouragement rather than condemnation.

Grant chose to take it as a compliment that no comment was ever made about his office. It was, evidently, exactly what his clients expected and nothing more.

...twenty-four...twenty-five.

Slipping on his glasses, Grant walked around the partition. He liked catching his new clients by surprise. He felt walking in on them unexpectedly put him in control from the very beginning of their relationship.

This time, it was different.

He was not expecting *her*. She was medium height with flawless skin. Her light brown hair shimmered in the shaded light, and there were traces of uncommon beauty in the delicate structure of her face and wide set of her eyes. Following her gaze, he was immediately intrigued by the smile that played upon her lips as she studied his office.

When she turned, his command of their meeting momentarily fell away, and the scripted phrases and intonations fled his tongue. It was only a temporary shift. Years of self-discipline returned the professional smile to his face, and he found the words that had served them so well in the past.

Although this lapse did not change the fact that she could be of no earthly use to him, Grant wondered why it became important to earn her trust and decided to use his kindest human voice.

The Interview

I closed the door behind me and stepped into the consultant's tastefully decorated office. Muted shades of brown, gold, and dark green blended perfectly with the polished walnut paneling that surrounded and divided the room. A large reception desk—without a receptionist—took up much of the outer section where I stood.

Well, it is noon…maybe she's out to lunch.

Unsure of what I was supposed to do, I glanced around the office. Two chairs faced the reception desk, and a small writing desk and chair were tucked into the corner to my right. The furniture against the longer wall to my left was a tea table covered with a white napkin.

Although slightly unnerved by the complete silence of the room, I found it warm and inviting. I instinctively felt I could happily spend the rest of the day there—except I wasn't visiting. Suzanne said every prospective client had an interview but impressed by the understated gentility of my consultant's office, I wasn't sure who was interviewing whom.

My examination of the paneling was interrupted when a man entered the room from the other side of the partition. I was immediately aware of his overall physical appearance; he was tall, well-built, and meticulously dressed in charcoal gray slacks, a long-sleeved white shirt, and a tie. However, all that perfection faded into the background when I saw his face and the way the lamplight caressed his cheekbones, the angular shadows beneath them, and his mouth—at once both sensitive and austere. Above the dark-rimmed glasses that made him appear more mysterious than scholarly, strands of bronze and gold fell softly over his forehead. Remembering Suzanne's description, I knew he must be Gregory Gates. I understood instantly how a woman could lose track of herself just looking at him.

His voice, however, did not match his undeniably masculine appearance. It was low-pitched, but his sentences were more rhythmic than traditionally spoken. I found it mesmerizing and distracting at the same time. Although he chose his words carefully, it was evident that English, American English anyway, was not his first language.

"Mrs. Taylor, forgive me for not being present to receive you when you arrived. My name is Grant Gates, and I am your admissions consultant. May I pour you a cup of tea?"

"Yes, thank you."

Ah, Gregory's brother. If Gregory looked better than this, perhaps Suzanne was right to warn me. To stop from staring, I continued looking around the room and realized it reflected his calm professionalism perfectly.

"I'm, um, afraid you've caught me admiring your office."

"You approve of it?"

"Oh, yes...very much. It's deceptive, though, you know. At first glance, it appears to be just a nice office, but when you look at the details, you realize that it is quite remarkable."

Smiling, he said, "That is as nice a compliment as I have ever received. Thank you."

He removed the napkin with a small flourish. The tea table was charmingly laid with a gilt-edged tea set, a small plate with toast triangles, and a crystal dish containing a golden spread that looked like marmalade.

"Lemon, sugar, milk?"

"Yes, no, no. Thank you."

"Good," he said, handing me the teacup, his fingertips barely touching my own. "If that was a test, you passed."

His smile and the touch of his hand caught me completely off guard.

"I'm glad to hear it," I mumbled. *Oh damn, why was I mumbling*? I was the prospective client. This was supposed to be *his* interview.

"I am sure, Mrs. Taylor, given your previous responses, that you will probably turn it down, but let me also offer you a toast point with our brand of bitter honey," he said, spreading a thin layer of the sticky golden stuff on a small triangle. He lifted the plate from the table.

I shook my head. Not even to be polite would I be able to choke that down.

"No, thank you. I don't even like regular honey," I protested.

"I understand," he said. "Many of our clients tell us it is an acquired taste. Are you sure, not even a little bit?"

He set the serving dish down and picked up a teaspoon. Touching the tip of the spoon into the honey, he offered it to me.

I didn't know how to refuse him. I reached for the spoon.

Unexpectedly, he pulled it away from my hand.

"Say, please," he said teasingly.

Becoming annoyed at having to say "please" for something I didn't want in the first place, I looked beyond his glasses and into his eyes.

"Please," I said, unable to conceal my reluctance.

His brilliant smile dimmed as he handed me the spoon. Wanting to get it over with, I closed my eyes and quickly licked the tip of the spoon. The flavor of the bitter honey lit up my interior senses. Gasping in surprise, I opened my eyes and saw him gently smiling at me as though he knew I would love it.

Sipping from my teacup, I had only one thought as the tea carried the warm deliciousness of the honey down my throat. *This...this is the taste I want in my mouth when I die.*

I could not resist smiling back at him.

"I may like the toast after all...please."

Lifting the dish again, he said, "*If* that was another test, you have passed again."

"Was it?" I asked, adopting his teasing tone.

A brief, enigmatic smile was his only response. He walked toward the reception desk. Before he sat down, he fixed his full gaze on me. There was a directness in his manner, a momentary searching in his expression, but it passed quickly. He motioned me into one of the chairs. Almost at once, the mood in the room changed. No longer the kind host, his voice became professional, and the lovely cadences disappeared.

"I think we can move on to the paperwork portion of our meeting, Mrs. Taylor—unless you have any questions right now."

I was disappointed that my teasing had been abruptly ignored, but based on what Suzanne had told me about the clinic's organization, I didn't have any questions…yet. I took another sip of tea and shook my head.

He opened a drawer and handed me a four-page questionnaire.

"For us to personalize your program, we would like you to complete this application for our records."

"This looks like a lot of information for a gym membership."

"I am sorry," he corrected, "GatesWay is not a gym. It is a health facility and spa. I, um, we hoped you wanted to make it part of your life, not somewhere you show up occasionally to exercise. There are plenty of *gyms* for that."

He put out his hand for the questionnaire, but I kept it.

"I know, I'm sorry. I just hate filling out forms."

"Most people do. Please feel free to skip any question that makes you uncomfortable. However, the more information we have, the easier it is to design an exercise program especially for your needs and allows us to personalize the rewards program."

"You mean there's a question in here that asks what I'd like on the ice cream sundae I get when I lose ten pounds."

I smiled to let him know I wasn't serious, but he still did not share my sense of humor.

"We do not reward our clients with food. Research has shown it is one of the problems with weight loss sustainability. We reward our clients with massages, pedicures, facials, and other treatments that enhance their appearance, all free of charge, as they meet their goals."

"Speaking of charges, I don't understand your billing system at all," I said, tapping the stack of colorful brochures on the desk. "Am I supposed to turn my credit card over to you so you can bill me whatever you want for the next six months?"

"We do not bill you whatever we want," he said, handing me a brochure. "This is our 'Weight Loss Payment Calculation Chart.' As you can see, we bill you according to your progress. If you decide meeting half your goal is enough and stop attending your classes and consultations, we are still obligated to bill you for the remaining contract time at that level of achievement."

After a moment, he added, "However, most of our clients do not discontinue the program even after they have successfully completed it. GatesWay Fitness Clinic and Health Spa is truly an oasis for many women. The most successful are occasionally offered jobs within the corporation so they may use their experiences and success to educate and inspire others."

Everything Suzanne said was true. I looked at the chart and noticed that the monthly charges declined as I met my goals. Still, it would be expensive, but the thought of Eric's surprised and pleased smile on his birthday was all it took to rationalize the cost. I moved to the little desk in the corner. Clicking on the lamp, I began filling out the form.

Rising quickly, he said, "Please let me know if you have any questions. I will be on the other side of the partition to…allow you some privacy. Please help yourself to the refreshments."

Unable to resist, I ate the rest of the toast and honey. Again, the sensation of pure joy flooded through me as I sipped my tea.

I looked enviously at the empty chair behind the reception desk. Although I loved my job, at that moment, I thought nothing could be better than working here, drinking tea, and nibbling honeyed toast all day.

I pondered the possibility. That particular position may not be open, but perhaps somewhere else in the facility? Suzanne liked working here, and it would be one more reason to make their fitness program work. A new body, a new job in the most beautiful building I had ever seen—*and* all of Eric's kisses I could handle—could I really be that lucky?

Optimistic and full of happy plans, I began filling in the blanks, circles, and checkboxes of the questionnaire. It started off normally enough, but the questions soon became specific: "Did I have any children, how old, how delivered, and did I plan to have any more?"

"Excuse me, Mr. Gates, but what is the point of all this information about my personal medical history?"

I thought I heard him sigh, but there was no hint of irritation in his voice.

"Mrs. Taylor, although this is not a public medical facility, we do have clinicians on the programming staff. Certain medical conditions and client expectations can affect our exercise recommendations. We want you to be healthy for life, not thin for a few weeks. But, as I said, please do not answer any questions you are uncomfortable with."

After the medical questions, the form took another turn: "What colors do I prefer? Sounds? Favorite perfume, candlelight or low lamplight, and what genre of music did I like?" It was as though they were asking me to unlock the secret workings of my soul, and I didn't like it.

"Umm, Mr. Gates, why do you want to know how I feel about candlelight? Or music? And why is the cologne I bought my husband important? I'm sure a *clinician* doesn't care about that information."

This time, I heard him laugh softly. His sense of humor had returned with his melodic voice.

"No, you are right about that. Our clinicians do not care about the answers to those questions…but the spa consultants do. They work very hard to make our clients feel at home, and those questions allow them to personalize the reward treatments. As I have stressed before, Mrs. Taylor, you need not answer any question that makes you uncomfortable, but if you dislike vanilla and your meditation or massage room is filled with vanilla-scented candles, you will only have yourself to blame. The questionnaire is for your benefit, Mrs. Taylor, not ours."

I nodded toward the partition. *One point for you, Mr. Gates.* His explanation calmed my suspicions, and I answered nearly every question on the form…even ones I normally would have skipped.

On the last page was an agreement requiring me to abstain from 1) all alcoholic beverages except three ounces of red wine per week; 2) over-the-counter drugs with the exception of low-dose aspirin; 3) tobacco products or any product that was inhaled into the lungs with the exception of prescription medications; and 4) more than four ounces of caffeinated beverages per day and all beverages containing added sugar. Lastly, I had to agree to submit to any and all urine and blood tests to confirm my compliance.

Suzanne had not mentioned this. Other than switching to decaffeinated tea, the agreement would not affect me too much, and I didn't mind signing it...except for the part about testing. Again, it seemed like they were crossing an invisible line.

"Mr. Gates."

The clicking of his keyboard paused.

"Yes, Mrs. Taylor."

"Is the agreement one of the optional questions?"

I heard the scraping of his chair. A moment later, he stood next to the partition.

"Yes and no. Yes, because we would never ask you to sign any document that would distress you, but keep in mind that our only measure of success is your success. The agreement is to inform you today that you may have to make adjustments to your lifestyle to achieve your goals. Then, no, it is not optional if you would like to experience the highest reward levels because we always test the day of your spa reward. If you are willing to consent to these terms, I promise you the rewards will be worth any of the small sacrifices requested here."

"Do most of your clients sign this?"

"Yes, because in the beginning, they all believe it's possible. However," he searched my face as if mentally checking off a list, "I do not think it will impact your current lifestyle since you do not smoke, do not drink to excess, and are not taking any non-prescription drugs."

"How do you *know* that?"

"At your age, if you smoked, you would have little lines, like parentheses, on each side of your mouth when your face is relaxed. You do not. And you do not drink to excess because I can detect the odor of alcohol nearly a block away and would have known it the moment you stepped into my office."

"Yes, but who drinks in the morning?"

"I am not talking about this morning. If you had consumed any alcohol in the last forty-eight hours, it would leach out of your pores as perspiration and be highly detectable. Since you did not drink over the weekend, odds are you do not drink much at all."

"Anything else, Mr. Wizard?"

"Well, that is Dr. Wizard to you, and yes, since your eyes are clear and the pupils are not unnecessarily dilated in the lamplight, you are articulate, and your hands are not shaking, I can safely assume you do not indulge in any recreational drugs. Again, if you did, you would have done so over the weekend."

Impressed at the accuracy of his analysis, I signed and dated the form.

"If that was a test, Dr. Wizard, you passed."

He smiled, and I was struck again by how handsome he was. Blushing slightly, I handed him my nearly completed questionnaire. Only one question was left unanswered. There was no way I was going to tell him how often I had sex. I could have lied, but I wasn't sure what a good lie would be, and "anniversaries only" wasn't one of the multiple-choice options. Smiling to myself, I thought *I might have to revisit that question in August.*

"Thank you," he said, glancing at the back of the application. "Mrs. Taylor, based on our discussion, I believe GatesWay can assist you in achieving the success you seek, and I am delighted you will be joining us. I will escort you to our financial consultant, and she will get everything in order before you meet your program designer."

"I have to pay before I play?" I asked lightly.

"Every time," he answered in the same tone.

We walked silently for several moments, but my impressions of the clinic kept bubbling up to the top of my mind. The beauty that graced each level of the building was so new to me that it was impossible to pretend this was something I did every day.

"It is so lovely here, Dr. Gates, the various architectural touches, the way the light changes from one area to the next, and it's not only that, but the mood also seems to change."

He didn't respond, so I added, "It's almost like walking through scenes of a play. The lighting and the furnishings all seem designed to make you feel…well, inspired, I guess, without being aware of it."

"Why do you think that?"

"I took a couple of courses in visual art and theatrical set design when I was in college, a long time ago."

He stopped at the financial consultant's door.

"I think you are giving us far more credit than we deserve, Mrs. Taylor. We are doctors, not interior decorators, but now I am curious. How do you feel?"

Facing him, I wished time would stop so I would never have to look away. As captivating as any perfect work of art, his face was a myriad of expressions all at once: expectant, amused, and attentive, yet with a palpable tension that demanded an honest response.

"Very happy to be here, Dr. Gates."

"Well, that is good to know. I may have to send the lighting technicians a thank-you note."

I put my hand on the door.

"Mrs. Taylor?"

"Yes, Dr. Gates."

"Please call me Dr. Grant. There are five other Dr. Gates in the facility, and I do not want you to forget that you are mine, I mean, my client."

I nodded, but before I could answer, he turned and walked back down the corridor.

Inexplicably, I wanted to hear his voice again. I tried to think of something clever to say, but when I did, he'd already disappeared around the corner. The taste of bitter honey still lingering in my mouth was irrevocably connected to his name and the lilt of his voice, and I knew I would remember that afternoon for the rest of my life.

As soon as he was out of her line of sight, Grant's smile faded into grimmer lines. Only years of staying alive by expecting the unexpected had kept the look of disbelief from his face. None of the nearly three thousand women who had walked through their doors ever mentioned the correlation between the lighting and the rooms. Of course, they admired the furniture and how the different areas were arranged, yet no one noticed the subtle distinctions in lighting or questioned the reasons they liked being at GatesWay.

Why was she different?

He, more than anyone else in the colony, knew how a single curious mind could affect the colony's safety.

Taking the nearest employees' exit to the catwalks, Grant scanned the building to make sure no one was around to see him. He grabbed the black metal railing with both hands and fought the urge to kill her. Recalling the light and shadows of her face, he found himself calculating the different ways he could lure her into one of the empty rooms where he could sedate her and devour her at his leisure.

The image of the gold ring on her left hand flitted through his mind. A married woman with a job and family couldn't just disappear. Well, *she could*, but inquiries would be made. A quick risk assessment put killing her out of immediate consideration. Nevertheless, he had to do something. In the facility for less than an hour and, she suspected—out loud—that certain areas were designed to elicit a specific response. Allowing that level of awareness to continue unmonitored was more than dangerous; it was reckless.

What else would she notice in the days, weeks, and months ahead? And why now, when they were so close...

Working with a non-negotiable deadline, Grant knew he could not allow anything—or anyone—to delay or distract his brothers from achieving their objective on time. His hands tightened and twisted on the rail. He tried to imagine them on her neck but instead saw the way her eyes brightened when she smiled. His hands slowly relaxed.

She would see *nothing*.

As her consultant, he controlled her program, and as the facility's director, he controlled nearly everything else. He would order temporary lighting adjustments and find ways to keep her too busy to notice anything he did not want her to see. At present, her observations had not done them any harm. After all, what did she say? Her soft voice echoed in his mind, *"Very happy to be here."*

Of course, she felt that way. She was *supposed* to want to be here. Her sense of well-being and pleasure was only the beginning of a calculated strategy that went much further than she could imagine. From the moment a client walked beneath the blue and white awning, she existed as a butterfly in a glass jar in which the facility controlled her thoughts, emotions, and, to some extent, her pleasures—and their clients rarely left disappointed.

From conception to completion, Grant reflected on the last four years and allowed himself to enjoy a silent moment of success. Keeping their secrets safe was a suitable finale for his service and sacrifice. And nothing, not even a nascent desire to remake GatesWay's newest client into the Lyostian idealized image of Persephone, would be permitted to risk the colony's mission or threaten the façade of unquestioning obedience he'd spent a lifetime perfecting.

Letting Caroline Live

It had been a long, thoughtful walk back to his office. Calm now and thinking it through, Grant decided it would be enough to adjust the lights and move a few things out of her way.

Her?

What was her name? Grant thought for a moment. *Oh, yes. Carrie.*

He didn't like it. It was just a piece of a name without meaning. Sitting at his desk, he looked up her financial records, *Caroline*. Yes, that was much better. Someday, he might ask her if he could call her Caroline. Maybe she would call him Grant. He rationalized that by breaking down the barriers of formality, perhaps she would come to him with her suspicions before voicing them to anyone else. It was a highly probable conclusion, but he couldn't wait that long. Something needed to be done now.

Howard.

Yes, Grant.

Adjust the settings on the illumination panel in areas H12, 14, and 17 from warm to cool by twenty degrees tomorrow, forty degrees Wednesday, and back it down to twenty degrees on Thursday. I will let you know when to return the settings to optimum illumination levels. Blend the connection grids gradually. And Howard, I do not want to detect one flicker.

May I ask why, Grant?

Yes. Someone noticed.

Wouldn't it be better to neutralize...?

Howard, are you arguing with me?

No, no, no, Grant. Not at all, never. I was just suggesting…options.

Don't. Neutralization should always be the last option, Howard, never the first.

May I ask who?

No. I will monitor the situation. If it escalates, we will take care of her.

We?

Of course.

Thank you, Grant, thank you. I'll get started right away and I promise, not one flicker.

Yes.

For reasons he did not fully understand, Dr. Grant Gates decided to let Mrs. Caroline Taylor live a little longer.

Measurements

It only took five minutes for Eileen Geiger, the financial consultant, to process my membership application.

Handing me the credit card receipt, she said, "If you would like to continue after six months, Mrs. Taylor, we will charge you on a monthly basis."

"Do most members continue their membership?" I asked.

"Oh my, yes. GatesWay becomes an integral part of their daily routine. We help them stay focused, and they help us stay in business."

"So, it's the fitness clinic that pays the rent around here, not the spa services?"

"I can tell you haven't seen the spa side when you ask that question. It's usually booked weeks in advance, and we charge more for some services than anywhere else in town." She shook her head in wonder. "These women pay it without blinking. I haven't been here long enough to try everything, but I've heard the massages are to die for."

"Well, I guess that is something to look forward to. Are there any other services I should know about?"

"Since you asked, and I don't get a commission for this, we do have the finest OB-GYN facilities in the city here. With so many women as members, it really made sense to offer routine examinations as well. We also provide limited obstetrical services, but only to the fourth month when expectant mothers are referred to a doctor with hospital privileges. Three of the meditation rooms are also examination rooms making it convenient for our clients."

"You're right. That does make sense. Maybe I'll think about that, too. Thank you for mentioning it."

"You're welcome. Please let me know if you need anything else." She pressed a button on her desk. Scarcely a minute passed before my escort arrived.

I leaned toward her. "Why am I escorted everywhere?"

"Once you've been issued a wristband, you'll have access to the lobby, lockers, and exercise rooms, but it will seem like a maze around here until you get used to the floor plan. Besides," she said, "if you didn't have an escort, how would you know where to go next?"

Realizing she was right, I turned to follow my escort, noticing for the first time that he wore the same type of eyeglasses as Dr. Grant.

Something to ask Suzanne about.

Stopping in front of an office nearly identical to the one I'd just left, my escort pulled out a chair for me.

"You will be issued your first wristband here, so I will not have the pleasure of assisting you anymore today, Mrs. Taylor."

I smiled and nodded, but before I could thank him, Dr. Grant's shorter, slightly broader twin entered the office. I knew from Suzanne they were not actually twins, only brothers, but if you discounted that this one also wore glasses and wasn't as handsome, the family resemblance was striking. Despite their similarities, the main difference between the two Dr. Gates I had met so far was that this brother seemed infinitely more agreeable.

"Good afternoon, Mrs. Taylor. I am Dr. Garrett."

I noticed right away that he spoke without the singsong cadences of Dr. Grant.

"We are happy you have chosen to join GatesWay, and I am here to help you pursue a healthier lifestyle as efficiently as possible. In a few minutes, my assistant will assess your current health status, and you will determine your personal goals. Afterward, we will meet again to design a program to help you achieve those goals. I promise you," he said smiling, "you won't be bored."

"Thank you."

"When you step into the measuring salon, you will see a dressing room to the right with hospital gowns in every size. Please leave the gown open in the front; it will be more convenient for you."

"Excuse me?" *Was I going to have to take my clothes off for this?*

"Yes, Mrs. Taylor?"

"How much do I need to undress for these, um, measurements?" I looked down at my two-piece suit, blouse, pantyhose, and high heels.

"Well, of course, that is completely up to you. Under no circumstances do we want you to feel uncomfortable. However, the more accurate our measurements, the easier it will be to track your progress. In the future, you may want to wear clothes that allow better access to your body than those you are wearing today."

"Okay…thank you."

"Please stand on the pedestal when you are ready, and Andrea will be in to assist you."

Although the teal blue and white carpeting gave the measuring salon a tranquil atmosphere, I didn't trust it. I knew that lurking somewhere was that horrible white medical scale that clanged ca-chunk, ca-chunk as it announced every increment of your weight to the world like a hammer on your heart. And, as if that humiliation wasn't enough, it was always followed by the grating sound of the metal slide on the balance lever as it was pushed relentlessly to the right, adding ounce by ounce until the bar reached a perfect balance. Experience had shown me that it was always worse than you thought it would be and always embarrassing. Just because it wasn't in plain sight didn't mean it wasn't hiding behind a curtain somewhere—as it should—being far too ugly to be in this beautiful room.

The dressing room was decorated with fresh flowers in a crystal vase and as lovely as the rest of GatesWay. In spite of what I suspected was going to be a humiliating ordeal, I found myself starting to relax. I flipped through the white paper bags on the bench until I found an L and an XL.

Well, Carrie, how optimistic are you today? I chose the XL. *Better a little loose than too tight.*

Removing everything but my "old lady panties," as Dan called my work lingerie, I opened the bag and pulled out the hospital gown. The soft fabric in my hands was unlike any hospital gown I'd ever seen. Pale teal with a white swirl, the silken fabric slid smoothly over my arms and wrapped around my shoulders. Pulling the ties snugly beneath my breasts, it was the most flattering and feminine garment I had worn in years.

I left the dressing room, stepped onto the small pedestal in the center of the room, and saw myself infinitely reflected in the mirrored panels. At the sound of a chime, a tall young woman entered wearing a white lab coat and carrying a clipboard.

"Hi," she said as she walked up to me. Her loosely falling blond curls bounced a little with each step. "I'm Andrea, Dr. Garrett's assistant. Did he tell you what we are doing today?"

"Measuring me?"

"Yes, but that's just numbers, speaking of which," she glanced down at the floor and wrote something down. Walking over to the doorframe, she said, "Please stand up straight and don't look directly into the light."

She slid a laser up the side of the frame until it appeared on the opposite wall. Looking up at it, she wrote something else down. When she pressed a button, the red light disappeared.

"Could you step from the pedestal for a moment? I need to turn the scale off."

"This is a scale?" I asked incredulously.

"Yes," she laughed. "Height and weight first."

"But what about the clothes I'm wearing?"

"Gown and panties, right?"

"Yes…"

"Already noted."

She removed a pair of calipers and a tape measure from her pocket. "Do you want me to do this, or do you want to help?"

"I don't understand."

"Well, I can either walk around, pinching here, measuring there, and be done. Or I can give you fair warning and say something like, 'Okay, I need you to move your arm now.'"

I laughed. "I'm yours, Andrea, have at it."

"It really is much faster this way."

She wasn't kidding, she *was* fast. Moving me around like an overgrown fashion doll, she pinched my waist and upper arm with the calipers. Using the tape, I don't think she left one spot unmeasured. Less than ten minutes later, I was sitting on a bench in the dressing room as she sat on the pedestal facing me with the clipboard on her knees.

"Well, Carrie, we have come to the moment of truth. For your height and body frame, your target measurements should be approximately one hundred twenty-three to one hundred twenty-eight pounds with a BMI of twenty-two to twenty-four percent. And that is a healthy weight, not runway model thin. We don't do anorexia here. You weigh one hundred sixty-four point two pounds, and your BMI is thirty-four percent. So, it is up to you to decide now what you would like to weigh." She paused to let the numbers sink in.

"Tell me, Carrie, how thin is the woman in your head?"

I thought for a moment. I weighed one hundred-sixteen pounds when I met Dan, but that was beach season, and I was starvation thin. I weighed one hundred and twenty-four pounds when we married. One year later, when I became pregnant with Brendan, I weighed almost one hundred and thirty pounds. It had been pretty much downhill from there. I couldn't remember "letting myself go." It was more like I'd lost track of myself with so much else to be responsible for.

How thin is the woman in my head? I mentally viewed our honeymoon photos and saw the girl in a red and white striped bikini on the sun-drenched coast of Bermuda.

I wanted her back. I took a deep breath and said, "Forty pounds."

She checked her chart. "That is a bit more than one and one-half pounds a week, easily accomplished in six months if you keep to the program."

"Not six months," I corrected her. "Four."

"Well, that's two and one-half pounds a week without any backsliding. That can be difficult for someone who hasn't taken fitness seriously in some time."

"If by 'some time' you mean nearly twenty years, then yes, you are right. But while I will commit to losing forty pounds in six months, I would like my program designed so I will lose it in four. That way, I have two extra months if my original goal proves too hard."

"Do you have a big date in four months? An anniversary, perhaps?"

"Uh, no." Then I remembered my earlier lie to Suzanne. "High school reunion."

"Ah, of course," she said. "I'm going to prepare my report for Dr. Garrett, and he will see you as soon as you are dressed."

Mentioning Dr. Garrett's name prompted me to ask a question that had been bothering me all afternoon. I was going to ask Suzanne, but….

"Andrea, how long have you worked here?"

"Practically since the beginning, nearly three years now."

"May I ask you a question?"

"Yes, if I may have the option of not answering."

"Fair enough. The eyeglasses, Andrea, why do all the doctors and escorts I've seen so far all wear those tinted glasses?"

She sat back down. "I don't have a medical degree yet," she said, "but I also asked that question when I started working here. Did you know that all the doctors are brothers?"

"Yes, a friend of mine told me."

"Well, all the escorts—and there are six of them, too—are cousins participating in a medical management program. GatesWay is a family-owned franchise, and they are interning here."

"What does that have to do with their eyes?"

"They all suffer from a somewhat rare congenital eye disease that causes photophobia, which means, technically, fear of light. They are not actually afraid of light, but bright lights cause them a lot of pain. Dr. Garrett said it's like sticking needles in your brain, and the glasses help block the light."

"But the glasses do not seem *that* dark. Their eyes are visible through the lenses."

"They are a lot darker than you think. The lenses work like a two-way mirror, but not quite. They block out nearly all the light on their side while letting you see their eyes from the observer or brighter side."

"What about the light from around the edges of the lenses? Doesn't that hurt them, too?"

"The frames are more curved than they appear. They aren't goggles by any means, but they aren't flat, either. And you will notice that there is little overhead lighting in the doctors' areas."

That was why Dr. Grant sat behind the partition when the desk lamp was on; it hurt his eyes. I instantly regretted making him walk around the partition to answer my questions.

"Well, I was just wondering. It seemed unusual that they were all wearing the same glasses, but now it makes sense." I started to close the dressing room door. "Andrea, last question. Why doesn't Dr. Garrett have the same accent that Dr. Grant has?"

"They all have that accent. When they talk to each other, it's almost like they are singing. They try to speak without it, but sometimes they forget."

I stood up. "Will Dr. Garrett come in here like you did?"

"No, they are very proper. He would never dare to presume when you are ready to see him. That door will take you into his office. If he isn't there, press the button on the corner of his desk. It was very nice meeting you, and I'll see you again in two weeks."

"Thank you, Andrea."

When I returned to his office, Dr. Garrett was already typing the data from Andrea's curly handwriting into the computer. Among the papers and files on his desk were a blue wristband, a small jar, and a candle.

"Mrs. Taylor," he said, "I am sorry I did not hear you come in. I've been designing your program. Please have a seat...I will only be another minute."

I waited as he tapped the keyboard. Then, he stopped abruptly and turned to me with an expression of concern.

"Mrs. Taylor, we want our clients to be successful in attaining the goals they set for themselves. However, forty pounds in four months is going to be harder than you may think right now. We worry about you losing weight too fast and how that will do three things to your body, none of them desirable. First, it can compromise your immune system because you are not taking in sufficient calories. Second, if you lose weight too fast, it is possible to lose muscle tissue with the fat, so although you may weigh less, you are less fit. Third, commitment to that rate of weight loss is difficult to sustain, disappointment sets in, the whole plan is jettisoned, and we never see you again."

"Forty pounds in four months, Dr. Garrett." Then, remembering how well it worked on his brother, I added, "Please."

"As you wish, Mrs. Taylor, but be sure to report any lightheadedness or fainting. If, during your exercise classes, you feel the least bit weak, stop, then try to go a little longer at the next session. If you push past your endurance level and hurt yourself, we will bench you until *we* decide you are healed. This is a health facility, not boot camp. Also, expect to be tired as your body adjusts to fewer calories, so please try to get at least eight hours of sleep at night. You will be less hungry if you are rested.

"Here is your class schedule. I understand you work full time, so most of your classes are before eight-thirty in the morning or after five-thirty in the afternoon. There is also one on Saturday mornings. On Saturday afternoons, the machine rooms are open from one to five with an on-site attendant for instruction and assistance. We are not open on Sundays."

He handed me a pamphlet with two numbers written on the front cover: Calories, fifteen hundred; Fat Grams, fifty. "This is your nutrition information."

"So, I can eat anything as long as I stay within these limits?" I asked.

"You can eat anything in this booklet as long as you stay within the parameters noted on the cover."

"This is a very thin booklet."

"Yes. I thought that was your goal."

"Ha!" I said, "Very funny." I couldn't keep myself from laughing. Everything was coming together. By the time Eric's birthday got here, I would be as thin and beautiful as humanly possible.

"As noted on your schedule, you are due back here in two weeks to assess your progress, check your muscle tone, and tweak any difficulties you may be experiencing. In the meantime, I would appreciate it if you would not use your scale at home to judge any weight loss, as they are often inaccurate. Let us surprise you in two weeks."

"So, I won't see Dr. Grant again?"

"Yes, you will meet with him once a month to review your overall satisfaction with your progress, the facility, and whenever you earn a reward. Now, just a few more formalities."

He pushed a form toward me. "This is a formal agreement stating that you want to lose forty pounds during your six-month contract and that you understand you will be charged accordingly."

I quickly signed my name. *No turning back now.*

"A couple of first-visit perks," he said, picking up the blue wristband.

"You must wear this, or you will not be able to get past the lobby without an escort. It will let you in all the rooms—there is a floor plan on the back of your schedule—that has this blue symbol in the corner. As you progress, your wristband will be upgraded to allow access to our personal trainer fitness rooms and other amenities such as the sauna, whirlpool, etc."

He picked up the candle. "We don't recommend that you exercise at home, but we do believe in meditation and visualization. While practicing the techniques covered in tomorrow's orientation in a quiet room at home, burning this candle may help reinforce the willpower we hope you will learn here."

"What happens when this candle burns out? Is there a place where I can order more?"

"The orientation session tomorrow morning includes a tour of the fitness and spa facilities, the spa gift shop, and juice bar." Lifting the jar and setting it in front of me, he continued, "And I would like to give you a sample jar of our bitter honey. Do you like it?"

"Yes, I do," I said, suddenly feeling shy and blushing. "Very much."

He tilted his head and smiled at me. "I'm glad. It's exclusive to our facility. We encourage our clients to eat a teaspoon a day on one slice of whole-wheat toast, one half of an English muffin, or drizzled on fresh fruit, preferably at breakfast."

"Or a bagel?" I asked, thinking how great it would taste on a toasted cinnamon raisin bagel.

"Mrs. Taylor?"

"Yes, Dr. Garrett."

"That booklet I just handed to you."

I looked at the booklet in my hands. "Yes, sir?"

"There are no bagels in there." Smiling as he said it took the sting out of his words.

"Right, of course not." I couldn't have felt sillier. *Oh yes, I could. It would have been far more humiliating if I had said that to Dr. Grant instead of Dr. Garrett.*

I didn't run into Suzanne before I left, but I emailed her my class schedule as soon as I could to determine how it meshed with her work schedule. I had missed her so much since she graduated that I found myself looking forward to a summer of long talks over no-bacon-bits, no-croutons, no-cheese, and low-fat-dressing-only salads.

Intentions

When I returned to my office, the "new mail" signal was blinking on my computer. The first one was from Eric. "Ninety-five days" was all it said. I wondered if I was going to receive nine-four more. I smiled at the thought of being on his mind at least once every day for the next three months. *Three months?? Oh, damn!* I had miscounted and thought I had four. *Fine.* I would keep looking better to him as I lost the final ten pounds. Echoing his enthusiasm, I responded with two words of my own: "…and counting."

More exciting than the confirmation of Eric's email was holding the GatesWay booklet in my hand. I felt empowered and loved this new and positive direction of my life. Changes were going to begin now.

Tonight.

As much as I loved them, my role as Dan and Brendan understood it was over. The last twenty years spent trying to meet every need, anticipate every desire, and be all things to them all the time was finished. The woman in my head was finally waking up. It was my turn. The slender booklet in my hands was a first step to reclaiming my life, and failure was not an option.

Recalling my conversation with Suzanne, I thought maybe she was right. *Perhaps somehow, in some way, I would rediscover my place in the world.*

On my way home, I stopped at the grocery store and bought fruit, salad vegetables, and a rotisserie chicken. Dan was standing in the kitchen when I came in with the bags.

"You're late."

"Yes, I had to stop at the grocery store."

"I thought you went to the grocery store on Saturday."

"I did, but I decided to change the menu."

"For tonight?"

"For the rest of my life."

First Day

"Welcome to GatesWay Fitness Clinic and Health Spa. My name is Natalie Brockman, and we are delighted you have chosen us to assist you in living healthier lives."

Looking around as if to make sure, she said, "We are all women here this morning, and that is the best thing to be. According to Genesis, without you, there would be nothing but a planet with animals, plants, and a guy standing around, probably with a stick in his hand, with nothing to do. I like to think that woman was created last because all that came before her was practice. The fact that we have sharp minds, soft hands, and know how to use them is just a bonus to our necessity for the survival of humanity. Yes, I know men are necessary, too, but think about this example for a moment. If you take five women of childbearing age and one virile man, you have the beginnings of a small society, and from such small societies, civilizations are built. However, if you take five virile men and one woman of childbearing age, the odds are higher that the species is likely to cease to exist. So, never take your role as a human female for granted, and don't let anyone else do it either.

"I've seen your charts and know that many of you have set ambitious goals, and I want you to succeed. After all, your success is as important to us as it is to you. So, I am going to talk a little bit about the GatesWay diet plan—there isn't one.

"You've each received a booklet listing the foods we recommend. You have suggested daily consumption limits on the front cover, and it is up to you to fill your meals with the most nutritious food you enjoy. One way to do this is what GatesWay calls 'eat like you are immortal.' Eating like an immortal takes a long view of the cumulative effect of what you eat and how food affects your body longer than the thirty to sixty minutes you actually spend eating every day. When you start thinking rationally about what you eat, you will realize that you don't have to eat everything you see or eat it all right now. As an immortal, you will always have another opportunity for that chocolate bar, that second piece of cake. Always remember, what you put into your mouth will either help you toward your goal or keep you from achieving it. Think before you choose.

"Thank you for listening to my little pep talk. If you could take one thing away with you this morning, I would like you to love the woman in the mirror. Visualize her face in your mind when you are tempted to eat something you shouldn't, or skip a class, or decide you don't have time for yourself, but also visualize her when you keep your appointments, attend class, and step on our scales to find that you've lost weight and inches. Ask yourself, is she worried about you, or is she proud of you?

"Before Ellen takes you on a tour of our facilities, I would like a moment to speak with each of you, so don't hurry out. Thank you."

Sipping a small glass of orange juice, I watched as Natalie met everyone and made notes on her clipboard.

Then she turned to me. "Mrs. Taylor?"

"Yes."

"Do you have any questions about the presentation?"

"No, Natalie. It was what I expected, except for the 'eat like an immortal' technique. That was new."

"Ah yes, Dr. Grant contributed that. He says most people eat like they are balls in a pinball game, bouncing from one meal or snack to another without realizing the cumulative impact. He believes everyone should eat slowly, taking the food into their minds as well as their bodies. Americans, he says, don't do that. They all eat like they are dining at fast-food restaurants, whether they are or not."

"Dr. Grant isn't American?"

"Yes, they're technically Americans, but they are from a military family and were raised all over the world, spending a lot of time in Malaysia or Indonesia...I get those places confused."

"Are any of them married?"

She laughed. "Just for the record, you are the fourth woman to ask me that question this morning. The answer is no, but also yes."

"Okay, I'll bite. What does that mean?"

"No, they aren't married...yes, they're all engaged...even the interns. Once they achieve a certain status, they will return home to marry the wife their family has chosen. They are quite strict. I've been here since the beginning, and there has never been a hint of impropriety with anyone connected with the facility."

She looked at the line forming by the door. "Oh darn, we are holding Ellen up. I need to ask you one quick question. What's your mantra?"

"My mantra?"

"Yes, you know, 'you can't be too rich or too thin,' 'one minute on the lips, forever on the hips,' something verbal that will motivate you to stick to your program."

Thinking for a moment, I broke out into a big smile and touched my lips. "Nothing tastes as good as being kissed feels."

"Ooh, good one," she said, writing it next to my name.

Unexpected

A couple of days following his interview with Mrs. Taylor, Grant began to notice her perfume in the corridors and realized how much he liked it. He could detect an underlying sweetness of the honey she was now eating regularly, and the combination made her scent easier to distinguish from the facility's other clients. Grant also noticed he was in the halls or standing behind the mirror whenever she was taking a class. He told himself she was a new client; he was *supposed* to monitor her in case she was having any difficulties with the routines. But, watching her while hidden behind the glass, he couldn't help but admire her natural grace as she moved in time to the exercise forms.

His requested modifications to the lighting had gone smoothly, so if she thought of it at all, she would suppose that her first impression was just her imagination. He intended to reintroduce the original design gradually, and he needed to gauge when it would be wise to do so. Since no one would dare question his whereabouts on any given day, he watched her as often as his duties would allow. As predicted, it only took two weeks until everything was back in place. He listened to see if she noticed, but she gave no sign of realizing she was now as helplessly caught in their bell jar as every other client at the facility.

Despite his vigilance, she occasionally caught him by surprise.

Leaving class one afternoon, she saw him standing in the hall. She smiled and waved at him as though they were in high school, and he half expected to see her carrying textbooks. Nodding in her direction, Grant fought the urge to look behind him to make sure she wasn't waving at someone else.

That evening, as Grant reviewed his client files for the upcoming week's appointments, he removed Caroline's file from his desk drawer. Since she was too old for consideration as a prospective mother, he hadn't paid much attention to her application when she returned it to him. He skimmed the front page and frowned. She was even a couple of years older than he thought, making her completely ineligible for the colony's plans. Good for her, bad for them—and for his research. Unwilling to share his concern regarding her observations with his brothers, he considered using her for some of his preliminary testing as a cover for watching her more closely, but based on the information in her file, he could not justify that level of involvement.

Well, safer for her if I don't.

Continuing to review her questionnaire, he noted she had not been content with just answering yes or no to many of the questions. Some of her comments were candid and insightful, and a few were embellished with stars, swirls, and asterisks. Grant smiled as he read.

Husband, son, hmm, seventeen, college soon, no answer on number thirty-seven. He glanced at Andrea's report and approved the program Garrett designed. He began to close the file when his eyes were drawn to Natalie's note regarding her mantra. The words surprised him; he had never heard that phrase before. Curious to discover how common it was, he decided to bring it up at dinner to get a consensus of its popularity.

Waiting until everyone was sipping their honey-sweetened tea, he said, "I heard a new mantra today."

"Oh, let me guess," said Gregory, "'You can't be too rich or too thin.'"

"No."

"Well?"

"I was waiting to see if there were any more guesses."

Garrett spoke up. "One of my new clients' mantra is 'live, love, lose.' Not bad."

"Or," interjected Gordon, "how about 'nothing tastes as good as being thin feels?'"

"So, that is where she got it."

"That's it?"

"No, but close. Her mantra is 'nothing tastes as good as being kissed feels.'"

"Oh, I like her version better."

Gregory laughed. "Please tell me she is young and single."

"No. Married and mother of a seventeen-year-old son."

Garrett was curious. "Then why is that her mantra? If she's married, isn't she already being kissed? And if she isn't being kissed, why is she still married? So, if she's married and being kissed, then who else does she want to kiss her?"

"All good questions, but too philosophical for me, Garrett. I was just wondering if she made it up or if it was in common usage."

No one else had ever heard that precise combination of words. Grant was gratified they didn't realize that he'd dropped out of the conversation as Garrett's questions tumbled over in his mind...*who indeed*?

Returning to his office to update her file, Grant went back to the section with the missing answer. The question, "How often do you engage in sexual relations?" was left blank—not a scratch out, remark, or drawing. Grant did not know why that bothered him, except Garrett had a point. Based on the possible interpretations of her mantra, either she was losing weight to get her husband's attention—who should be thanking his god every day he woke up next to her—or she was losing weight to get the attention of someone else...someone who had kissed her.

Grant thought of little else all weekend. The following Monday found him once again standing in the hall when she came out of class. Ostensibly making notes on a clipboard, he waited for her to notice him.

"Hi, Dr. Grant."

She looked radiant. Already slimming down and glowing from the exercise, she smelled so delicious that, for a moment, Grant had a problem finding his tongue.

"Good afternoon, umm," he glanced down at the file in his hands, "Mrs. Taylor."

"You have my file?"

"Yes," he answered, trying to sound casual. "I wanted to ask you about your mantra. It's ah, new to me." He waited for a moment and read it aloud as though he hadn't memorized every word in the file.

"Nothing tastes as good as being kissed feels." He looked at her and smiled. "It is very original."

"Thank you, but I didn't make it up. I adapted it from something else."

"So, you like being kissed?"

"Doesn't everybody?"

Grant's only memories of kisses were from a blind nurse, and so long ago, he couldn't remember what they felt like.

"Well, yes, of course, they do. I have never heard a mantra phrased exactly that way, and I wanted to verify that it was written correctly. I hope it encourages you to be successful, Mrs. Taylor."

She didn't move. Looking down, she said shyly, "Well, you know, Dr. Grant, sometimes it's enough encouragement to know that someone wants to kiss you. Sometimes the actual kiss is just a bonus." When she looked back up at him, there were tears shining in her eyes.

She smiled through them. "Must go home now…always a zillion things to do. Goodnight, Dr. Grant."

A quick wave, and she was gone.

No, he thought, watching her walk away, *not a chance*. He would not hurt her. Writing "too vulnerable" on the inside of her file, he closed it and promised himself he would stop noticing her. He had determined she was not dangerous. In fact, she was acclimating quite well to the facility's routines and had not made any further suspicious observations. The need for constant surveillance was over.

Poised to return her file to his desk drawer, Grant hesitated. There was something about her that brought back his idea of slowly seducing the most likely prospective mothers. He recalled the tears in her eyes, and although she was not a candidate under any circumstances, he could still exploit her vulnerability to test specific stimuli. A woman whose tender feelings were so easily read would be an ideal subject. If she recoiled or rejected certain behaviors, then he would discard them, but if her response was positive, he could use the successful techniques on his clients who met the selection criteria.

It was possible…he mused. Taking a new file folder, he wrote on the tab: Human Experiment of Actualizing Relationships through Bonding and Encouraging Acceptance through Submission. It was a pretentious beginning, but he could not see any downside to this approach. Although convinced of the value of his research, Grant was still not ready to share his experiment with the rest of the colony. Final decisions would not be made for two months, and he could use that time to devise tests to prove his hypothesis. Keeping his plans to himself also had one fundamental advantage: no one would know if he failed.

Oh, but if he were successful, then his new brothers would have mothers who loved and wanted them. For their first year, they would live in the light of their mother and feel her love. Regardless of what else happened or what they had to endure for the rest of their lives, they would always have that place in their minds to escape to. No one would be able to take away the memory of her love.

It would make them strong.

It had been more than ten years since Grant cared whether a human lived or died. Resting his head on his hands, he recalled Caroline's trusting eyes looking up into his and sang Anya's song of protection.

First Reward

Grant kept the promise he made to himself. He wasn't noticing her as much anymore. After a decade of unrelenting self-discipline, denial was more than a habit; it was a way of life. He had been assigned some interesting prospects in the last few weeks and was focused on charming them. Still, Caroline had been so successful that it was only fair to reward her for outstanding progress during their second program review.

When his next appointment called to say she would be late, he had some extra time, and it seemed natural to him to prepare Caroline some tea and toast.

Shyly entering his office, she was, to his eyes, lovelier than ever, even in those ugly workout clothes all the women wore. He forgave her when he noticed how they hugged her body, outlining every curve and enhancing every shadow. For the first time, Grant wondered what she looked like without them and decided that regardless of the tile she chose, she would receive a programmed shower massage, *his* programmed shower massage.

Dr. Grant stood as I entered the room.

"Mrs. Taylor, I have been looking at your file, and I am pleased to see that you have made outstanding progress. An eighteen-pound weight loss together with a reduction of body fat that is even more impressive—and with no resulting loss in muscle tissue. It isn't a reduction rate we recommend, but you've done well, and that kind of success should be rewarded. Would you like that?"

Smiling, he waved at the crystal bowl containing small colored tiles in front of him like a magician.

I couldn't resist smiling back at him. "Well, Dr. Grant, while a reward is nice, I am happier with the way I look and feel than any reward you have in that bowl."

"Thank you. That is exactly how we want you to feel. Being healthy is its own reward, and that realization will encourage your continued success. However, we like to offer incentives to our fitness clients as they make serious inroads toward their goals by providing an opportunity to experience spa services that may not be a part of their regular routine. So, please let us share your success by pampering you a bit."

Rainbows flashed across his desk as he swirled the tiles in front of me.

As before, when he offered me a taste of the bitter honey, I didn't know how I could turn him down. Closing my eyes, I reached into the bowl and chose a teal-colored tile. I handed it to him.

"Good choice," he said, looking at the code card in front of him. Noticing the question in my eyes, he added, "We change it every week, so our fitness clients experience a variety of our spa services instead of choosing their favorite over and over." He consulted the list again. "Mrs. Taylor, you chose the double massage and an hour in one of our meditation rooms."

"What's a double massage?"

"A full body massage followed by a shower massage. We always schedule a meditation room after a double massage because it can be…quite relaxing."

"How long does it take? I work during the day."

"Two hours, one hour for the massages and one for meditation."

"Question."

"Yes, Mrs. Taylor?"

"Can you call me Caroline?"

"Yes, I can, Caroline. Was that your question?"

"No. What?" I took a deep breath. *Why do I always feel so self-conscious around this man? And why did my name sound so nice when he said it?*

"Okay, well, you see, I'm not sure I would be comfortable with someone giving me a massage in a shower, even if it was a woman."

Looking at me with barely suppressed amusement, he sat back in his chair and didn't speak for several moments. I could feel a hot blush staining my cheeks.

"Mrs. Taylor…Caroline," he said, "no one will be with you during the shower massage. The masseurs use oils and lotions during the massage, and there is a certain aromatic bonus when followed by a warm shower. It prolongs the effect of the physical massage by slowing the heat loss from your muscles. The showers are located between the massage and meditation rooms, so it is a one, two, three experience."

I looked at him doubtfully. It sounded more complicated than one, two, three.

"If you don't enjoy it, Caroline," he said slowly, glancing at the tiles in the bowl, "I promise to find you a reward you will like."

There was a seductive undercurrent to his words. My stomach immediately filled with butterflies. I had trouble breathing, and it was an effort to keep my voice even.

"I'm sure it will be lovely."

Continuing to regard me with an amused smile, he said, "Caroline, I have a few minutes before my next appointment. Would you care for some tea and toast?"

Remembering he hadn't offered me tea the last time I was here, I thought it might be part of the reward.

"That would be lovely, too."

A few minutes later, we sat in the visitor chairs and used the receptionist's desk as a tea table. As he reached for his cup, I noticed the scars on his fingers for the first time.

"Oh, Dr. Grant."

I instinctively took his hand in both of mine. Horrified at the level of pain he must have endured to incur so much scar tissue, I gently traced the white lines inside his fingers.

"What happened to your hands?"

I quickly became aware that my voice was the only sound in the room. I looked up and saw him staring at his hand in mine as though my concern had somehow embarrassed him. I was instantly ashamed.

"I'm so sorry, Dr. Grant, that was unforgivably rude of me." I pulled my hands away from his, picked up my workout jacket, and started to stand.

"No, please, we still have a few minutes. Please, don't go," he said.

I sat down slowly. Picking up my teacup, I tried to pretend that I had not asked such a personal question that was so obviously none of my business.

"I'm sorry," I repeated.

"No, forgive me, I overreacted. It was, quite simply, a childhood accident so long ago that I don't notice them anymore. The scars are part of who I am." He put his cup down. "I cannot even remember the last time anyone asked me about them. I hesitated because I did not immediately understand what you meant.

"It is quite all right, though," he said, smiling. "Please feel free to hold my hand anytime."

Or not. Irritated because I had gone from being stupid to hysterical to rude all in the space of about five minutes, I concentrated on silently drinking my tea.

"What were we talking about? Oh, yes, scheduling your reward. I'll check the computer and see what is available." Getting up quickly, he disappeared behind the partition.

I heard the rapid clicking of the keyboard. "We have next Monday or Wednesday afternoon at three o'clock. Are either of those days convenient for you?"

Remembering Dr. Bennett was attending a seminar Wednesday afternoon, I answered, "Wednesday at three o'clock will be perfect."

A few keystrokes later, he was standing next to the partition. "You can call me Grant if you would like, Caroline. I understand that might be a little informal for you, but perhaps you could try it out sometime."

Knowing I wasn't ready for that, I only nodded.

He checked his watch. "I am sorry to end our little tea party, but my next appointment is due in a few minutes. Thank you so much for joining me. Perhaps we will do it again soon."

"Yes, thank you," I said, retrieving my workout jacket. "And thank you for the reward...I think. I'll let you know more about that after Wednesday."

I attempted to smile as I fled the room.

She asked *him* to call her Caroline. It wasn't the name everyone else called her; it was rarer, more personal. Now he could say it aloud whenever he saw her, instead of just saying it to himself.

Grant tossed the tile back into the crystal bowl, noting that the aqua-colored tiles were for facials that week. Oh, well, a minor misunderstanding, but to come so far in such a short period of time, Caroline surely deserved more than that. *And* she had touched him—his horrible hands—with such care as if they still hurt him. Well, not in the way she meant. But she voluntarily touched him, with concern in her voice, and her finger on his hand was almost a caress. For that kindness, he would have given her the moon.

Grant sat in her chair and luxuriated in the warmth of her body as it crept into his own. Picking up her teacup, he placed his lips exactly where hers had touched the rim and slowly sipped the last few drops. Reliving every moment of the afternoon, he felt her fingers move gently over his hand as it was cradled in hers. When the tea was gone, he held the cup against his heart and mentally calculated the seconds until three o'clock the following Wednesday.

Seeing Suzanne on my way out, I smiled and waved. "Suzanne! Guess what? I have my first spa reward next Wednesday."

"Great! What tile did you choose?"

"The teal-colored one."

"You will love the facials here; it will feel like you have new skin."

"It isn't a facial. It's something called a double massage." I blushed at what I originally thought it meant.

"Well, maybe they changed the list since yesterday because when my mom picked out the same color, she got a facial."

"Does she have Dr. Grant?"

"No, she has Dr. Grayson."

"Well, maybe someone got the lists confused. Anyway, it's official. Next Wednesday afternoon, I am going to be pampered for the first time in my life. I can hardly wait!"

"I'm so glad you are happy here. You shine now, you know? Your skin, your eyes, you're so different from the overworked, slightly frumpy lady behind the desk. Oh, Caroline, you are beautiful, you know!"

She bubbled over in her way of hyperbole, but it sounded so nice I didn't argue with her.

"Thank you," I said. Raising my eyebrow, I added, "I was frumpy?"

"Yes, but only the nicest definition of the word."

"There are no *nice* definitions of that word."

Giggling like two schoolgirls, we walked toward the parking lot.

"Oh, Suzanne," I said, hugging her, "I love you. You saved my life."

Reward Day

I set the alarm back an hour on my spa reward day. I wanted to get to my office early so I wouldn't feel guilty for bugging out at two-thirty. Plus, I wanted to scrub and exfoliate every inch of my body so I wouldn't gross out the masseurs. The spa booklet described the massage as having three sensory elements: touch, aromatherapy from the oils and lotions (my choice was GatesWay's signature honey scent—*not* vanilla), and sound (I chose Spanish guitar). The booklet also said I should wear whatever made me feel comfortable.

What did that mean exactly? Thong, bikini, nothing?

The experience of a full-body massage was new to me, but I didn't want everyone in the spa to know. Searching my lingerie drawer, I found an ivory satin camisole set my much younger sister had given me the previous Christmas—two sizes too small. Now it fit perfectly. I folded the soft fabric and slipped it into my purse.

Energized by the excitement of my afternoon of pampering, I tackled the daunting job of reviewing forty graduate files, answered at least as many emails, and updated Dr. Bennett's calendar for the fall semester. Having lunch at my desk, I was out of the office at two-thirty sharp, guilt free.

Anticipation

It was impossible that he would have to wait all day to see her. What if she didn't come? Things change at work…delays happen…accidents. At the possibility of anything hurting her, Grant's heart pounded in his chest. He walked into his examination room and splashed water on his face. Pressing the damp towel against his eyes, he wondered what had happened to him. At what point had she become so precious that mere imagination could cause him anxiety? Once again, he sensed her soft fingers on his hand and knew the answer.

He'd spent the day working on anything and everything that would keep his mind occupied. Squelching each glance at his watch or the clock on the computer, he tried to ignore the seconds endlessly counting down in the back of his mind that needed no earthly confirmation. Even so, he knew he could not wait until three forty-five to see whether or not she walked into the shower room.

Grant's initial design for the NAFTRAM buildings did not include many windows. They were hard to keep clean, natural light wasn't flattering to any woman over fourteen, and even while wearing their glasses, daylight tormented the doctors' and interns' eyes. Local building codes, however, required windows, so there were thin bands of darkly tinted glass encircling the building on the second and fourth floors and full-length windows on the sixth floor.

As the seconds ticked closer to three o'clock, Grant decided not to wait any longer.

The sight of Grant standing on a ladder in front of the windows on the fourth floor was so unusual that Gordon stopped immediately.

"Grant?"

"Gordon."

"Can I help you?"

"No. I am quite capable of checking the interior window ledges myself," Grant said, holding the small rectangle of black welding glass out of Gordon's line of sight. As he peered through the glass, he saw Caroline step out of the white Honda and walk toward the awning.

"Is there something wrong?"

"Yes," Grant said, surreptitiously slipping the glass into his pocket. Wiping his hands together, he climbed down the ladder. "The window ledges are quite dusty. I am going to have to speak to Garrett. Is there anything I can help you with, Gordon?"

"No, I was passing by and saw you on the ladder."

"Well, thank you for your kind offer of assistance." Grant picked up his clipboard, tilted his head, and, within Gordon's hearing, asked Howard to remove the ladder and told Garrett to arrange to have all the window ledges dusted that evening.

Grant turned toward the nearest exit with the clipboard tucked under his arm.

"Grant was where?"

"On a ladder, checking the window ledges for dust."

"Dust?"

"Have you ever known any of us to care about dust? Think about all the tunnels we've lived in and the few aboveground colonies. No one has ever dusted, let alone gone looking for dust. No one."

"Gordon," Gregory asked seriously, "who do you think he *really* is?"

"I don't know my brother, and I don't want to know...and neither do you."

Reward Day — Part II

It had been two hundred and twenty-two hours, fifty-six minutes, and thirty-seven seconds. Grant walked quickly through the spa reception area, his footsteps counting *thirty-eight, thirty-nine….* Ostensibly looking at the clipboard in his hands, Grant was also looking over the top of his glasses and deliberately stepped in front of her.

"I am so sorry, Mrs. umm, Taylor." *Why did she smell so good today…didn't her car have air conditioning?*

"Caroline," she reminded him.

"Caroline. Yes, please forgive me for being momentarily distracted." *Momentarily distracted all day.*

"You're forgiven."

"Thank you." Not quite ready to let her go, he pretended ignorance. "Well, what is it going to be today? Hair, nails, or toes?"

I couldn't believe he said that. Whether it was anticipation, fear of the unknown, or the novelty of doing something just for me, I hadn't been able to calm down all day. I was more than a little embarrassed he did not remember.

"It's my, it's my 'chose a tile out of the bowl' spa reward day…the double massage."

I saw something finally register. "Yes, Caroline, you are right. Again, please forgive my distraction. I hope you will enjoy it."

Another polite smile, and he was off down the corridor.

I stopped at the receptionist's desk and gave her my name.

"It's the first door on the left."

I stood there so long that she repeated, "Mrs. Taylor, it's the first door on the left."

"Yes, I heard you."

"Do you have a question or need an escort?"

"No, it's just that when I met with Dr. Grant last week, he arranged this spa reward, but I just saw him, and he'd forgotten all about it. I am just a little surprised he didn't remember." I spoke slowly, realizing that I was no longer excited and a little annoyed that he had totally killed my buzz.

"Are you one of Dr. Grant's admission clients?" she asked quietly.

"Yes."

"He saw fifty of you last week, and fifty of you the week before, and fifty of you this week. And next week, he will see fifty more…and then he will see all two hundred over again. Also, please remember, he is the clinic's executive director. Never think he doesn't care about you because he does, but until you've been here a little longer than what? Two months?"

"About that."

"He won't remember you every time. Sorry. All of our doctors are very busy. However," she said, lightly touching my arm, "I'm sure he would like to know you were distressed because he forgot your reward. Shall I tell him?"

"No, of course not. I've never had a massage before, and I thought it would be as special to everyone else as it is to me. I'm sorry, I'm just being silly."

"Not silly at all. I understand. You should hurry, though; they can't start without you."

The difference between the massage room and everywhere else I'd been in the building struck me immediately. Illuminated only by the reflection of spotlights on the pale wooden walls, the room was a soothing study of shadows in a Zen-like setting of sage, tan, and ivory. The eucalyptus plants lent a fresh edge to the honeyed warmth of the room, infusing a sense of serenity that banished all thoughts of Dr. Grant from my mind.

There were two doors, one to the dressing room and another, a pebbled glass door, led to the massage room. Changing out of my work clothes, I tied the camisole's ribbon closures across the back and slipped on the matching lace tap pants.

I looked in the mirror. *Nice*. Angie had good taste, even if she had been a little optimistic about the size. I wasn't thin yet, but I was thinner.

Knocking softly on the glass door, I was surprised when it was opened by my interview escort. I smiled tentatively at him, but he gave no indication of remembering me.

Grow up, Carrie. You are one of at least twelve hundred women. How are they supposed to remember you?

I sighed. I was accustomed to blending in with the woodwork, but as I looked and felt better, my self-confidence was returning. *Someday*, I thought, *someday, they will remember who I am.*

"Mrs. Taylor," said the second intern, "would you like a headset or prefer we play the music aloud in the room?"

I knew I would feel less nervous if I wore the headset. That way, I could lie down on the table, close my eyes, and pretend to be blissfully unaware.

"The headset, please."

Handing it to me, he explained, "With the headset on, you will not hear us, but we will hear you. I will touch your shoulder here," he lightly touched the top of my right shoulder, "when I want you to turn over. That way, we won't disturb your enjoyment."

"Front or back first?"

"Please lie down on your stomach."

"Okay."

He touched my shoulder. "Mrs. Taylor?"

"Time to turn already?"

"No, ma'am. Do you mind if I untie the camisole? I don't want to get any lotion on the fabric."

"Will you tie it back when you've finished?"

"Yes, ma'am."

"I don't mind."

Slipping the headphones on, I stretched out as gracefully as possible on the massage table.

Covered with warmed muslin sheets, the sound of Spanish guitar in my head, and the scent of the honeyed candle surrounding me, I closed my eyes and let my mind drift. One of the interns loosened the ties and opened the back of the camisole. Together, they moved slowly from my neck to my calves, ankles, and feet, never pausing at the same time and not touching anything covered. I became warm and drowsy, relaxing into the moment. When the masseuse lightly touched my shoulder, I turned onto my back, sad it was almost over. Starting with my fingers, the blissfulness began again until they finished with my toes. At this point, I couldn't feel anything but a warm, tingling sensation in every muscle. My mind was at peace, but my body was singing.

Thinking they were finished, I opened my eyes and started to remove the headset, but my interview intern gently smiled and shook his head.

More then, I thought, putting the headphones back into place. He touched my shoulder, and I rolled over on my stomach. The ties of my camisole fell loosely at my sides.

I began to drift again, but this time it was different. Their fingers feathered up and down my back, arms, neck, and spine. They tapped down the outside of my legs and up the inside, timing their rhythm to my heartbeat. The lithe movements of their fingers shook me from my dreaming state to a sudden awareness of their hands, slippery and smooth, on my body. The strings of my camisole were retied, and I turned over at the tap on my shoulder. I kept my eyes closed now, not because I was relaxed, but because I was afraid they would see how aroused I was by this technique.

The feathering, stroking, and tapping continued relentlessly. I struggled to breathe normally and thought if Eric were here, I would teach him a thing or two, and if he asked nicely, I would teach him some more. *Oh, and he would ask nicely. Heck, he would beg.*

Two taps on the shoulder signaled they were finished. I removed the headset and, with their help, slowly got off the table. The intern I knew handed me a white laundry bag and pointed toward the door. "The massage showers are this way," he said.

"Thank you, that was lovely."

Lovely! I could barely walk and hoped the shower massage would calm me before I went home and had to explain to Dan why I was tearing off his clothes.

The shower room was empty except for a single shower stall and a small bench with a stack of sage and ivory towels. The glass shower door was sandblasted in a swirl design, and the shower, floor, and walls were tiled with white and gold marble. The only illumination in the room emanated from two narrow silver bands of light near the ceiling.

I set the white bag on the bench and noticed a small note on top of the towels.

To start the water, please place your feet and hands on the blue tiles.

To stop the water, remove your hands and feet from the blue tiles.

Thank you.

Opening the glass door, I stepped into the shower hoping it would alleviate some of the tension that had built up during the last part of the massage. I removed my lingerie and tossed it onto the bench.

Standing behind the silver glass tiles decorating the upper half of the shower room walls, Grant watched Caroline toss her lingerie on the bench. He couldn't see her clearly with the lights on and reminded himself to be patient. No woman had ever walked out of the shower before the massage was over.

Grant had not watched his brothers. It was the standard first reward massage, and Howard knew what to do, but Grant could hardly bear the thought of them touching her and fought the urge to scan their minds or send lightning headaches so they would think of little else but the pain. It was enough to ascertain that she wore lingerie during the massage. They would not see her as he would or hear her response. Someday, he promised himself, he would touch her, too.

It was unlike any shower I'd ever seen. Without controls or a showerhead, it was little more than a tile box. Looking closer, I saw hundreds of small holes drilled into square ivory tiles divided in half by a row of blue glass on the left and right sides of the shower. Two parallel vertical rows of blue glass were on the floor. Following the instructions, I put my feet and hands on the blue glass. Two things happened simultaneously. The lights dimmed, and hundreds of water jets hit me at once. Shocked, I pulled my hands back. The lights came on, and the water stopped.

Okay.

Knowing what to expect, I placed my hands back on the blue glass. The lights went out and the water spray began again. At first, the shower jets went up, down, and around, soothing my now very limber body. A moment later, the spray changed to droplets of honey-scented soap that were nearly overpowering in such a small space. As I breathed in the honeyed mist, the tingling in my body seeped into my mind. Warm water drove the fragrance into my skin from my neck to my ankles and mingled with the residue of the massage oils and lotions.

Nothing in my life had ever felt this wonderful, and I gave in to the calming sensation of the water. Then, without warning, the jets changed. My breath caught in my throat. The shower began to dance over my body, replicating the end of the massage, but now there were no clothes protecting the more sensitive areas. Up and down, increasing pressure, increasing speed, the jets deftly moved from one sensitive area to the next. I was caught and enslaved by a sensation I never dreamed possible. I started breathing in short gasps as the water teased my body relentlessly. Just when I believed I could not endure another moment of such exquisite torture, the jets from the center of the shower floor were activated, and I bit my lip to keep from screaming as the pressure from the water geysers exploded upward, and all the built-up tension in my body fell like rain against the glass.

Grateful for an experience beyond my realm of expectation, I closed my eyes and whispered, "Thank you, Grant."

When I moved my hands away from the walls, the jets sprayed a warm mist into the air. I shook my head to clear my mind.

This had to be the best-kept secret on the planet. Talk about an incentive! I may never eat another thing.

I dried off and, slightly chilled, reached into the white bag. I couldn't feel anything. Thinking it was empty, I pulled my hand away. Caught in my fingers was a delicately woven pale rose caftan. Slipping it over my head, it fell around me like a hush of warm air.

Grant was not surprised when the shower stopped abruptly. Of course, she would test it; it was her first time. When she placed her hands and feet on the blue glass again, Caroline's shower massage began in earnest. At first, he wanted her clean—everywhere—and covered her with honey-enriched lather. To erase his brothers' handprints, he rinsed the soap away by writing his name over and over on her skin. Monitoring the sensors within the blue lines that indicated the shower patterns she liked from the ones she loved, Grant played with her reactions, watched how she moved her body, and listened to her breathe. When he was certain she could not stand another moment of his hydrographic caress, he released the floor controls. Not taking his eyes from her face, he saw her bite her lip and gasp for air.

A few moments later, he heard her whisper, "Thank you, Grant."

The unexpectedness of her voice caught him off guard. He knew she did not know he was there, but hearing her gratitude and the gentle way she said his name, every torturous moment of the day vanished.

As she slowly stepped away from the blue tiles, he enveloped her in a heated mist so she would not be cold. He did not move as she dried herself and slipped into the caftan he had chosen for her to wear. It was, as he imagined, beautiful on her.

I placed my camisole set in the empty bag. My feet barely touched the floor as I walked into the meditation room. Looking around, I couldn't help but smile. Nothing in this facility was what you expected. Unlike the elegance of the lobby or the introspective atmosphere of the massage room and shower, the colors in the meditation room were all muted and dreamy. The way the faded blues, greens, and grays blended with the whitewashed paneling reminded me of the sleeping porch of my aunt's beach house.

Low lights shone through shimmering lace panels framed like windows. A white embossed coverlet and pale blue pillows covered the bed. Beautiful and serene, the room seemed to have been designed just for me. Two candles burned on the little table next to the bed, and headphones and a note lay on the pillow.

We regret the audio system in this room has not been completed.

Please wear the headphones for your pleasure and to aid in your meditation.

Thank you for your patience.

I wasn't sure I could take much more pleasure, but I slipped on the headset and glanced at the clock; it was five minutes past four. I had nearly an hour to figure out what had happened. Two minutes later, the lights dimmed, and air gently flowed through the lace panels like a breeze.

Expecting the same classical guitar arrangement as my massage, I was surprised to hear much softer notes played randomly, like synchronized wind chimes. I smelled salt in the air, and the cry of a gull echoed through the music that melted into the sound of waves breaking against the shore, lulling me to sleep.

I opened my eyes. Above me, the blue and white sails of my catamaran ruffled in the light wind. Standing on the canvas bridge above the rolling grey-green water of the gulf, I caught a breeze and flew parallel to the shoreline. A young man on the beach waved. I brought the boat about and tacked it to shore. Tall and tan, he deftly caught the thrown rope, and together we pulled the sailboat above the waterline. The wind had blown his hair into a wild brown nest, and overlarge aviator sunglasses hid his eyes, but I recognized the crooked grin I'd loved for years. I ran toward the towel on the beach, but he caught me after two or three steps. Rolling together in the surf, I could feel him press my body into the hot sand. Pinned like a butterfly, I tasted salt spray on his lips as his face blocked the sun. Lost in the sound of the waves and the touch of his hands, the memories of that sun-drenched summer washed over me, and for the second time that day, I was carried to a place I believed no longer existed in my world.

Grant waited patiently until she was asleep before entering the meditation room. He hung her work clothes neatly in the bathroom, but before he could leave, he pressed the fabric against his face to drown in her scent—but only for a moment—and turned toward the door. He planned to ignore her and just walk out. He couldn't stay. He had already punished Gregory and Garrett for lingering with clients while they were resting. He understood the attraction but could not understand their willingness to take such a risk...until today.

Today, Grant could not prevent himself from breaking his own rule.

Arranging the curtain over the mirror, he knelt silently beside the bed. Closing his eyes, his hands gently memorized the contours of her softness as he recalled her voice saying his name. He heard her breath quicken and felt her temperature rise. For the first time since arriving in America, Grant pressed his mouth against a woman's skin and tasted the sweetness of their honey as it effused from the pores of Caroline's neck and shoulders.

Powerless to raise his head from her pillow, his hands never left her body. Her heartbeat quickened as she grew tense, and a small cry escaped her throat. Her skin blushed against his lips, and her body trembled beneath his hands. With a small smile and a sigh, she turned on her side toward him.

Grant would have given everything he had to climb into the bed, gather her to him, and feast on the ambrosia that now covered her entire body. Everything...except the respect of his brothers. That is what a moment's loss of self-control would cost him, and then she would be lost to him forever. Only the promise that this would not be the last time he touched her enabled him to get up, brush the creases from his clothes, and straighten his tie.

Looking down at her, he bent over and picked up her hand. Lightly pressing it to his face, he swore she would be his. He wasn't sure how it would happen or even if she wanted him, but that was irrelevant. The taste of her was in his mouth, and her softness was forever in his memory.

Grant quietly backed out of the room. Touching his forehead to the door, he unknowingly echoed his father's prayer.

Please, blessed Anya, mother of us all, please. I will do anything.

I woke up slowly. That my body responded to relived memories did not surprise me; what puzzled me was the ease and naturalness of my response. Tears filled my eyes. I wondered how my life had gotten so twisted around that those memories of half a lifetime ago brought me more pleasure than anything in my present life. I thought about Eric, and as exciting as it was, a purely physical relationship with him would never be enough to fill the aching emptiness in my life after Brendan left. There was no future in it and, other than the provocative distraction it created, no real purpose either.

Too relaxed to move, I rested until I heard a chime and looked at the clock. It was nearly five o'clock and time to get dressed. For a moment, I couldn't recall where I'd left my clothes, and I hoped I wouldn't have to go looking for them. I walked into the small bathroom, and although I didn't remember seeing them when I came in, I found my clothes hanging on the back of the door and my purse on the vanity. Quickly checking the clock again, I realized there were only four minutes left and decided to ponder such mysteries when there was more time.

I was dressed and folding the gown across the foot of the bed when I heard a knock on the door. Expecting an escort, I opened the door and saw Dr. Grant standing in the hall. I caught my breath.

"Mrs. Taylor, did I startle you?"

"Yes, no, I was…um…expecting someone else." It was happening again. *Why did this man totally unnerve me?*

"Who?"

"Anyone else…an intern or one of your assistants. I'm not sure how to get back to the lobby."

"That is why I am here."

"I was told you were very busy."

"I am, but I was angry with myself for being too distracted earlier to remember that today was your well-deserved reward day. Then I recalled that I promised you if you did not like it, I would find you a reward you would like. I am here to keep my promise, Caroline, or did you like the double massage and meditation time?"

He sounded genuinely sorry, and I wondered if the receptionist had said something to him, but I was too shy to ask.

"It was lovely and much more, um, invigorating than I expected."

"Good. I hope you will consider it an incentive to continue your fine progress toward your goals." He looked closely at me for a moment. "Caroline, have you been crying?"

"No, sir," I lied.

"No, Grant."

"No…Grant."

"Please sit here for a moment," he said, leading me to the gray chair and ottoman. He brought the desk chair over for himself.

"Sometimes, Caroline, a massage brings more than toxins to the surface; it also relaxes some women to the point where the walls they have built around their innermost feelings temporarily dissolve, and the time spent in the mediation room helps them sort out those feelings. Occasionally, women make life-changing decisions in these rooms. For others, it is only a short rest before the walls go back up, and nothing truly changes.

"So, if you had a moment where you faced an issue you have been denying exists, I ask that you do something with that confrontation to help your life. Do not consider it a weak moment and return to whatever is making you unhappy. Remember, sometimes the only thing standing between a woman and her happiness is herself…and I, well, I would be personally gratified if you used this experience as an opportunity to make a positive change in your life. It is *your* life, Caroline."

"I'll do the best I can, um, Grant. Thank you." I smiled at him, determined not to start crying again.

"You're welcome," he said, helping me out of the chair. "Besides, Caroline, you are far too beautiful to cry. Positive changes," he admonished as we left the room, "no more tears."

Walking down the hall, his words, "I would be *personally* gratified," and "You're too beautiful," echoed in my ears, and for the first time, I wasn't just one of Dr. Grant's two hundred clients. Instead, I felt like he saw me—the real me—and liked what he saw. My heart beat with a little thrill of happiness. From that moment, it was not the woman in the mirror or Eric that I visualized for inspiration, but Dr. Grant. In our first interview, he said my success was his success. After everything he had given me that afternoon, it was the least I could do for him.

Walking as close to her as he dared, Grant watched her face as he led her through the corridor to the main lobby. Sensing her shift of allegiance, he smiled to himself.

Yes, it was only a matter of time, patience, and planning. The seed he planted at their first meeting had taken root, and when the flower he held that afternoon bloomed, he would have all of her he wanted.

Grant took the stairs of the catwalks two at a time. Turning into the hall toward his office, he found Grayson waiting for him.

"Grant."

"Grayson."

"You are smiling."

"Is that a problem, Grayson?"

"No. An anomaly. Dare I ask?"

"Not yet. I am considering a new challenge and still working out the details."

"Tell me, Grant. I'm always curious as to what you find challenging."

Grant did not want to banter with Grayson. He neither liked nor trusted him and wanted this conversation over.

"As you know, Grayson, we have many tasks facing us in the next several months that the collective expects us to complete successfully. I have broken them down into phases and am considering them one at a time. As we discern the most efficient solutions, we can share them with the other colonies, comparing outcomes and moving forward together with the best methods."

Knowing Grayson had no imagination or talent for brainstorming solutions, Grant continued, "And, as you are so curious, Grayson, I will be happy to inform the collective of your desire to collaborate in the pursuit of these solutions."

Grayson did not understand how Grant did that. Turn a perfectly innocent conversation into a commitment from him to the collective for what was, essentially, Grant's job. Implementation was what he was good at, and with Grant as his enforcer, they had the most obedient and successful colony in the NAS. Everyone knew their place and did their jobs. Grayson was not going to do Grant's.

"No, Grant. I leave all the designing to you, but perhaps you should approach Garrett or Gordon since they will be involved in many of the tasks necessary to meet the collective's expectations."

"Excellent suggestion, Grayson. I will tell them you recommended that I solicit their input. Thank you. Three heads *are* better than one."

By the end of the conversation, Grant was still smiling, and Grayson was wondering how he was going to placate Garrett and Gordon for placing them in Grant's path.

Grant's Dream

Grant sat at his desk and gently pulled the folded silk from beneath his shirt. He crushed the fabric in his hands like rose petals, releasing Caroline's fragrance into the air. As the memories of the gentleness of her finger tracing the scars along the inside of his hand, the sound of gratitude in her voice, and the beauty of her body washed over him, Grant recalled the last time he had felt such hope. He was almost nineteen. With his medical degree in hand, he had traveled home for a visit before his first assignment. Those few summer days changed the trajectory of his life forever, but before the firestorm destroyed everything he loved, he remembered the feeling of completeness that surrounded him as he stood at the edge of a small lake with his eyes closed, memorizing the sounds and smells of the oasis as desert winds brushed against his hands.

Tonight, he imagined Caroline next to him. Sitting together beside the pool of water surrounded by palms with the moonlight casting their shadows on the sand and the tent pitched beneath the trees. Unable to keep himself from making his vision a reality, he took a piece of paper from the printer tray and began sketching the scene exactly as he saw it in his mind. Knowing what would have followed had she actually been there, he turned the paper over and began another sketch. As impossible a dream as it was, he could not stop imagining being with her.

His hands trembled above the sketches. He had to have these drawings in his life where he could see them…*touch* them. In his mind, they were not mere pencil drawings but paintings on canvas, beautifully framed and hanging on his wall. It had been a long time since Grant had painted anything for himself, and he could not begin now—it was late, and his brothers were expecting him downstairs—the paintings would have to wait.

Tomorrow, he promised himself.

Walking into his examination room, Grant gazed longingly at the silk caftan. Taking one last breath, he tossed it into the incinerator shaft and washed his hands and face—twice.

That night, Grant dreamt of Caroline for the first time. She looked slightly different: she was younger, smaller, her skin darker, her eyes lighter, her hair long and sun-bleached; and, in this dream and all the dreams he ever had of her, she was pregnant. It did not matter that her appearance was altered. It was always Caroline's voice saying his name and her gentle touch against his skin. The taste of her perfumed the air, and in his dreams, she was his beloved.

Grant returned to his desk early the following morning and revised the sketches slightly to resemble his dream. He called the nearest art store at ten o'clock sharp. Ordering frames, canvas, paints, and brushes, Grant bought everything he needed to transform his imagination into something tangible. Emailing Monique, GatesWay's receptionist, he told her to page him as soon as the package arrived.

Less than an hour later, he was standing at Monique's desk.

Smiling as she handed him the box, she said lightly, "Art supplies, Dr. Grant? Have you taken up a new hobby?"

His expression impassive, he looked down at her.

"Ms. Robichaud, have I ever made any personal remarks to you?"

"No, Dr. Grant."

He did not move his eyes from her face.

"I'm sorry, Dr. Grant."

"Yes," he said, turning toward the double doors.

Monique knew as well as any of the staff that no one got the chance to annoy Dr. Grant twice and waited for Dr. Gabriel to fire her. By the end of the day, when he had not come out or called her into his office, she started to relax. She loved her job, the clients, and *some* of the doctors were so nice.

Feeling like she had been given a reprieve, she promised herself to be even more professional and circumspect with regard to Dr. Grant in the future. She didn't want to risk losing the best job she ever had.

Grant had forgotten her existence before he reached the elevator.

Hoping to carry the supplies into his office unseen, Grant became concerned when he ran into Garrett in the office corridor.

"What's in the package, Grant?"

"Just some prints for my office."

"I thought you painted your own. That mural in Gregory's office is fantastic. I keep waiting for the girls to walk out of the wall and into the room."

"So does Gregory."

"Ha! I bet he does, too!" Garrett laughed and pointed to the box.

"Can I see what you've bought?"

Escaping into his office alone, Grant turned in the doorway and said, "No, not yet. I think I am going to remake the frames. I will show them to you as soon as I have hung them up."

Grant picked up the sketches from his desk, took them into his examination room, and closed the door. Glancing at the two-way mirror on the wall to his right, he removed a piece of black felt from the carton and taped it over the glass. Within fifteen minutes, Grant had fashioned his examination room into a rudimentary art studio. To disguise the smell of the paint, he lit a large candle outside the door. He didn't want any more questions.

The paintings were just one of the two alternate realities of Caroline that Grant designed to keep her in his life when he could not be with her. Needing something to fill his time while the paint dried, Grant began building a virtual reality. Synthesizing his dreams, memories, and imagination, he created a world where he and Caroline existed together in the only home he had ever known: the desert. Although he knew he could never have her, Grant instinctively sensed that she belonged with him, and it was important that those early memories include her and that she was a part of the life he'd loved.

The dream sequence was also a tribute to the world his parents never knew: a husband, a wife with child, together with affection, gentleness, peace, and commitment. This illusion of a dream fulfilled acted on him like a drug. It kept him sane as she waved shyly at him before disappearing out of his sight into the world beyond the facility's doors—a world he could not control.

Creating alternate realities was a skill he'd perfected in the last few years and was an integral part of their clients' rewards. In the colony, talents and skills were shared, and he didn't restrict this unique talent to their clients. Grant also created fantasy dream sequences for his brothers who, too busy to indulge in their personal interests during the day and confined to the facility at night, found certain versions of the virtual world very enticing.

Gregory was always reenacting and directing a movie he had seen, requiring alternative actors and actual film footage. Sharing what he saw with Gordon, the brothers had endless discussions about which actor or actress would be better or how this or that scene should progress. Garrett's love was sports, and football was his favorite. To keep it interesting, Grant occasionally changed the teams and plays around, "forgetting" to tell him. Garrett's exuberance the day after finally scoring a touchdown always gave him away, and Grant would start working on a different set of plays. Gabriel preferred gardening and his dreams contained fields of flowers, orchards, and gardens with cultivated roses. Without being asked, Grant varied the seasons according to the calendar, and Gabriel looked forward to the challenges each new version brought. Only Grayson declined a dream sequence and kept whatever fantasies he possessed to himself. Grant, however, had gleaned enough from his unguarded thoughts to know they involved genocide and mass human destruction. As much as Grant might share some of the feelings behind those thoughts, he was relieved he was not asked to design Grayson's personal holocaust.

Standing in front of his easel with the images so vivid in his mind, it only took a few days to turn his imagination and desire into art. While the paintings were drying for the last time, he took the wooden frames and painted them randomly with silver and gold, adding a coat of black paint. When the frames were dry, he hit them carefully with a hammer, just hard enough to depress the wood, exposing the metallic paint. Finishing with a high gloss acrylic sealant transformed the painted wood into ebony from which ripples of gold and silver shimmered like moonlight on a black lagoon.

Just before tacking the paintings into the frames, he took a thin brush and signed them.

Grant looked at the signature. The overlapping Ts representing his real name was something he could barely admit to himself. The closer he came to Caroline, the more he felt like the son his father always hoped he would become. If he had no other reason to care for her, he would always be grateful that Caroline helped him find his way back to that part of himself.

Once the paintings were fully assembled in their frames, Grant dismantled his makeshift art studio. He tossed nearly everything except the paint thinner into the incinerator chute and removed the fabric from the window. No one asked why it was up, and he knew no one would. He had heard his brothers discussing it among themselves, and the consensus was that none of them *really* wanted to know what he was hiding in there.

Initially, Grant planned to delay hanging the paintings until he was sure the paint smell was out of the room. Impatient to have them where he could see her, he decided if anyone noticed the odor, he would simply blame it on the new frames.

Once mounted on the walls of his office, he backed away and removed his glasses. They were exactly what he wanted: the impossible dream of her. Forever together, the small family sat beside the moonlit desert lake, and he could lose himself in their happiness any time he wished. He smiled at the thought of showing her the paintings someday—not telling her the identity of the artist—to get her reaction. He tried not to think how much he wanted her to like them. He would not tell her who they were, but maybe, someday, she would know and find pleasure in their happiness, too.

A few days later, Garrett walked in and smelled the paint.

"Can I see them?"

"Sure."

Garrett slipped off his glasses, looked at the paintings, and noticed the signature. "I thought you said they were prints. These are original paintings."

"Well, yes and no. They are prints overlaid with brushstrokes to look authentic. I would have preferred the originals, but they are not currently for sale. I have my, um, feelers out if they ever come on the market."

"Ha! Feelers!" Garrett laughed and shook his head. "You know, Grant, there are some people here who say you don't have a sense of humor…they don't know you very well."

"Well, there are some people here who believe they know me all too well," Grant said slowly.

"Um, yes, well. That's true."

Wanting to change the subject, Grant asked, "Well, do you like them?"

"Oh, yes…a little moody for me…but beautiful, and the frames set them off perfectly. But, you know, you're the expert on this sort of stuff. Oh, and speaking of things you are an expert in, we really need to discuss the new game plan you designed…how am I supposed to get through that defensive line? I'm blocked every time."

"Yes."

"Ah, come on! It's been every night for a month. A hint?"

Grant smiled. He liked Garrett almost as much as he liked Gabriel. They were good brothers who rarely tested the limits of his patience or resented his position within the colony.

"Lateral to the left."

"Really? That's all?"

"No, that isn't all, but it will get you started."

"Okay. Thanks, I think."

On his way out, Garrett tilted his head. He turned and looked at Grant.

"Grayson would like to meet with you in the main tunnel in fifteen minutes…if it is convenient."

Grant stopped smiling. He tilted his head and nodded to Garrett, who walked quickly out the door.

Garrett didn't know why Grayson wanted to meet Grant *in the main tunnel* during the middle of the day, but he knew it couldn't be good. He liked Grant. However, he didn't understand how someone who did what he was capable of doing could also appreciate the delicate relationship illustrated in his new artwork. There were more sides to Grant than he had eyes, and Garrett wanted to stay on his good sides. He knew what happened to those who didn't.

Images

As depicted in the paintings he looked at far too often, Grant believed Caroline was his. He wanted her with him *almost* more than anything, but she was a client—a *married* client—any kind of personal relationship was more than impossible. It was suicidal. Despite being fully aware of the consequences, he had given up his efforts to ignore her and, as often as he could, watched her classes to hear her voice, her laughter, or just to see her smile. Her scent was now a living memory. He could tell exactly where she had been on any given day, and at night, he roamed the facility searching for her shadows.

Beneath his watchful gaze, Caroline slimmed down, and her skin acquired a healthy glow. Already beautiful to him, he regarded each change with critical approval and adjusted her program to work on areas that were being stubborn. She was unaware that every time Garrett altered her exercise program, it was a direct result of Grant sculpting her body to reflect his idealized image of her.

"For what?" Grant asked himself in anger and frustration. "For her *husband*?"

Then he would see how well she responded to his fine-tuning, and he didn't care who else saw her. As long as she lived in his eyes and smiled when she saw him, it was enough.

For now.

Knowing what she looked like without them, he wished he could buy her clothes. Not that he wanted her dressed, but if she had to wear clothes, shouldn't they be beautiful? He hated the drab, overly human things she usually wore. He wanted to wrap her in soft, flowing fabrics that caressed her skin, letting her shape set the curves in what she wore instead of the other way around. Stealing time between appointments, he designed clothes for her to wear. Too dear to incinerate, he placed the sketches in a special envelope in her file. From time to time, he glanced at the drawings and visualized her wearing his designs, smiling at him, and touching his face as gently as she'd touched his hand.

Seeing no way to move forward, he did not indulge in his fascination with Caroline often; it was not useful and made everything else seem empty by comparison. Instead, he saved her for those days when he needed to be reminded of the little humanity he possessed and how, out of that, he was transforming the kindest creature he had ever met into the most beautiful woman he had ever seen.

Needing an occasional dose of reality when his desire threatened to overwhelm his judgment, he would focus on her wedding ring and think how that slim gold band with its paltry bit of carbon prevented him from stealing her away, taking her deep into the tunnels, and keeping her there for his pleasure...and hers. He knew enough about the physiology of human women to keep her physically sated, but the tunnels were dark. They would frighten her, and she would try to leave. He had no doubt he could force her to stay, but then she wouldn't want him, wouldn't smile at him anymore, or caress him with her gentleness. He knew she would fight him, and then, as a matter of survival, he would kill her.

Only the thought of Caroline sleeping forever with the others in the serai stopped him. Even when his disfigured hands ached to touch her, he kept his distance. His role in the deaths of the women who would never leave haunted him and held him back. If she did not want him, he could never want her, and the possibility of her ever wanting him was nonexistent.

Grant pressed his hands against his eyes. *It was a pretty hell*, he thought, *that he had created for himself.*

Origins

Eric's daily emails counted down the summer, and it was finally Thursday, the twelfth of August. I was still a little shy of my original goal, but I was fit and weighed less than I had in eighteen years. My hair—longer and highlighted—looked like I had spent the summer on the beach instead of working out five or six days every week.

I stopped at the grocery store on the way to the Marriott. After getting the keycard, I put fruit and a single birthday cupcake in the little refrigerator. I set the candle and robe from the spa gift shop next to the bed to complete the room. We agreed to meet at seven-thirty in the morning, but I planned to arrive an hour early to make sure everything was perfect. Feeling slightly wicked, I called from our room and left a message on his pager: the number "224" and nothing else.

Everything I envisioned in May was coming true; Eric would be twenty-five, and I would be as beautiful as humanly possible. Law school didn't start until the middle of September, and I was looking forward to a month of secret trysts. Even if that was the extent of our relationship, a month of Eric's kisses would be a delicious reward for a summer of controlled hunger. Although it was Eric's birthday, I had scheduled a nine-thirty appointment at the spa for my second incentive reward. I could have arranged the facial for a different day or time, but I wanted to have something to do—somewhere to go—so I could make a graceful exit in case the morning didn't work out as well as I'd hoped. If it did, I would return after my appointment looking radiant. After all, the room was ours until two o'clock.

Picking up supper on my drive home, I thought of Dan, and my smile dimmed. As I lost weight, I'd hoped he would find me more attractive, but that had not happened, and feelings of dread threatened to overwhelm me each time I thought of Brendan leaving for college. I reminded myself that I would soon have a flood of new students who needed looking after, and I still had two more months at the spa. I was sure Dr. Garrett could find something interesting for me to do to keep my newfound body in shape…maybe kickboxing or Zumba. *Something with music.* Hard music that would make me too tired in the evenings to think, to wander aimlessly in Brendan's empty rooms, or constantly check for an email that wouldn't be, shouldn't be, sent. I wanted to be too tired to feel, night after night, so desperately alone.

My alarm went off at five-fifteen. Dan was used to me getting up before him, but not before sunrise. "What's going on…why are you getting up so damned early?"

"A new exercise class I've wanted to get into finally opened up, and I want to try it out. Go back to sleep. I'll wake you in an hour when I leave."

"How much longer are you going to that gym? I mean, you look great, but you should quit so you won't wake me up so early."

"Don't you want me to be healthy?" I asked softly.

"Yes, but I would rather you were fat again and lying beside me than skinny and running off somewhere all the time."

It was the nicest thing he'd said to me in five years. "Dan…."

"Wake me in an hour. I'm going back to sleep."

I sighed. The day wasn't beginning quite on the upbeat I'd hoped. After showering, I dried my hair in Brendan's bathroom so I wouldn't disturb anyone. Carefully applying my makeup, I slipped into my workout clothes and smiled at the mirror.

No one will think you're Eric's mother now.

"Dan, it's time to get up."

"Okay, okay," he muttered.

I didn't know what kind of car Eric drove, so I wasn't prepared to see him sitting in the lobby. Without a flicker of recognition, he stared past me, looking for the woman he'd left in May. The last thing I wanted was a reunion in the lobby. Thankful for my dark sunglasses, I glided past him and went up to the room. Lighting the candle, I changed my clothes and twirled in front of the mirror. Smiling in anticipation, I dialed the lobby's courtesy phone.

"Room 224, zero days."

I'm Your Man

"How long have you been here?"

"I just arrived."

"How? I've been watching the door for fifteen minutes…I hoped you'd be early."

"I know. I walked right past you. I didn't trust myself to greet you in the lobby."

"Wait, the only person who came through there was a blonde in workout clothes."

"Guilty."

"Wow, Carrie, you were hot!"

"Were?"

"Yes, in the workout clothes, you were hot, but now," he said, taking me into his arms, "You're gorgeous and so thin."

His eyes traveled to my mouth.

"Is it okay to kiss you now?"

My hand slipped behind his head, and I brought his lips to mine. I felt like a young girl when he picked me up and carried me to the bed. Without much introduction, he took off his shirt, and I gasped at what three months of training in the Florida sun had done. Sliding out of my robe, his eyes widened appreciatively as well.

The physical attraction between us was intense and immediate. I didn't talk. I didn't want him to talk. I wanted his lips, his hands, and his body against mine. This was the moment I'd dreamed of for an entire summer of tearful graduations, too-short vacations, hours of bike pedaling and dance classes, months of telling myself that hunger can be managed, and only managing it with the hope of being with this beautiful young man *who wanted me*. His desire was the only validation I needed.

I luxuriated in the warmth of this embrace.

"Recovering okay?" he asked, slightly out of breath.

"Yes," I gasped, "but I am not sure the room will."

Laughing, we surveyed the wreckage of our lovemaking from the bed to the floor and back again. "Well, next time, we will try to stay in one place," he said.

"Only if we must," I answered, slipping into my robe.

I closed the bathroom door and checked myself in the mirror to see what repairs needed to be made. Everything except my lipstick was still where it belonged. I began brushing the tangles out of my hair when my hand froze.

He hadn't used anything.

Everything had been so immediate that I didn't ask, and he didn't hesitate. I felt faint and put my hand on the vanity to steady myself. This could be the stupidest thing I'd ever done. I thought he would have…but he didn't…and I hadn't brought anything with me. Mentally reviewing my personal calendar, I calmed down. I should be okay for another week or so before we needed to discuss "being safe" options.

Another week of this? The thought banished the fear from my mind. I looked in the mirror and giggled.

Returning to the room, my delightful anticipation was immediately diverted by the sight of Eric waving the room service menu around in front of the open windows.

"What's wrong?"

"That candle, my gosh, Carrie, what was that?" he asked, both arms fanning the air. "Essence of stinkweed?"

"No, it's called Bitter Honey. It's a lovely fragrance. I'm sorry you don't like it." I mentally crossed off offering him any honey for breakfast. Then I remembered the cupcake.

"Wait, I do have something that might take your mind off the candle." I opened the little refrigerator and saw he'd already been there. I looked up and smiled. "Did you like your birthday cupcake?"

"Yes, it was delicious."

Picking up the remote, he turned on the television.

I left the window open but closed the curtains. There was altogether too much sunlight in the room. I started putting the bed back together as he changed channels, looking, I supposed, for some sports news. I glanced at the clock next to the bed. It was only half past seven. I sighed.

This could be a long morning.

"Room service?" I asked, retrieving the menu.

"Hey, that would be great! Just eggs, bacon, hash browns, and white toast, it can be part of my birthday present."

He caught my hand and pulled me into his lap.

"You know, Carrie, this may be my best birthday ever."

Without leaving his arms, I called room service and added two pieces of whole-wheat toast, no butter, no jam, orange juice, and tea. Leaning against his shoulder, we watched television as we waited. I wasn't quite old enough to be Eric's mother, but it was hard not to feel like Mrs. Robinson. When the waiter arrived with breakfast, I was sure if I'd been wearing one of my regular house robes, he would have automatically believed that was exactly who I was and not his, not his…what?

Girlfriend? Lover? Groupie?

I gave the waiter a nice tip. I wasn't sure what my role was, but at least I would be generous.

I apologized when Eric realized there was no butter or jam for his toast. Despite my earlier decision, I offered him some honey. After one whiff, I was glad I hadn't handed it to him. He looked like he would have pitched it through the wall and into the next room. I quietly called room service.

"How can you eat that stuff?" he asked incredulously. "It smells vile."

"Well, to be honest, I usually don't like honey either, but I love this. I have it every morning for breakfast."

With his eyes glued to the television, he said, "That's okay, Carrie, just remember to brush your teeth before we get back in bed."

I sat quite still. I'd never experienced chills up my spine and butterflies in my stomach at the same time. Every warning bell going off in my head was battling with the desire to wreck the room with him again. My fingers moved up his arm, and I knew which part of me was going to win this round. Finished with his breakfast, he snaked his hand through the opening in my robe, easing it from my shoulders as he pulled me into the bed.

"Now," he said.

"Now?"

"Now is the time for you to brush your teeth. I'll wait." Releasing me, he leaned against the pillows, his blue eyes bright with anticipation.

I closed the door and looked at myself in the bathroom mirror. *Be careful what you wish for, Carrie.*

Taking the toothbrush out of my cosmetic bag, I brushed, flossed, and used the hotel's little bottle of mouthwash. Hoping I'd removed all evidence of the bitter honey, I returned to the room. The TV was still on, but Eric's eyes were closed and didn't open until I turned the television off.

Eric smiled slowly.

"Carrie, I've waited so long." Reaching for my hand, he pulled me on top of him. "I've imagined you like this every night for three months, and this is so much better than I ever thought it would be."

He was more affectionate, going slower. I could tell he was trying to please me, but although his lovemaking was wonderful, something was missing, something not quite as *I'd* imagined. Deciding I was overthinking it, I closed my eyes and abandoned myself to the pure physical sensation of him, and, as he'd promised me three months earlier, it *was* glorious.

Wonderfully exhausted again, I looked at the clock. It was later than I thought. Luckily, the spa was only five minutes from the hotel, but I still needed to shower and change back into my workout clothes.

"Where are you going, Carrie?" he asked as I got up.

"I have a spa appointment at nine-thirty, and I must run."

"Skip it. I've...we've waited a long time for this."

"I know, but I don't want to miss anything that makes me look as beautiful as I feel right now."

"Are you coming back?"

"Yes. Two hours at the latest…we have the room until two this afternoon. Can you stay?"

"No, I'm meeting my parents in Cincinnati this weekend and still need to pack. I can stay until eleven, though, so why won't you stay with me?" He yawned as he reached for my hand.

"Sweetheart, I can't…but why don't you stay and sleep a while? I'll request an eleven o'clock wake-up call." I sat on the bed next to him and brushed the hair away from his eyes. "You were here very early this morning," I said softly.

"Hmm, good idea." He half opened his eyes. "Do you think we can do this again in a couple of weeks?"

"A *couple* of weeks?"

"Uh-hmm," he said sleepily. "The ball club wants me in St. Pete until the end of the month. After that, I'll have a couple of weeks before school starts."

"That would be great," I said, looking at his perfect body at rest. It was so tan against the white sheets that I could trace the outline of nearly every muscle, and my fingers ached to do so. But I was running late, and missing a spa reward meant that I would have to explain why to Dr. Grant, and babysitting sleeping young men was not worth that conversation, not even beautiful sleeping young men.

An unexpected pang of conscience struck me as I hurried out the door—but not for Dan. I did not believe he loved me enough to care, but there was another man's opinion that was far more important. An unsuspecting accomplice to that morning's deception, the thought of Dr. Grant's certain disapproval cut me to the heart.

Protocols

As summer grew to a close, Grant had other matters on his mind to distract him from Caroline's whereabouts. He had chosen his ten prospective mothers, all young, unmarried, and charmed by him. He met with them often, serving tea and honey while he listened as they prattled on about their hobbies, books, films, or jobs, offering consolation and encouragement in equal amounts as needed. He did not flirt with them but touched their wrists, looked deep into their eyes, smiled softly, and said goodbye reluctantly. As the time for their all-day spa rewards drew nearer, most were thoroughly smitten with him, and, seeing the desire in their eyes, Grant smiled to himself. So far, his experiment was going precisely as projected.

In fact, everything throughout the facility was going well. After nearly four years of preparation, testing, and rehearsal, the week for which the colony was created progressed smoothly. Grant designed a special spa "treatment" for each of their prospective mothers to keep them occupied, relaxed, and under the clinic's total control from the moment they walked in until they went home five hours later. Their spa day began with breakfast or lunch, complete with Grant's specially blended tea to aid in their enjoyment of the full-body massage techniques choreographed to soothe their muscles and mind, followed by a warm, calming shower massage. Deliberately developed not to arouse, the treatments enhanced feelings of well-being so these few chosen women would be receptive to the dream sequence Grant had programmed for them.

Each evening that week, the doctors reported on the two procedures they performed. Grant was gratified to learn that the serum and the Reconception protocols established the year before were being implemented without any problems.

There was a general feeling of reverence in the colony. Sixty prospective mothers meant sixty new brothers waiting to be born. Every morning and evening, Anya's song of protection echoed through the corridors. Twelve voices together as one prayed that their brothers—and their mothers— would live.

Head to Toes

I ran through GatesWay's double doors.

"Hi! Carrie Taylor," I said, slightly out of breath. "I'm scheduled for a facial at nine-thirty."

"Yes, Car…rie…Tay…lor," she said, drawing out each syllable as she looked down the list. After writing my name on the back of a test card, she handed it to me with a lancet.

"Here you are."

"Oh, right." I pressed the lancet against my finger and put a smear of blood in the center of the test square for her records.

"Bethany's station is number three. Enjoy your facial, Mrs. Taylor, and have a nice day."

Trying not to smile too broadly, I said, "It's been pretty nice so far."

"Yes, ma'am," she said, handing the next client a lancet and test square.

Predominately decorated in GatesWay's signature colors of aquamarine and white, the salon was a beauty technician's paradise. To impart a sense of privacy in a room containing thirty stations, each station was contained within an oasis of light surrounded by darkly tinted glass walls.

After locating station three, I picked up the now-familiar white paper bag and went into the changing room. Coordinating with the station numbers, I put my purse in locker #3A, piled my workout clothes on top, and slipped into the teal and white kimono. Returning to Bethany's station, I saw Dr. Garrett on the other side of the room. He strolled through the unlit aisles of the salon, talking with some of the clients and technicians and nodding at everyone else.

As I sat down, I caught the mirror's reflection of Dr. Garrett talking to a lovely girl with long blond hair. She was listening and smiling up at him.

I smiled, too. I knew a crush when I saw one.

I was surprised when she walked up to me.

"Hi, Mrs. Taylor. My name is Bethany, and I am happy to be your aesthetician this morning. Please relax, lean back, and let your mind wander a bit."

"Not a problem. My mind wanders all the time on its own anyway."

"Oh? Any special reason why it would be wandering today? Or does it wander every day?"

I blushed. "Well, it might be wandering a little more today than usual," I said, trying not to giggle.

She smiled and whispered conspiratorially. "Well, there's nothing like good sex to make your complexion glow."

That was a little too much information. I tried to protest, but undaunted, she turned the chair around.

"See?" she said, "You are still glowing."

I glanced at my reflection. She was right. Embarrassed, I quickly looked down and tried to think of a way to change the subject. I glanced back at the mirror in time to see her nodding to Dr. Garrett.

"Yes, you are absolutely right, Dr. Garrett," she said.

As I watched, he flipped the little card he was holding in his hand over. It was one of the blood test cards. Smiling, he tossed it into the small blue box he was carrying.

"'Absolutely right,' Dr. Garrett?" I inquired after he turned away.

"Oh, he was just reminding me to ask you if you wore contacts and, if so, to take them out." She glanced around for a moment and whispered, "I forgot to ask a client yesterday. Her facial could have damaged her eyes if she hadn't told me."

Looking at my face in the mirror, she asked brightly, "So, do you wear contacts?"

"No."

"Great! Then let's get started."

After lowering the chair into a reclining position, Bethany washed off all my carefully applied makeup. It was the only thing that made me happy I wasn't meeting Eric afterward. I had brought repair cosmetics with me that morning but not enough to start from bare skin. Bethany began by dipping her fingertips into a velvet lotion and making small circles over my face and neck. It felt so luxurious, and I gave myself up to memories of the morning as she delicately patted pink gel into the few lines on my forehead and around my eyes. I tried to keep from smiling as she massaged my neck, shoulders, and upper arms. Tilting my chin up, she finished with long strokes from the base of my neck and up the sides of my face to my temples.

Preparing for that morning's surgery, Grant looked up when Garrett knocked on the door.

"Grant, one of your spa clients today is not pregnant."

"Did we miscalculate?"

"No, it wasn't us. I talked to her. It seems her fiancé had to go out of town unexpectedly. Believe me, she seems almost as frustrated as we are." Smiling, Garrett continued, "You could say she is all dressed up with nowhere to go, gestationally speaking."

Grant did not return his smile. Ten were few enough, but starting with nine put him one short. Then again, it also meant one less woman might die, and he decided it could be for the best.

"Well, we know we will lose some of the embryos, and it's too late to find someone else. It will be fine."

"But."

"But what?"

"There is an unexpected pregnancy. Apparently, she did it without our, um, encouragement. There is the barest trace of the enzyme, but it's there."

"One of my clients?"

"Yes. A little older than the others. Her file indicates she's been married about twenty years."

Nearly half of Grant's clientele had been married for twenty years; it was one of the reasons finding ten was so difficult.

"Married twenty years! Too old—especially the male—she will miscarry the first week. Too risky and against selection protocols."

"Yes, but listen, Grant," Garrett's voice became conspiratorial, "I have reason to believe the baby isn't her husband's."

"Why?"

"The way she keeps blushing. No wife still blushes after nearly twenty years of marriage, and besides, she married young. Bethany, her aesthetician, indicated she practically admitted having an affair." Garrett's voice became serious. "Grant, regardless of the age of the male, you need one more, and we should not waste this opportunity. As you say, we expect to lose some, so we should start with as many as we can."

Grant reluctantly nodded in agreement. The completion of their mission was the colony's number one priority. It had been a very successful week, but it was Friday, and the last day the serum would be effective. Garrett was right. He needed a substitute.

"My morning or afternoon appointment?"

"Afternoon. It will allow us to 'surprise' her with an upgraded spa treatment."

"Do we already have a dream sequence for her?"

"Yes, I checked. She had her first reward massage a little over a month ago."

"I don't like it, but we need her." Hiding his annoyance at this change of plans, Grant wrote a short message on a monogrammed notecard and handed it to Garrett. "Give her the good news, and I will see her this afternoon…and Garrett."

"Yes, Grant."

"Thank you for bringing this to my attention."

"You're welcome, Grant."

Bethany's soft voice interrupted my blissful reflections of the morning.

"Mrs. Taylor, now that your facial massage is finished, I will apply a clay mask. Your skin will tighten as the mask draws out impurities. It may feel a little strange, but the tightness will only last a few minutes. Afterward, I will wash the mask off with warm water, followed by an astringent and a wonderful moisturizer. You will be pleasantly surprised, ma'am, to find that your skin feels as soft and smooth as your silk robe."

She patted a thick paste on my face and placed cucumber slices on my eyes. I heard someone call her name, and she walked away. A few minutes later, she removed the mask with warm cloths. The astringent stung a little but was quickly soothed by the cooling lotion. She twirled my chair toward the mirror.

"Feel the difference?" she asked.

I couldn't believe it. My face was so soft and, as she promised, smooth as silk. I looked in the mirror. For the first time in my adult life, I looked younger without makeup.

"Wow, Bethany," I said. "You are good." I smiled at her in the mirror. "I look every bit as beautiful as I feel today."

"I'm so happy you are pleased, Mrs. Taylor." She reached into her pocket and handed me a note. "Dr. Grant dropped this off for you during your mask treatment."

"What? Dr. Grant was here?" I looked around quickly.

"Yes, ma'am. Well, he didn't come into the spa area exactly. Dr. Garrett brought it over to me." She frowned and asked, "Anything wrong?"

"No, of course not," I smiled. "I was just surprised. I don't have an appointment with him for another two weeks."

Unable to contain my anticipation, I tore open the unaddressed envelope.

I am happy to inform you that your spa reward has been upgraded to our Head to Toes Spa Treat for exceptional progress. I hope you will enjoy the additional spa services we have arranged for you this afternoon. - Dr. Grant

"Bethany, what's a Head-to-Toes Spa Treat?"

"Really? That's what it says?" She seemed genuinely surprised. "You must have been really good. What did you do? Lose like fifty pounds or something?"

"Not quite. But I've worked hard to get where I am in a short period of time."

"Well, congratulations. To answer your question, the H-T treat is the facial, plus lunch, a full-body massage, shower massage, meditation, and concludes with a pedicure. We want you to leave us today feeling pampered from head to toe."

My heart pounded. I didn't hear a word she said after "shower massage."

"That, that will be wonderful," I said, trying not to grin. "This day keeps getting better and better."

"Well, Mrs. Taylor, I hope it will be one you'll always remember."

"Thank you, Bethany. Um, where do I go from here?"

"I'll be happy to escort you to the massage therapy section. Lunch will be waiting for you in the dressing room. A little chime will indicate when the masseurs are ready for you, so relax and enjoy. I am sure you deserve all the attention you're getting today."

"I'm not so sure about that. I think Dr. Grant is just being kind."

"Well, I have only worked here a short time, but of all the words I have heard used to describe Dr. Grant, 'kind' is not one of them."

Looking around as if she'd said too much, she added quickly, "But of course, our clients believe all the doctors walk on water, so I'm sure you're right."

Bethany

Dr. Gabriel did not like listening to his staff's conversations. However, as the facility's human resources director, it was his job to ensure their clients received the special attention and courtesy they expected and, more importantly, were paying for. The staff had specific instructions regarding customer service and personal grooming: they must act like professionals, look as good or better than the work they performed on their clients, and their comportment must be above reproach. Discretion regarding the doctors, staff members, or other clients was mandated, but, above all, they must never endanger a client's health. Accidents, even those that could happen anywhere, were not tolerated. In return, they were paid very well.

Gabriel had listened to Bethany McWilliams's conversations all morning. She had been careless the day before, beginning a facial without determining if the client wore contact lenses. Had the woman not spoken up, it could have led to dangerous consequences, resulting in a lawsuit. That was precisely the sort of accident they could not afford. However, she had performed flawlessly this morning, and Gabriel hoped he would not have to fire her. With her morning's facial appointment nearly over, Gabriel turned back to his computer and listened with only half an ear.

"Well, I have only worked here a short time, but of all the words I have heard used to describe Dr. Grant, 'kind' is not one of them…but of course, our clients believe all the doctors walk on water, so I am quite sure you're right."

Gabriel tilted his head and summoned Grant and Howard. Smiling at her comment, he began preparing the separation documents and severance check.

Returning to her station, Bethany saw Dr. Gabriel and Dr. Grant standing in the hall. She felt a sinking sensation in her stomach. She thought she had dodged a bullet yesterday, but she had not.

"Bethany," said Dr. Gabriel, "I regret that we cannot continue your employment at GatesWay Fitness Clinic and Health Spa. The omission yesterday regarding the contact lens could have resulted in tragic consequences. Unfortunately, we feel you have not grasped the serious level of attention we require our staff members to provide to our clients."

He withdrew an envelope from the pocket of his lab coat. "Please accept this severance check with our gratitude for the satisfactory work you performed for us until yesterday. Howard is waiting for you at your station to help you pack your things and escort you to your car. May I please have your wristband?"

Bethany knew carelessness was unacceptable at this facility. She had been surprised when she managed to get through yesterday without having this conversation, so while it was not wholly unexpected, she was disappointed. Of all the salons where she had worked, GatesWay was the nicest. Sighing, she removed the dark blue band from her wrist and handed it to him.

"Yes, Dr. Gabriel. I understand, and I'm sorry."

She took the envelope and, opening it on her way back to her chair, was impressed to find a check for two months' salary. Seeing Howard at her station with a cardboard carton at his feet and his arms crossed over his chest, she closed the envelope. It was her own fault; she knew the rules.

Walking back to Gabriel's office, Grant turned to him with an amused smile.

"She actually told a client I wasn't kind?"

"Not exactly. She told a client that she had never heard you described as being kind."

"Well, that is probably true."

"Irrelevant."

"Yes."

"With that comment today and endangering a client's eyesight yesterday, she poses too much of a risk."

"Yes."

Gabriel knew full well that the client's comment would have been met with nearly the same response from any of the staff and not enough to be fired for alone, but it meant she was becoming irresponsible. "So," he said to Grant, "letting her go today kills two birds with one stone, um, check."

Relating to Gabriel her assistance to Garrett that morning in confirming the details of his afternoon appointment, Grant disagreed.

"Three," he said.

Head to Toes — Part Two

Lunch was delicious. Caught up in the thoughts of the morning as I sipped my tea, I realized the only thing I was wearing under the salon wrap was the black lingerie I'd bought for my rendezvous with Eric.

If my only choice is to have a massage with or without lingerie, I'm definitely wearing what I have. It probably isn't the first time they've seen lacy black underwear on a client...at least it's new.

I expected the same masseurs as my previous session and was surprised to see two different interns. Acknowledging I had only met two out of the six interns, I knew it was presumptive to expect familiar faces. However, the difference didn't end with their appearance. Soundlessly, they helped me out of the wrap and onto the table and handed me the headphones. Knowing GatesWay probably kept progress notes on everyone, I assumed they knew my preferences from my first massage and didn't want to interrupt the soothing atmosphere with talking.

Once again covered with a warmed muslin sheet, I closed my eyes, listened to the music, and, like last time, pretended I wasn't really there with two strangers touching my body.

I relaxed into the musical rhythm of the massage, the fragrance of the candle, and the scented oil. Swirling together, these sensations lulled me into a dreamlike state where the hands stroking and pressing my muscles did not exist outside my mind. I was sure that the dream would go on forever as long as I didn't open my eyes. Not even the touch on my shoulder interrupted the illusion, and, turning on my back, the massage followed the same pattern. I was only aware of the soothing pressure on my hands, feet, and neck and drifted even more.

I fought to stay awake.

Too soon, I felt two taps on my shoulder, and the spell was broken. Still slightly dazed, they carefully helped me down and back into the wrap I had worn all morning. Tying the belt, I was surprised when one of the interns said, "I am so sorry about the scratch, Mrs. Taylor."

"What scratch? I didn't feel anything." I looked down at my stomach and saw a small bandage slightly below my navel.

"I'm very sorry, ma'am," he said, opening the door.

"I'm sure it's fine," I said, not asking how it happened. *If I didn't feel it, how bad could it be?*

Walking into the shower room, I smiled slightly in anticipation. Everything was the same…even to the small white bag leaning against the towels on the bench.

I stepped into the shower, removed my lingerie, and tossed it toward the bench. Standing on the blue lines, I placed my hands on the blue tiles and waited for the lights to dim and the water spray to begin.

And waited.

I stepped off the blue tiles and, as though rebooting a computer, stepped on them again and put my hands against the walls.

Nothing happened.

I was becoming more disappointed with each passing moment. My body was still relaxed from the massage, but my mind was actively engaged as I pressed the tiles searching for the right spot. When pressing didn't work, I lightly pounded the tiles and stepped harder with my feet.

Silence.

I couldn't go back because I was concerned I would interrupt another client's massage. I didn't want to go forward because I was unwilling to give up the shower experience that still haunted my dreams. Feeling trapped, I leaned my head on my arm and said, "Please."

Seconds later, the lights went down, and the shower began. At first, I was worried I wouldn't be able to relax, but I was wrong. It only took a few minutes for the warm soapy water to melt my confusion, and I gave myself over to the fragrance and rhythm of the shower as the music I had listened to during my massage was played upon my body.

Like fingers dancing over invisible strings, the pressure of the water slid, swirled, rose, and fell. The constantly repeating melody, accompanied by a hundred pulsating harmonies, washed over me until my fingers trembled on the tiles. I pressed my hands harder against the walls, not wanting it to stop. The increasing intensity of the water streaming at me from all directions and the inescapable music in my mind crashed together in a crescendo of resounding joy. I was no longer flesh but a finely tuned instrument upon which a virtuoso had played his final masterpiece.

My hands slid slowly down the blue lines of the shower, and as the lights came up, a warm perfumed mist embraced me. Breathing deeply, I shook my head in gentle wonderment. I had never felt so calm, so sure, so serene. The power of the music that resonated throughout my body answered every question about my life, and I realized that Dr. Grant was right. My life belonged to me—not Dan or Eric or even Brendan—and encapsulated everything I was at that moment: beautiful, timeless, and rare.

The mist began to evaporate as I moved my feet from the blue tiles. Reaching for a towel, I carefully avoided the bandage as I patted myself dry. I turned the paper bag upside down and stared in awe as a fragile cascade of red and gold silk floated over the white bench. Delicate enough to have been woven from spider webs, I lifted the gown carefully with both hands and, in one flowing movement, dropped the towel as a swirl of red and gold enveloped me from my neck to the floor. Stepping over my lingerie as though the black lace belonged to someone else, I walked out of the room feeling like an empress.

The Substitute

Grant had not seen Caroline all day. He walked past her morning class and did not detect her perfume. He hoped she was not ill, but there was no time to check his email with everything he had to do that day. When she didn't come in for her noon class, he made a mental note to follow up with her on Monday and find out why. He would be quite stern with her if he found out she skipped the day without an excellent reason. He knew from experience that if a client skipped one day, she would skip two and then three until she no longer attended her classes at all. He wasn't sure what he would do if Caroline never came back.

Hesitating outside the door of his last surgery for the week, Grant prayed. He didn't want to harm these women, but they were the Lyostians' only hope for survival. Grant reminded himself that he had developed the least invasive procedure possible and reached for the door handle.

Entering the darkened meditation room, he did not pay attention to the still form on the bed. The virtual dream headset covered most of her face—she could be anyone. The red and gold robe lay like a whisper over her body, enveloping her completely except for the edge that was discreetly pulled back to reveal a small area below her bikini line.

Grant looked at the intern. "Is it viable?"

"Yes."

"What do we know?"

"Laparoscopic examination shows active cell division indicating human male, under thirty."

"In position?"

"Yes. Do you want me to remove it?"

"No. Now that I know it's viable, I will take care of it myself. You may leave after you set the vials and syringes on the table. Take all the equipment with you. There are others waiting."

"The headset?"

"I will dispose of it when I leave. It is her dream. It would not make sense to anyone else."

"Wouldn't it?"

Grant heard the intern laugh as he closed the door.

The intern had a point. The names and scenarios changed, but the story was always the same. The virtual dream sequences were recordings of the dreams following the client's first shower reward. They were always vivid, predictable, and direct.

Grant glanced down at the woman on the bed. All day he had thought of her as "the substitute," not because he had been too busy to learn her name, but because until this moment, it was immaterial. Lost in her dream, his last prospective mother moved her head, and the headset tilted away from her face.

It was only when he leaned toward her to straighten the headset that Grant recognized who she was, and the reality of what he was going to do to *her* hit him like a physical blow.

It was the face that Grant saw nearly every night in his dreams. Noticing the natural glow of her skin and inhaling the fragrance he had formulated especially for the showers that week, Grant understood why she had missed her noon class. She was being groomed for him.

He pulled his hands away and backed into the room. He wanted to turn around and walk out, but he dared not leave her now. One of his brothers would finish the procedure, and he couldn't bear to let anyone else touch her.

"What am I going to do with you, Caroline?"

He had to think. He walked around the bed, admiring the way the silk caressed her body. Remembering how she looked those few short months ago, he shook his head. Her loveliness then could not be compared with the beauty that now lay so submissively in front of him. Without warning, Garrett's hints of a possible affair, the intern's words "male under thirty," and Caroline's mantra came together in Grant's mind, and he finally understood the reason that brought her into GatesWay that spring afternoon.

"Oh, Caroline, was that why you worked so hard? So that someone new would love you…would kiss you?" He sighed as he looked down at his hands. "I hope *he* deserved you."

As different as she was to him, she was still like the other women who walked under their blue and white awning, thinking all they needed to do to be loved was lose weight, exercise, get a haircut or a facial because they believed it was their fault they weren't appreciated and not the neglect of the men in their lives who were even more blind than a Lyostian at noon. Despite being the most powerful creative force on the planet, these women asked for so little and accepted even less. For Caroline and the other fifty-nine prospective mothers, their faith in GatesWay was not misplaced; each had been found desirable by a human male.

Not wanting to disturb her dream, Grant gently readjusted the headset. He touched the softness of her hair, and the backs of his fingers lightly stroked her cheek. At that moment, he realized that she meant everything to him. Beautiful, her body newly pregnant and healthy, she was his prize for a decade of research, planning, and discipline: a living trophy, the symbol of his success. Even with the small snake of a laparoscopy tube lying on her abdomen, she was perfect. This was the last day. Her son would be the culmination of the next generation reconceived at this facility. Grant felt a sense of justice in the knowledge that Caroline would be the last woman he loved in the only way he could.

Grant checked the second hand on the clock against his watch. Once he bathed the fertilized egg in the serum for one minute with the first syringe, he would then use the second syringe to add the neutralizing agent to effectively halt the DNA conversion. Finally, he would remove the tube and close the incision. For the next thirteen weeks, he and his brothers would secretly watch their new mothers, change their classes, give them small amounts of a hormone-enhanced formula of bitter honey, and request additional blood and urine samples. During their constant observation, the Lyostians would hope and pray that if a prospective mother carried their hybrid brother to term (and Grant knew the chance of that was statistically slim), she would not die or suffer brain damage from any embryonic toxins entering her bloodstream.

Grant closed his eyes. The thought of losing her that way was almost unbearable to him. He knew the procedure would make her infinitely dearer to him, but he also knew the risk he was taking. Even if she survived, she would never forgive him, never touch him again, and never…care. As painful as that future was, Grant knew the truth was worse.

She would hate him.

He had endured hatred from the moment he was born, but now, when he believed there was a chance for something different, it had been taken from him. Although the established protocols were unchangeable, he recoiled at the thought and, for a moment, considered doing nothing. He would tell his brothers the sac was impermeable or remove it and say it was a mistake. No one would know, not even Caroline. He could decide the risk of exposure was too great; a married woman was against the selection criteria. If he did nothing, he could give her and the baby a future…a human future.

But could he let her go?

No. He could not.

Grant knew he had to try. Howard had the laparoscopy photo. Even if he persuaded Howard to destroy the photograph, lying in a collective consciousness was difficult. The layers of deception necessary to escape detection made it all but impossible, and he doubted Howard could maintain it for any length of time. Eventually, everyone would know, and someone, Grayson or Gregory, would notify the collective; sanctions would be requested and approved. He could lose his standing within the collective and with it, lose her forever.

Regardless of his feelings, he could not walk away. Every phase of his life had been encoded for this moment when he could act for the continuation of his species. Not trying would violate the fundamental reason for his existence. Having no real alternatives, Grant considered the consequences of doing what he had been born to do.

From what he had learned from her questionnaire and eavesdropping, he knew she had a neglectful husband and a son who, stereotypical for most American male adolescents, had rejected mothering since the day he turned thirteen.

Why not give her a son who would cherish her for the rest of her life? Didn't she deserve a reward, too?

His eyes lingered on her face, and he saw her smile. He turned again to the clock. Why was he hesitating? He should have already left. He knew he was stalling because he did not want to hurt her, but there were no alternatives. It was mandated. He could not disregard the protocols he'd developed for his species' survival. Choice did not exist.

He turned toward the table to prepare a syringe with the serum when he heard her sigh.

"Oh, Eric."

He could tell by the way her back was beginning to arch what part of the dream she was experiencing.

"Eric," she sighed again.

Ah, that was his name, the human who had claimed this body as his own. The man who had loved yet failed to protect the perfect biological mystery of her. These men of earth were reckless, taking for granted the loveliest and most fertile creatures of the universe and leaving them, vulnerable and alone, to fend for themselves.

At the thought of anyone hurting her, the small human part of him rebelled. His hand became a fist, and the fragile vial was crushed. In his anger, Grant's breathing became rapid and shallow. He remembered the softness of her skin, the taste of her in his mouth, her body's grateful response beneath his hands, and the sound of her voice whispering his name. Drowning in the fragrant images of her, changes he did not believe possible began happening to his body.

He had thought about her and hesitated too long. She was beginning to release pheromones brought on by her dream, and he knew he would not, could not, leave now. He had enhanced enough virtual sequences to understand what was happening to him but wondered at the unexpected waves of heat that caused a tightness in his chest that made it difficult to breathe. What little air Grant could force into his lungs was saturated not only with her pheromones but the candle scent that infused these rooms. Through the haze caused by this onslaught of raw passion, the calm mask of Dr. Grant Gates fell from his face as another option occurred to him.

Grant picked up the threaded needle from the tray. Gently removing the tube, he made two quick sutures below her skin, brushed a medicated adhesive over the small incision, and replaced the bandage.

He looked at his watch; he had almost waited too long. Only minutes were left to affect the embryo. Even if he were capable of walking out of the room, there was not enough time to obtain another vial. The standard procedure took less than fifteen minutes, and had she been anyone else, he would already be in his office making notes in her chart. But she wasn't anyone else, and he was still compelled to complete his mandate. However, in the collective knowledge of his species, it had not been done this way for nearly one thousand generations.

He knew the mechanics of the act, but all of his early training told him he could not do this without her permission. It would violate the basic tenet of his existence to assault her. He knelt at the head of the bed and, bending over her, brushed the headset away.

"Say, please," he whispered against her ear.

"Grant?"

"Yes."

He was gratified to discover that she was conscious enough to know who he was and what he was asking.

"Oh, please."

She wanted him to love her. He quickly removed his lab coat and folded his clothes across the chair. Moving cautiously, he bent down and kissed the space above the incision where his son would soon be sleeping and reverently pulled back the other edge of her robe. Because he had removed the headset to watch her face, she was no longer in the dream sequence, and Grant was unsure what her reaction would be as he lowered himself onto her. Embracing her, he heard her catch her breath and felt her back arch under him. It was a welcome he knew he did not deserve and had no right to expect.

As he moved in her, certain human concepts he never understood became crystal clear: desire, ownership, territory, and war. He finally understood why some men would go to war and kill their brothers to protect what belonged to them—to have this joy and to keep it safe. Grant had owned very few things in his life, but he knew he would own this moment and protect this woman as long as he lived.

No longer a dream or a promise and forever linked by this memory, Caroline was his.

A quickening life force drove every thought from his mind until wave after wave of exquisite pain washed over him and through him. As the last shudder left his body, her arms came up and pulled him down to her.

When the tightness in his chest finally eased, Grant realized that her arms encircled him, cradling his head against her soft breasts.

When had she moved her arms?

He panicked. How long had this version of the Reconception procedure taken? He would have believed two minutes; he would have believed two days. He looked at the clock.

There was still time. Grant was grateful there was no need to leave right away and relaxed into her softness. Slipping his hands under her head, he looked at her face. Her eyes were closed, a small smile played about her lips, and her breathing was even. She was still asleep and wonderfully his for thirty more minutes. He knew she would probably sleep longer than that, but he did not want to be there when she woke up.

What if, when she saw him, she remembered?

Grant didn't believe he could endure the look of betrayal he would see in her eyes. Carefully unfolding her arms from his neck, he kissed the palms of her hands and laid them on the bed. He stood up slowly and gently lowered the edges of her robe.

Gathering up his clothes, Grant went into the small bathroom to wash and dress. Afterward, he ran some warm water, pressed a few of the colored buttons, and a softly fragrant soap filled his hands. He knew he could use a cloth to bathe her, but he wanted to remember the feel of her skin, its indentations and textures; each touch would be a part of these few moments. Regardless of whatever happened to him, no one would be able to destroy this memory.

Pulling away only one section of her mother's robe at a time so she would not be cold, he used his bare hands to remove the lingering traces of his body on hers. In gratitude and appreciation for all she was to him now, he wiped the soap away gently with one hand while using the other to pat her skin dry with a small towel. Like polishing a work of art, it was not so much an act of self-preservation as one of worship.

With few minutes to spare, Grant put the pieces of the vial, the unused syringes, and the rubber tubing in the toxic storage bag and dropped it into the hidden incinerator chute located at the head of the bed. Unwilling to have her slip back into her dream of Eric, he set the headset on her pillow. He meticulously scanned the room to verify that nothing was out of place and no evidence remained of the crimes he'd committed that afternoon. Slipping on his glasses, he straightened his coat, picked up the empty lab tray, and walked toward the door.

"Grant." His name was a sigh on her lips.

She knew. He was completely undone. He rushed to her bedside, ready to confess everything and beg for her forgiveness, ready to do or say anything to keep her from hating him, from leaving him and never coming back. That he risked her life was an act in which he had no choice; that she might take herself out of his life was an outcome for which he had no defense. Kneeling beside her, afraid to touch her hand and dreading the accusation he would see in her eyes, he slowly looked up at her face.

Her eyes were still closed.

"Yes, Caroline."

"Thank you," she whispered.

Those two words decided him. Grant's forehead touched the edge of the bed as he thought of ways to keep her safe. He would tell her everything so she would not be scared, he would watch over her and the child, and afterward—if they survived—he would make sure they were somewhere no one could harm them. Repeating his silent promises to her and to himself, he stood up. Knowing how sweet she would taste, he did not trust himself to kiss her face. Instead, he lifted her right palm, pressed it to his lips, and placed it on her heart. Grant's eyes never left her as he picked up the tray from the floor and quietly backed out of the room.

Glancing quickly up and down the corridor, he smiled. There was no one there who would wonder why it took him over an hour to complete a fifteen-minute procedure. He turned toward his office and stumbled. His hands trembled, and he began to have trouble breathing. Tilting his head, he located each member of the colony. Satisfied no one would see him, Grant walked unsteadily to his laboratory, closed the steel door, and tried not to scream.

The thudding pain in his chest rivaled the flashes of excruciating lightning in his head. Falling to his knees, he clawed at his tie and the front of his shirt. Gasping for air, Grant waited either for the pain to ease or to die. He rolled over onto his back and closed his eyes.

What was happening?

Trying to distract himself from the agony racking his body, Grant searched the collective's archives and gradually understood what his sense of duty and his desire had cost him. Focusing only on the memory of the unexpected joy of her body welcoming his, Grant smiled through the pain and realization of having just signed his own death warrant.

A Thousand Voices Singing

The meditation room was the same, and I welcomed its restful serenity. A tray of tea and toast sat on the small table. Sitting down in my beautiful robe, I felt every bit as delicious as the food I was eating. The day was turning out so perfectly that I even forgave the shower—it had more than made up for its earlier difficulty.

Yawning and feeling cozy, I slipped on the headphones. Hearing the gentle guitar music and seagulls calling, I smiled.

Oh, yes. I want this dream again.

When my eyes closed, the boat was already racing the wind, but I was not sailing alone. Eric stood on the bridge next to me as we sped along the shoreline. Tan and strong, he held me close, almost possessively, and I leaned against him as the sun warmed us both.

Aiming the white hulls at a spit of land, he drove the boat onto the beach. The sound of breakers beating against the shore competed with our laughter as he began untying the strings to my bathing suit. Hearing faint voices drifting in and out, I turned my head and scanned the beach for a radio, but Eric's hands had loosened my suit, and we were falling onto the sand.

Feeling his arms around me, I sighed, "Oh, Eric."

His blue eyes shining with desire hovered teasingly above mine, and my body curved slightly against the sand.

"Eric," I whispered.

Becoming aware we were not alone, Eric pulled away from me. As he stood up, a butterfly alighted on my stomach, and the gulf breezes brushed my hair away from my face. The familiar smell of honey suddenly surrounded me, and Eric's silhouette dissolved into Dr. Grant.

A feeling of joy flowed through me. I didn't want *him* to leave. He was the wellspring of every pleasure I'd experienced in the last three months. As Eric's face faded, my desire for him also disappeared. There was no room for Eric in my dream of Grant.

A familiar voice whispered, "Say, please."

"Grant?"

"Yes."

It *was* Grant. My heart, my mind, and my body responded at once to his unspoken request.

"Oh, please."

Eager to embrace him, my body rose to meet his. Possessed by the scent and strength of him, reality retreated into shadow. Catching my breath became impossible as we tumbled in the surf. Waves crashed around me, pushing me relentlessly out to sea. Unsure if I was dreaming or dying, my mind flickered for a moment.

This…this is how drowning must feel.

Catching sight of a life raft floating above me, I reached up and, hugging it to my chest, heard a thousand voices singing.

A Dream Within a Dream

The chimes of the small clock roused me from my dream.

Wow, had I really slept for two hours?

I wasn't surprised. I had been so excited about seeing Eric that I had gotten very little sleep the night before.

Ellen knocked on the door as she entered the room. Before I could sit up, she was setting fresh tea and refreshments on the table.

Picking up the other tray, she asked, "Did you rest well?"

"It was quite…wonderful," I said, meaning every word.

"The H-T treat *is* a special delight. I'll be back in thirty minutes to escort you to your pedicure. I need to check whose station you're in, so please rest here until I come to get you."

"Well, don't forget me. I'd stay here all night if you'd let me."

"No, I won't forget you," she said, closing the door.

I stood up to pour myself a cup of tea and immediately sat back down. Not just because I felt lightheaded, but also because I was a little uncomfortable, *there.*

Hmm, well, Eric had been enthusiastic.

There was also the shower massage, but that hadn't bothered me at the time. Now, however, I felt a bit tender. Walking slowly to the tray, I poured green tea into the cup and picked up a piece of honeyed toast. As I bit into it, the warmth of slightly melted honey triggered the memory of my dream of Dr. Grant. I barely had time to set the cup down before my knees folded, and I fainted.

It was only for a few minutes, but I couldn't remember ever fainting before. I stood up carefully, walked to the bathroom, and put a dampened towel against my face. It smelled so nice that I immediately felt better.

I was sitting at the small table when Ellen returned.

"It's down the hall, station eighteen," she said, leading the way.

As I followed Ellen, I relived the morning's excitement, the surprise of having a spa day, the unforgettable massages, and my dream within a dream. Feeling more than pampered, I felt I was finally in charge of my life and laughed a little as I imagined robbing a bank so I could have this every day.

Knowing there was more to come, I entered the spa area smiling as I realized that it had been one of the top ten best days of my life.

As she turned to go, Ellen touched the silk of my robe.

"This is so beautiful," she said. "All of the kimonos for the spa clients have been exquisite this week, but this is the most magnificent I've seen. It makes you look like a queen."

"Well, I certainly feel like one today," I said, delicately settling myself into the salon chair.

Risk Management

Leaning slightly against the wall next to the double doors leading to the lobby, Grant focused on breathing evenly. Caroline would be coming out any moment now. He had to know if she remembered…anything…so that he could respond accordingly and dissuade her from believing the truth.

He saw her and smiled, but she was too busy admiring her pedicure to notice he was there. Easing slowly away from the wall, he deliberately stood in her path.

Distracted by my glittering pink toenails, I nearly ran into Dr. Grant on my way to the lobby.

"Did you enjoy it?" he asked.

Recognizing his voice from my dream, I felt myself blushing.

"Excuse me?"

"Your Head-to-Toes spa day, was it what you expected?"

Something was not right. I could not form one coherent sentence. Afraid of what he might see in my eyes, I was too shy to look up at him. Staring at the pocket of his lab coat, I stammered, "Yes, um, thank you for upgrading my spa reward, Dr. Grant. It, it was the best day I've had in a very long time."

"Well, that's something then, isn't it? But you worked so hard. Well, good," he said, tapping the folder in his hands. "I see you have a yoga class on Monday morning."

"Yes, sir, six-thirty…bright and early." *Well, early, anyway.*

"Good. Please stop by my office afterward. Not to get your hopes up, er," he opened my file as though unable to remember my name…again. "Mrs. Tay… Caroline, but I may be in a position to make you an offer you can't refuse. I will have more information on Monday morning."

"Oh, okay, I'll see you then," I said, still staring at his pocket. I wasn't sure I would be able to leave if I looked at his face.

Walking hurriedly through the double doors, I thought about what he'd said.

What could he possibly offer me that I did not have today? The moon?

I saw Suzanne talking to Monique in the lobby. We walked out together, and she told me she'd had a spa day, too.

"What was *your* favorite part?" she teased.

"You, first."

Grinning, we said simultaneously, "The shower!"

Laughing, we walked to our cars. I wasn't being entirely truthful with her, though. Like comparing sea mist to a tsunami, the shower wasn't anything compared to my dream.

Standing behind the tinted windows of the lobby doors, Grant watched the only woman he would ever love vanish into the late summer sunlight.

Challenges

On the way back to his office, Grant looked down at the file in his hands and sighed in relief. She didn't remember what happened, or perhaps she believed it was part of her dream sequence. He knew her ignorance should make him grateful. Still, there was something about the anonymity of the situation that bothered him. Although she had said "yes" to him, she probably dreamed it was Eric loving her with his body.

He didn't want to dwell on what that bit of anonymity was costing him. The pain in his chest had subsided and the worst of the lightning flashes had faded, leaving a dull ache behind his eyes. He wanted nothing more than to retreat into the tunnels and rest. She was gone—there was nothing left for him aboveground.

Grant walked into the salon's empty locker room. He had one more task before closing the file on Carrie Taylor, client, and opening a new one for Caroline Taylor, prospective mother. Taking a black plastic bag from the custodial closet, he went to locker #3A. It only took a second for the flash of red and gold to disappear into the black bag. Needing to return her chart to his office and dispose of the bag's contents, Grant thought to Gabriel that he would be delayed and would meet him outside the tunnel dining room.

Walking into his office, he glanced at the stack of files on his desk and decided he needed an assistant. He was finished watching her through glass walls and catching her in the hallways. He knew he could keep her busy enough so she wouldn't think the job was an excuse to hire her for observation purposes. The more he considered it, the more sense it made. He remembered the few times she had been in his office and how empty it seemed when she left. If she took the job, she would be here almost every day, and maybe, if he was subtle, she would let him take care of her. Grant wasn't sure how large a role her husband, son, or lover played in her life, but what if he could—through a level of controlled affection, conditioning, and manipulation—separate her from them?

His thoughts tumbled ahead. If he could convince Caroline that he was the only one she could trust, wouldn't she confide in him, doing what he suggested, encouraged, or told her to do? And, if she obeyed him, taking the precautions he asked of her, wasn't the possibility of her giving birth to the colony's offspring greater? And finally, if she trusted him, and he gently let her know what to expect would she, could she, be glad of it?

He pulled out the datasheet from the experimentation file he'd compiled regarding compliance through submission, but that was before she was a prospective mother. Her current status changed the entire experiment. Since the beginning, he had tracked her response to every overture he'd made since he began noticing her.

What if he continued doing that?

What if she actually gave birth and wanted the child? Nurturing him and loving him? Then the results would no longer be based on a theory—or an experiment—he would have created Persephone's blueprint, not from paper theory to manipulated realization, but through actualization to a detailed report.

If he succeeded, wouldn't this be something the colony—no, the entire collective—could use? He would continue strengthening the relationships with his other prospective mothers, but Caroline would be his baseline. He would design a timeline of expectations and outcomes using Caroline Taylor as the single focus of a new experiment to validate his theory of psychological manipulation and control to create a compliant colony mother: a fully aware human mother with all the developmental advantages that position entailed. He would share the successful methods and techniques with his brothers for use in establishing relationships with their prospective mothers as test cases.

Grant smiled for the first time that afternoon.

As an experimental subject, he would be able to keep her close to him without any questions from his brothers as he exploited her human vulnerability to broaden the colony's usefulness to the collective. Couched in those terms, not even Grayson could object.

Grant's confidence knew no bounds as he walked into his examination room to toss her red and gold mother's robe into the incinerator. Reaching deep into the bag, Grant grasped the silk with his left hand.

It was still warm.

He pulled her robe slowly from the bag. Touching the soft fabric brought back the memory of her skin next to his, and, knowing it was a mistake but unable to stop himself, he lifted it to his face and inhaled. Drifting throughout the bouquet of fragrances that was delightfully her lingered another scent that was, undeniably, his. Unable to move, he didn't know how long he stood there holding the silk against his face, reliving every moment of the afternoon.

In those few moments, Grant's objective changed. He could not treat her dispassionately and analytically. She was his Caroline, not a mouse in a maze. He had wanted her from the first moment she touched his hand, and he saw kindness in her eyes, a mother's eyes, directed at him. Now she was carrying the promise of his child inside her. As long as that promise existed, he would still be a part of her. Perhaps he could make her... *No. It was preposterous.* He looked down at his ugly scarred hands and remembered who, and what, he was.

No, he concluded, she would never love him, but if he was extremely careful and unrelentingly manipulative, perhaps he could make her love the child. Wouldn't that be enough? Producing a compliant, loving mother was what was important, and it would be his only goal if it were possible to forget the taste of her and the welcoming embrace of her body.

Descending the catwalks to the tunnels, Grant was already devising a thousand little ways to bind Caroline to him through psychological control and dependence. Still, her innate gentleness and trusting eyes kept interfering with his plans. He tried not to notice how his hands trembled when his thoughts strayed to the red and gold robe folded neatly and lying at the bottom of his safe. The black bag where it rested held a secret he was willing to kill to protect.

Arriving at the dining room before Gabriel, Grant waited outside the door and overheard Gregory talking to Gordon.

"Yeah, made her say 'please.'"

Grant abruptly walked into the dining room. "Excuse me."

"Oh, hi, Grant, you would have loved this. Your last client today, I was supervising the shower massages; you know they've been glitchy lately."

"Yes."

"I stalled it for five minutes after she stepped in to see what she would do."

"And...."

"Well, at first, she seemed a little out of it—"

"Which is exactly how she was supposed to feel."

"Yeah, I know. Then she was confused, and after that, she got a little angry. Finally, she laid her head against the wall, all pitiful-like, and said, 'Please.' I timed it perfectly. Five seconds later, the lights went out, and the water came on. I wanted to stick around to see what would happen if I turned it off again, but I had to prep for my afternoon procedure."

"So, Gregory, you took my last prospective mother and, defying a sequence that I had designed, implemented, and in execution had been successful all week, you did what? You 'teased' her? What if, at four minutes, she'd had enough of your teasing and left?"

"But don't you see? That was the beauty of it! Five minutes was the perfect amount of time to take her from acquiescence to arrogance to asking for it. I would have said begging. It would have been more accurate but would have ruined the alliteration."

Grant stared silently at Gregory's triumphantly grinning face and thought to himself, *What if she had left? What if she had said 'to hell with it,' gathered up her things, and walked out?*

Despite Gordon's presence, Grant was barely able to keep his rising desire to kill Gregory in check. His hands itched for Gregory's neck not only because of his lack of respect toward a prospective mother but, more importantly, also for nearly robbing him of something that had become infinitely more precious to him than his own life.

Neither Gregory nor Gordon missed the flash of anger behind Grant's eyes.

"Oh, come on, Grant, it wasn't a big deal, and it didn't change anything. I mean, really, did it?"

"Not this time, Gregory. If it had, you and I would be having a different and more one-sided conversation."

Monday Morning

Checking in fifteen minutes early for my six-thirty Monday morning yoga class, I was surprised when Patti asked for a urine sample.

"Really? I had a spa day Friday, and they took a blood test."

"I am sorry, Mrs. Taylor, but our computer randomly picks names every Monday for the week. I know you were tested Friday, and you are not the first client this has happened to this morning. I have asked Dr. Garrett to check the system. Of course, you can refuse if you'd rather not, but I will have to mark that on your chart."

"Umm, wait a minute, Patti. I'll do it, no problem. I didn't expect it, that's all…and *it is* Monday morning. I'll take care of that right now." I hurried off toward the ladies' room.

That was close! There was no way I was going to miss an opportunity for another experience like last Friday.

Grant looked down at the list in his hand. Out of the sixty prospective mothers they had tested so far, only two did not show evidence of the Lyostian enzyme, indicating the embryonic cells were impermeable when the serum was added. All of his operations were successful.

He knew at least half of his prospective mothers would come to work for him if given the opportunity, but he wanted Caroline. Over the weekend, his confidence had returned with his strength. He believed he could control her emotions and manipulate her into caring for him and, by extension, for the child. However, that outcome would only be possible if he was allowed to take care of her, monitor her activities, and watch for signs of miscarriage or worse.

To accomplish all that, he needed her in his office.

Dr. Grant smiled at me from behind the reception desk as I sat across from him. He was so close I wondered if he could hear my heart pounding. The memory of my dream had haunted me all weekend and made it difficult to think of anything else. The email I'd received from Eric was full of plans for our next rendezvous, but I didn't know how to answer it. Since Friday afternoon, I'd felt disconnected from everything. I felt as though I existed in a balloon that was only tethered to my life by four thin strands of ribbon. The one holding me to Dan was frayed almost beyond repair, the one to Eric was growing slimmer by the moment, and Brendan would soon be letting go of his. The strand attached to my job and students was the one I depended on to keep me grounded, and I wondered what would happen if that last ribbon broke. Amid all this uncertainty, Dr. Grant's melodic voice was a welcome intrusion into my thoughts.

"How are you feeling this morning, Caroline?"

"Well, other than it's Monday, and I've got a new semester starting soon, everything's fine, Dr. Grant."

"Ummm, when you left Friday night, you looked happy and relaxed. Did that feeling linger over the weekend, or was it just a short break?"

"It must be lingering. I've been sleeping really well these last few nights, except...."

"Except?"

"Well, I know it sounds strange, but since Friday, I hear singing just before I fall asleep."

"Like a recording?"

"Almost. At first, I thought it was a radio, but no, it's just weird. In that half-second, while slipping from being awake to being asleep, I hear voices singing."

He made a note in my file. "Does it annoy you? We could give you something to help you sleep."

"No, it's beautiful, almost like I am being sung to sleep. I don't recognize the music, but I've started looking forward to it."

"That's good. We don't encourage sleep aids, even natural ones."

"Well, if I've talked myself out of a full-body or shower massage," I said, blushing slightly, "I may have to reconsider."

"Well, Caroline, one of the perks of being my assistant is that you can have a massage whenever there is an appointment available. But, um, the shower massage computers have developed a synchronization glitch and are being repaired. The regular showers are still operational, however, if you ever wish to freshen up. Is it a position you might consider? Of course, it's only until the first of the year when my regular receptionist returns from maternity leave. At that time, however, if you wish to continue working here, I think you would make an excellent representative. It is up to you, but you will need to begin next Monday. Please let me know as soon as you decide."

He looked down at the list of names in his hand. "There are others who might be interested, but I will wait to hear from you."

I could not have heard him correctly. "Are you asking me to work for you?"

"Yes."

"As what?" I blurted without thinking. It took a full two seconds to recover my manners. "Excuse me, I mean, what will my duties be?" Not that it mattered, but was it possible that he was asking me to sit in this lovely room with him, five days a week, for the next four months? *That really couldn't be the job, could it?* I held my breath.

"Primarily, the administrative duties include acting as my secretary, assistant, and receptionist, and I hope you can make a nice pot of tea. When I meet with prospective and current clients, you will serve tea and toast, then, while new clients are completing the questionnaire, answer their questions, escort them to the financial consultant, make up a file with the signed documents for my review, and enter the pertinent data into the computer. You will also keep my calendar and schedule new and established client appointments as necessary."

He made notes on a small piece of paper. "These will be your hours, and this is your salary. Any medical issues that can be addressed at this facility are at no charge. However, if you go anywhere else, you will have to pay those charges yourself."

I looked wordlessly from him to the piece of paper and back.

He smiled at me from across the desk. "Thank you for your kind consideration of this new position, Caroline."

I was clearly being dismissed. "Thank, thank you, Dr. Grant," I stammered, standing up.

"Thank you…Grant?" he offered.

Too dazed to argue, I smiled gratefully.

"Thank you, Grant."

With no clear memory of leaving his office, I found myself standing in the locker room staring at the paper in my hand. *Nine to four…almost double the salary.* Sit in that beautiful office, enjoying massages during my lunch hour or after work or before work, tea and toast all day, *and* the best part, I would be Dr. Grant's assistant. He was always so busy. I knew he needed an assistant, and maybe he needed *me.* I would make sure he never regretted hiring me. I would be careful of the lights, learn how he liked his tea, listen to everything he said in his extraordinary voice, and, well, maybe he would let me take care of him a little. If I could do that, even for only four months, it was still a dream come true. The heat rushed to my face. *Well, maybe not that particular dream,* but it was everything I'd wished for since meeting him that warm afternoon in May.

Despite my enthusiasm, one question kept circling in my mind… *Could I really leave my job at the university?*

Using my nervous energy all summer, I'd updated everything from student files to cleaning out years of archived emails. With a few extra hours this week to pull some loose ends together, and if HR started right away, I was confident no one would be too inconvenienced while they looked for my replacement.

I stared at myself in the mirror. I couldn't believe it. I assumed I would work at the university forever. What a difference fifteen minutes with Dr. Grant could make! I'd gone from being anxious about the start of another school year to walking on air. And who knew? Perhaps his regular assistant would not return in January; many women did not resume working after having a baby, at least not right away.

Wouldn't it be wonderful? What if I never had to leave?

I was so captivated by these happy thoughts that it never occurred to me to turn the position down. Caught up in the excitement of mentally drafting my resignation letter as I drove to work, I failed to hear the fourth ribbon snap.

Thank you, Grant. Her soft voice echoed in his memory.

In that moment of innocent acquiescence, Dr. Grant Gates began planning the deconstruction of Mrs. Carrie Taylor. He saw it in her eyes and heard it in her voice. She would not refuse him. The first silken thread had been cast and caught. There would be others, one or two a day. He would lie to her, bring her flowers, watch her, listen to her, manipulate, and shelter her until she was as helplessly his awake as she had been asleep.

Grant looked at his watch. It was eight o'clock when she left his office. She would be at work at eighty-thirty. Checking his calendar, he picked up the telephone and called Monique.

"Ms. Robichaud, I am expecting a call from Mrs. Taylor. Please put her through and hold my nine o'clock appointment for five minutes. Thank you."

At one minute past nine, Grant felt he was on the right path when Caroline called to accept the position as his secretary, assistant, receptionist, and tea maker. Yet, with all his foresight and planning, he hadn't realized that each silken thread that bound her to him also connected him to her, intricately weaving their destinies together. Although Grant was unaware of it that morning, he no longer journeyed alone.

Reviewing the List

"Carrie Taylor? Isn't she a little old, and doesn't she have family here? Why did you pick her? She's a dreadful risk."

"I did not pick her, Grayson. She was not supposed to be there."

Gregory agreed with Grayson. "She has a husband, a son, and, apparently, a boyfriend. Aren't you a little concerned that might be too much competition, even for you?"

Grant closed his eyes. *Maybe I should give her up.* He could stop the pregnancy. A day or so of bad cramps and it would be over. He could put something in her tea or give her a "vitamin" shot; it didn't matter. She would never know the truth, and wouldn't it be better anyway? She didn't want more children, did she? No. There were no plans for another child on her admission form. He should ask for permission to terminate her pregnancy and let her go. Unbidden came images of her smile when she saw him, the smell of her hair, and her skin was so soft that his hands ached slightly at the memory. No. He wouldn't ask. He knew the drugs would hurt her and kill their son, and he was unwilling to destroy that physical connection to her. Unless it was to save her life, terminating her pregnancy would have to be their decision or hers; it would never be his.

He opened his eyes. "I've already lost one," he said. "Why two if it is unnecessary? She has agreed to be my receptionist, maybe I can—"

"Seduce her?" Gregory asked, laughing. "Can we please watch that? Please? I love a good comedy."

"I was going to say 'convince' her, Gregory, before you interrupted me."

Gabriel watched Grant's face. Although he could not read his thoughts, he had a good idea of what they were. *He likes her. Maybe he can convince her. What, besides everything, have we to lose? On the other hand, we also have everything to gain.* Gabriel believed he understood Grant's anxiety. He had already lost two embryos himself and would do almost anything to prevent a third.

Gabriel decided them. "I agree we shouldn't abort her pregnancy unless we have to. Grant, if you think you can convince her," he said, looking at Gregory, "you should try. Just have a hypo close by in case she needs sedating, and then, well, we will do whatever is necessary. She wasn't planning on having more children, was she?"

Grant glanced down at her admission form as though he didn't already know the answer.

"No."

"Then, that's settled."

"Yes."

Happy that all ten of his embryos were still viable, Garrett looked up from the list. "When do we tell them they are pregnant, Grant?"

"We will retest in three weeks. Everyone who is still pregnant will be told the following week, so they will expect a break in their cycle and justify a change to less strenuous classes. We must tell them in a confidential—but pleased—manner, establishing minimal physical contact so they will comfortably share any anxiety or difficulties with us. Above all, we must act warm and caring while remaining professional in all respects."

After a general assent, his brothers' voices, discussing the status of their other prospective mothers, faded into the background. Grant closed his eyes and prayed silently.

Forgive me, Caroline. I could not let you go.

The News

Working for Dr. Grant was everything I'd hoped it would be...*almost.* After the nervous excitement of the first few days wore off and the job eased into a routine, I began to feel a little displaced. Although he treated me professionally, the gentle camaraderie in our client consultations was missing, and I didn't know how to get it back. Realizing that the dynamics of my relationship with him had shifted from paying client to paid employee, I wondered if his kindness was only customer service. Every hour, the dream of him drifted further away, and the loss tore at my heart. Determined not to let him know, I smiled whenever I saw him and worked hard to be the best assistant he ever had.

On Thursday of my second week, Dr. Grant entered the office looking preoccupied and went straight to his desk. He stopped me as I was leaving at noon to meet Suzanne.

"Caroline, I was wondering if you would return after your last class today. I want to review some office procedures with you, and I have appointments out of the office the rest of the afternoon."

"We can talk now if you'd like," I said, even though I didn't want to miss lunch with Suzanne. We worked in the same building now, but our schedules were difficult to coordinate.

"No, I have an executive meeting. You cannot stay this evening?"

"No, sir, I can stay, no problem. I was just trying to make it easier for you. If I have to stay late to meet with you, then you have to stay late, too."

"Yes, well, it does seem that I live here sometimes. So, you will return after your four o'clock class?"

"Yes, sir."

"Yes, Grant," he corrected.

"Yes, Grant."

As I hurried to meet Suzanne, I realized there wasn't a noon executive meeting on his calendar. I made a mental note to ask him about it. If it was a regular meeting that wasn't ordinarily written down, then, as his receptionist/assistant/secretary/tea-maker, I should know about those meetings, too.

My afternoon class ran long. I rushed back to the office still wearing my workout clothes and went directly to my desk. Waiting for him to return to the office, I was startled when, at one minute past five, I heard a faint whirring sound, and the partition behind me unexpectedly disappeared into the ceiling. Swiveling around, I found myself sitting directly in front of Dr. Grant's desk.

Not wanting to intrude upon his privacy, I hadn't inspected his side of the office and believed it to be dark and uninteresting. However, without the partition in place, the highly polished paneled walls shone without the partition, complementing the two beautifully executed desert landscapes hanging behind his desk. To the left of the paintings was a recessed door that I assumed was his private washroom.

I started to stand.

"Where are you going?"

"To turn the rheostat down. I don't want the lights to hurt your eyes."

"You've been doing that all along, haven't you?"

"Yes. It doesn't bother me. The laptop is backlit."

"Thank you."

"You're welcome. Where did the partition go?"

"Into a space above the ceiling; it works on a variation of a garage door mechanism."

"Did you design that?"

"Yes. It was a solution to a problem."

"Like the rheostat," I said. Turning the dial, I watched the shadows in the room deepen. "A perfect solution to a painful problem."

Like you. Grant glanced over at the partially opened drawer; the edge of the hypodermic syringe was barely visible. Without the partition in place, he could catch her if she screamed or tried to escape. Fashioned like a trigger on a gun, he tightened his finger around the curved lever under his desk and silently locked the door.

"Oh, speaking of problems and solutions," she said, "is there a reason today's noon meeting wasn't on your calendar? Perhaps your other assistant knew all the regular meetings, but I don't know them yet, so if you would give me a list of the meetings you attend that aren't normally on your calendar, I would appreciate it…you know, to avoid confusion. I want everything to run as smoothly as possible while I am here, Dr. Grant. I don't want you to regret hiring me."

Interesting that she should speak of regrets. Grant looked at her and considered all the possible outcomes of the next twenty minutes…or five. *Yes. Everything he hoped for could all come crashing down in just five minutes.* He took a deep breath.

"Thank you, Caroline, that is an excellent suggestion, but all my appointments are on my calendar. This was an unscheduled meeting. We were all free, so we took the time to meet." He smiled at her efficiency. "I'll be sure to keep you more informed."

"Thank you. I don't want to disappoint you, Dr. Grant. I know you had several candidates for this position, and I'm happy you chose me."

"Are you?"

"Oh yes. I've wanted to work here since the first day I walked in."

"By here, I assume you mean here at the facility."

"No, sir. Here, in your office."

"Well, thank you for saying that." Watching her expression carefully, he asked, "Caroline, what will it take for you to stop calling me sir, or Dr. Grant, and call me Grant as I have asked you to do?"

"I guess I just need to work here a little longer."

Avoiding his eyes, she looked at the paintings behind his desk. Smiling slightly, she added, "And get to know you a little better."

Is it possible, he wondered, *that she likes me?* He wanted to discount it, but all the markers were there. She blushed when she looked at him and couldn't seem to find anywhere to put her hands. He watched her eyes linger on the paintings behind his desk and saw pleasure in them. Feeling confident of the outcome, his smile began to resemble that of a tiger spotting a lone gazelle.

Not understanding the full meaning of his smile, she smiled back.

Ah, such trust. Altering his original plan to make it more challenging, Grant decided to let her choose.

"I am not sure that will be possible, Caroline, because one of the items on my agenda to discuss with you this afternoon is your pregnancy."

"My, my, what?" she stammered.

He continued as if he had not heard her. "As you know, we take prenatal health care seriously at GatesWay. We will reschedule your classes, start you on a vitamin regimen, and increase your lunch hour so you can rest. If you wish, I, or one of the other doctors, will be happy to act as your obstetrician until your fourth month so your appointments will not affect your work schedule—"

"Wait a minute, wait a minute. Please stop. Are you saying I'm pregnant? How do you *know* that?"

"Your last blood test indicated the presence of a protein associated with pregnancy. I am so sorry, I thought you knew. Have I distressed you?" Grant stood and brought her a cup of his specially blended calming tea. Returning to his chair, he opened the drawer a little wider.

Her hand trembled as she brought the teacup to her lips. Contemplating the pale brown liquid, she did not notice that he scrutinized every expression that crossed her face. He watched as dread and confusion played havoc with her emotions before settling on pure fear.

"Distressed? Me? Oh, of course not. Hmmm, could you please direct me to the nearest bridge that I can throw myself off of? How tall is this building anyway?" Unable to continue speaking, she set the cup on his desk and covered her face with her hands.

Grant came around the desk, picked up her wrist, and looked at his watch. He hoped his attention would reassure her, but at his touch, the shaking in her hands became more pronounced, and her heart rate shot upward. Afraid of increasing her anxiety, he released her hand and sat back down.

"Caroline," he said gently, "talk to me. I am a doctor, and I care about you. This was unplanned?"

I could only nod my head. What was I going to say to him? I was so embarrassed, humiliated, and scared. Eric's baby…what was I going to do with Eric's baby? Seduce Dan? And my body, oh, I finally have a shape again and now a baby? What would that mean? Another thirty or forty extra pounds? I briefly considered an abortion, but not even my newfound vanity would consider that alternative. I just needed a few minutes. I put my hands on my lap, closed my eyes, and leaned my head against the chair. Two tears leaked from the outer corners and made a tortuously slow slide toward my temples.

"What are you thinking, Caroline?"

I was too devastated to lie. Without moving or opening my eyes, I said, "Just reviewing my options, Dr. Grant. I, I didn't know. You surprised me."

"We treasure mothers at this facility and believe their mental health must come before their physical health. That said," he paused, "GatesWay is not an abortion clinic."

I nodded. "I don't really consider that one of my options."

"Is there anything I can do to help you right now?"

The cadence of his voice brought back memories of the first day I'd met him, our tea party when I held his scarred hand, our discussion when he told me I was beautiful, and, lastly, my dream of him. Taking this job just to be near him, I'd deluded myself that he'd hired me because he wanted to be near me, too. And now a baby…Eric's baby. My beautiful dream of Grant would always remain a dream. Feeling something precious was irretrievably slipping through my fingers, two more tears slid toward my temples.

Grant planned to convince her that he could take care of her, but her grief caught him off guard. He never intended to hurt her and didn't understand why having the baby of someone she had gone through so much effort to please upset her. Aching to comfort her, it was only by keeping his hands firmly on his desk that he was able to stay in his chair.

Watching more tears fall from her eyes, however, breached Grant's endurance level. He got up quickly and carried her to his side of the desk. Sitting down, he held her head against his shoulder.

"What can I do, Caroline?"

"Forgive me."

Grant's mind whirled. *Forgive her for what? Had she changed her mind?* He controlled the apprehension in his voice.

"What is there to forgive?"

She pulled his head down so she could whisper in his ear.

"That it isn't yours."

It was impossible that she said that. With his heart in his throat, he asked, "Did you wish it to be?"

"I had a dream on my spa day, but it felt so much more than a dream, Dr. Grant; it was the most beautiful, wonderful experience…that we, um, that we…you know."

"Made love?"

"Yes."

"And that was all right with you?"

She placed her hand on his chest and sighed, "Oh, yes."

Each whispered word was more inexplicable than the last. He glanced at the syringe. Briefly closing his eyes, he prayed he wouldn't need it.

"Caroline," he said, his breath warm against her cheek. "It was not a dream, and…and the baby *is* mine. Please forgive *me*."

What had I done? There was tenderness in his voice, he was holding me so close, and that afternoon hadn't been a dream. In a moment of time that had grown more precious in memory, Grant Gates wanted me.

I couldn't look up. Knowing it was just as likely Eric's baby as Grant's, my hand resting on his chest became a fist as I tried not to cry.

I felt the gentle pressure of Grant's lips as he kissed my hair.

"Please, forgive me," he asked again.

Lifting my fist, he kissed each finger as he loosened it and, laying my flattened hand back on his chest, covered it with his own.

"Why so quiet, Caroline?"

In his arms and breathing the familiar scent of him, I had never felt so safe, but it was a security I did not deserve. Realizing my vanity had cost me the only man who really cared for me; I had nothing left to lose by telling him everything.

"Because it might…might not be yours." My voice broke, and my tears fell on his starched white shirt. "It might be someone else's."

"Ah, it is someone else's as well."

My head snapped up to meet his eyes. "You are going to have to explain that."

"It is late. Perhaps we should finish this discussion another time."

"I'm not moving until I understand whose baby I'm carrying, Grant."

"So, I am finally Grant now, am I?"

"I feel I know you better." I put my hands gently on each side of his face. "That was really you? In my spa-day dream?"

"Yes, Caroline," he whispered. "Tell me you forgive me, please."

"There is nothing to forgive. It was the most unforgettable experience of my life because you were there. But Grant, I don't understand. How can the baby have two fathers?"

He looked at me solemnly.

"I will tell you as much as you need to know right now, Caroline, but I see this as a series of discussions if that is acceptable to you."

"Can we sit like this when we 'discuss?'"

"As long as you are comfortable sitting this close to me."

"Why wouldn't I—"

"Shh," he said. "Do not say anything, and please, stay until I finish. Then I will answer all your questions."

Grant considered for a moment how much he could tell her without needing the syringe to stop her from screaming and running out the door. He should have rehearsed something, but her obvious affection had taken him by surprise. Trusting that affection, he decided to stay as close to the truth as possible.

He lifted her chin so he could watch her face. "Caroline, I want to say I care about you more than you know and I, well, I offered you this job because I hoped you might like to be here. I thought that if you got to know me, you might…care for me someday, but also so I could watch you and that you might share your pregnancy with me. I have dreamed of children, Caroline, and it makes me happy that you are pregnant with my child, happier than anything in a very long time. So, before I go into any further details, I want you to know that I cherish you both."

"Grant, I care for you—"

He placed his finger on her lips. "Shh. However you feel right now, what I have to say will not be easy for you to accept."

Grant gently brushed the hair from her eyes and hoped it would not be the last time he touched her face while she was still alive.

"I am sure you have noticed subtle differences, voice inflections, light sensitivity, little things that make my brothers and me seem foreign to you. And it is true, Caroline, we *are* foreigners."

"Really? Natalie said you were Americans."

"We are—legally—and you are not supposed to be interrupting."

"Sorry, I don't understand."

Grant held her as though these were the last few minutes he would ever look into her eyes.

"We have had different beginnings, you and I, different cultures."

"I know. Natalie said your family lived somewhere on the other side of the world."

"Not this world."

"I still don't understand."

"Think about it, Caroline."

It only took a moment. I sat up quickly.

"Wait, Grant, are you saying I am having a 'close encounter' here?"

I stared at his handsome face. His eyes watched me like he was waiting for me to dissolve into hysterics, but I didn't. I tried to laugh and couldn't. I wanted to move, but my body seemed frozen. It wasn't Grant or even fear that held me, but incredulity mixed with a sense of undeniable truth.

"Not exactly, Caroline. We have been on Earth for thousands of years. In our attempts to achieve a balance between your species and mine, we have been interbreeding with humans as necessary to adapt to this planet by incrementally combining our DNA."

His explanation was so straightforward that it was hard not to believe him. Of the dozens of questions tumbling through my mind, I could only focus on one. More disappointed than horrified, I asked, "Is that what we did, Grant? We interbred?"

"Only in the strictest clinical sense." Reaching for my hands, he pressed them to his face and whispered, "Oh, Caroline, loving you was the greatest experience of my life."

I gently pulled my hands away.

"Are you afraid of me, Caroline?"

"I don't want to be, Grant. I just want to understand, so bear with me for a minute." I took a deep breath and tried to clear my head. "I was pregnant with another man's baby, but when you made love to me, it became your baby?"

"He."

"What?"

"*He* became *our* baby, Caroline. If the replicating cells lacked the Y chromosome, you would have already miscarried."

My hands slid to my abdomen. *Another boy.* Visions of blue and white, baby giggles, flashing eyes, and chubby toes swirled through my mind. I couldn't stop a small smile from my lips. Grant took my hands again, and this time, I did not resist.

"Please do not be afraid, Caroline. I promise I will never hurt you. I only want to be close to you, to be a little part of your life…and perhaps the baby's life, too. This may be the only child I will ever have." His voice dropped, "If he…."

"If he…?"

"Survives."

"But Grant," I could not keep the edge of panic from my voice. "Why wouldn't he survive?"

"Several reasons, but primarily for my age and your age, the miscarriage rates are off the charts in this situation."

"How old are you?"

"In earth years, twenty-eight. Biologically, I am closer to forty. If he lives, it will mostly be due to the strength of Eric's, um, contribution."

I was stunned. "How?" I whispered.

"Oh, Caroline," he said with a smile. "You talk when you are dreaming."

"Then there are no secrets?"

"No. Not between us. Not anymore."

Grant set me on my feet. Pulling a stethoscope with an attached amplifier out of his lab coat, he lowered the waistband of my tai chi uniform and slowly moved the bell over my abdomen. When he found the sound he was seeking, he marked the area with his finger and removed the headphones. Then, slipping from the chair to his knees, he kissed the skin above his son's heartbeat.

He looked up at me.

"You will let him live?"

Although the glasses hid his eyes, I felt all the raw intensity of a loving father asking me not to kill his son. Overcome by the emotion behind his words, my eyes filled with tears. I nodded my head slowly. Standing, he pulled me close to him and buried his face in my neck.

"Thank you, Caroline."

Lifting me carefully, we sat back down in his chair.

In his singsong voice, he told me about the serum, the DNA sequencing, and how he and his brothers had each chosen ten of their clients to reconceive by changing the DNA of the human embryos. The only difference was that the others were altered surgically, but overcome by his feelings for me, Grant disregarded the established protocols and made love to me as a man.

All I heard was that Grant cared for me, desired me, and the rest of the information faded into the background as impossible. Resting in his arms, however, the ramifications of my pregnancy became real, and I wondered about the strange child growing within me. Lost in my thoughts, I heard Eric's name.

"What?"

"You have to tell Eric. The sooner, the better."

"He won't want to know."

"It does not matter. He is the first father and should be told."

"Do you give that advice to the other mothers?"

"No. For them, it is irrelevant. There is no second father. Most are not even aware they are pregnant, and I will not stop theirs," he said. "But I would do that for you if you decided to stay with him. It is not what I want, Caroline, but your well-being is important to me. I want to give you every opportunity to understand what having this particular child means and what you are doing to your life."

"What do you mean? Grant, if not for you, I would feel so alone. I would still be pregnant with very few happy options."

"Perhaps, but you would still have a normal human life. This isn't going to be easy, or particularly safe, for you at any stage."

"But you don't understand. I would probably be scheduling an appointment at an abortion clinic or adoption agency…either of which would probably haunt me for the rest of my life…or I would be a single mom living on alimony from one man and child support from another while I raised a child neither of them wants. Do you realize my personal horror of having to explain that to Brendan? Do any of those options sound remotely more desirable than the one you chose when you loved me?"

"All of them would be safer for you."

"Possibly…but none of them include you, and no one makes me feel as safe as you do." Recalling the contents of Eric's most recent email, I added, "But because it is, as you say, important, I'll tell Eric tomorrow."

I sat up and teased him. "You're taking a big risk, you know. He might make me an offer I can't refuse and then how would you feel?"

One look at his face told me how he would feel, but "It will be as you wish" was all he said.

Grant pressed the hidden latch that opened the door and watched her walk down the hall. He smiled as he returned to his desk and reviewed the events of the afternoon. Her concern for the child was genuine. His research indicated that would only happen if she accepted the baby as hers, but it was her promise to let the child live that allowed Grant to let her leave his office. Opening his experiment file, he confidently checked off several items on the projected trajectory arc.

He wasn't worried about Eric's reaction. He knew exactly how that little scene was going to play out tomorrow. But, on the slight chance he miscalculated, Grant knew other ways—more permanent ways—of taking care of *Eric*.

Once again, he saw the expression on Caroline's face when she realized she was carrying his child. He would move heaven *and* hell to secure that happiness for his son, and no mere human DNA donor was going to stop him.

The tiger's smile slowly returned to his face as he closed his desk drawer firmer and a little louder than necessary.

The Decision

My mind reeled with Grant's confession. I have no memory of walking to my car, unlocking it, or getting behind the wheel. Unable to lift my hand to turn the key, I stared through the windshield at the blue and white awning. Everything was true. My wonderfully impossible dream wasn't a dream at all, but the awakening was not of loving a man but loving a monster.

The two plus two of my observations and suspicions finally made four. Despite their carefully groomed exterior, Grant and his brothers were not human. I knew I should call someone, the newspapers or the police, anyone who could stop them, but I could not make myself move. Despite the payphones in the mall, I knew anonymity was impossible. No one would believe me without proof, and the only evidence I had was my child. What if they began their investigation by killing my baby? Would they then search out all the other pregnant women in the facility and kill their babies, too? I knew Grant and his brothers would fight to protect them. Innocent women and babies could perish, and I would be the one pointing the guns and knives in their direction.

Even if I survived, everything I'd experienced that afternoon in Grant's office would be destroyed. Affection, tenderness, and joy would be replaced with blood, death, and the unrelenting sorrow of knowing our son was only the first of many to die. Once again, I heard the anguish in Grant's voice as clear as if he were standing before me.

"You will let him live?"

It was "yes" then. It had to be "yes" now.

"I have dreamed of children, Caroline…."

Reliving the feeling of Grant's lips on my neck, his arms holding me, and the beat of his heart beneath my hand, I sought another heartbeat. My hand slid to my stomach.

Are you a man or a monster?

Smiling, I shook my head. He was neither. He was just a little baby boy with his eyes closed, perhaps dreaming fantastical dreams of his own, who trusted me.

Only my silence kept him alive.

Gently stroking my stomach, I whispered, "Sleep, little one, sleep, and dream. I won't let anyone hurt you…or your father."

Uncertain what the next day would bring but determined to guard Grant's secret and my son's life, I turned the ignition key and refused to be afraid.

Repercussions

"You did what?"

Grant looked calmly into Grayson's stricken face.

"It seems quite plain to me, Grayson, that having just shared the memory of my conversation with Mrs. Taylor, your question is superfluous."

"But you let her leave the premises! Has it occurred to you that once she has two minutes to think about it, she will go to the police? Or contact the FBI or NASA? Who knows what a woman with that kind of knowledge will do?"

Grayson's outburst continued as the rest of the doctors filled the small room. When he paused for a moment, Grant answered him.

"I know exactly what she will do."

"No, I don't think you do. Are you fully prepared to kill her when she comes back here tomorrow with her husband?"

"No, Grayson, I am fully prepared to kill them both. However, that will not be necessary."

"Are you sure? What time is she supposed to come in?"

"I have given her the day off to discuss the matter with the baby's father."

"WHAT!! Have you lost your mind?"

Grant grew still. For a moment so brief that most of them believed it was their imagination, the air reverberated throughout the enclosed space.

"No, Grayson, I have not. In fact, I have been putting my mind to very good use. Even before Mrs. Taylor was presented to me as a substitute, I had been exploiting her innate vulnerability as a test subject in my experiment on manipulation techniques. Now that I have daily access to her, I have continued refining the response cues that have proved the most successful. It is my intention to prepare a report for the collective delineating methods to generate receptiveness in prospective mothers, thereby increasing the probability of their compliant acceptance of our offspring."

"Why didn't you tell me?" demanded Grayson.

"I thought I just did. However, to answer what I sincerely hope will be your last question this evening, such an experiment is time-consuming, and I was not sure it would be possible, nor was I certain Mrs. Taylor was the best test subject. She was, after all, not among those originally chosen. After witnessing her lack of panic this afternoon, however, I am encouraged to pursue it through to success. Do not look so worried, Grayson. I am sure the next time we see Mrs. Taylor, she will be alone. Quite alone."

Grayson stared as Grant turned and left the room. Despite Grant's parting words, fear oozed from every pore in Grayson's skin. They all felt it and understood that the entire North American operation depended on the discretion of one human woman and the confidence of a single Lyostian drone. The odds were overwhelming, and several wondered if they should begin preparations for escape if the worst happened.

Calculating how long it would take to get a transport, Gregory looked at his brother, but Gordon gave a quick shake of his head. He was the only one who recognized the pulsating ionized charge for what it meant: there was no escape. If GatesWay failed, the collective would destroy them all.

Resolution

It had just started to rain when I met Eric in a tree-sheltered section of the quad. Huddling together under Dan's golf umbrella, we walked to the nearest covered bench.

"Why here? Why aren't we going up to your office? It's like two steps away and dry," he said as we sat down. Using the umbrella as a curtain, his finger traced the edge of my collar. His eyes traveled further down.

"We can go up there later," I lied. "I just wanted to talk for a moment, and we won't be interrupted here."

He smiled at me, and I recognized the longing in his eyes. *What had I been thinking? But I hadn't been thinking…desire is not thought, but action awaiting an opportunity.*

Ah, but that was before. The woman who sighed beneath his touch was not the woman who spent yesterday afternoon in the arms of Grant Gates. I would always be grateful for Eric's affection, and although I no longer thought of the child as his, any paternity test would prove me wrong.

"Okay, but I'm getting drenched, and there are things I would rather do than sit *here* getting wet with you."

His eyes smiled into mine to make sure I understood his meaning. Smiling back cautiously, I prepared myself to walk into an emotional minefield. I knew Grant was right. Eric should have the opportunity to acknowledge his son, but it wasn't going to be easy—on either of us. I fully expected one of the two typical reactions; the only thing I was unsure of was how humiliated I would feel afterward.

Gazing past him into the rain, I said softly, "I'm pregnant, Eric." I waited a few moments to give him some time to collect his thoughts before looking back at him.

When my eyes found his, they were expressionless. His smile had faded. "Not…hap…pen…ing."

He said it as though he could make his son disappear if he denied him in as many syllables as possible. Total rejection. Typical reaction number one. I waited for the "you're married, are you sure it's mine?" accusation, but it never came, and I was grateful not to have to debate my marital love life with him.

"No, it isn't happening. I just wanted you to know in case you had any religious objections." *Or if you loved me…and wanted us…the only offer I wouldn't refuse.*

"In theory, yes," he said, "but in practice, I have no objections. At this stage of my life," he rationalized, "it's the best choice. And for you, too. I mean, don't you have to worry about birth defects after a certain age?"

I hated the relief that showed so plainly on his face, and I sensed he hated it, too, but not enough. I smiled as I remembered Grant's gentle kiss and his gratitude when I told him I would not stop my pregnancy. I looked at Eric and knew the only thing standing between me and the living hell that would soon have become my life was the knowledge that Grant was waiting for me. My heartbeat quickened. *Grant was waiting for me.* The longing to be with him was greater than any reason to stay. I stood to leave.

Mistaking my smile, Eric said, "Well, now that we've gotten that out of the way, when can I show you my new apartment?"

So young. As gently as I could, I touched his hand and said, "Goodbye, Eric."

As I expected, he did not come after me, and it was just the sound of my hurried footsteps echoing against the red brick buildings as I whispered in the rain, "Thank you."

A Matter of Confidence

The tension in the facility was hard on everyone. Only Grant appeared oblivious as he went about his daily routine. Preoccupied with their own sense of impending doom, no one looked at him closely enough to notice that his hands were never in sight. As the day edged toward midafternoon with no sign of Caroline, Grant kept more and more to his office.

What if he had miscalculated? What if she did not care about him? What if…what if she lied? Betraying them to the authorities was not the worst outcome—Grant was always prepared for such a contingency. However, his words of warning echoed back at him, "I assume you know the penalty for any brother who puts the colony at risk." Nothing they did to him, neither the slow death of banishment nor the quicker death in the Sidereal Chamber, would hurt as much as losing her, losing the chance to hold their child and have the joy that might have been theirs lost forever.

Regardless of whatever punishment the collective chose, Grant knew he would go to his death willing to risk it all again just to feel the single caress of Caroline's fingers on his skin.

He had purposely assigned Howard as the client escort of the day, and it was not until four in the afternoon that he sent Grant the message that Carrie Taylor was in the lobby. Alone.

Discreetly follow her to the elevator but let her come up by herself. Thank you, Howard.

Um, Grant?

Everything is fine.

Grant dimmed the office lights and raised the partition so he would see her the moment she entered the office. With his head down and supported by his hands, he could look over the rims of his glasses. Having memorized every expression on her face, Grant knew the one he wanted to see.

The door opened slowly.

Silhouetted by the shaded lamps in the hallway, he saw hope in her eyes as she searched for him in the darkness of the room. Suppressing a smile, he sighed as he raised his head.

Silent Rain

The partition was raised when I returned to Grant's office that afternoon, but the room was so dark I could barely see him sitting at his desk with his head in his hands. He looked up slowly as I closed the door. I could feel his eyes staring into me as he tried to read my heart.

"Are you okay, Caroline?"

"Yes, Grant."

"Did he want the baby?"

"No, he didn't want the baby."

"Did he still want you?"

"Oh, yes."

"I see."

He stood as the partition dropped soundlessly back into place.

Taking my hand, he led me through the door behind his desk. What I assumed to be a washroom was actually a small medical office. The examination table in the center of the room was surrounded by pale yellow walls and stainless-steel cabinets. The only item on the polished countertop was a small tray holding a single syringe.

He turned toward me. "This is the second time I have had to do this today."

"Do what?"

"Abort one of my reconceived embryos."

"You lost another one?"

"Yes, she…she started miscarrying, and it is easier if we tell them the truth. That they were pregnant, and now they are no longer pregnant. She will have some discomfort for a day or so, but then she will be fine. At this stage, there is little chance for any adverse reactions from her pregnancy."

Speaking tonelessly as though he was very tired, he added softly, "It will be like it never happened."

He began unbuttoning my raincoat. "Here, let me help you."

"I don't understand. Help me with what?"

"Undress. I need to inject the drugs directly into your uterus."

"What are you talking about? What drugs?"

"For the abortion, Carrie."

"What? You brought me in here to kill my baby?" Bewildered, I grabbed the lapels of his lab coat and looked into his face.

"Why?"

He took my hands from his coat and brought them together between us. "You said you would go back to Eric if he still wanted you. When you said he did, I thought that was the offer you couldn't refuse. I was going to give you back your life, Carrie. I want you to be happy."

I jerked my hands from his grasp.

"Thank you, Dr. Grant, for being so thoughtful, but please understand—and engrave upon your brilliant brain now and for all eternity—that one, I *am* happy, and two, I will never willingly consider a life that does not include this baby. Now, stop upsetting me, or my doctor will get very angry with you. He *cares* about *us*."

I turned and walked out of that horrible yellow room.

The Show

Looking through the two-way mirror above the counter, Grant smiled triumphantly at the brothers he knew were standing there.

Grayson immediately transmitted Grant's success throughout the colony. The built-up apprehension within the facility dissipated as his brothers breathed a collective sigh of relief. Two of the three witnesses smiled at each other; the third continued to stare through the window.

"I can't believe he did it! Did you see that?" Gregory asked Gabriel.

"Yes…but a little too melodramatic for my tastes."

"I know! I kept waiting for the violins to come up."

They noticed that Grayson was unusually quiet. "What is it, Grayson?" Gregory asked. "Didn't you enjoy the show?"

"Yes and no. Despite Grant's fondness for dramatic tension, I'm still concerned about her. She's a little too independent. She *is* still married and could decide to pass the pregnancy off as her husband's. At least until he is born…I don't think antennae run in the Taylor family. But we continually risk exposure if she starts to miscarry and goes to a hospital, especially if her husband is involved. Just working here isn't enough. We need to keep her here to make sure the child is born here and, if the worst happens, that she stays here—indefinitely. In the meantime, we need to observe her more closely to find out why she cares so much about her pregnancy. As Grant said, such information would be useful not only to better influence our current prospective mothers but those at other facilities as well."

He was silent for a moment, then thought privately to Gabriel.

When she leaves, go to Grant's office. Tell...no...ask_him if he thinks he can separate her from her mate. After this victory, he'll be ready for another challenge.

Where will we put her? Gabriel asked.

That will be his problem.

Trust

Grant closed the examination room door firmly. Standing by the partition, he watched the reflection of Caroline's face on her laptop screen, looking, by turns, furious and scared. He was willing to accept a lot of pain for using her so abominably and put his hands lightly on her shoulders.

"I don't think you should touch me right now."

He lifted her wrist. Her heart was beating a little too fast for just anger, but why else?

"If I apologize, will you stop being angry at me?"

"You cannot apologize for wanting to kill your own son."

"Eric did."

"He didn't apologize. He just thought it was for the best. 'Not a good time for a child in either of our lives,' he said."

She was quiet for a moment. "Men…and apparently all men, whatever their species, are quite careless with their unborn children. They don't understand that for most women, from the moment they know they are pregnant, that tiny heartbeat becomes the most important sound in the world—not something to be casually silenced or ignored."

His hands tightened on her shoulder. "Think whatever you like about me, Caroline. But understand fully that I am neither careless nor casual when it comes to you or our child. That I am willing to sacrifice him for the sake of your happiness should tell you how much I care about you. That I am willing to confess that I would have rather died myself than walk into

231

that room and kill my own son should tell you how much I love and want him."

Turning her chair around, he knelt and looked into her face.

"I *hate* that room, Caroline. Our unborn brothers die in there." The strain of the day crept into his voice. "To walk in there with you, knowing that I was only minutes away from breaking my own heart, was the hardest decision I have made in my life. You see, I…I thought it was what *you* wanted. Please forgive me."

"How many have you lost?"

"Three."

"So quickly?"

"Better earlier than later for the mothers. If I am going to lose them, I would rather it be now."

The anger in her eyes became concern, and Grant dared to hope that she still cared for him. He saw her glance at her computer screen and back at him.

"Dr. Grant, it appears you have no more appointments this afternoon. What should we do about that?" she said softly.

In relief and gratitude, he tugged on her hands and pulled her down onto his lap.

Sitting on the carpet with his back to the partition, he whispered, "I thought I had lost you, Caroline, and when you said he didn't want the baby, I thought I had lost you both. It was my greatest fear; you will never understand what kind of hell today has been for me."

"I'm sorry. I wanted to tell you I never planned to see him again as soon as I came in, but you didn't ask that. Then you scared me when you took me in that dreadful room." She shivered slightly. "And I meant what I said in there. I realized after I left yesterday that the baby and I are a package deal. That means you must take us both, or you can't have either one. So please," she said, stroking his cheek gently, "please consider that, Grant, before you start caring about us too much."

"I am Grant again?"

She smiled and nodded, nestling her head against his shoulder.

He leaned into the corner, holding her tightly against his chest, his right hand on her abdomen where his son safely slept. She closed her eyes and relaxed in his arms. Not wanting to disturb her, Grant sat silent and unmoving until she had to leave. Even then, he did not rise from the floor but watched her until she closed the door.

He meant what he said, too. Despite the level of control his brothers thought he had in manipulating her emotions, he would have, had she wished it, killed his son in front of them. For her, he would have disobeyed their mandate and risked his own life. Grant was no longer sure upon whom he was experimenting, what he was going to do now, or what he would be allowed to do if his brothers became aware of how close he had come to murdering one of their own.

That she understood most of the implications of her choice and still returned to him indicated she cared about him and her pregnancy. "The baby and I are a package deal," she'd said. Did he want that responsibility? She worked here, wasn't that enough? Wasn't sharing her pregnancy with her nearly every day and holding her in the evenings before she went home enough? Wouldn't the memory of her softness beneath him be enough?

No.

Grant leaned his head back against the partition. At what point, especially when her pregnancy entered its most dangerous phase, would having her out of his sight and touch drive him mad with anxiety?

Soon, he sighed, *very soon.*

The Request

Gabriel's signature echo intruded into his thoughts.

Grant, are you in your office alone?

Yes.

As he stood up, Grant mentally reviewed the list of improvements he planned to make over the long weekend. The most important, a new partition, would necessitate a chair large enough to accommodate both of them since he would not be bringing her back into his section of the office again. The colors were all wrong, too. They suited him, but he didn't consider it *his* office any longer. She was here now, and he wanted the room to reflect her presence so he could imagine her with him when he was working alone.

Gabriel entered without knocking, and Grant was not sure he liked the look on Gabriel's face.

"Congratulations on handling that situation so well this afternoon, Grant. The way you controlled her response, making her want *and actually defend* her decision to keep the child, was quite impressive."

Grant saw Gabriel smile at the memory of a mother wanting their offspring. It was a dream they all shared.

"It was a risk, but I set it up before bringing her into the exam room. Pity for her that she is so tenderhearted and oblivious."

"Yes, but great for us. If there is one compliant human mother, there might be others, and if the child survives, he will have a mother who cares for him."

"Yes, Gabriel, so many ifs...."

"So, the experiment is working?"

"Yes. As you observed, my methods have encouraged her to care for the child because," he laughed softly, "she thinks I care for her. Which I do, of course; she is one of our mothers. Manipulating human women is easy because they are so susceptible to kindness that they mistake it for a myriad of other nonexistent emotions."

"Yes. Umm, Grant, how far are you willing to take this experiment? Just how much time are you willing to invest in it?"

There was a tension in the question that was absent from Gabriel's previous comments, and sensing a trap, Grant responded cautiously.

"As far and for as long as the colony deems it useful."

"Grayson...."

Grant's eyes narrowed to mere slits. "Yes, Gabriel, please tell me what Grayson wants now."

"I understand your skepticism, Grant, but please hear me out. Grayson wants to know if you would consider accepting the task of separating her from her mate and bringing her here to live."

Grant stared at him. "Excuse me? Why does Grayson want that?"

"I know it's unusual—"

"It's not only unusual; it's also dangerous."

"Yes, but she's the only one of our prospective mothers who is married. Grayson believes the danger of exposure is far greater if she starts to miscarry or carries the baby to term and her husband takes her to a hospital. We are watching the other mothers and, through your example and notes, hope to start developing closer, if not as honest, relationships with them so they will come to us if they experience any difficulties. However, the fact is she has a husband, which could mean unpleasantness if we cannot extricate her—the kind of legal unpleasantness we all want to avoid. So Grayson believes she should live here for observation, at least until she has the child.

After that, we'll see…when she sees. Anyway, since you handled her so well this afternoon, he thought you might be able to isolate her from her family and persuade her to move here. If you don't believe you can do it, do you think she would trust one of us?"

Although Grant's face did not change, his mind was racing down a hundred paths at once. After a few moments, he said reluctantly, "I will do it. As you saw today, she came back here to me. She didn't go home or just call or ask to see anyone else at the facility. Of course, observing her behavior in a non-professional setting *will* make our report stronger, but where am I supposed to put her? She has to *want* to stay."

"You're the architect; design something. There is that entire storeroom area above the garage we don't need anymore. Only five levels straight down, it's practically under our feet…or—"

"Or where? There is no other space available except the sixth floor, and we don't want her to have access to the roof, nor am I willing to take her deep into the tunnels. There is far too much for her to see," Grant said, looking down at his hands.

"True on both counts. The storage area it is, then. Will you need any help in arranging things?"

"No, Gabriel, thank you. Just provide me with an account number, please, and tell Grayson I'll take care of it: her, the extrication, and the creation of a human habitat. Yes," he said, smiling slightly, "I'll take care of it *all*."

"Even if…."

"Yes, even then."

Later that evening, Grayson met Gabriel in the conference room alone.

"So, he thinks he can persuade her to live here?"

"Yes."

"Where will she stay?"

"In the storage room above the garage."

"Good place for her," Grayson said, smiling briefly at his own joke. "What was his manner of acceptance?"

"Twofold, I would say. He seemed intrigued by the idea of adding a new dimension to his experiment with the added challenge of besting another human competitor."

"I knew it would appeal to his vanity."

"Vanity?"

"Look around, Gabriel. All the beauty you see in this facility is by his design because he thinks it makes up for his ugly hands. No amount of perfection will ever erase those scars or what they represent, but that doesn't keep him from seeing every challenge as another chance at redemption. He will stop at nothing now, including murder, to separate her from her husband."

"Do you think he will hurt her?"

"No, I think he will give her everything a human woman desires."

"Everything?"

"Oh, yes. Everything. Except her freedom. But by the time she realizes that it will be too late…for her."

Betrayal

Verb: be·tray Pronunciation: bi-'trā
Etymology: Middle English, 13th century
Definitions: to lead astray; a disloyal act; to fail/desert; to prove false.

Yes.

I confess to all the above definitions. It was not my original objective, but the act of betrayal is not always premeditated. It can result from a series of small, innocuous steps that, building upon decisions made from lack of choice or self-preservation, must lead irrevocably to a conclusion that was never intended yet seems, in retrospect, inevitable.

Individual contrition is not part of the collective's emotive range, but she will be my last thought, the single hope of my final whispered prayer.

Forgive me, Caroline.

From the private journals of Grant Gates, Ph.D., M.D., A.I.A.
Executive Director and Resident Psychologist
GatesWay Fitness Clinic and Health Spa

Tuesday Morning

Returning to work following the Labor Day weekend, I found the entire office transformed. Soft summer hues of white, blue, and gray replaced the autumn greens and golds. The walls, newly painted a slate blue from the ceiling to the paneling, blended perfectly with the dark blue carpet. Even the furniture was different. A new oversized leather chair and ottoman with ivory and blue suede cushions occupied the far corner, and an exquisite antique writing desk had replaced my bulky reception desk. The tea table was set with a pale blue and gray tea service with a bamboo design. Everything was perfect, not a cushion out of place. I twirled in the center of the room. I could not have felt more at home if I had designed it myself.

Although the new furnishings were beautiful, the most notable change was the partition. To make the front room brighter without adding more incandescent light, Grant replaced the dark wooden panels with mirrored horizontal segments set inside a filigree frame of golden bamboo.

Grant entered the office carrying a crystal vase filled with fresh flowers while I was arranging things on my new desk. Feeling slightly shy in the face of all the beauty surrounding me, I could only whisper, "The office is lovely, Grant."

Countless rainbows decorated the polished surface as he placed the vase on my desk. Lifting my hand to his lips, he kissed the palm.

"Good morning to you, Caroline…to both of you," he added before walking behind the partition.

"Did you get a new desk, too?"

"No. It was for you."

It was all for you, he repeated in his mind, touching the only new addition in his office. Hidden under the top edge of his desk was a small rheostat that controlled the light within the partition's two-way mirror, allowing him to change the opaqueness of the panels on his side from impermeable black glass to a completely clear window.

He could look at her whenever he wished, and, just as important, he could read the screen of her laptop. An emergency off-switch on the floor quickly darkened the window if she—or anyone else—needed access to his office.

Grant was not proud of his surveillance tactics, but to comply with Grayson's request, he had to know her contacts, how close her relationship was with her husband, and whether she still corresponded with Eric. He didn't think she would lie to him, but until the day she was completely his, trusting her was the only luxury he could not afford.

"Th-thank you. The room was beautiful before, but this, well, I'm overwhelmed."

"I'm happy you approve of the changes, Caroline."

Later that afternoon, he saw her get up from her desk and walk toward the partition. His foot immediately touched the floor switch, but he did not turn to look at her.

"Grant," she said softly, as though not to disturb him. "I'm going to my step class in a few minutes, but I," she paused, waiting for him to look up, but although he stopped typing, he made himself keep his eyes on the screen.

"I wondered if you would, umm, be here afterward."

Still refusing to look at her, he glanced at the papers on his desk. "Was there anything particular you wanted?"

"Umm, yes. Over the weekend, I considered some of the things you said, and I hoped we could 'discuss them further,' like you promised."

Grant detected disappointment in her voice at his indifference and started counting to ten.

"It's…it's okay if you have a meeting or something. I'll just go straight home. Maybe we can talk tomorrow."

Nine, ten. He looked up at her and smiled. Tilting his head a little, he said, "Carrie, do I have a meeting on my calendar for later this afternoon?"

"No, sir."

"No, Grant."

"No, Grant."

"If you want me to wait for you after class, then, of course, I will," he said. Taking her hands in both of his, he added, "I would have suggested it myself, but I thought you would be tired. It's been a busy day."

There it was…the predictable smile and audible relief from the reassurance that he cared about her. Grant smiled inwardly. *So easy, Caroline.*

"Thank you. It would be great just to sit and talk for a few minutes. And you're right, of course. We've been so busy I feel I have missed you all day."

As she turned toward the outer office, Grant watched her hair swirl around her neck and bounce on her shoulders. He turned on the partition in time to see her caress one of the pillows, and Grant's heart twisted a little at the happiness on her face when she unexpectedly paused at the door and blew a kiss in his direction.

"I'll be back in an hour," she called.

His head still tilted, he thought to Gabriel, *Did you catch all of that?*

Every word and gesture. So, how long before she's eating out of your hand?

What makes you think she isn't already doing that?

He heard Gabriel's laughter.

Well, if she isn't doing it now, it's clear she's thinking about it.

Tell Grayson she will be here. Two weeks at the most.

Why wait two weeks?

Because, while I will separate her from her husband, I do not think she would—and we would rather she didn't—leave her son. When he goes away to college in two weeks, the loneliness of not having a child to care for any longer will actually help with maternal acceptance by making her feel needed again. If I encourage Carrie to leave him now, then she will feel guilty nurturing another child. If I wait until he leaves her, a new child will give her an outlet for her maternal feelings.

Good thinking. That's why you're the psychologist, and I'm the accountant. So, two weeks, then.

Yes. As you know, a lot can happen in two weeks.

Gabriel understood. *That is sadly true. I heard you lost another one today.*

Yes. Gordon took care of it for me.

Better early than late.

Yes.

Six left, including hers?

Yes. You?

The same.

As Gabriel's echo faded, Grant looked at her empty chair through the glass.

Was this, then, the price of keeping her? Having to refer to her as "Carrie," a name he detested, to his brothers; analyzing and trivializing every sweetness of her feelings for him; ridiculing her joy of him and reporting her every move? Worst of all, must he continue treating his beautiful Caroline as a microscopic specimen? Was it the only way?

Yes…for now.

Unwilling to destroy his son and return Caroline to her husband's care, he had no alternative but to do or say whatever was necessary so the colony would allow him to watch her, touch her, hold her, and, one day soon, bring her here to stay.

Not trusting one minute of the time she was out of his sight, the hardest thing he did every day was allow her to walk out of his office, even for an hour for class or lunch at the mall with friends. It was torture to let her out of his sight, just as it was torture to treat her indifferently when she was in his presence. Overcoming this pain, as he had conquered every pain in his life, he focused on surviving one more day.

Impatient for her return, Grant left his desk and straightened the immaculate room. Knowing she would shower after class and thinking she might be cold, he took a small quilt out of the ottoman and folded it over the back of the chair. He brewed a fresh pot of his favorite tea, and because he knew she would be hungry, he prepared honey and crackers. Lastly, he moved the tea table closer to the chair where he could serve the tea without leaving her.

Shading the candle so he could remove his glasses, Grant also took off his lab coat and tie. He checked the time and sat down to wait. Leaning his head against the soft leather, he tried not to count the seconds.

I showered quickly after class, and although I wanted to run, I made myself walk back to the office so I would not be sweaty and out of breath. I didn't want to be that way for Grant. I wanted to appear calm, the way he was, always in command. Reaching his office, I took a deep breath and slowly opened the door.

"Grant," I said softly to the darkness.

"In your chair, Caroline," he replied just as softly.

Closing the door, I heard the cushions sigh, and the scent of bitter honey filled the air. Two strong arms came out of the darkness, picked me up, and carried me to the chair.

"Tomorrow, when the lights are on, you might practice walking from the door to your chair so I can wait here for you."

I pulled his head down to mine.

"Our chair," I said. Then I noticed he wasn't wearing his glasses. "Oh, Grant, you don't have your glasses on. How did you find me? Can you see at all?"

"Yes, perfectly. Much better than in the light. To prove it to you, open your mouth."

Doing as he asked, a cracker with honey was placed precisely on my tongue. Delighting in its sweetness, all I could think of was how being with Grant made the simplest pleasures wonderful.

"Good?" he asked.

"Oh, yes," I said. "Only a cup of tea could make it better."

He placed one of the new teacups in my hand. Bringing it to my lips, I recognized it as the tea I had the first day I met him. "Hmmm, more crackers, please," I asked, and he handed me the saucer.

"Have your eyes adjusted to the candlelight yet?"

"Yes, I see dark shapes, but details are escaping me. It may take a few more minutes, seeing that I'm not an alien or anything amazing like that."

He took the saucer and teacup out of my hands and pulled me close. "Caroline, there is no one more amazing than you."

I wanted him to hold me forever, but my rumbling stomach gave me away, and he handed me the saucer again. By the time I finished eating, I could see fairly well for a human and saw him without his glasses for the first time.

In the flickering candlelight, Grant's face was a study of angles and shadows. There were no words then, and there are none now, to describe how breathtakingly handsome he was to me. Beyond classic male beauty, he possessed a sense of tightly controlled power that sharpened his features. Sitting so close to him in the darkness, I realized that for all his outer calm, he was an irrepressible force to be reckoned with. I had a moment of panic when I considered how helpless I would be if he ever turned that brilliant fire against me…helpless because it would never occur to me to fight back.

I could not keep the fear from my eyes.

"Do not be afraid of me, Caroline, please. I promised you I would never hurt you."

"But you could, so easily, couldn't you?"

"Oh, yes, you are quite fragile, but it is impossible. Hurting you would destroy me. Whatever else you believe about me, please believe that I will never allow anything to happen to you or our son."

I did believe him. Despite the extraordinary nature of our relationship, I felt safe with him. Even in my dream, I trusted him. I lifted my hand toward his face.

"Grant, may I touch you?"

"May I touch you?"

"Yes, but I asked first."

"Yes, Caroline, you may touch me," he said, taking my hand and kissing it. "Gently, and tomorrow, it will be my turn."

Hearing those words—a simple spoken promise—the stars realigned in my sky, and this room of dark shapes and shadows became the universe to me. I would keep up the appearances of my marriage if I had to, but any life outside this office would be a calculated pretense. Facing my own personal truth, I knew the only life I wanted was one that included him.

"Yes, Grant."

Barely making an impression, my hands glided softly over his face. His forehead was smooth and warm; the high, slightly angled cheekbones were prominent and sharp. I traced the bridge of his nose and moved lightly over eyebrows so finely arched they felt like feathers beneath my fingers. I slowly tracked the curves and shadowy hollows of his face to the firm muscles of his jaw. Like a sculptor, my hands followed the arch of his neck and moved around the quiet strength of his shoulders, finally coming to rest on his chest.

His breathing was so shallow I thought he had fallen asleep. I kissed my right index finger and touched his lips. He caught my hand and pressed it against his face.

"That was the nicest thing anyone has ever done to me."

"The very nicest?" I asked teasingly.

"Yes," he said, "The nicest…but maybe not the most earth-shattering. Another record you hold."

I smiled for a moment, lost in those memories. So quiet and relaxed, he seemed content to let me reminisce, but I was aware that time was passing and there were things I needed to know.

"Grant, may I ask you some questions now?"

"Yes," he said, handing me another cup of tea. Getting one for himself, he settled into the cushions like a rajah while I, like Scheherazade, sat next to him on my knees.

"Grant, Andrea said that your family has a genetic history of photophobia. Is that true?"

"Yes, photophobia is the correct term. We are afraid of light because when you have four pairs of eyes—"

"What did you say? You have four pairs of eyes?"

"Yes, Caroline," he admitted, "we said 'no secrets.'" His confidence in her wavered with each admission, and he wondered how much he could tell her before the truth of what he was would send her running away from him forever.

"Can I see them?"

"You cannot see them?"

"Only flashes when the candlelight strikes them."

That's not candlelight. Aloud, he said, "Perhaps someday, but it seems that any light bright enough for you to see them individually would hurt too much for me to have my eyes open."

"Oh, okay."

Grant could not miss the sound of disappointment in her voice and was intrigued, not for the first time, by this woman and how her mind worked.

"So, as I was saying, when you have four pairs of eyes, they assimilate a lot of light. Imagine four times as much light coming in through your eyes at one time."

"That would be blinding."

"Yes, it is, and excruciatingly painful," he said, grimacing. "As our star was slowly dying, our species evolved to let in more light by increasing the number of irises and lenses to our eyes. This evolution resulted in our possessing both monocular and binocular vision—"

"I'm sorry, what?"

"It means we can see different things from each eye or the same thing with both eyes simultaneously. That's possible because the pupils of our eyes are smaller than yours and float independently on the surface of the eyeball, each connected by its own optic nerve to the brain to let in as much sight and light as possible. Your moon, at its fullest, is twice as bright as our white star toward the end of her existence. Cooling with each passing century, we could not wait for her to die, destroying our only food source and leaving us in darkness. With regret, we had to leave Lyos, our mother, because she could not nourish us. Calculating the precise timing of space portals, we sent research probes to other planets to determine their ability to sustain our life form. Dividing our dwindling population among these life-giving worlds, the elders directed my ancestors to this planet about a hundred thousand years ago."

"But Grant, that was our stone age. If your ancestors were so intelligent, why isn't your species ruling the earth instead of humans?"

"We would be, but your planet with its bright star forced us underground. We were blind creatures in the daytime and only able to venture out on moonless nights. Unfiltered sunlight will always be too bright for us, but through centuries of trial and error, we've adapted to human circadian rhythms: walking around during the day, first in candlelight, then artificial lighting while wearing glasses with photosensitive lenses."

"They hide your eyes?"

"No, they focus our eyes, so they move together. Anyone looking from the other side of the lens only sees one pair of eyes. But when we remove our glasses, our eyes can move in eight different directions at once."

She was quiet for several moments. Afraid of what she might be imagining, Grant wanted to bring her back to the present.

"Does that scare you?"

"A little," she confessed, "but I am more worried about our son. Will he have four pairs of eyes as well?"

"Perhaps, that is still unknown."

"Will he be more like me or more like you?"

"He will be more human than the rest of his generation."

"Why?"

"The added human DNA of my mother."

"So, you're half human. Or almost half?"

"No," he said. "The last two hundred generations have been reconceived from the same serum, the strength of which has never varied, allowing only minimal DNA from our mother. Our son will have my mother's DNA in addition to yours, which will make him slightly more human than any of his brothers."

"And ...."

"He will have all of my memories up to the moment of reconception and the cumulative knowledge of our species. One of the only comforts I have is that he already knows how much I care for you and will love you for both of us."

"And the other comforts?"

"Because of that little bit of extra human DNA, he will live longer than most of his generation. The last is more selfish—and the one that makes me wish I could stay with you— is watching him become a leader of his generation and the generations to follow."

"Who will he lead?"

"If he survives, our son will lead seven generations of human hybrids against those who commit dangerous crimes against our planet. We will try to make changes peacefully, if possible, but humans are not peacefully led, so it may come to war."

"But why human hybrids?"

"Three reasons. One, we need your lifespan. My generation only lives fifteen to eighteen years after reaching maturity. Our biological clocks slow down as we pass twenty-five, and by the time most of us are thirty, they have stopped altogether."

"And the rest."

"Die sooner."

"Is that why you said you *wished* you could stay with us? Not because you were going to send us away or go home to be married, but because you are going to...to...."

Grant watched sadness descend like a thundercloud over her beautiful face.

"Grant...die?"

"Yes."

His decision to confess this to her was vindicated by the strangled sorrow in her voice, and he gathered her in his arms.

"Everything dies, Caroline. It is only your species that wastes so much of the precious time you are alive, dreading the time you won't be. We are not going to do that, are we?"

"No, Grant," she whispered, fighting back the tears.

Her face betrayed her words. Grant knew she could not generate such an instantaneous response if she did not feel the corresponding emotion. She genuinely cared for him—it wasn't just the child. Hoping against hope, he held her as close as he dared and kissed her eyes.

"I told you once before, Caroline, you are too beautiful to cry."

To fight down my rising panic over losing him, I focused on imitating his calm acceptance. To distract us both (me from becoming hysterical, him from having to deal with it), I asked him about the history of the Lyostians once they landed on Earth.

"That brings me to reason number two," he answered, "we need your light tolerance. It was the brilliance of your sun that nearly killed us, Caroline. When our probes measured your biosphere, we were ecstatic that your star was so strong. It would sustain us for millions of years. However, we miscalculated our reaction to so much starlight and were blinded by it. So blind that many of us died trying to escape it by stumbling into the paths of beasts we could not see. Until our depth perception adjusted to the way your atmosphere bends light, we drowned in rivers or fell from cliffs. We were smaller, only about two-thirds the height we are now; our skin was nearly translucent, and our eyes much more delicate. Compared to humans, we are a scientifically advanced species, but without weapons to defend ourselves, we were a helpless people until we found caves. Going deep underground, we recovered slightly, only to discover there was nothing to eat, just large animals who thought we were food.

"The only help we found was from a species of ant that lived on the remains of the carcasses the cave animals brought in for their young. They took pity on us because we shared their capability for telepathy and fear of the world above ground and shared some of the food they raised. It became a symbiotic relationship. On the darkest nights, we would go out and bring them dead and decaying flesh, and we would feast on their fungi and whatever soft fruits we could find. We thrived underground and built vast cities of interconnecting tunnels, rooms, and catacombs. Keeping careful records, we created a calendar of when your moon was waning or new and went out as freely as we could.

"Gradually, we realized our two species were becoming intermingled. Our close relationship with the ants had little effect on them, but the food they produced contained microscopic traces of their DNA, and we began to mutate. After approximately twenty thousand generations, our telepathy evolved into a collective consciousness. It did not take long, about fifteen thousand generations, for us to adopt their hierarchical system, and our society became organized and stratified. Such mutations helped us adapt to this planet, and our numbers slowly and steadily increased, but twenty-five thousand generations later, our genes mutated again, resulting in fewer females being born. As survival is our strongest instinct, the desire to preserve the females of our species gradually became a form of worship. Our deity, initially possessing both male and female physical attributes, slowly lost all its male characteristics, taking on the aspect of a pregnant female, the life-giver.

"I am sure your society would call it sexist and crude, but a pregnant female represented another generation…another chance for our survival. As every male in each succeeding generation is our brother, every female became our mother, and we adored her. All of us cared for the females of our generation and gave them the best of whatever we could find so that they would live, mate, and produce offspring as long as possible. But all that special care did not save our mothers. It was the arthropod mutation. We learned too late that most ants are born male unless receiving an additional chromosome through mating—a chromosome that did not make it to our particular end of the constantly evolving Lyostian gene pool.

"You must understand, we were desperate. Our species was facing global extinction, and we would have failed our objective. Without a way to bring more Lyostian females from other planets, we were doomed. So, on the darkest nights, we crawled to the surface…"

"And kidnapped human women," I said evenly.

"Yes," he whispered. "We had no choice, Caroline; it was the only way we could survive. But it wasn't human women we wanted. We needed the female progeny of what your archaeologists call Neanderthals."

"Why? Was there something wrong with humans?"

"Yes, your brain cavities were too small."

"But not now?"

"No, by taking their women and female children, Neanderthal males had little alternative but to mate with female homo sapiens, thereby enlarging the skulls of your entire species. Almost everyone has a bit of Neanderthal in their DNA, as do we. It is one of several ways we have tried through the last forty thousand generations to decrease the arthropod DNA while increasingly acquiring a more human appearance. Some of these DNA combinations have been more successful than others, but we are still connected in many ways to the insect world. Ants—and I have to also say we—see humans as unthinking destroyers, powerful pests which must be controlled and no longer allowed to waste the resources of this planet."

"And ants will take over the world?"

"No. They are quite good at breaking anything organic down to its smallest parts, but they are not interested in the world above ground. With the exception of their decaying flesh as a possible food source, ants have no interest in humans. They are just something to avoid. The ants want the subterranean back. For all they have done for us, we have promised not to destroy their extensive tunnel structures or return underground."

"Did you ever try talking with humans? Perhaps they would understand."

For a moment, he looked very tired, but his voice did not change. "Yes, we tried, Caroline. It would have been so much easier for both of our species if humans had given us half a chance at any time in our shared history. For millennia, whenever we found groups of humans or they would find us, we would cry "Cymmerya, cymmerya," which is our word for peace, but they did not understand—or want to. We were smaller than most humans and, lacking any inborn aggression, easily overpowered. Chased across continents by one human tribe or another, we were forced to return to our underground colonies to survive. There we stayed and planned for the day when we would be strong enough to rise out of the darkness to claim and protect the planet we love."

The enormity of what he was saying washed over me. Expecting the same honesty he had shown throughout our discussion, I asked, "Are you planning to *kill* all of us, Grant?"

Understanding the ramifications of her question, Grant took a deep breath. Softening his voice slightly to calm her, he said, "No, it is our belief most humans will repent and join us. We will make them understand, Caroline, that we must preserve the planet for our children and their children; it is not just for us. We are fortunate there are so many human organizations dedicated to that same objective. When the time comes, we will reach out to them first for mutual support."

Her face relaxed into an expression of relief.

"So, there's hope for my species after all."

"Of course, we prefer peace, and there is always hope. We would rather work with humans than against them." It was Grant's hope that would be the only lie he had to tell her that day.

Smiling mischievously at him, she took one of his hands and placed it on her stomach.

"So, we are saving the planet, you and I, together?"

Knowing that he could not have said it any more truthfully than that, Grant pulled her close, whispering, "Yes, Caroline, that is exactly what we are doing."

Soundings

Checking Grant's calendar the following morning, I saw he was booked from seven in the morning to eight-thirty in the evening every day for the rest of the week. I was looking forward to scheduling our next "discussion," but there was no way I could stay that late. Dan had questioned me a little too severely when I got home the night before, and it wasn't seven-thirty yet. Despite my feelings for Grant, I still had to live with Dan, and my response, "Don't you want me to be healthy?" was starting to sound a little repetitious, even to my ears. His angry reply, "Not if I have to live on hamburgers for the rest of my life," was justified. My commitment to a healthier lifestyle should not be harmful to his health, and neither should my desire to be in the presence of the flesh and fire that was Grant Gates.

Although he was supposed to be in a meeting with Dr. Garrett, Grant entered the office at his usual time and set a jar of honey with a V4 label on my desk.

"Good morning, Caroline," he said. "We've created an enhanced version of the bitter honey for our remaining mothers. I wondered if you could taste it and give me some feedback."

"Would you like me to taste it now?"

"Do I have an appointment right now?"

I quickly glanced back at his calendar. "Well, yes, you have a consultation in Dr. Garrett's office that started three minutes ago."

"Then, no. Schedule the taste evaluation for the first available fifteen-minute block."

"There's nothing available for the rest of the week. Do you want me to move anything around?" I asked, trying to keep the hope out of my voice.

"No. It will have to be next week. Just find the first fifteen-minute block, please, Caroline."

Although he smiled when he said it, he sounded like he was tired of talking to me.

"Absolutely, Dr. Grant, no problem."

"Caroline."

"Absolutely, Grant, I'll take care of it."

"Thank you." Glancing down at his watch, he turned and left the room.

I didn't see him again until noon on Thursday. He walked in carrying fresh flowers and, without a word, took the vase from my desk. Going to the sink in his examination room, he exchanged the slightly fading flowers for new ones. I barely had time to thank him before he walked out the door.

I was early to work on Friday morning, having just finished my extraordinarily successful seven o'clock weigh-in and measuring session with Andrea. I opened the door to the office, and just as I turned on the lights, Grant came around from his side of the partition, startling me.

"I'm sorry, I didn't know you were here," I said, quickly dimming the lights.

He took my gym bag and set it on the floor. Taking my hand, he led me to our chair and pulled me into his lap.

"How are you feeling, Caroline?"

"I'm fine, we're fine," I said, smiling up at him.

"Do you mind if I check?"

"Do I have to go back, back there?" I said, my eyes glancing in the direction of the examination room.

"No. Do you think you will be comfortable lying flat in your chair? You can rest your head on the cushions."

"*Our* chair will be perfect." Feeling shy, I asked, "Should I take anything off? I'm quite layered here, you know."

"Would you be more comfortable in your workout clothes? There would be fewer layers to deal with."

"Yes, I think I would."

"I'll go back to my desk…call me when you are ready."

"Thank you. It will only take a moment." I started to unbutton my jacket and self-consciously looked around. "Grant, do you mind if I lock the door?"

"Not at all, though I am not expecting anyone this early."

"I know, but…."

"Of course, Caroline."

Sitting at his desk, he adjusted the light in the partition panels so he could observe her through the glass. Although lust was impossible now, he could not help but feel he was invading her privacy, but, in a medical sense, such clinical observation was justified. He would be able to see if anything or anyone was hurting her.

Removing his glasses, he scanned every inch looking for a slowness of movement here, a bruise there, mentally cataloging each view for comparison later. In the first bloom of her pregnancy, there were few discernible changes, merely a slight roundness he knew was not there a month ago. A casual observer would never notice.

Neither would her husband.

He watched her move the chair cushions around and smiled at her attempts to look both relaxed and alluring. She did not need to try so hard. He had been irrevocably hers from the first moment she welcomed him, found joy in him, and held him, breathless and mesmerized, in her arms.

"Grant," she called out softly.

"Be right there," he said, busily entering random data on his keyboard as he got his emotions under control. It would scare her away if she knew how much he cared for her. It was too soon; he had to bind her to him a little more.

Just one more week until everything was ready. Then he could tell her the truth and ask her to join him—but not in the tunnels. Taking Gabriel's suggestion, he had knocked out walls and spared no one, least of all himself, in the design and construction of a citadel of beauty and security. He could not build her an oasis but hoped that when she saw what he created for her, *for them*, she would understand how much he loved her.

The clicking of his keyboard stopped. I heard a snap, and candle scent instantly perfumed the air.

Walking through the semi-darkness, Grant lifted the quilt that lay on the back of the chair.

"Are you warm enough?"

"Yes, thank you."

He rubbed the stethoscope's bell quickly across his hand so it would be warm on my skin. Gently lowering the waistband of my workout pants a little below my navel, he moved the bell, then stopped, listened, and looked at his watch.

Even in the dim light, I could see his smile and knew everything was fine.

I smiled back as he picked up my hand and kissed it. Then, regretted as soon as it was said, I asked impulsively, "Do you kiss the hands of all your prospective mothers like this?"

He set my hand down and looked at me for what seemed an hour but was only a few seconds.

"Yes, I do, Caroline," he said quietly. "They are all precious to me. They may not understand exactly why I do it, but it is quite effective...as you well know."

Humiliated almost beyond endurance, I rested my arm over my eyes to hide the tears and fought for control.

"I'm sorry, I don't know why I said that. I didn't mean...." I was struggling to sit upright when the room went black, and I heard his glasses hit the top of my desk.

"Don't move."

I froze in the darkness. Although I could still smell the candle, I could not even see its burning wick. A glimmer of my earlier apprehension trickled back into my consciousness, and I began breathing in short gasps. I knew Grant was watching me, but I could not erase the fear from my eyes or my mind.

"Yes, Caroline, I kiss their hands. It is important that they trust me and will come to me if they have any difficulties rather than go to a hospital where I cannot help them. Most think it is a quaint, old-world affectation; others believe it is a romantic gesture, but I do not care what they think as long as they trust me."

His voice was behind me, in front of me, and to the side, but always between me and the door. Regardless of his intentions, escape was not an option.

"However, and I want you to understand this thoroughly, while I treasure each of them more than my own life, I do not," his breath was warm in my ear, "kiss them like this."

I was suddenly aware of his skin brushing against mine as I was lifted from the chair. I heard the ottoman bounce off the wall, and a moment later, I was lying on the quilt-covered carpet. Grant placed a cushion under my head and slowly, as if he had all day, caressed and kissed every exposed inch of me. When he reached the area below my navel that made him smile earlier, he pressed his ear against my stomach, listening. Bringing his hands down the sides of my body, they paused on either side of my hips. His lips pressed the skin above his son's heartbeat with more love and tenderness than I believed possible from a man of any species. I knew that some women went their entire lives without being kissed like that, and I was thrilled at the thought that one day, he would love me enough to kiss my mouth that way.

There was no shyness in his voice as he helped me into a sitting position and asked, "Any more questions this morning, Caroline, or shall we get to work?"

Silently, I reached toward him. My fingers feathered over the hard muscle of his shoulders down to his flat stomach. I leaned my head against his chest and located his heartbeat. Then, pressing my lips against his skin, I kissed him with all the love and tenderness he had shown our son.

"You cannot possibly mean that," he whispered.

I sat back and looked in the direction of his voice.

"But I do mean it, Grant. You have no idea how much I care about you."

"Tell me how much," he asked. "Tell me now."

Although I could not see them, I knew each of his eyes was intent on some area of my face.

Unused to being the focus of so much scrutiny, I bent my head forward until it rested on his shoulder. "I just want to crawl inside you and stay there…forever, Grant."

He could not miss the sincere affection on her face or the hope and heartbreak that hid beneath her words. *No*, he decided. He would not hurt her like that. Not even to secure a mother for his son would he lie to her—or himself—by pretending that a world existed where he could be her happily ever after.

"I do not have a forever to give to you, Caroline," he said slowly.

"As long as you can," she said, "it will be enough."

Gathering her up in his arms, Grant pressed his face into the softness of her hair.

"Thank you for that, Caroline," he whispered.

After a few moments, he released her. Picking up his clothes, he moved behind the partition to dress. Adjusting the lighting so she could see, he asked, "Think we can put the office back together for my eight-thirty appointment?"

"I'm sure we can. What time is it?"

"Eight-twenty."

He watched her as she stood up quickly and tossed a cushion into the chair.

"Race you!" she said.

Grant could not miss the happiness in her words and approved of the way her laughter echoed in the newly soundproofed room. Nodding to himself, he opened her file and made a note on her chart.

Shortly before noon, I heard Grant's voice behind the partition.

"I know you like to leave a little early on Friday, Caroline, but I was hoping we could continue our discussion. Of course, if you have plans, I certainly understand."

"No, no plans," I said, mentally postponing my eight-item to-do list. "But I thought…." I glanced down at his calendar. Although yesterday it was completely booked, now everything after three o'clock was clear. Changing direction mid-sentence, I asked, "Would you like to do the taste test then also?"

"Isn't that scheduled for Monday afternoon?"

"Yes."

"Tell me, my dear, would you rather have one meeting with me or two?"

I didn't hesitate. "Two," I said.

"So, yes?"

"Yes…Grant."

"Thank you."

At noon, we started to leave the office together, but Grant glanced at his clipboard and turned back toward his desk. Not wanting to be late for my class, I hurried out alone. Leaning briefly against the closed door, the joy of the morning possessed me, and I had to fight the urge to twirl, dance, and skip down the dimly lit hallway.

Grant turned the new deadbolt in the door after her and sat at her desk. He had barely enough time to walk behind the partition when her early arrival interrupted him before he could review her emails. He observed her activities through the partition when he was there, but he had been out of the office for several days supervising the construction of her apartment as well as his other responsibilities—such as meeting his prospective mothers in Garrett's office. It was inconvenient, but he didn't want her to feel self-conscious. None of them were as beautiful to him, but they were all considerably younger, and he knew that was her most vulnerable spot, the only one for which she had no defense.

As soon as he sat down, he quickly opened all three of her email accounts: GatesWay, her college email, and her personal dotmailusa address. He didn't care about the emails she received; it was the emails she sent that interested him. Installing a keystroke capture program on her laptop over the weekend, he'd deciphered her passwords and created hidden saved-sent files for each of her accounts. Those were the files he wanted to review.

The emails to Dan were mundane household comments or concerned Brendan's move to his university the following weekend. While he noted several emails from Eric, she had not opened any of them. Unable to erase or read them without detection, he could, and did, add Eric's email address to the spam blocker. If she emailed him—and after the events of the morning he doubted she would—she would never see his response.

Working his way almost to the end of her personal account, he saw an email from Suzanne Bradford. His hands temporarily hesitated above the keyboard. Anne Bradford was one of Gregory's prospective mothers. Immediately suspicious, Grant checked their client list and found no Anne Bradford listed.

Reading the history of Suzanne's emails, Grant's suspicions were not only confirmed, but he became alarmed at the dynamics of their relationship. Realizing that they were closer than friends, though not quite the confidence level of mother and daughter, it was clear that Caroline was protective of her. This could become a serious problem. Caroline might be willing to risk her own life for their child, but he knew if she became aware of Suzanne's pregnancy, she would try to do something about it— something that could endanger everyone.

He needed to talk to Gregory immediately.

Grant sent her email links to his email account so he could check them from his computer. To avoid raising Caroline's suspicions, he put everything back the way she liked it and closed the laptop. Tilting his head, he located Gregory in their private lunchroom.

When Grant entered the lunchroom, he sent the two interns out and faced Gregory alone.

"Gregory, I want to inquire about one of your mothers."

"Which one?"

"Anne, also known as Suzanne Bradford."

"I know."

"What do you know?"

"That I shouldn't have selected her because she works here, but she was perfect…and Gabriel was allowed to select Monique, so I thought it would be all right."

"That is not my problem right now."

"What is?"

"She and Carrie are apparently best friends—in the worst possible sense."

"But the age difference, I mean, they can't be that close."

"Didn't you look at her resume? Suzanne worked with her for two years before coming here. She is the one who told Carrie about us and convinced her to join. Carrie, on the other hand, feels especially protective of Suzanne. Her emails are full of motherly advice and concern."

"What do you want me to do?"

"Stop Suzanne's pregnancy."

"I won't do that. You stop Carrie's."

"And how, exactly, is that supposed to make her less protective of Suzanne?"

At that moment, Grayson, Garrett, Gabriel, and Gordon joined them. Gordon, the last to enter, locked the door. They didn't need the interns' input on this particular issue. They all knew selecting mothers from the facility's staff was forbidden because the employees knew each other too well. Little changes, even the slightest pregnancy bump, would be obvious to women who watched other women's waistlines for a living.

"A problem, Grant?" asked Grayson.

"Possibly. In preparation for extricating Carrie from her family and friends, I searched her emails for the less obvious entanglements and found this one."

"Was this the only one?"

"The only one I cannot neutralize myself. That is why I wanted to talk to Gregory."

Grayson looked around the room. "There are reasons we have rules concerning who we select as prospective mothers. Gabriel approached me first about Monique, and that specific exception was approved. However, Gregory," Grayson turned his steely gaze on him, "you did not request an exception. So why did you deliberately disregard our rules and select a member of our staff as a prospective mother?"

Gregory did not fear Grayson's authority. After all, they had elected him as their colony leader, and they could depose him just as easily. He served at their pleasure. He knew Grayson could request punishments, but that knowledge did not make him cautious.

"Ah, Grayson, I needed one more. Most of my clients are too old or married. I had nine good prospects, and since Suzanne has a serious boyfriend, I thought, 'Why not?' I didn't know she knew any of the other clients except her mother, and she ended her membership last month. When I verified Suzanne's family would be in Europe until the first of the year, it made sense. I mean, really, she was a gift horse."

Gregory gradually became aware that his voice was the only one he could hear. As though someone had pressed a mute button, there was no other sound in his head. He looked around at his five brothers. Each pair of eyes in every face was focused on him, yet all he could hear was silence. The terror of abandonment by the collective consciousness that exists within each Lyostian struck Gregory like a wrecking ball. He was banished. Even in the midst of his brothers, he was alone. Pressing the heels of his hands to his eyes, he dropped to his knees.

"Please, please don't do this. Talk to me, please, someone talk to me. I'm sorry. I know I should have asked for an exception or inquired if anyone had a prospective mother they would share with me. I was so careless. For the love of Anya, mother of us all, please don't do this. Gordon, my brother, talk to me...please...Grayson, I'm so sorry."

Gordon looked at Grayson. "You are not punishing Grant. He chose a married woman, which is also against selection rules."

"I did not choose her," Grant said. "And I would never have chosen her. She was just in the right place at the right time and was presented to me as a substitute."

"You knew she was married before you reconceived the embryo. You could have refused," countered Gordon.

"That alternative was not possible as it violates our mandate. Garrett and I discussed it, and we believed it was my duty to try. Since we had this discussion when reviewing the original success list, I will not spend my time justifying it now. Moreover, it should be noted that I am committed to seeing this complication through to conclusion as well as using Carrie as an opportunity to research methods to encourage maternal acceptance. Methods, I might add, that appear to be working with other prospective mothers." He looked at Grayson. "As *you* requested."

Grayson nodded. "Through Grant's efforts, we are establishing stronger relationships with our prospective mothers." He glanced down at Gregory, who had not moved or stopped begging for forgiveness.

"We work together for the survival of our colony and the future of the collective. We do not endanger that survival by breaking the rules to which we have all consented without discussion and approval. Don't you agree, Gregory?"

Gregory nodded.

"And do you also agree that referring to our mothers in anything less than glowingly respectful and endearing terms is blasphemous?"

If possible, Gregory cringed even more and nodded again.

"As we are now at forty percent of our original number of prospective mothers, I cannot advocate stopping anyone's pregnancy. Gregory, I want every move Suzanne makes, as well as any changes to her work schedule, instantly forwarded to Grant so he can circumvent any possible meetings between her and Carrie. It will be easier when Carrie is living here and we can control her movements, but right now, all we can do is monitor them to keep Carrie and Suzanne apart. Grant, you will see to Carrie's emails and work schedule?"

"Of course."

"Gregory."

"Yes, Grayson."

"Never again, Gregory."

"Yes, Grayson, I understand. Thank you, my brothers." *And thank you, Anya, mother of us all.*

His brothers left the room. Gordon stood outside the door and waited as Gregory, kneeling alone with his hands pressed to his eyes, prayed for forgiveness.

Dreaming Time

I waited for Grant, but he did not arrive at three, or three-fifteen, or three-thirty. Thinking I might have misunderstood him, I decided to wait until four before leaving. At four-fifteen, he had not returned, nor had he called. At four-thirty, I turned down the lights, rested my head on my arms, and closed my eyes.

At five-fifteen, Grant slowly opened his office door expecting anger, disappointment, or the silence of an empty room. He was completely disarmed to find her asleep at her desk, tousled like a schoolgirl at her books. The lights were dimmed, and he knew she was waiting for him. *She was waiting for him.* Grant allowed himself a few moments of happiness as he walked back to his desk. Quietly opening her file, he added another checkmark to the trajectory arc. She was almost his. With total confidence, he lifted her in his arms and carried her to the chair.

I awoke in Grant's embrace.

"You're late," I said sleepily.

"And yet, you are still here," he replied.

"Of course. You said you would be back."

Looking over his shoulder, I saw a delicious dinner of honey, toast, tea, and strawberries with a light golden cream. "You brought this for me?"

"Yes. Such patience should not go unrewarded."

"'We do not reward our clients with food,' you said."

"Yes, I did. But I am not rewarding you with food. I brought you dinner because I hoped you—"

"You knew—"

"I hoped you would still be here."

He dipped a strawberry in the cream. "Try this."

It was light but intense, with the taste of honey, melted marshmallows, and vanilla ice cream spun together. It was irresistible.

"Oh my, Grant. Whatever this cream is…write it down as my favorite food ever. Does it go on everything?"

"It could, but it blends best with strawberries."

"Don't you want anything?"

"Ah, no, just tea for me. I will have dinner later with my brothers."

"Will it be better than this?"

"There is nothing better than this," he said softly, looking at me and not the food. "But it brings me to a subject I am afraid might make you angry."

My hand, holding a piece of honeyed toast, stopped in midflight and dropped to my lap. "What is it, Grant?" I asked, trying to keep the dread from my voice.

"Caroline, it is not as bad as that," he said quickly. "At least, I don't think it is."

I knew it. He had not forgiven me. My heart began breaking as I waited for him to say that I was expecting too much from him. I took a shuddering breath and willed myself not to cry.

"Just tell me what it is. Please."

Looking up, I expected to see his "doctor" face but saw only concern. "Andrea emailed me your stats this afternoon. You've lost another four pounds and are just a few millimeters away from your optimal BMI."

Relief washed over me. I couldn't believe I had been so wrong. The world wasn't going to come crashing down after all. I smiled at my silliness.

"That's good, isn't it? I mean, it's been five months, and I'm less than four pounds away from my six-month goal. Really, I'm not angry I didn't lose it faster."

He took my hand. "Caroline, I applaud your perseverance and hard work. Although you were lovely the first day you walked into this office, you are breathtakingly beautiful now. But I must ask you to stop following the nutrition limitations Garrett gave you. I am going to change your classes so that your workouts are less strenuous and emphasize stretching and toning. It is important to me that you set aside your original goals and think of what your child needs."

He closed his eyes for a moment. "Will it bother you to do that? For him? I know I am asking a lot of you, but would you mind doing this for us, just for the next few months?"

I was stunned. Not because he had asked me to give up my carefully planned and highly successful diet and exercise regimen but because he thought that surrendering my goals for his son would upset me. *He* was worried about *my* anger. I stood up and lowered the rheostat to complete darkness. As I'd practiced, I returned to the chair and sat down exactly where I had been. Placing my hands gently on the sides of his face, I removed his glasses.

"Grant, you are my doctor, and you are my baby's father. I will do whatever you think is best to make our baby healthier and keep him safe."

Pulling me close to him, he rested his head on mine and said, "Are you sure the 'woman in the mirror' isn't going to be disappointed?"

"Oh, she left soon after I started taking classes here."

"She did? What image replaced her?"

Grant immediately regretted his question. *How are you going to feel when she says Eric?* He made a conscious effort not to react, no matter what she said.

"You."

"What? Me?"

"Yes. You were always in my head, smiling if I was doing well or being stern if I ate more than a few bites of anything that wasn't in the book." She smiled up at him. "You can be quite strict, you know."

Suddenly it was imperative that he learn why she cared what he thought of her so early in their relationship.

"But why, Caroline?"

"In our interview, you said that my success was your success, and I wanted to give you that. Your encouragement during our discussion after my first spa reward made so many things seem possible. It was important to me even then that maybe, on some level, I could be responsible for a little bit of your success…your happiness."

Her response was so matter of fact that it had to be the truth and wrung from him a confession as well. "And now, Caroline, how does it feel to be responsible for all of it?"

"But I'm not, Grant. At last count, I'm only responsible for about fifteen percent. But you know," she said, placing her hand on his chest, "that's quite a lot."

"If you think of it that way, it is twenty percent today. That is why I was late."

"Oh, Grant, I'm so sorry."

"You mean that, don't you? After this morning, I wasn't sure."

"Well, I do mean it because, after this morning, I am sure."

Glad for the change in subject, he said, "You said I could touch you."

"That was pretty thorough touching."

"Did you feel uncomfortable?"

"No, it was wonderful. But, um, I think you may have missed a few places."

"Yes. I am saving those for later."

"Later?"

"Oh, yes."

"Promise?" she teased.

"Be very careful, Caroline, of the promises you ask of me." Picking up her hand, he whispered, "I take promises quite seriously. Both those I make and those I extract." He smiled in the darkness and kissed the palm of her hand. "But yes, in this instance, I do promise."

I shivered slightly as anticipation, excitement, and delight competed with the icy touch of apprehension at the base of my spine.

"Cold?"

I nodded. It was easier than any other explanation.

"Turn around and finish your dinner. I'll keep you warm."

I leaned against his chest as I finished the tea, toast, strawberries, and cream. When the saucers were empty, we rested together, my head on his shoulder just above his heart, his right hand resting lightly on my abdomen.

"It's dreaming time," I said.

"I don't understand."

"Early evening, it's my favorite time of the day…I call it dreaming time. The day hasn't quite surrendered the light; the night hasn't quite conquered the day. It's best in summer, when it lasts for hours, lots of dreaming time."

"What do you dream of, Caroline?"

"What did I use to dream of, or what do I dream of now?"

"You dream differently now?"

"Oh yes," I said, smiling slightly. "Before, I dreamt how wonderful it would be if Dan came home just once and said, 'Hey sweetheart, what would you like to do tonight?' and I would imagine the things we would do together…silly things, romantic things, you know, just sharing the joy of each other in the ease of the half-light. But you know," I swallowed back sudden tears, "he never has."

"Fool, then, to have missed one moment of you."

"No, blind. He never wanted *me* in his life, only *my role* in it. It hasn't been a marriage so much as a semi-successful stage play."

He held my hand next to his eyes. "And now?" he asked.

I turned my palm toward his face. "I don't have to dream it, Grant; I live it." I brought my lips just close enough for him to feel their warmth.

"Grant, will you do me a favor?"

"If I can."

"Tell me when it's okay to love you," I said softly, "I don't want to miss one moment of you."

He pulled away a bit and looked into my eyes. "Caroline, *you* love *me*?"

"Oh, yes."

"And our child," he said, "do you…could you ever…love him, too?"

Grant grew very still; so much depended on her next words.

"I've loved him since the beginning. Even before I knew he existed, he was part of the dream of you."

As if she were a bubble that, if pressed too hard, would burst, his hands began to tremble.

Speaking barely above a whisper, he asked humbly, "Caroline, may I touch you?"

She stood up and locked the door.

"Yes, Grant."

After she left, he held the quilt to his face.

She loved him.

Not as a Lyostian loves from necessity and gratitude, but as a human loves: freely from desire and choice. His analytical side felt vindicated; the experiment worked, and now she would obey him—but everything that was human in him rejoiced. For the first time in twenty-eight years, a sliver of light entered a dark and dusty room that Grant thought was closed to him forever.

Taste Test

Scheduling appointments for moms looking for exercise classes now that their children were returning to school made me sentimental. I remembered with fondness the shopping, the nervous excitement of the "first day," and the prideful sadness of watching Brendan learn his way, step by step, as I lost him a little more each year.

Seeing him grow up in my mind, I thought about the hectic weekend I'd spent running all over town getting everything he needed to take to college. There was the official dorm list — and the unofficial Mom list — which added up to a lot of shopping. However, drifting beneath the anxiety of Brendan leaving home, the tension of mall traffic, and endless errands was Grant's singing voice echoing in my mind, making me lose my place in whatever was going on around me. Daytime did not move fast enough, and the nights crawled as I remembered and relived every moment of our dreaming time: every look, every touch, every sigh that was honey-scented and cloaked in sepia-tinted candlelight.

Checking my schedule, I saw Grant had switched my step aerobics class for a ballet barre class that met on Tuesdays and Thursdays at noon. When he mentioned it to me, I asked him to change it because that was the only time I could meet Suzanne for lunch, but he said there was nothing else available. I was disappointed but not too worried; I would see her eventually. After all, the building was only so big.

Promptly at three o'clock, I brewed a fresh pot of tea for the taste test and set the V4 honey and spoons next to the teapot. At five minutes past three, Grant walked in with a small tray of thinly sliced toasted focaccia bread, plain crackers, and orange slices.

"Let the tasting begin," I said, laughing.

He smiled and removed a familiar jar of V3 honey from his pocket.

"We can do this in one of two ways: blindfolded," he said, loosening his tie, "or with the lights off. You choose."

"Either way, you will have to feed me, or it's going to get all over my fingers."

"Of course," he said, "I promise to clean you up if you get sticky."

I thought for a moment. "Well, you would probably want to see my whole face instead of just my mouth, so I vote for lights out."

"Excellent point. You have beautifully expressive eyes."

"Thank you. Are you going to taste the honey, too?"

"This honey is formulated strictly for our mothers."

Grant kissed the top of my head, and while I got comfortable in the chair, he pulled something else out of his pocket. At first, it looked like a small camera, but when he pressed a button, everything went dark.

"Grant?"

"Well, I had to do something this weekend to keep busy," he said, adding in a softer voice, "What did you do, Caroline?"

Leaning back, I reached my hand out in front of me, and he caught it in midair. "I helped Brendan get ready to go to college next Saturday. It was a lot of shopping and driving, getting his clothes together, and packing suitcases and boxes. And I spent every moment of it missing you."

I tried to pull him toward me but realized he was completely rigid, and the hand that held mine was nearly crushing my fingers.

"What's wrong? What did I say? Grant, I can't see your face. Tell me what is wrong. You must…now, please."

"Caroline."

Oh, no. It was his stern doctor voice. What had I done to deserve that voice? It cut me to the heart, and a small sob escaped my throat.

"I did not change your classes so that you could spend your days off running all over town. You cannot possibly, in one breath, tell me you have put your child at risk and, with the next breath, say you were thinking about me. Haven't you been listening to me at all? Have I not made it perfectly clear to you that this is a high-risk pregnancy, and you could miscarry at any time?"

"Yes, yes, Grant, you have. I didn't think I was hurting him. I would never do that. I, I just had to help Brendan. He's leaving on Saturday, you know. Leaving me...."

I tried not to, but I started crying. First, because I had ruined the afternoon; second, because there was an edge of indifference to Grant's reprimand that made me feel alone; and third, because my sweet son was on his way to college in a few days and on his way to his own life forever.

Grant gathered me up as he would a ragdoll.

"Shh, Caroline, shh. I know you were just being a good mother, but you should let Brendan do some things for himself, or he will be lost at college without you. You don't want that, do you? Especially when there is someone who needs you much more now...someone who will never leave you all alone."

"I know, Grant, I'm sorry. It's hard, you know, trying to be what everyone needs you to be."

"Then stop," he said, his breath against my ear. "Make it easier on yourself, Caroline. Please just be what *I* need you—who *we* need you to be. Try to put us first, at least for a little while."

"I will, Grant. Please don't be angry with me."

"Then don't scare me. Or torture me. Yes, it is more like torture, being helpless in fear and powerless to stop it."

He handed me a cup of tea. "Here, drink this and rest for a moment while we think about how much we care for our son. Perhaps he will hear us, and together we will make him stronger."

Cradled in Grant's arms, I directed the love I felt for his father to our child. His head resting on mine, Grant sang softly, gently caressing the skin above his sleeping son.

When he stopped singing, I whispered, "Why do I never want to leave you when we are like this?"

"Because your heart knows this is where you belong."

Before I could respond, he stood up and settled me into the chair.

"I promised to get back to Gordon, the facility's chemist, about the honey as soon as possible. So, shall we give it a try?"

"Of course." I was relieved my carelessness had not spoilt the *entire* afternoon. "Where do you want me?"

"Oh, Caroline, that is a question…and an answer…for another time. However, for the official V4 GatesWay Bitter Honey taste test and evaluation, just stay exactly where you are.

"We will try the rosemary focaccia first." I heard the spoon tap against the jar. "Do you want me to place the bread in your mouth or in your hand?"

"My mouth, please."

The honey was delicious, but the focaccia was too flavorful, competing with the honey— not complementing it. "On a one to five scale, it's a three. The bread is too herb-y."

"Thank you, now this."

Same bread, but the new honey ignited fireworks in my senses. The way honey and the herbs mingled made each more delicious than either would have been alone. The combination that before was a boring three became a five plus.

"Oh, Grant, that's magical."

"Now that you have discerned a distinct difference, we will not go back to the V3 formula. This time, let's try it on plain crackers."

"If you lighten the room a bit, I'll be able to feed myself. This must be tedious for you."

"As you wish."

I might as well be eating pure nectar. It was more than honey. It tasted as though all the flowers in the world had been sifted for their essence and distilled into a single drop of paradise.

I looked up at Grant.

"Gordon made this?"

"Yes, on a basic molecular level, he did. It is the V3 honey with additives to enhance the nourishment our children need to complete their development. We want to know if you think mothers would like it as much or better than the V3 formula."

"Grant, never in my life have I tasted anything this delicious. They'll love it, but I warn you, keep the jars small unless they are allowed to eat all they want. If you tell them it's good for them, I'm sure they will eat nothing else or add this to everything they eat."

"Good. I'll email him now."

"Grant, is there more? Or do we have to give the rest back to Gordon?"

"I think he can spare another spoonful," he answered from his office.

I put some of the focaccia, a few crackers, and most of the orange slices on a saucer and drizzled honey on top of everything. As I picked up the sweetened morsels, the honey dripped onto my fingers.

Laughing at my clumsiness, I said, "Grant, tell Gordon not to worry; once the mothers have tasted this, he'll have to kill them to make them stop eating it."

Pressing send as he heard her last sentence, Grant closed his eyes and prayed, *Dear Anya, mother of us all, I hope not.*

Gordon's Flower Syrup

Smelling the sweetness on her fingers, Grant went into his examination room and returned with a dampened towel. As promised, he cleaned her hands and brushed all the crumbs back onto the tray. Taking the remnants of the taste test into the examination room, he quickly closed the door and lit a fresh candle, gratefully inhaling its clean fragrance. The V4 honey was much too sweet, and he was glad she would only need a little of it every day. He gave her one cracker with the V3 so that she would smell like Caroline again, instead of Caroline covered in Gordon's flower syrup.

"This isn't the other kind."

"I know. Gordon is not sure what would happen if you ate too much, so it is best to follow the original guidelines of one teaspoon a day—until we ascertain any side effects. You can still have as much of this as you would like."

"Is it also my job to report any side effects?"

"It would be helpful, but we are not sure they would be consistent. The V4 may affect each mother differently. For instance, although we have made discreet inquiries, you are the only one who has reported hearing voices before you fall asleep. Just for my notes, do you remember the first time you heard them?"

"For the rest of my life, Grant," I said softly. "At the end of my, um, our dream, I thought I was drowning, and I saw a life raft floating above me.

To save myself, I wrapped my arms around it, and as I hugged it to my chest, I heard voices singing."

"That was not a life raft, Caroline."

"Yes, it was…it was you."

"You knew that?"

"Not at first, but later, when I thought about it. I only feel that kind of peace when I'm with you."

He sat next to me in our chair. "Lean against me, Caroline. It is our dreaming time. Is there anything you would like to do this evening?" he whispered.

"May I have a cup of tea and just stay like this? Talk about our son and dream together before…before I have to go home?"

"Of course," he said, handing me a teacup. "For as long as you can stay. Was there anything you especially wanted to know?"

"Just a few things. What did you mean when you said earlier that he would never leave me alone? Won't he want to go off to college, too?"

"Yes, but he will not leave you; you are his colony. He will live with you, go to college nearby, and find work close by as well. He will stay with you until the collective calls him."

"When will that be?"

"This is the first generation, so they will be with their mothers or a colony until they are twenty-five, then our son will lead his brothers in our efforts to reclaim the planet. Now that we have protocols in place to successfully reconceive human hybrids for six succeeding generations, NAFTRAM's U.S. operations will cease on the last day of December. On the first day of January, we will begin on another continent. In six years, we will have a nascent army all around the globe working and thinking as one."

"He will be mine only until he is twenty-five?"

"He will be yours forever, Caroline, but he must leave when he is called. However, if you would rather not keep him," he said slowly, "there are others who will raise him. We have colonies where many of this generation's offspring will be cared for."

"Orphanages?"

"Only in the broadest sense. He will be nurtured far more lovingly there than children in most human homes."

"He would grow up to hate me."

"He already loves you more than anyone else until he dies, regardless of what you decide. You have raised one son. Perhaps you are not interested in raising another, especially one who comes with…special challenges. It will be your decision. I am so grateful that you have chosen to let him stay inside you, Caroline, that I will never hold it against you or blame you for one moment if you decide to let him grow up in a colony rather than raise him yourself."

He didn't mean it. I knew he didn't mean it, and I knew I would never let his son go to a colony alone. The sorrow of losing him after twenty-five years would overwhelm my life, but if that was all I could have, I would take it, whatever the price to myself. I turned and placed my hand against the curve of his face.

"You are a terrible liar."

"No. Actually, I am a very good liar, Caroline. I was not lying when I said I would not blame you."

"Hush," I said, putting my fingers on his lips. "If we come safely through this, you know I would never let him go. Never hear him laugh? Miss seeing the world through his eyes, regardless of how many there are? Not being able to hold him or be there to answer his questions as he discovers the world? Never once be able to think, 'he is just like his father,' or tell him that? How can I leave those joys to others when I am his mother? When he depends on me? Needs me? Loves *me*?"

I touched my forehead to his.

"And Grant, even if all that were possible, how could I give away the only piece of you I will ever be able to keep?"

I could not see his eyes, but I didn't have to. He crushed me to him and buried his face in my neck.

"What can I give you, Caroline? I know humans want things. I will give you anything, anything that will make you as happy as I am at this moment."

A desire for "things" was pretty much out of my life now; I just wanted to be somewhere I could care for our son without fear. Raising him with Dan was impossible, and going to my family was out of the question. They would never understand. I had to disappear.

"I want us to be safe, Grant. If we survive, you must see that we disappear."

"It's already been done."

"What? When?"

"Before I left you the afternoon of your…our…dream, I promised to take care of you. When I saw your name on the list of successful procedures, I began making arrangements for new identities, bank accounts, papers, the official medical records you will need through the years, and, well, house keys. It is not what I would have built for us, but I have arranged some modifications that I hope you will like."

I was momentarily stunned by his generosity and the depth of his love for his son—and me. He did all that before knowing how much I loved them both.

"Will the other mothers disappear, too?"

"It will be one of their options," he said reluctantly. "Some die, Caroline; others are, for one reason or another, unable to care for their offspring or do not wish to keep them. That is why we have nurturing colonies; we cannot risk losing any of this generation. They will have the most experience, education, and training, so we must save as many as possible. Staying with their mothers is our first priority. As I mentioned earlier, it completes their development."

"Any chance I'll run into the other mothers at the supermarket?"

"No."

If everything Grant said was true, rejection by their mother had to be the most hurtful thing in their lives. Fearing it may be a tender subject, I asked, "Grant, why don't their mothers want them?"

"Our children are not fully developed when they are born. Human babies would look strange, too, if they were born at the end of the first trimester. But unlike human embryos, hybrid cells are genetically programmed to multiply and mature at twice that of humans so they can survive outside the mother's body."

"I know you're a doctor, Grant, but three months doesn't seem nearly long enough to make a baby."

"It wasn't, but we had to find ways to protect our mothers. The longer our children stay inside their mothers, the more dangerous it is for both of them—and our children need their mothers. We discovered the best way to do that was to encapsulate the embryo and accelerate the cell division. However, this rate of development requires that they are born at thirteen weeks because they need more nutrition than they are able to absorb living within their human mother. Although they are fully developed mentally, their bodies are small and fragile. They require their mother's milk for an additional six months after they are born to complete their physical growth and DNA sequencing. It is the same nine-month gestation period, just reached in different phases."

"Are there mothers at the colonies to feed the babies whose mothers can't feed them?"

"Not always. One of the things Gordon is developing is synthetic mother's milk. What we have so far nourishes the children to full physical and mental development. However, it does not always complete their DNA sequencing."

Without waiting for my next question, he said, "I have told you enough today. To tell you more right now might confuse or frighten you. Oh, Caroline," he said, pulling me close, "I missed you so much this weekend, and before I have to let you go again, I just want to hold you and, what did you say the other day? Feel the joy of you? Please."

"Yes, Grant."

I turned slightly so I could put my hand on his heart and rest my head against his shoulder. I had more questions, but we would get to them eventually, and I knew the answers would not confuse or frighten me if he held me like this. Nothing in the world could be as bad as that.

More Answers

I was looking forward to meeting with Grant after my last class the next day, but he had consults scheduled past seven-thirty. Going straight home, I received more attention from Dan because I wasn't late.

"Hey, Brendan," he called upstairs, "there's a mom sighting, and it isn't nine o'clock yet. We may have dinner tonight after all!"

Still wearing my workout clothes, Dan looked at me as though he had not seen me every day for the last four months.

"You look good," he said. "Whatever you're doing over there is working. But you needn't go through all that trouble, Carrie. You've always looked good to me."

I recalled all the work I'd done and how hard it had been to get to where I looked and felt healthy again. The months spent on exercise machines returned to me with memories of aerobics classes, dance classes, the fear of each weigh-in, and dreading the calipers in Andrea's hands because I hadn't done enough. Then I remembered the appreciation in Eric's eyes, Grant's kind words, and gentle caress. Although I knew it was a mistake, I couldn't stop myself.

"Looked good enough for what, Dan?"

"What do you mean?"

"Just what I said, 'looked good enough for what?' To ignore? To push away? To hurt in so many little ways until I just didn't care anymore? Is that how good I looked to you?" My head began to throb, and I realized if Grant were here, he would be angry with me for getting upset. Hearing his doctor voice in my mind, I took a deep breath and backed down.

"I'm sorry, Dan, I don't mean to be cranky, let me start dinner. I'll feel better when I've eaten something."

Throughout my rant, Dan looked at me like I was talking in a foreign language, and my words had no relevance to him at all.

"Cranky, huh? Well, where I'm from, we don't call that (air parentheses) *cranky*; we call it an entirely different word that starts with a (air parentheses) *B*." Walking away, he began clicking the remote, looking for the golf channel.

I knew that when dinner was over, he would use my show of temper as an excuse to go down to the basement and start drinking. Later, he would come to bed smelling like a saloon, and I would breathe the fumes of stale cigarette smoke and bourbon all night, which, he would claim, was my fault. Knowing how Grant would feel about that, too, I vowed to sleep in Brendan's room as often as necessary for the baby's sake.

I'm sorry, littlest, I thought to him later that night as I moved as far from Dan as possible to get a breath of clean air. *Just one more week, then we'll sleep in your big brother's room.* I wiped my tears away with the edge of the sheet.

He won't even know I've gone.

The following morning, I found a jar of V4 honey on my desk. Although it did not have a label, I recognized it by its darker color. On it was taped a note: *ONLY one teaspoon per day.*

I picked the jar up and found a note from Grant underneath it.

Fruit and crackers in the refrigerator.

I looked up. *Refrigerator? Since when was there a refrigerator in the office?* Almost as if he predicted my thoughts, there was another note with an arrow drawn on it taped to the partition. My eyes followed the arrow's direction to a narrow black box that blended so well into the dark paneling as to be nearly invisible. Set against the wall next to the tea table, it could have been anything from an expensive air cleaner to an audio system. Inside was a series of small drawers, each containing a bag of sliced fruit or vegetables. In the unrefrigerated section was a drawer with several bags containing crackers and thin slices of bread. There were also some jars of the V3 honey with another note from Grant: *Please consume one teaspoon of this last. Thank you.*

Preparing a small breakfast, I sat down and opened Grant's calendar for the day. Right away, I noticed two consultation appointments scheduled in Dr. Garrett's office. It only took a moment to realize what those consults were and why they were in Dr. Garrett's office. That was where Grant met with his other mothers. I checked his calendar and saw that Grant had been scheduling his consults outside this office since the week I began working for him.

Why was he hiding them from me?

I passed my hand over my stomach and wondered which one of them would be sitting here if Eric's birthday hadn't been August thirteenth. My questions continued to spiral downward. Which of them would be sitting in our chair? Who else would he be kissing in the dark? And the most hurtful thought of all, which one would be spending my dreaming time with him?

I told myself I had no reason to be jealous; didn't I have a husband? Didn't I have Eric's obvious affection as well? Then I remembered the list of names in his hand and realized "Taylor" had to be near the bottom, yet I was the first one he asked. I was probably the oldest of his prospective mothers—the highest risk—yet I was the one he wanted. He told me he cared for his prospective mothers more than his life, and I doubted he cared for their children less than mine. He would never treat them any differently than he treated me. I had witnessed his grief over each loss as I knew he would grieve with me if the worst happened.

I rested my head on my arms. I didn't know why he inconvenienced himself for me or why he was so tenderly attentive. All the little extras he'd arranged for my comfort, the chair, refrigerator, flowers, and his willingness to examine me here instead of his medical office. That he cared for me, I could not deny. No one had ever been so patient, so kind, or made me feel so desirable, but I also knew, without a doubt, that he was treating the others the same way.

Yet *I* was *here*.

To prove my point, he walked in only a moment later, holding a colorful mixture of late summer wildflowers wrapped in green tissue paper. As he reached for the vase, I stopped his hand.

"I'll do this," I said, "you're very busy today."

"Yes, but I do not mind, Caroline. You do not like that room."

"No, I don't, but I realized this morning that I have several more reasons to love you, and with that comes trust…and forgiveness."

Glancing down at the open jar of honey and saucer, a small smile touched his lips. "If I had known that a refrigerator would make you feel this way, I would have bought one sooner."

"As nice as it is, it isn't the refrigerator."

His smile faded. "Then please say what you are not telling me, Caroline."

I turned my laptop toward him and pointed out his consultation appointments with Dr. Garrett.

"This, this, and this," I said, scrolling down his calendar. "This one and these you have today." I looked up at him. "Those appointments are with your other mothers, aren't they, Grant?"

"Other prospective mothers, yes," he said quietly.

"And you're meeting them in Dr. Garrett's office to spare my feelings?"

"Yes, Caroline," he whispered.

"See? Several more reasons to love you," I said, kissing his right cheek. "Trust you." I kissed his left cheek and, looking up into his eyes through my lashes, said, "And if there was anything to forgive, then to forgive you anything."

I leaned into him and kissed the hollow of his throat. A faint groan escaped his lips, and he carried me to our chair where he held me and sang songs in words I did not understand.

Forgotten in the darkness, the wildflowers lay on the carpet where they had fallen, the crumpled tissue concealing their delicate stems, now crushed and broken.

Anticipation

I did not expect Grant to be in the office on Thursday. Although no office appointments were scheduled, he had marked out the entire day. I went to my ballet barre class at noon. It was my favorite because afterward I always felt taller, my legs, arms, and fingers elongated and elegant. It was an excellent class for pregnant women, at least in the beginning. I giggled as I imagined myself trying to execute a *grand plié* when I was eight months pregnant with Brendan.

Brendan.

In just a few days, Brendan would be in college, and, with the brief exception of high school football camp, he would be gone from under my roof for the first time. Gone from my supervision, my protection, my big-as-the-sky mother's love I'd felt since the moment he was placed in my arms. The fact that he would most likely walk away from me without a backward glance made me both lonely and proud.

Oh, littlest, I wish you could have known your big brother. I sent my newest son an image of Brendan, grinning with a trophy in one hand and a football in the other.

Reminiscing, I rested my hand on my abdomen. It was still as flat as it was a month ago, but when pressed just a bit, I could feel a roundness that had not been there before. A thrill went through me.

Grant will be so happy.

My excitement left little room for sorrow for one eaglet fleeing the nest when another one was on the way.

Remembering that Grant examined me the Friday before, I thought perhaps he would want an update. Eager to share my discovery with him, the following day, I dressed in a loose-fitting top and elastic waist skirt. Checking his appointments that morning, I saw he was free after noon and fought the temptation to add my name to his calendar.

Opening the refrigerator to get the V4 honey, I noticed salad vegetables and a few cheese slices. I couldn't remember ever seeing Grant eat anything resembling animal products. Thinking about it, I'd never really seen him *eat* anything. He only drank tea while I dined on honeyed toast, strawberries, and cream.

Lighting the candle in his office had become part of my morning routine. Its fragrance was the essence of love to me that infused the air of every memory of him, every memory of us.

Sipping tea and nibbling toast and honey in the fragrant half-light, I entered data on my computer and believed myself to be the luckiest woman on earth.

Grant.

Grayson.

Status on Mrs. Taylor, please.

I am going to ask her to move here today.

Probability of success?

Of moving in today? Zero. Of being here on Monday, one hundred percent.

You can't be one hundred percent sure.

Hello, Gregory. And yes, I am quite sure.

That she is going to leave her husband, friends, family, and life to live here just because you asked her?

We need her here. She will be here. On Monday. Really, Gregory, I cannot say it any simpler than that.

Is her room ready?

Yes, Grayson. A couple of rooms, actually. She will need somewhere to sleep, eat, bathe, and a room for nursing.

We have a nursery.

Yes, but humans require privacy to bond with their newborns. Please keep in mind that these rooms must look as non-threatening and human as possible. She would expect a nursery. Remember also, Grayson, she has to want to stay to make this transition successful.

And you will be…?

Wherever she wants me to be. She trusts me. If, at first, she is more comfortable with me there, I have arranged a small bench in a curtained alcove. If she prefers to be alone, then I will be in our rooms.

Well, I hope you haven't packed.

Thank you, Gregory, I have not. I hope it will not be necessary. Working with her has provided enough 'togetherness' as far as I am concerned.

How long before you control her completely?

Emotionally, that is nearly accomplished. However, I will not have physical control of her until the baby is born, and I can threaten to remove him to motivate her. I assure you she will be a compliant mother to her offspring, and these methods will be useful in encouraging compliance in other mothers.

Gregory interrupted again. *Do you really think you can do that? Completely undermine her human independence and guarantee that she will voluntarily commit to nurturing a child whose only purpose in life is to grow up and destroy her own species?*

Yes.

I don't know what is more far-reaching, Grant, your arrogance or your dreams.

Thank you for your confidence, Gregory, but I think you will find that all you really need is a little leverage.

Monday, Grant?

Monday, Grayson.

Grayson waited until Gregory's signature echo faded from their conversation.

Grant.

Grayson.

I am gratified that everything is working according to our plan, of course, but I think there is one thing you are forgetting.

And what would that be, Grayson?

Your exit strategy. As we have seen in the past, human women can become quite attached....

I have already prepared the groundwork for my leaving her. So, you see, Grayson, I did not forget.

How?

I told her I was dying.

Not for years!

Of course, Grayson, but it's a classic exit strategy.

But will she believe it?

She already does. Because she knows we are different, she believes whatever I tell her about us. Besides, a shortened life span makes her more caring and patient while simultaneously destroying any long-term expectations she may harbor.

Brilliant.

Yes. Is there anything else you think I may have forgotten, Grayson?

Uh, no...damn.

Something wrong, Grayson?

Another lightning headache. I'm going back to the tunnels for a while.

Yes. I hope you feel better soon.

A Matter of Commitment

Grant had not been in the office all day. Considering how many things there were to do to get Brendan moved out—and in—the next day and unwilling to do anything that would endanger the baby, I'd planned to leave that afternoon by three. My to-do list was huge. Recalling Grant's suggestion, I phoned Brendan and gave him half of the items on the list. The fact that he agreed to it without any hesitation made me wish I'd given him a few more.

Working through lunch, I was slightly starving by two-thirty and preparing some cheese and crackers when Grant walked into the office.

"You are still here?" he asked. "With all the errands I'm sure you need to run before tomorrow, I thought you would want to get an early start." He looked at me and, using his serious doctor's voice, added, "So you do not overexert yourself."

"I did, but then I remembered what you said about letting Brendan do some things for himself, so I gave him half the list."

"And?"

"And he seemed happy to help."

He glanced at the food in my hands. "Hungry?"

"A little."

I fumbled with the wrappers. "Um, I thought you would be in earlier, so I worked through lunch."

He took the food out of my hands. "Why did you stay?"

"It's Friday."

"Yes. Is there something special about Friday?"

I tried to look down, but he was standing too close. The blood rushed to my face. *How could I tell him I wanted him to examine me without sounding like an idiot?* I couldn't. Grant was right; there *was* a lot to do. He obviously wasn't interested in me or my pregnancy right now. He could examine me next week or whenever it was convenient for him. It didn't have to be today.

"You're right, Grant. I should go; there is much to do." I smiled and held up two fingers. "And, I promise to be careful and not do anything strenuous or lift anything heavy. Scout's honor."

He caught my hand with the fingers still raised and gently folded them within his grasp.

"Not yet, Caroline," he said quietly.

"Why 'not yet,' Grant?" I asked, slightly out of breath.

His lips were warm against my skin. "You cannot leave yet. I still…," he said, kissing my forehead. "Need to…." He kissed my cheek. "Examine you."

So relieved, I threw my arms around his neck.

"Oh, Grant, I thought you had forgotten or that it wasn't important to you. It's the reason I waited."

"You wanted me to examine you?"

"Yes! Wait until you feel him. I think he's gotten bigger."

"The chair or the examination room?"

"The chair—" I was about to add, "or the examination room," but he cut me off mid-sentence.

"The chair it is then."

He walked to his side of the partition. "I'll wait in my office while you get comfortable. If you are cold, use the quilt and let me know when you are ready."

"Yes, sir."

"Yes, Grant."

"Yes, Grant," I repeated. "I'll only be a minute."

"Fine."

Comments, Grayson?

Just a few. I agree your emotional domination is nearly complete. But, um, I'm not the psychologist, Grant, but I think you should interact more with her—be more engaged. As you said, she has to want to be here with you.

Grayson, she smells like rotten flowers, and I kissed her, twice. How much more interactive or engaged *do you think I need to be?*

Until she gives birth and begins nursing, I'd say whatever it takes. Sorry, but she's your client, and it's your experiment. Now that everything is falling into place, her continued cooperation is your responsibility. I'll talk to Gordon about the V4 formula. Maybe he can make it less revolting.

Oh yes, please talk to Gordon. I am sure he would do anything *to make this easier for me. Don't do me any favors, Grayson, or he will have her smelling like composted syrup.*

You have a point.

Thank you.

Grant?

Yes.

I don't want to regret this.

It's too late to speak of regrets, Grayson. It has become a matter of commitment to the colony, the collective, and our unborn brothers.

To her?

Only as an inconvenient means to a successful conclusion.

Still designing solutions to the colony's problems, Grant?

As ever, Grayson.

During this conversation, Grant watched Caroline undress, but while he shared his thoughts with Grayson, he did not share the view. Now giving her his full attention, he noticed that although he had not asked her, she had removed everything but her lingerie, and he was able to scan her for a comparative analysis.

Oh, yes.

There was a discernible roundness to her now. Her breasts were a little fuller, her hips a little rounder. His hands ached to touch her. Then he remembered Andrea's email and opened Caroline's file. Looking over the email, he wrote down the numbers from Caroline's most recent measurement session, found a measuring tape in his top drawer, and, smiling in anticipation, watched and waited.

He had not told Grayson the truth. She didn't smell like rotten flowers at all; she smelled like all the flowers in the world to him. The nectar Gordon distilled to mask the level of estrogen in the V4 formula made her smell too sweet, but the honey she consumed directly afterward mellowed it out perfectly. The mingling of her scent and the candle fragrance was slightly intoxicating to him. It was doubly hard to be distant and cold to her when all he wanted to do was wrap her in silk to warm her skin and taste her at his leisure. He already knew that once he relocated her to the facility, he would feast on her for the rest of his life.

"Grant," she said, "whenever you're ready."

He smiled at her choice of words, but his voice was calm. "I'll be there in a minute, Caroline."

Picking up the measuring tape and piece of paper, he pressed a new button on the underside of his desk. The room went utterly dark. Only the candlewick shivering from the force of the cooled air indicated any sign of life in the room. Grant stood up and began to undress.

"Grant," she said, "I can't see anything."

"I can. You are not afraid, are you, Caroline?"

"Well, it's just that I am nearly naked and—"

"I know."

"And I think I forgot to lock the door."

He laughed softly. "Such trust, Caroline, such trust." He turned the deadbolt in the door. "Better now?"

"Yes, thank you."

"Are you thanking me for locking you in a dark, soundproofed room?"

"No."

"No?"

"No, I'm thanking you for locking me in a dark, soundproofed room with you."

"My presence makes the difference to you?"

"It's why I'm still here…because you are here."

Her trust got to him every time. Her complete and unreasoning faith touched the one tender chord that remained within him. It was like she was his own mother who knew him so well that she unerringly caressed his most vulnerable spot, bringing him to his knees and wringing an honesty from him that was not always in his best interest.

"Caroline, may I touch you?"

"Yes, Grant."

Not wanting to frighten her, he said, "I have removed most of my clothes."

"Umhmm. You're warmer without them. Though it's hardly fair," she laughed, "with no lights on."

"Maybe next time." As much as he wanted to make these few moments with her last all night, he did not want to keep her too late. "Do you mind if I take some measurements? I want to compare them with Andrea's recent ones."

"Okay. Just a minute."

He heard the metal hooks unfasten.

"It won't be the same if I am wearing this." She placed the folded lace on the floor next to the chair. "Do you want me to stand up?"

"Yes, it will be easier that way and quicker, too."

"That's exactly what Andrea says."

She held her arms away from her body as he measured her chest, waist, and hips. After months of measurements, she wasn't shy about it anymore.

"How am I doing?"

"Well, I hope you won't be disappointed to learn that you are rounder by a fraction of an inch in your chest and hip; your waist is the same."

He hesitated. He wanted one more measurement, but he wasn't sure how to broach the subject.

"Are we finished measuring me?"

"Um, no. There is one more thing I need to measure while you are standing up, but I am not sure how to ask."

"It works best, in such cases, if you just tell me what you need me to do."

"Can you raise your arms so that I can, hmm, weigh your—"

"Bosoms?"

"Yes. If you prefer that word."

"For comparison?"

"Baseline," he said.

"Like this?" she asked, putting her hands behind her head.

"Yes, just like that."

He came up behind her and, lifting her arms, kissed the inside of her wrists and placed her hands behind his neck.

"Stand up straight, just like your grandmother always told you."

His hands gently held the wonderful weight of her, and, in his mind, he saw Caroline smiling at him while feeding their son. His breath caught at the force of his emotional response of pure joy. That was his true objective— not the experiment, the colony, or the collective—but that one moment in time when *she smiled* at him as she held their son in her arms.

Appreciating the delightful way her body felt against his, Grant realized that he continued to choose her. First as a lover, a mother, and now, separating himself from his brothers, a mate. He wondered *when*, not *if*, these choices were going to kill her, him, or all three of them.

Sighing, he brought her hands down and wrapped his arms around her to warm her. "Thank you, Caroline."

"You're welcome, Grant. It was quite nice, actually. Should I expect an exam every Friday so I will know what to wear?"

"For the next four weeks, yes, then a little more often as his birth gets nearer."

"As often as you like," she said. "Should I get back in the chair now?"

"Yes, of course, I didn't mean to keep you standing so long." He lifted her and set her down in the chair.

"Comfortable?"

"As comfortable as possible in our chair alone," she said. "But I will wait and hope for better things."

"Cold?"

"Just a little."

He spread the quilt over her. Lifting only the corner he needed, he lightly pressed her abdomen. She was right. The fetus had grown to the size of a small lime. A third larger than he expected, Grant was glad the darkness hid his face.

"I will be right back," he said, replacing the corner of the quilt.

"Grant?"

He could not miss the sound of concern in her voice. "Everything is fine, but I left the stethoscope in my lab coat," he lied. "Two seconds."

Grant picked up his stethoscope from the floor and returned to his office. Her file was still lying open on his desk, and he looked for the preliminary DNA report. All the markers were there; it was a Lyostian, not a human child. He was a trained geneticist—there were no errors in the report. Perhaps the increased size was due to the V4. He didn't wish to scare her by ordering an ultrasound now, but there would be a sonogram during next week's exam. He had to know exactly what was going on. There was more than just Caroline and the child to protect. It would ruin his professional credibility within the colony if his brothers suspected the truth. Grayson would report it, and the governing hierarchy would reassign him—if it did not kill him outright. Any control over their lives that he possessed would be destroyed, and he would lose everything. Refusing to accept that outcome, Grant was determined his child would be the genetic twin of every other child born in November, one way or another.

"Grant," she called from the chair, "can I help you look?"

"Got it," he said. "The lab coat was underneath everything else."

Kneeling beside her, he lifted the quilt, warmed the bell in his hands, and listened. At twice the number of beats per minute as a human fetus, his son's heart echoed joyfully in his ears like hummingbird wings.

He smiled at her. "Your baby is very strong. Here, listen to his heartbeat."

He handed her the earpieces, and as she listened, he saw the look of happiness and love he had imagined earlier.

"Oh, Caroline, we love you so much." The forbidden words, torn from the very heart of him, echoed in the room. Still kneeling, he touched his forehead to her body and, pressing the heels of his hands against his eyes, began singing prayers to Anya to protect her and their son.

Grant's Labyrinth

When he finished praying, I rested my hand on his hair until he raised his head.

"You love me."

"Yes, Caroline."

In the silence following his words, I understood that this was not the impassioned declaration of a lover but an acknowledgment of something I had always known. I reached out and touched his face.

"Grant, please sit with me if you have a few minutes. I've missed you this week."

He wrapped me in the quilt and settled me into the chair. Holding my hands in his, he said, "I know, I'm sorry. We've been renovating some of the space in the building, and I supervise all the architectural and interior design."

"You? You designed all of this? This spiraling maze of rooms and corridors?"

"Not a maze exactly, more like a labyrinth."

"There's a difference?"

"Oh yes, a major difference. A maze is composed of tricky angles, asymmetrical and broken, containing many false turns and traps. A labyrinth is a thing of curved beauty and symmetry. It has only one path but twists, so you cannot see too far ahead. It slows your progress but inspires you to keep moving toward the center with the promise of a sacred garden, fountain, or moment of truth. It then unwinds in the opposite direction, making the time for anticipation and reflection the same. Didn't Garrett give you a floorplan when he met with you?"

"Yes."

"If you look at it closely, you'll see what I mean. Or I could show you one evening when the facility is closed. Give you a real tour."

"That would be wonderful, Grant."

I looked at him through misty eyes. "Is there anything you can't do?"

"Drive," he said. "I can't drive here. Even in the dark, oncoming headlights kill my eyes."

"That's okay," I whispered. "We already have everything we need."

The afternoon was fading, and I wanted to distract myself from the responsibilities that waited for me at home.

"Grant, you said the boys whose mothers cannot nurse them will go to the colony's orphanages. What happens to them? If their DNA sequencing isn't complete, doesn't that make them different from the others?"

"Yes. Because our genetics are tightly controlled, if their DNA is imperfect they will not be allowed to breed."

"How will they keep them from doing that?"

"Think about it, Caroline," he said slowly.

I stared into his face. "They neuter them?"

"Yes, but chemically, not surgically."

"Grant, that's terrible."

"No, it doesn't mean in our culture what it means in yours. For nearly a thousand years there have not been enough females, and most of our males never mate. Chemical castration makes it easier for them to bear that limitation and encourages cooperation within the colony. They accept their societal roles, as we all do, working hard to make each colony a success. Without the distraction of desire, they are creative and focused."

"But aren't they considered less than the men with fully sequenced DNA?"

"There is no 'less' in our culture because each position is integral to the structure of the collective. There are different roles, but all are regarded as equal because our mandate is to work together to benefit the colony, thereby enhancing its chance for survival. That said, some hierarchies are more critical to survival than others, but because each hierarchy is necessary to move forward, we are one: one voice, one mind, one purpose. We are equal but not interchangeable. However, because we have had no choice but to depend on evolving versions of the Reconception procedure for hundreds of generations, chemical castration is an irrelevant but established procedure. You see, until you, Caroline, no one in our history had successfully mated with a human female for hundreds of years."

"You mean, until 'us,' Grant."

"Yes, Caroline. Until us, we believed it was impossible, and it may yet be. We will not know the child's true genetic makeup until he is born. There are consequences for not following protocols."

"Speaking of consequences, does anyone ever rebel, or is there even a choice?"

"Most of us are fitted to our assigned responsibilities which enables the colony to move forward by our individual abilities and talents. We are not clones. We are brothers, each with slightly different human characteristics that make some of us more suitable for one role than another. Rebellion occasionally happens—we are *partly* human. If the issues cannot be settled within the colony, then the discontented are...reminded of their place within the social structure of the collective. If such reminding is unsuccessful, then our brother is given the choice of being punished, exiled, or killed."

"Join or die?"

"It usually never goes that far. Unlike humans, our greatest loss is the support of the other members of our society. Exile is death to us. We do not only lose contact with our brothers and our mothers but also the collective consciousness of our ancestors. It is like unplugging your computer. Without that connection, it is just a box of lifeless electronics. That is what exile is to us: not an adventure or refuge but an existence of agonized abandonment and silence, which is worse than death. The truth is, each of us fears banishment so much—even for each other—that we work together so no one is forced into that position. "But sometimes," he said, glancing at his hands, "compromises cannot be reached." He shuddered slightly at the thought of the never-ending silence that was the worst hell he could comprehend.

"You said brothers and mothers, did you ever have sisters?"

"Our culture does not have a word for sister. Because they mature earlier than males, females of one generation are prospective mothers for future generations."

"What about fathers?"

Grant briefly closed his eyes. "Until quite recently," he said, kissing my forehead, "the word 'father' has been a verb, not a noun. But that will change with this new generation."

"How?"

"Remember the first reason for hybrid humans was for your longevity, and the second was for your light tolerance? The third reason is because, like humans, hybrids will be able to breed with human females at will—and without suffering serious side effects."

"But won't that make their children half human? Eventually eradicating the Lyostian DNA?"

"No. Using Lyostian germline cells, the DNA sequencing is complete. The only difference between the fathers and offspring will be the minor amount of DNA of the mother. The generation being born now will produce hybrid humans with their own DNA structure. There will be generation after generation of hybrids, all part of the collective, all thinking as one. With no reason for conflict, they will move forward with survival as their primary goal and caring for their mother, the planet Earth, as their singular occupation."

I was stunned but not repulsed. "I won't live to see that, will I?"

"No."

"Good," I whispered.

"But that brings me to a subject we need to revisit."

"My death?"

"No, mine," he said. "Biologically, we are all aging, but I can feel myself weakening. My brothers do not sense it yet, and I must keep it from them as long as possible. They cannot know the details, Caroline. It would mean separation and exile if they discovered I defied standard protocols. Ah, well, your Bible says the wages of sin is death, or a stroke, in my case."

"You can joke about it?"

"I am still luckier than most. Some of our distant arthropod cousins die of cardiac arrest as soon as they mate. Others are even more unfortunate. They get eaten alive by the females as soon as she is done with him."

"Well, we do get the munchies from time to time." *I can be brave, too, you know.* "How long?"

"Long enough to see you hold our son, probably a few months past that, but that will be all I can hope for."

He pulled me closer and rested his head on mine. "And I do hope for it, Caroline. I'll just feel a little more like his grandfather than his father by then."

"There is no hope for us if I lose this one?"

"What? What do you mean by that?"

"Well, I thought if I miscarried, I would hunt up Eric and try to get pregnant…with both of you, again, but only on the condition that I can be totally conscious during the, um, procedure."

The room was so still I could hear myself breathe. Grant's voice broke the silence.

"Do you want to hunt up Eric again, Caroline?"

"No, of course not. In fact, I can't bear the thought of anyone else touching me. But Grant, I would…endure it…if it was the only way I could have your child."

Grant sighed.

"Why would you do that?" he asked. "Why, if you miscarried, wouldn't you run out of here with your life still intact like this was all a bad dream? It is what we let the other mothers do who miscarry. And there is no 'trying again.' If your body rejects the first one, it will surely reject the second, or third, or the, well, please do not ask me to explain how I know this."

"All right, I won't ask…if you make me a promise."

"Yes?"

"Please don't ever ask me 'why' again, Grant. This has never been, or could ever be, a 'bad dream' for me. Don't talk anymore about dying, and don't talk to me about leaving; to me, they have become synonymous. I believed I was dying that Friday afternoon, and I didn't care because I knew I was with you. The hardest thing I do every night is go home because I worry that when I come back the next day, everyone will be gone. I've had dreams like that…*those* are my bad dreams."

As he listened patiently, he casually lifted my wrist to check my pulse and slowly kissed each finger, one by one. When I finished talking, he nodded to himself and said casually, "So, don't go home."

I was incredulous.

"Don't go home?"

"No. Do not go home tonight, do not go home ever. I could justify keeping you here. You are high risk and need round-the-clock observation by your…doctor."

"Live here?"

"Yes."

"Do you live here?"

"Yes, it is our colony."

He wanted me here…with him…everyday…and all night. Was that possible?

"Grant, I've been married for twenty years. How can I just leave?"

Even as I said it, I knew I'd been thinking about divorcing Dan since realizing Jack Daniels was his first love. Brendan was the glue that kept our marriage together, but he was leaving for college tomorrow. ROTC would take care of him for the next four years at UNI, and then the Marines would have him for the rest. He didn't need me. Dan didn't really want *me*, and he certainly didn't want another child—of any species.

Grant was silent as I struggled inwardly. When I looked up, he said, "I only have six more months, Caroline, maybe less. Will you not stay, live with me, and be my love?" he asked.

I took a deep breath before answering. "Nothing on this earth would make me happier, Grant, but why? I'm here almost all the time. I love you; you have me. Your son is safe. Why do you want me to live here?"

Even in the darkness, I could feel him looking at me steadily as if deciding what to say.

"Do you see that door, Caroline? You walk through it every evening. Until I see you the next morning, my imagination tortures me with everything that can harm you. Even when you are here, you are a mirage if I cannot touch you—hear your voice—and I am even less than that unless you touch me. I know it's hard to understand, but until I see you, I doubt your existence, and only the touch of your fingers on my skin keeps me from doubting my own, for I am not real—even our son is not real—unless you touch me."

It was a confession I never expected to hear from anyone. I took his hand and slowly caressed each scar on his fingers. "It seems, Grant, that we need each other...need *us*."

"Yes, Caroline, please."

There was no heart in me to refuse him. "Brendan leaves for college tomorrow. I'll be here Monday morning, doctor's orders."

"Thank you, Caroline. What time in the morning shall I send the ambulance?"

"Ambulance?"

"To bring you here. You could, for instance, call about seven-thirty and cancel your yoga class because you felt unwell. As your doctor, I would then decide to dispatch our ambulance to bring you here as a precautionary measure."

Monday morning? Dan ran late on Mondays, but he was always gone by eight. One thing about him, he never missed work because of his drinking; he just missed everything else.

"I'll call at eight o'clock. What do I need to bring?"

"Our son."

"I wouldn't go anywhere without him," I laughed.

Grant was silent for a moment. "You mentioned Eric earlier. Do you think he will come looking for you?"

"No...not after I left him sitting in the rain. Quite truthfully, I have no idea where he is right now. I haven't heard from him in weeks."

"Well, just to be thorough, why not bring everything with our logo or name? Brochures, t-shirts, and anything else you have. I will delete all your credit card transactions tomorrow." Smiling, he added, "Why make it easy for either of them to find you?"

It occurred to me that although this was the first mention of me living with him, it seemed he had been thinking about—no, actually planning—this move for some time.

"Is there any reason, other than the obvious, Grant, why you don't like them?"

"I am not sure what you mean by 'the obvious,' Caroline. If you are referring to the fact that they will still be here to love you when I am dead, then yes, but I have other reasons. My dear, you were beautiful the first day I saw you. That Dan, because of his neglect, or Eric, because of his youth, made you feel you were somehow less than the delightful, intelligent, loving woman you are angers me. I know how hard you worked to meet Eric's expectations, but he doesn't know—nor does he care—because somewhere in his male human heart, he believes you *should* have made those sacrifices for him, that he somehow *deserved* them. If he didn't feel that way, he would never have let you go. And, well, during the time you've been here, has Dan...oh, Caroline, I know I have no right to ask—he is your husband—but it was the only question you did not answer on the questionnaire."

I knew what he was asking.

"No. Dan only wants to make love to me when he is drinking, and I will only make love to him when he is sober. The reason I didn't answer the question is that it was too humiliating to write the truth. I always believed it was my fault because I wasn't thin anymore, but that couldn't be the reason because nothing has changed. He just doesn't want me. I don't know if he ever did." Overcome by the heartbreak of all those years of longing and begging for kisses, I put my head in my hands and wept quietly for the marriage that might have been.

Grant pulled my hands away and lifted my face to his. "Don't cry, Caroline, over what is past," he said. "Things that have happened are memories, and memories can only hurt you if you let them. Regret nothing. Let the ghosts of dead dreams go, and don't waste any more love or affection on someone who doesn't love you in return. Love me, Caroline, love our son. We love you. Your touch, your affection, and your thoughts are worth more than gold to us."

Holding me close, he took both of my hands in his and placed them on my abdomen.

"You are the center of my labyrinth, Caroline, my sacred garden. We have the future with us now, and we will go forward from here as three."

At that moment, as if to emphasize his father's words, the baby moved. We caught our breath at the same time, and Grant pressed his lips against the back of my neck.

"You are the most precious thing in the world to me. Please stay," he whispered.

I turned to face him. "I promise I will be back on Monday, Grant."

In the awkward silence that followed, I realized he hadn't been speaking to me.

Grant stood by the door. Mentally following her down the hall to the elevator, he heard the chime and the closing of the doors. She was gone. Every empirical reason for letting her leave was sound; it was another step in a sequence of prescribed events that would lead to the desired outcome. Nevertheless, there was not an ounce of him that did not want to run after her, bring her back into his office, lock the door, and keep her there for all time. Safe, that was really all he wanted, just to keep them safe.

Unable to follow her, he forced himself to turn back toward his desk to update her file and reclaim his clothes. He glanced at the partition to straighten his tie, but it was not his reflection mirrored in the glass. Instead, another man's face, silhouetted against a smoke-filled sky, looked back at him. The love and compassion Grant saw there wrenched his heart.

But it was the pity in his father's eyes that brought him to his knees.

Brendan

Dan was quite wonderful while we helped Brendan load the car. He even tried to give Brendan a few of his CDs, but when Brendan predictably declined, Dan laughed and gave him forty dollars so he could buy some new music of his own. It was a typical take-your-kid-to-college day: packing the car, driving for hours, unpacking the car, and setting up the room. Brendan didn't want us to stay but didn't seem to want us to leave either. I tried to keep my promise to Grant, but it was difficult to let Dan and Brendan carry everything. I've never been the kind of person to just stand around and supervise, and I knew Dan would notice and ask why.

When Brendan's roommate, Jeremy, showed up parentless, we helped him unpack his car. With only one trip left, I let the boys and Dan carry the boxes and laundry hamper while I stayed outside to wait for them. The weather was warm, and I was sweating, so when I saw a small, shaded park near Brendan's dorm, I went over to rest and wait there.

Tall pines, slate, and river rock created a simple but striking seating area in the center of a beautiful garden. As I was thinking how enchanting it would be to sit there with Grant during our dreaming time, I felt something on my arm. I thought it was a mosquito and started to swat it until I saw the colorful wings and stopped. A few seconds later, I saw more butterflies land on me. Holding out my arms, it wasn't long before I was covered in dozens of beautiful butterflies from my shoulders to the palms of my hands.

"Mom," said Brendan, "don't move. I've got to get a picture of this." He ran back to his room to get the new digital camera we gave him as a graduation present.

Dan and Jeremy stood next to him, and I heard the shutter click several times.

"Mom, you can't see this, but there's like fifty butterflies hovering above you as if waiting their turn."

It was the first genuine smile I'd seen on his face all day.

"This is so cool," he said, snapping a few more photographs.

Dan started walking toward me, and I knew he intended to brush them off. Rather than risk him hurting any of them, I shook my arms.

"Sorry guys," I said, "lunch is over."

Brendan's roommate looked at me, and I heard him whisper to Brendan, "Does your mother have diabetes?"

"I don't think so."

A moment later, Brendan asked, "Mom, do you have diabetes?"

His new roommate looked mortified.

"No," I smiled and looked at Jeremy. "Why do you ask?"

"They were, well, they were eating your sweat. They usually only eat nectar, so I wondered if there was any reason you would have a lot of sugar in your system. I'm sorry…it isn't any of my business."

"How do you know so much about butterflies?" I asked.

"My godparents got me a butterfly kit one year for my birthday. You get a big box and some caterpillars and watch the transformation. I thought it was pretty cool at the time, and so I did a little more research," he said, looking back at the park. "I've just never seen that happen before and wondered why they did that."

"Well, I do eat a little honey every day for medicinal purposes."

"It must be pretty strong."

I put my arm around Brendan, who, for once, did not push it away. "It is. That's why I only eat one teaspoon a day."

Jeremy nodded as though my answer made sense to him.

They had to report at fifteen hundred hours, so we left shortly after lunch to give the boys some time to become more acquainted. I hoped they would be good friends. Although the U.S. was at war in Kosovo, the president promised it wouldn't last long. Even with soldiers stationed all over the world, I was still thankful he was going into the ROTC program—they would keep him busy. There isn't a lot of downtime when you are training to be an officer in the U.S. armed forces.

On the way home, I remembered how, only a couple of months earlier, I'd hoped that Dan and I might grow closer with Brendan in college, but that was impossible now. Nothing between us would ever change. To prove my point, Dan switched the radio from the soft rock we were listening to earlier to the country music station he preferred; it was almost as though he forgot I was sitting next to him.

I turned to look out the window and hardly recognized the reflection staring back from the glass. The latest country hit faded from my consciousness as I tried to untangle my feelings.

Who are you?

A month ago, those answers came easier: wife, mother, daughter, sister, valued employee, and friend. Now, all those identities seemed faded and blurred as though they belonged to someone else. An unfamiliar fear of the future arose in me. My life was changing in ways I could neither control nor predict, and each path forward was uncertain.

What would happen to me if I accepted Grant's offer and then miscarried? If I stayed with Dan, I could pretend nothing had happened and pick up the pieces of my life. Grant said he loved me, but there were other mothers who needed his attention. Eric was out of my life, and if I left Dan and the worst happened, I would lose Grant, too. Everyone I loved would be gone, and the prospect of that kind of loneliness was almost too unbearable to contemplate.

Of course, I could stay with Dan and work at GatesWay until the baby was born and then decide, but what if I went into labor and Grant couldn't help me? The baby was as real to him as I was, and I knew every night I went home caused him indescribable anxiety. It *was* torture, just as he said, and my heart hurt at the thought of what two more months of that level of stress would have on his health.

I looked back at my reflection for answers but found only another question.

What do you want?

I thought of my last option. I could follow my heart and accept Grant's invitation. The memories of the many ways he cared for me gave me every reason to believe him and trust that he would not abandon me if I was no longer one of his prospective mothers. As heartbreaking as it would be, at least I would still be with him, which was what I really wanted. The baby seemed to read my mind because he suddenly flitted around inside me like one of the golden butterflies. If there had been any question at all as to what I should do, that slight movement settled it. I was willing to take a chance on my life, but not his, and only Grant could save him.

Grant's words from last night echoed in my memory: *You are the most precious thing in the world to me.* It was possible our baby was the only reason he loved me. However, even if that was true, it was still the kindest—and the most intense—love I had ever experienced. I would not, could not, give it up.

Grant had promised to protect me as I had promised to protect our son, and there was only one way for both of us to keep our promises.

I had to forge a new identity: stronger, wiser, braver.

Regardless of how I spent the rest of my life, however long or short it might be, I vowed never to regret this decision. I would leave Dan and stay with Grant as long as possible. His son and I would leave when we had to and make it on our own with whatever help Grant could arrange for us. It was the most dangerous path, but it was the only one that led to the life and love I envisioned for us.

Glancing at my reflection again, I saw I was smiling. Having Grant's son at my side as we made our way through the world did not seem a hardship at all; it would be an adventure. Watching the countryside flash by the car window, my confidence returned. We would have a future together—even if we had to carve it out for ourselves.

Arriving home, Dan went to the basement, and I put my decision into action. Under the pretext of cleaning up after Brendan's departure, I put everything with the GatesWay logo in a black plastic garbage bag. In went the workout clothes and t-shirts, and the little things like the visor, water bottle, business cards, and brochures. I mixed dirty clothes with clean clothes. It didn't matter. I was sure Grant would destroy the entire contents. Instead of taking the bag to the garage, I carried it to the front closet so I could grab it when I left Monday morning.

Monday morning.

Just the day after tomorrow, and I was never coming back. I looked around at the house full of my things. Lovely things, but what did I need? I went upstairs and found the biggest purse I had that could not be mistaken for a tote bag. First, I put all my jewelry in it. There wasn't much, but some of it was my grandmother's, and I was not going to leave it for the next woman Dan married to wash, cook, and clean for him. I had no doubt there would be someone else, sooner or later, filling my role in his life.

Probably sooner.

Going into Brendan's room, I pulled out a couple of his favorite storybooks left from his toddler years and found two small blue baby blankets at the back of his closet that still had tags on them. I opened the box where we'd tossed all his stuffed animals. Glancing at the mostly new toys, I picked out a small bunny. Then I felt, rather than saw, Dan's shadow in the room.

"Mooning over your soldier son already?"

Looking up, I noticed that his eyes were starting to glaze over. Treading cautiously, I said, "Yes, I guess it's a mom thing."

Keeping it light, I continued, "And you know, I'm thinking about all the extra space in this room. I could move my scrapbooking stuff in here and have a larger work area in the sewing room. What do you think? I'll leave everything the way it is now, but just move a few things around so there will be less clutter."

"Well, don't get so caught up in your (air parentheses) *mom thing* that you forget to fix dinner." He turned around and headed back down to the basement.

Had I ever?

I put the bunny on top of the books and blankets in the purse. Then I considered my sewing room full of fabric and notions, scrapbooking supplies, books, and magazines. I called my five closest friends, inviting them to a craft sale at noon the next day, and told them to bring plenty of cash.

My fabric collection was legendary among my friends. Surveying the unopened bags, overflowing project boxes, and cabinets full of fabric and supplies, I realized it had all been purchased to fill the great gaping hole in my heart where love was supposed to be, but it had never been enough. Although it represented thousands of dollars and hundreds of hours of my life, it all seemed so worthless now…but maybe it would not be worthless to my friends.

After making tacos for two, I cleaned the kitchen. On my way upstairs, a sharp pain caused me to miss a step.

Okay, no more tacos.

I took the fabric out of the cabinets and closet in the sewing room and moved boxes of patterns, thread, and two sewing machines into Brendan's room. Setting the last machine down, I felt another pain. My ears started ringing, and the room dimmed.

Damn.

I sat down on Brendan's bed, my head between my knees.

Okay, okay. Enough.

Recalling everything I had done that day, I realized how disappointed Grant would be if he knew. Hearing his doctor voice in my mind, I stopped trying to turn Brendan's room into a fabric store.

Needing to relax, I took a warm shower and went to bed. My butterfly woke me up shortly after midnight, fluttering and turning. Perhaps he is dreaming, too. I placed my hand above his heart and mentally hummed,

"As Time Goes By." It had been Brendan's favorite lullaby, and eventually, we both went back to sleep.

Feeling better Sunday morning, I dabbed a bit of color onto my face and dressed in a loose t-shirt and jeans. Making some breakfast for myself, I opened a new jar of honey and suddenly realized that in just twenty-four hours, I would be eating breakfast with Grant. My mind took flight. When I came back to earth, I was still staring at the honey jar.

I should pack this, too.

I decided to wait. It was going to be a long day, and having a little honey on crackers after everyone left would make waiting so much easier. Despite my careful planning, all I really wanted to do was run out the door and into Grant's arms but now wasn't the time.

Sequences, Caroline, sequences. Have patience. First this, then that.

When Dan came down, I told him my friends were stopping by after lunch to help me clean the sewing room and move some things into Brendan's room.

He grimaced. "Then I'll be downstairs all afternoon repacking the camping gear. Brendan left it all in a pile again. When we have the next garage sale, remind me to set this stuff out."

He grabbed two breakfast sandwiches out of the freezer, nuked them, and, pausing at the top of the basement stairs, said, "Let me know when they leave."

I took a tray with tea and cookies upstairs. By the time I set it down in Brendan's room, I was out of breath and had to rest. I felt so tired.

From all that work yesterday. I tried to shake off sudden feelings of guilt.

Hearing the doorbell, I hurried downstairs. Not wanting to miss anything, they all arrived on time. Leading the way, I pointed to both rooms, sat in Brendan's desk chair, and said, "Have at it."

They looked at each other and back at me.

"All of it?" asked Vicki.

"Yes."

"The sewing machines, too?"

"Yes."

"Anything." It was a confirmation this time, not a question.

"Anything you want," I answered.

"How much?"

"Whatever you think is fair."

Vicki's eyebrows came together in sudden concern.

"Carrie, are you dying?"

I smiled until I realized that all their faces wore the same expression.

"No, I'm not dying (*well, not today anyway*). It's just with Brendan off to college, I'm thinking about taking some classes myself, and well, I'll need somewhere to study. Or, depending on how generous you ladies are today, I might buy a red convertible and see the world."

They were not fooled. Anne put her hand on mine and said, "You're leaving Dan, aren't you?"

Caught off guard, I whispered, "How did you know?"

"We always thought it was just a matter of time. You don't seem...I don't know what the right word is, Carrie, but you've never seemed *connected* to Dan or he to you. You should see yourselves at a party—even sitting next to each other—the space between you is like a dead zone. We want you to be happy. Tell us how we can help."

Tears burst out of my eyes like a fountain. How lucky I was to have such wise and rare friends. They had always understood and, although blissfully unaware of my plans, were totally aware of my reasons.

Laughing through the hiccups of my sobs, I said, "Well, I guess it depends on how much you buy today."

"Do you plan to go back to your family in Florida?" Katie asked.

"Yes," I lied. "At first, and then probably up to Savannah or Charleston. I have friends and extended family there, too. I haven't thought it through yet. I just know I have to do this."

"Well, ladies," said Anne, "let's clean this place out."

With no arguments, they emptied the rooms of everything they wanted. The only thing I did not understand was the Singer featherweight that Kira set at my feet.

"What? You're leaving the featherweight? It runs perfectly, you know."

"Carrie, all of us want this machine, but we've decided to leave it for you. You will need it for your next sewing room and to remember us by."

Laughing like teenagers, we folded fabric and packed shopping bags. It didn't seem like I was leaving my life, but that it was leaving me, and I felt so much lighter that I didn't mind watching it go. Looking at the sewing machine at my feet, memories of the Halloween costumes I had made for Brendan came back to me, and I was grateful.

I may need it after all.

"This isn't nearly enough, but here," Val said, handing me a pile of twenty-dollar bills. "It's $2,500, not enough for a convertible, but it will get you to Florida and give you time to build a different life."

Five hundred dollars each. Then it hit me. That was the maximum amount of money you could withdraw from an ATM in one day. They all knew what I was going to do before they came.

At four o'clock, I went to the basement and gave Dan the "all clear" message, but he did not answer. Opening the door to his den, I found him napping on one of the sleeping bags. By the time I had returned to Brendan's room to clean up the remains of my sale, I was gasping for breath.

"Slowly, slowly," I said to myself.

I scattered a few pieces of leftover fabric between the two rooms so it would not look like anything was missing. Picking up the tray, I walked to the top of the stairs. Before I could start downward, my little butterfly, which had been so quiet all day, rolled over and fluttered.

The last thing I heard before everything went dark was the breaking sound of the teapot and cups hitting the first-floor landing.

The crash must have roused Dan because I heard him call my name through the haze.

"Carrie, Carrie, are you all right?"

A cold cloth wiped my face. Slowly, the ringing in my ears began to subside, and when I opened my eyes, Dan was looking at me with his face so worried and caring. I had not seen that expression in his eyes for a long time.

"What happened to you?"

"I guess I fainted. I've been feeling weird since I ate those tacos last night. Have you been okay?" I asked as I struggled to sit up.

"Yes, I'm fine, but let's get you into bed. Can you stand up?"

"I don't know yet."

"Well, let's not be in a hurry to find out. You weigh so little now I bet I could pick you up." He slid his arms underneath me and carried me to bed. "Thank goodness you fainted at the top of the stairs. I would hate to have to pick you up in pieces like the broken china."

"Yes, I need to get that," I said, trying to sit up.

He pushed me back onto the pillow. "No, I will. In fact, I'll take care of dinner, too."

"Well, okay," I said, "but I'm not hungry. I've been eating cookies all afternoon."

"Just let me know. I'll fix myself a sandwich and be back to check on you in a little while."

I stared at the ceiling. That was unexpected, the fainting spell *and* the fact that Dan was not only mostly sober but chivalrous, too.

Well, no more tacos for me. Ever.

Just then, another sharp pain went through me, and I couldn't deny the premonition that I'd forced to the back of my mind all day. I was losing my baby. Unsure of what he could—or would— do, I restrained myself from calling Grant.

I remembered his words: "Fully one-half of our mothers will miscarry in the first four weeks."

Grasping at straws, I thought it might be something else.

Oh, please, let it be anything else.

In my mind, I saw the hurt in Grant's eyes. He would not blame me but himself for loving me instead of following protocols. Tears fell from my eyes when I remembered that caring for me was costing him his life, too. Losing our baby was turning his love, hope, and sacrifice into pain and sadness for *nothing*.

I closed my eyes and let the tears course down my face. Then there was a flutter and another and another as though the baby was trying to comfort me. I gently patted my abdomen.

"Thank you, little butterfly."

As I drifted to sleep, I heard voices singing.

I was surprised when Dan woke me up with a kiss on my forehead. "How are you feeling this morning?"

"Better," I said, "but I don't think I'll go to work."

"That's a good idea," he said. "Let the students figure out their own problems today."

I opened my mouth to say something and closed it. With everything going on with Brendan, there just hadn't been a good time to tell him I'd quit working at the university, and now wasn't a good time either.

I glanced at the clock. It was only seven o'clock, and he was already dressed.

"Why are you going in so early?"

"Oh, sorry, I thought I told you. I have a breakfast meeting at eight, so I'm going to try to knock out a few emails before then. Just call me if you need me to pick up anything on the way home."

"Okay. Thank you."

He stood at the doorway and smiled at me, and I remembered all the years I would have given anything for a smile like that from him.

Too late. His footsteps seemed to echo down the hall, *too late, too late.*

I rested there until I heard the garage door close. I stood up to take a shower, but something did not feel right. Filled with dread, I turned and stared at the few flecks of blood on the sheet. My ears started ringing, and I sat down quickly. I didn't have time to faint. I had to call Grant and let him know that our charade had become all too real.

I could not wait until seven-thirty. Calling the spa, I changed the message for Dr. Grant to say I would miss my morning yoga class because I was having severe cramps. I set the phone down and slowly walked into the bathroom.

The rushing water of the shower mingled with my tears and blood on the stall floor. I shook my head at my moment of foolish optimism last night.

"Goodbye, little butterfly," I said, choking on the words.

Toweling off carefully, I put on a loose sundress and left my bedroom. I looked at the purse I had readied only thirty-six hours before and barely controlled my hysteria. I had to be calm. I wasn't sure how much the ambulance interns knew, and it wouldn't help to act like the hysterical, crazy woman I was on the verge of becoming. Closing my eyes to the storybooks and bunny, I removed my wallet and put it in my pocket. I held tightly to the banister as I walked downstairs into the kitchen and took the jar out of the refrigerator. Opening it, I put a small amount on the tip of a spoon and tossed the jar into the garbage.

It had only been fifteen minutes since I called the spa, so I knew the ambulance I heard in the distance had to be for someone else. I dragged the bag from the closet and unlocked the front door. Unable to remain standing, I held onto the stair rail and slowly lowered myself to the floor. Feeling nothing but the cold, hard tile beneath me, I touched the spoon to my lips so the delicious scent would overpower the reality of everything I was losing. As I closed my eyes, a sunbeam shone through the skylight and, reflecting off the diamond in my wedding ring, cast an arc of color onto the white stone floor.

The ambulance sounded closer. Thinking that someone else in the neighborhood was hurt, I said a short prayer for her survival. For myself, I had little hope.

Grant's honey melted like warm gold on my lips as I waited for my life to end.

A Call to the Spa

Grant awoke at three o'clock that morning. There was something wrong. He truly believed she would call as promised, yet as the time grew nearer, he couldn't help but feel as though he was exploding in a hundred directions at once. Unable to sleep or work, he paced the dark corridors and waited. When Andrea paged him, he met her outside Garrett's office and tried not to let the relief show on his face.

"Sorry to bother you, Dr. Grant, but Mrs. Taylor specifically requested that I tell you she would miss her yoga class this morning because she was having severe cramps. I don't know why she asked me to bother you when her chart indicates that would be expected at this time."

"Yes, I see. Well, it is Monday…perhaps she is using it as an excuse for sleeping in this morning. I'll speak to her later. Thank you."

Refusing to panic until he saw her, Grant strode toward the elevators and slightly tilted his head. Two interns immediately rushed to his side and then ran to get the white room ready. Stopping in his office long enough to get the darkest pair of sunglasses he owned, Grant took the elevator to the garage level where an ambulance was waiting and slid into the front seat.

Expecting another intern, Harris could not believe his eyes. Never before had a doctor ridden in the ambulance.

"8828 Decker Court."

"Sirens and lights?"

"Yes. Stop for *nothing*."

Grant's scarred hands formed a fist. If Dan had hurt her, he would hunt him down and, with pleasure, deliberately and mercilessly exterminate him as something that had forever forfeited its right to live. Lyostians did not understand the abuse human men were capable of toward the mothers of their children or a society that would condone it. His son would punish human men with the retribution that kind of arrogance warranted.

Only then did he realize that his son was probably dying or already dead. The pain was almost more than he could bear, but he was a doctor, and he knew—and she knew—what the odds were. They had just hoped too much. The only thing he wanted to do now was save her life. He would let her go back to her husband if that was what she wanted. The extraction procedure would make her uncomfortable for a few days, but she would fully recover if the formic acid had not affected her brain. If she was already affected (and he knew the odds of that outcome as well), he would keep her sedated in one of their underground rooms where he could take care of her, and she could not hurt herself. The rooms he had prepared for her, when he thought they had so much happiness to look forward to, would be dismantled and destroyed.

Grant was out of the ambulance before it stopped moving. Bursting through the front door, he froze at the threshold and stared down at the woman he loved, lying still as death in a pool of shattered light.

Broken

The honey was still in my mouth when Grant took me in his arms.

"Caroline, open your eyes. Are you in any pain?"

"Not anymore," I said, sobbing. Grant lifted me from the floor and carried me into the back of the ambulance before the driver had time to remove the stretcher.

"My spa stuff," I muttered, pointing to the black bag by the door. The driver ran to the door and returned with the plastic bag in his hands.

As Grant stepped into the back of the ambulance, he said, "Put the bag up front with you. I'll stay here."

Laying me down carefully, he kept one arm under my neck as his other hand went under my dress and gently pressed my abdomen. There was no movement at all. No longer sobbing, tears streamed down the sides of my face. He smoothed my dress and gently kissed his son goodbye.

Sighing, he lifted his head and reached for my chart. "Tell me what happened since Friday. Leave nothing out. No matter how small, every detail is important."

His voice was so distant and remote that my despair was complete; his affection *had* been because of the baby, and in losing one, I had lost them both. I tried to answer his questions as tonelessly as he asked them but couldn't do it without breaking down.

"I was so careless, Grant. It was all my fault."

The professional mask slipped a little from his face. "Caroline, you can't cry right now; you must tell me everything. I promise," he said, kissing my forehead, "I will let you cry all you want later."

Yes, but I will be crying alone. The other mothers who had not failed needed his attention now.

"Talk to me, Caroline. What is causing you the most pain?"

"That you will leave me, and later, when you let me cry, you won't be holding me. I, I will be crying alone."

"Oh, Caroline," he said in his singsong voice, "I will hold you like this until I die."

Believing him, I told him everything...almost. Brendan's trip to UNI, packing the car, trying to supervise but carrying boxes up and down stairs, walking all over the campus, how I thought it was the damn tacos and nothing serious. I told him about moving the sewing machines and going up and down the stairs nearly a dozen times, the lightheadedness and fainting that I thought had nothing to do with my pregnancy. I knew he was hearing everything he'd told me not to do. I waited for his anger, but it never came.

"Caroline," he whispered in my ear, "were you trying to have a miscarriage?"

There was no accusation in the question, no sense of blame in the tone of his voice; he just wanted to know.

"Noooo," I wailed, "I was just being stupid thinking I could do everything and take care of everybody so that I could leave." Then I remembered the storybooks, baby blankets, and the bunny—the part I could not bear to tell him—and moaned in despair over what could have been.

"What is it?" Grant pulled the dark curtains over the windows and took off his glasses so he could search my entire face at once. "Try to stop crying, Caroline. I cannot help you if you do not tell me where you are hurting or what is hurting you."

"It's the bunny," I said.

"What bunny?" Suddenly, he looked as though an inevitable horror had finally clicked into place. Taking a deep breath, he put his glasses back on and pulled me into his arms.

"Tell me about the bunny, Caroline," he said gently.

With no defenses left, I told him how happy I'd been picking out books, finding the blue blankets, and choosing the toy and how those memories were crushing me now as they sat abandoned in an empty hallway because I would not need them. The relief was so plain on his face that I thought he didn't understand.

"No," he said, "I understand two extremely important things that will help me accept this loss. The first is that, so far, you are not mentally compromised, and since we are nearly there, I will see that nothing hurts you ever again. The second, which is the only happiness I will hold on to now and forever, is that you didn't do it on purpose. You wanted to hold him, read to him, and play with him—you already loved him that much. I cannot tell you what knowing that does to me. Thank you, Caroline, thank you."

He held me in his arms until the ambulance stopped moving. When the backdoors opened, he was Dr. Grant again. His sudden professionalism destroyed my momentary peace, and despair consumed my heart.

I expected to be taken to one of the meditation rooms, but I was wheeled into a blinding white operating room. Two doctors were already there, their faces hidden by glasses and surgical masks. They could be anyone. As soon as the doors closed, the lights in the room dimmed. Two interns removed my dress, replaced it with a hospital gown, and lifted me onto the table.

"What are you going to do?" I asked.

A voice I didn't recognize said, "We have to remove the embryo at once. If it ruptures, any toxins released into your bloodstream will harm you, and you may not recover." Although he continued talking to me, he glanced up at Grant and said, "You will not be able to have any more children if it becomes necessary to remove the entire uterus."

"What? Is that the only way? Can't you induce contractions or something?"

"We could, but the contractions needed to complete your miscarriage could compromise the integrity of the fetal sac, which must be avoided. It could also take nearly an hour, which we feel is too long. You don't understand, Mrs. Taylor. We have lost women as a result of this kind of infection before, and we don't," he said, glancing at Grant again, "want to lose you."

"Dr. Grant," I said, turning to him, "please just induce…it has to be so small…it won't rupture, I will be so still. Please, can't we try that first? I want to try that first."

"Mrs. Taylor, the risk—"

"Is mine."

Not just yours, his face said, but he smiled gently as he explained, "You still don't understand. The reason inducing takes so long, and why we usually have to remove the uterus, is that while the embryo is growing, it attaches itself, more than any human embryo ever does, to the mother. Comparatively, the human embryo attachment has the strength of your little fingernail; the embryo you are carrying now has the connection strength of your entire fist. Inducing drugs just do not work."

"Please," I said, my eyes begging him. "Please, Dr. Grant."

"Why, Carrie?"

"So I can have the hope of trying again."

"I told you, there is no 'trying again.'"

"Give me thirty minutes. If it doesn't work, you can operate." I closed my eyes, but the tears leaked through them. "Just thirty minutes, Dr. Grant. Please."

He tilted his head and looked at the other two doctors. Simultaneously, they tilted their heads to the side as if listening to something or someone. It was too quiet, and I grew more frightened with each passing second. Then, the two doctors nodded, checked their watches against the clock on the wall, and left.

Sighing in defeat, Grant said, "It will be as you wish."

His face a mask, Grant silently opened a narrow closet and removed an IV stand. Preparing the IV, he attached a tube to the bag and laid it on the table.

His finger traced the veins in my hand. "Carrie, this is going to hurt."

"I'm not afraid of needles. I've already had one baby, you know."

"Not the needle. The contractions will be hard, fast, and painful. Imagine the worst cramps you've ever had and quadruple them—exponentially. It will take too long if I give the drugs to you intravenously, so I am going to put the needle directly into your uterus. If you expel the embryo, we will stop immediately, and the pain will stop as soon as we remove the IV. If we put the drugs into your bloodstream, it will take longer to start and stop. Of course, this also means if it gets too painful for you, we will go back to our original procedure."

"Their original procedure."

"We are one, Carrie."

I thought of what this was doing to him, from the moment of his greatest joy to this heartbreaking performance for the benefit of an uncomprehending audience. I reached for his hand.

"Thank you for not leaving me here alone. It is something to remember, you know. That you were there at the beginning and now at the—" but I could not say the word. "Oh, Dr. Grant, I wish it could be any other way."

Grant looked down at her tear-stained face and saw death—first the child's, then hers, and finally, his. There was no way he could circumvent his responsibility to the colony. When Grant thought of her body lying in the serai, his carefully controlled emotional equilibrium began to slip.

The touch of her hand brought him back, and looking into her eyes, he no longer saw death but hope and trust. He kissed her forehead.

"I know, more than you do, how much you mean that. But you will never fully understand my regrets, even now, as I am going to hurt you more than you can probably stand; accept that I am doing it with all the compassion I have left in me."

He pointed to the metal rests near her feet.

"I am going to tilt the table to allow gravity to help. Please put your feet against these and be as still as possible."

He tried not to think about the restraints concealed under the edge of the table.

As gently as possible, he separated her gown at the waist and brushed his hands along her body, feeling every curve.

"Let me know when I touch the area where you felt the pain." His fingers slowly drummed downward from her navel ever so lightly until he heard her catch her breath.

"There," she breathed.

He nodded. It was where he expected it to be. He brushed her skin with a topical anesthetic. Slowly, as if feeling the pain himself, he inserted the needle until it met with the resistance of the outer wall of the uterus, then, pushing it a little further, he stopped. He attached the leader tube and turned the dial on the IV stand.

She shivered slightly.

"May I have a blanket?" she asked.

Without speaking, he reached over the table and pressed a button on one of the stainless-steel cabinets.

In less than a minute, Grant spread a warmed sheet across my chest and arms and another over my legs. In twenty seconds, I hurt; in less than sixty seconds, I thought there was nothing in the world beyond the pain. Nothing Grant said prepared me for this. He held my hand, but I didn't feel it. After three minutes, my feet slipped against the metal braces, and I realized I was bleeding. I looked up, and he would not meet my eyes. I looked at the clock.

At four minutes, I started hyperventilating.

He bent his head toward me. "Remember your Lamaze classes, Caroline? Let's begin with four shallow breaths and then two deep breaths. I will help you count."

I stared at the clock, and we counted.

At ten minutes, I had to stop counting because my lips began trembling. Looking worried, he leaned close to my ear and said, "Caroline, please, please let me turn this off."

"Fi-fi-five more minutes."

I didn't want to stop. Even hopelessly trapped in this cold white torture chamber, I knew as long as I was in pain, I hadn't lost him.

At twelve minutes and fourteen seconds, I saw rather than felt—because I could not feel anything but pain—my body convulse. Grant released my hand and switched off the IV.

By fourteen minutes and thirty seconds, I was breathing normally and being wheeled out of the operating room.

Although I had been awake for just a few hours, I was so exhausted that when the interns placed me on the bed in a meditation room, I fell asleep at once. I heard a chime and thought it was time for my pedicure...then I remembered. I tried to lift my hand to wipe away the tears, but it wouldn't move. Opening my eyes, I saw Grant holding my hand. The tube embedded in it was connected to a plasma IV.

"Before I answer any of your questions, you have to answer some of mine. First, tell me your name, the date, the sixteenth President of the United States, and your first conscious memory."

"Caroline Anne Taylor, October fifth, Abraham Lincoln. I am standing up in the front seat of my grandfather's car with my sister, and we are going to get donuts for breakfast."

"Which sister?"

"Leann."

He sighed in relief. "The fetal sac was intact, but I wanted to be sure that your memory was not affected before we talked. I am grateful for that, Caroline, because I didn't want you to forget...." his voice trailed off.

"You?"

"Us."

He glanced up at the IV stand.

"You lost nearly a liter of blood, more than we expected, or we would not have let you have your way. But, upon examination, it was the better of two options."

"Why? What happened, Grant? How did he die? What did I do wrong?"

"It wasn't anyone's fault, Caroline. He just wasn't attached securely enough."

Attempting a bedside manner, he said, "You know the embryo lives in a fetal sac, but it is not attached to you by an umbilical cord like a human embryo; the sac is complete. He grows by taking in nourishment from your body through little connections that anchor him here." He gently placed his index finger where he had inserted the needle. "Those connections do not detach until he completes that stage of his development and is born. That is why inducement drugs don't usually work. They worked this time because, for some reason, he wasn't securely attached, so, well, he didn't…grow."

"My poor little butterfly, I'm so sorry," I whispered. My throat filled up with unshed tears. I could barely meet Grant's eyes, but I had to ask.

"Was it my fault?"

I watched the struggle on his face as he decided what to tell me.

"We aren't sure. It appeared he had been firmly attached at one time, but something happened that detached two-thirds of the connections. Since these connections were formed in the first thirty-six hours following the Reconception procedure, he was unable to develop more. That he lived as long as he did, Caroline, was only because you took such good care of him."

"But he was so active on Saturday and Sunday, fluttering up and down and over, he felt so strong." My voice broke on the last word as I realized he wasn't moving because he was strong but because he was starving.

"Here," he said, setting a small bed tray with a cup of tea and toast over my lap, his lips just brushing the top of my head, "something to make you feel better."

The honey wasn't as dark as before.

I stared at the tray without moving. Nothing could have screamed what a failure I was more than this consolation offering. Bowing my head, I knew that if there had been anything left of my heart to break, it would have shattered at that moment.

"When your blood levels stabilize, we will move you to a more comfortable room. We are still trying to run a spa here, you know."

He tried to smile, but it seemed impossible.

I understood. Business was business. They had twelve hundred members; two hundred were his responsibility, and I was falling lower and lower on the clinic's priority list, hovering somewhere near the bottom with the sweet geriatric clients.

"You don't have to move me anywhere, Grant; once I'm stable, I'll just go home."

"Go home?"

"Yes, why not? I don't need your personal supervision. The reason for that no longer exists." Then, keeping my voice as toneless as possible, I said the words he had avoided all afternoon.

"He starved to death."

I don't think I could have hurt Grant more if I'd decapitated him.

"As you wish."

In my grief, I was relentless. "And you can stop being so nice to me," I said, handing him the tray. "I am not one of your prospective mothers anymore."

"Caroline, please don't do this," he whispered.

"Don't do what, Dr. Grant? Agree with you? Because you are absolutely right. You have a spa and a health clinic to run. And don't worry about me, I'll be fine. I'll probably need a few sick days, but I'll be back to work, bright and early, on Thursday morning."

"As you wish," he repeated. Grim, his mouth a straight line, and his eyes hidden behind his glasses, he nodded to me and left the room.

The moment the door closed, the torrent of tears I'd held back broke through, and I hugged the pillow to my chest.

"Oh, Grant, I'm so sorry," I said in a voice from somewhere so deep inside me that it sounded like a strangled bird. Inconsolable, I tried to come to grips with a reality that I had so confidently dismissed less than forty-eight hours ago.

I *had* lost them both.

Staring into the dark abyss that was now my life, I rocked dully back and forth, wondering once more who I was.

Window of Grief

Grant watched her soundlessly through the two-way mirror. Her reaction to the loss of her—their—child when she was alone was necessary for his experiment report. It was harder to endure than he believed possible. He wanted to go to her, hold and comfort her, but her voice echoed in his ears…she did not want him. Regardless of her words, he could not stand and watch her suffering much longer. Perhaps if she understood that he, too, was grieving, she could find a way to reach through her own misery to comfort him.

What if, in her sorrow, she left and never came back? Would he be made to find and murder her, too? Would the last word she ever uttered be his name screamed in terror?

The possibility was too great for him to deny.

He did not want to think of how execrable his life would become if it was only his connection to the child that she loved. Had he lost everything? At the thought of never again feeling her gentle touch, he prayed, *Blessed Anya, mother of us all, please protect her and give her strength.*

The hands that pressed against his eyes trembled for a moment as he added, *And please let her remember that once, for a little while, she loved me, too.*

An Unexpected Visit

Grayson's voice interrupted his prayers.

Grant?

Grayson.

Mr. Taylor is in the lobby demanding to see his wife. Take care of this. Now, please. He is being loud.

Of course.

Grant.

Yes.

I'm sorry. I know you put a lot of effort into your experiment with Mrs. Taylor.

It was not unexpected. She was high risk.

Yes.

Is she going home?

That is her plan.

What if she doesn't return?

I will do whatever is necessary to neutralize any threat against the colony, Grayson.

Pity to lose her.

Yes.

Are you in the lobby yet?

Two steps away.

Thank you.

Bad Monday

I hadn't been alone long when Grant stepped in without knocking.

"Caroline, Caroline," he said, brushing my hair back. Seeing my glazed eyes, he went into the powder room and, returning with a cool cloth, carefully wiped my face.

My voice hoarse, I repeated, "I didn't mean it, I didn't mean it."

"Caroline, stop, please stop."

He sat on the bed and gathered me up in his arms. He was so warm. The scent of honey was on his breath, and my body relaxed into his. After a few moments, he stood up and lifted my hand to his lips.

"I didn't mean it," I whispered.

"I know."

"How?"

"I'll show you sometime. But right now, we have a problem."

"Did someone else…?"

"No, not as bad as that. Dan is here and wants to see you. Now. I'm afraid he is being rather insistent."

"How did he know where to find me?"

He took a small jar from his pocket. I recognized it immediately.

"I threw that away."

"He found it. Caroline, we need a reason for you to be here with an IV attached to your hand. Appendicitis?"

"Already removed, see?" I said, pointing to a faded scar. I thought for a moment and realized I wasn't afraid of Dan. What could he do to me here? I had $2,500 in cash, and despite what I'd said to Grant earlier, I wasn't going home.

"We'll tell him the truth, Grant. I'm recovering from a miscarriage. This is a medical clinic and where the ambulance brought me."

It wasn't that I lacked imagination, but I didn't think the truth could hurt any more than it already did.

"Are you able to handle that?" he asked slowly.

"Will you stay and be my doctor?"

"I *am* your doctor, and yes," he said, "I will stay as long as you wish."

"Is that a promise, Dr. Grant?"

His eyes did not move from my face. "Yes, Caroline, that is a promise."

An intern escorted Dan into the room. I was surprised to see him carrying a shopping bag.

He walked up to me and took my hand. "How are you feeling, Carrie?"

"Better."

He dropped my hand and pointed to the telephone. "Well, it would have been nice if you'd called to let me know where you were. I started calling every freakin' ambulance company in the damned telephone book after nosy Norma next door phoned me *at work,* mind you, to ask what was wrong with you. If I hadn't gone home and found that jar with the clinic's name on it, I'd still be calling."

"I'm sorry, I just woke up. Dan, this is Dr. Grant Gates."

"Nice to meet you," he said, shaking Grant's hand. "Why is she here instead of a real hospital? I'm not sure our insurance covers this place."

"Our membership services include full gynecological care, Mr. Taylor. As this procedure falls under that umbrella, so to speak, there is no charge at all."

"Okay, so to speak, why is she here?"

"Your wife telephoned our facility this morning, informing us she would miss her yoga class due to unusually severe abdominal cramping. First suspecting appendicitis, we sent an ambulance to take her to the medical facility on South Kennedy. Upon the initial examination, we discovered Mrs. Taylor does not have an appendix, and because she was hemorrhaging, our interns brought her here. Regrettably, she suffered a spontaneous abortion. We performed an emergency D&C, and she is scheduled for release tomorrow morning.

"Don't worry," he said, looking from Dan to me, "she will be able to have more children."

Dan shook his head as though trying to clear it. "*More* children? Carrie, what does he mean, more children?"

"I had a miscarriage, Dan. But it didn't cause any permanent damage. That is what he means."

I saw Grant tilt his head and immediately heard footsteps in the hallway. Not seeing anyone pass the door, I knew the interns were standing in the hall.

"What's in the bag, Dan?" I asked, trying to distract him.

"Uh, you left your purse, so I brought it to you. I thought there might be something in it you needed."

Of course, he put it in a bag. Nothing in the world would make Dan Taylor walk through a spa holding a purse. I almost laughed at the thought.

He saw me smile and took it out of the bag to hand to me, but it tipped sideways, and Brendan's bunny fell out.

Dan froze at the sight of the toy. I knew then that he finally understood everything Grant and I had said to him. His face turned red, and he threw the purse across the room.

"How many, Carrie?" he demanded. "How many *other* men's children did you plan to have?"

"I didn't plan it, Dan," I said calmly.

"What a fool I've been! Wait—is that what was wrong with you yesterday? You were *pregnant*? Twenty years of thinking you were Little Miss Perfect, and now I find out that you are a..." he glanced toward Grant, "are nothing. And I am the world's biggest idiot."

He looked around the room.

"Well, I'm glad this place is free," he said, casting another glance at Grant, "because I'm going to the bank, and I'm closing our accounts, then I'm canceling our credit cards. You will have nothing from me. Not one damn thing. Do you hear me?"

"Yes, Dan," I said, looking at him. "I hear you. I am nothing...I have nothing. I'm sorry."

"You're *sorry*? I can't freakin' believe this. Why, Carrie, why? Every day I was there. Every damn day. I can't believe it...what a waste of my life! This," he said, pointing to the IV, "is unforgivable."

Grant's voice cut smoothly through the tension in the room. "As I mentioned earlier, we would like to keep her overnight for observation."

"You do that. In fact, I'll make it easy for you." He looked at me, his eyes flat and cold. In a low voice, he said, "Carrie, I don't care where you go, but don't bother coming home. As far as I am concerned, you have no home. Not tomorrow, not ever."

He turned to leave and pointed to the door.

"Well, doc," he said to Grant, "if I were you, I'd put a reserved sign on the door. I doubt this will be the last of her," his fingers made air parentheses, "miscarriages."

The sound of my hysteria caught him off guard, and he looked momentarily ashamed as Grant rushed over to me, offering me the teacup from the tray.

"Mrs. Taylor, please drink this."

I pushed his hand away. "No, it's not for me anymore."

Looking from Dan to Grant, I was devastated by my sense of failure. These men loved me for such different reasons, and I had let them both down so completely that Dan was right. I was nothing now...to either of them. As if to agree with me, Dan slammed the door on his way out. Grant followed more quietly with his head slightly tilted.

Neither of them looked back.

I felt my life crumbling around me, but when I thought of the love I would never know, the child I would never see, every dream in my life died. I removed my wedding ring and set it gently on the table as a mourner would lay a flower on a grave.

Folding my legs to my chest, I dropped my head on my knees and tried to appear as small as possible.

If I get small enough, maybe I will disappear.

Only One

The room was so quiet when I raised my head that I thought I was alone, but I saw Grant sitting at the desk across the room, his head slightly tilted, looking at Brendan's rabbit. I watched him set the bunny on the blue blankets and pick up one of the storybooks. Thumbing through the pages, he read a line or two, and, smiling to himself, he closed the book. Then he looked up at me, and I knew I had not lost everything.

"Feeling better?"

"A little. Why did you call for reinforcements?" I asked, referring to the interns in the hallway.

"Waves of perspiration were pouring from Mr. Taylor, and I was afraid he would become violent."

"Why?"

He smiled. "I told you I could smell alcohol a block away—he was only across the room. Hardly a challenge."

He sat on the bed beside me.

"Did you think he would hit you?" I asked.

"They weren't called to defend me; he couldn't hurt me. They were called to protect you." His fingertips brushed the side of my face. "So soft."

"Why would they risk a fight to protect me? I am nothing to them. I failed," I said quietly, "all of you."

Removing the pillow from my back, he pulled me against him and wrapped his arms beneath my breasts. "Caroline, the pregnancy failed, not you. And you are wrong. My brothers do not consider you 'nothing.' It is the dream of you that each one has carried since birth. A mother who not only wants to share our future but also cherishes the thought of it. You have entered our collective consciousness for all time to revere, inspire, and remember."

But it wasn't enough to save her. She knew too much, Grayson said. They could not risk her leaving the facility alone or going home. If she fainted, someone might call an ambulance. If she returned home, it could be even worse. They had seen the marks of violence on other women, and Dan's outrage had been broadcast throughout the facility. If his anger led to injuries, other hospitals might get involved, blood tests performed, and questions asked.

Who knew what she would say under duress or anesthesia?

Not even the threat of her death could induce Grant to share the delicate nature of their relationship. In mute surrender, he listened and set the necessary plans in motion. He had known from the first day he met her that her death was inevitable, but despite his current impaired condition, he could not explain why he was suddenly tired or why it hurt so much to breathe.

Deciding he had endured enough pain for one day, Grant looked at her pale, upturned face and thought, *tomorrow.*

Resting my head on his shoulder, I closed my eyes. Grant began singing, and his hands made long, smooth movements down my body.

"So beautiful," he murmured, his lips barely touching my skin.

For the first time during that anguish-filled day, I let his warmth and love encircle me. Feeling safe and calm, my hand slipped from resting on his chest to my lap. Tenderly caressing my abdomen as though it were an open wound, I felt a faint flutter. My hand froze. It was impossible. I had to be hallucinating. My golden butterfly had died. It happened again, stronger than before. I gasped in surprise.

Grant's head snapped up. "Caroline, are you in pain?"

Taking both of his hands, I moved them to my stomach.

"Do you feel this?" I asked, my eyes filling with tears. "Or am I just imagining it?"

Holding our breath, we didn't take our eyes from each other's face. Then, as if to take away all doubt, our son moved against his father's hands.

Grant sat very still. He tilted his head and lightly stroked the little bump under his fingers, and less than a moment later, there was an answering flutter. Grant looked at me, and I could tell he was mentally searching the collective's databases.

"Please don't move," he asked, getting up slowly.

"Where are you going? Please don't leave me. Oh, Grant, is this, is this bad?"

"I am not leaving you, and I don't know."

Almost immediately, there was a knock on the door, and an intern entered with an ultrasound machine. Lying perfectly still and barely breathing, I watched Grant place a small dab of jelly above the bump. As he moved the transducer slowly over my skin, a humming sound filled the silent room. Grant looked at the monitor, then down at his watch, and counted. The smile I loved returned to his face.

He motioned the intern to remove the sonogram cart.

I waited until the door closed and whispered, "What is it, Grant?"

"Well, Caroline," he said, still smiling, "I am fairly certain it's a boy."

"What?"

"Caroline, do you have a family history of twins?"

Twins? Oh no, not again! I wasn't sure I could live through losing another one.

In despair, I looked down so he could not see my eyes. "Yes, my mother had two sets of twins, one identical and one fraternal."

"Hmmm. I realize this is a personal question, and if you would rather not answer, I will understand, but that morning you were with Eric, how many times did you …?"

I blushed and looked up. "Twice."

"Over how long a period of time?"

"About an hour and a half."

He nodded. "About an hour and fifteen minutes apart?"

"Yes."

"There can be only one."

"One?"

"Yes, Caroline. Sometimes, when conception is not simultaneous, it can result in fraternal twins. One lower in the uterus than the other, which was the one we moved for the Reconception procedure. The one slightly higher was not disturbed and did not have to reconnect, giving it a slight advantage. Because they are nearly infinitesimal at that point in the development, we only found one during our examination. If we had followed protocols, they both would have died, and...."

"Me, too?"

"Statistically, yes."

"Why only one?"

"We are not sure...the information in our archives is still inconclusive. Identical twins will bond as brothers, indivisible from any other brother because they share the same DNA and a single consciousness. Gordon and Gregory are identical twins. However, since fraternal twins are encapsulated separately, they do not share a single consciousness. At this point, the cells are replicating so quickly that unless they telepathically connect on their own—which is difficult if they are not conceived simultaneously—they do not bond and see one as a threat to the other's survival, and they will fight, each trying to dislodge the other from their only food source, you."

"So that was what was going on inside me over the weekend, a civil war? All right here?" I asked, laying my hand over his.

"Yes," he said, "and you were about to become Atlanta, but I would not let you go down in flames, no matter how determined you were."

I felt the blood drain from my face.

"What is it?" he asked quickly.

"Did we? Grant, did I hurt him this morning? The drugs...?"

"No. If anything, this morning's experience made the survivor stronger. Because of the contractions, he would have literally dug in for dear life. He is healthier today than this time yesterday. So, right now, his chances are better than if he had been alone."

"Grant," I whispered, wrapping my arms around his neck, "I'm still pregnant." All of the fear, pain, worry, and despair of the day disappeared, and my heart soared.

He looked at me for a long moment and kissed my forehead.

"Thank you for that."

"For still being pregnant?"

"Well, yes, but more importantly, for your joy at still being pregnant."

"Well, this pregnant lady is hungry, and you are taking your life in your hands by holding me so close, I might nibble you."

"I have more than just my life in my hands," he said, his face reflecting all the stress and concerns of the day. He started to kiss me but tilted his head and sighed.

Setting me gently on my feet, he asked, "Do you think you can shower by yourself, or will you need help?"

"Will you be the one helping me?"

"No," he smiled, "not this time, anyway. I have to get you some dinner, or I might need to fear for some of my appendages, but I can get a masseuse to assist you. Maybe I should do that anyway; you might slip."

He looked at me as if calculating every conceivable way I could hurt myself.

"Grant, I took a shower all alone this morning without any reason to be careful, and do you think," I said, echoing his words of a mere seventy-two hours ago, "I would risk endangering the most precious thing in the world to me? I promise you I will be fine. Just be back as soon as you can."

I pretended to be stern.

"Don't make me come looking for you," I said, putting my hand over my stomach. "I'm a war veteran, you know."

"Yes, ma'am," he said with a mock salute.

After seeing her safely in the shower, Grant left the room and quietly closed the door.

Filled with a sense of gratitude he had never known, he knelt on the carpet. Crossing his hands over his chest, he lowered his forehead to the floor.

Thank you, beloved mother of us all, for protecting her from those who command me and would wish her harm. Thank you, too, for letting me live long enough to witness the joy in her eyes. In my unworthiness, I only ask that you continue to watch over her and keep her safe.

And the boy.

Please…and the boy.

Blessings of Anya

Grant stood inside the doorway to Grayson's office.

"You wanted something, Grayson?"

"I was reviewing your report…fraternal twins?"

"Confirmed."

"Remains?"

"Incinerated according to protocol. Why do you ask, Grayson?"

"Rare."

"It is difficult to know what is 'rare' at this stage."

"Unusual, then, at any stage."

"Perhaps. Blessed Anya watches over our mothers."

"And you, apparently."

"She does not find me ungrateful."

"Carrie Taylor will be our guest now, I assume."

"As requested."

"Are you being, um, kinder to her?"

"As I said, Grayson, blessed Anya, mother of us all, does not find me ungrateful. I will be taking her to the rooms I have prepared for her this evening. I will persuade her to stay."

"I understand she has no home to return to, so that shouldn't be much of a challenge."

"She still has friends, family, and monetary resources. She could choose to leave, but she will not. She believes I saved her baby today because I listened to her, and she trusts me now more than ever. Her husband disavowing her only makes it easier for us to avoid legal entanglements, unwanted inquiries, and further impromptu visits."

"True. Well, you've had a roller-coaster day, Grant. Seeing your emission regarding her happiness at still being pregnant, little evident dismay at her husband's defection, and her total faith in you, I'd say it was a lucky day for you both."

"Grayson, as pleased as I am that Carrie remains pregnant, I am quite sure 'luck' had little to do with it. Anya, mother of us all, is gracious, and l bow to her limitless mercy."

"Very spiritual of you, Grant. Unusually so."

"I am not unmindful that we are tied to this life by silken threads that grow thinner each day. If today's events have shown me nothing else, it is how precious a beating heart can be. If I seek guidance in humble gratitude for the mercy of that single beating heart, I am sure my brothers will understand and do the same."

"Of course, you are right, and we will. Follow up tomorrow?"

"As promised."

"Confirmation at noon?"

"Before then."

"Good."

Grant turned to leave, then paused for a moment.

"Sleep well, Grayson, to you and my brothers."

"And, um, to you, too.

"I do not believe sleeping is going to be remotely possible."

"Maybe she won't want you to stay."

"Perhaps, but that does not work to our purpose. I cannot observe her if I am not there. She must want me to stay. I will leave her little choice. Patience and guidance, Grayson, one cannot pray for enough."

"Um, yes. Until tomorrow, Grant."

"Yes."

Grayson waited until Grant closed the door and tilted his head.

Gordon, Gabriel, I would like to meet with you in my office. Just the two of you.

Yes, Grayson, they answered simultaneously.

When the three brothers were assembled, Grayson closed the door and waved Grant's report of the day's events and the embryonic cell analysis in their direction.

"What do you think of this miscarriage of Carrie's? How possible is it for a single reconceived embryo to divide into fraternal twins? And, if this is not possible, how plausible is it for a set of fraternal twins to be reconceived if only one of them is in place at the time the serum and neutralizer is added?"

Gordon spoke first. "I think the likelihood of either of those scenarios is small, but this is the first time this version of the Reconception procedure has been utilized at this level. Therefore, we do not have clear evidence of what is and is not possible. Actually, I am not sure they were conceived as fraternal twins. Twinning can occur up to fourteen days after conception, and a single embryo can divide into separate encapsulations. Also, some sets of identical twins consist of stronger and weaker individuals regarding their physical and mental capabilities; they are not clones. I believe that, as individually capsulated hybrids, they may not have recognized each other, and the physically stronger twin destroyed the weaker one."

"And there are the percentages to consider," interjected Gabriel.

"What percentages?"

"The strength of the serum seems to have a shorter shelf life than originally anticipated. We've lost more than half of the embryos reconceived in the three sessions from Thursday afternoon to Friday afternoon. That percentage is significantly higher than the earlier sessions. In fact, it has become so noticeable that in the future, the serum will be distributed in smaller, biweekly deliveries. If there were anomalies, especially from Friday's procedures, I would suspect the serum itself rather than the relationship of the twins."

Gordon could see Grayson wasn't convinced. "What do you want to do, Grayson?"

"I want a full DNA test run on Carrie's remaining embryo."

Gordon paled. "But to do that, you would have to abort—"

"Yes."

Gabriel was horrified. "No! You can't. First, it violates our mandate; second, Grant will never agree; third, why would you destroy the child of the only mother who, at this point in time, truly wants one of our brothers? And fourth, you said yourself that we would not stop anyone's pregnancy."

"And," said Gordon, "you don't have cause. Killing a healthy brother to satisfy your curiosity is not cause, Grayson; it is blasphemy. Of course, we can always seek another opinion. Why don't we ask Grant how he feels about it?"

In the face of their opposition, Grayson quickly did the math. Gregory would side with Gordon, and Garrett would support Gabriel. As soon as Grayson realized he would most likely be standing alone, he swallowed quickly.

"No, that won't be necessary. Um, now that I know more about the um, percentages, and ah, other considerations, I realize that I was just being overly cautious. We don't have to mention any of this to Grant. He has enough on his plate as it is."

Willing to be gracious, Gordon said, "I agree. It is a trying time for all of us right now, and there is no reason to burden anyone with additional anxieties."

"Rightly so," added Gabriel.

They left Grayson in his office alone to consider how close he'd come to possible sanctions—or worse. As they walked down the hall, Gabriel smiled at Gordon and said, "I think Grayson owes you one."

"No, Grant does, but don't tell him. It would take less than two seconds for him to understand the full ramifications of Grayson's proposal. Then all hell would break loose in our small colony, and I mean that literally. I think I know what Grant is capable of, and no one, *no one*, Gabriel, neither child, mother, nor brother, would escape alive."

Gabriel nodded.

No one except her, he thought.

Hell

The shower washed away the evidence of the day's pain and despair. I said a prayer for the baby I lost but felt too blessed to mourn his death. Unable to go back and save him, I could only move forward and prepare for the one who still lived.

Stepping out of the shower, I realized I didn't have any clean clothes. I opened the cabinet and found several white terrycloth robes. Slipping into one, I walked out of the bathroom. The room was so dark I didn't see Grant sitting in a shadowy corner until the bathroom light glinted off his eyeglasses. I turned it off immediately.

"Grant?"

A spotlight above the bed illuminated a beautiful iridescent green silk kimono. I smiled in his direction. "How many dragonflies did you have to kill for this?"

"None," he answered. "When they heard it was for you, they insisted we take their wings as a gift."

I hesitated to remove my robe like I was on a stage, yet it would look silly to take the kimono and run back into the bathroom and turning my back to him just seemed rude.

"If you would like, Caroline, I will avert my eyes."

"All of them?"

"Well, most of them."

I turned and hung the terrycloth robe on the hook at the back of the door. Grant was standing next to me before I could lift the kimono from the bed.

"I'll help you with that. I should have hung it up so you wouldn't have to bend over." He wrapped the kimono around my body, smoothed the fold, and tied the sash at my back.

"Do you like it?"

"It's the loveliest thing I've ever worn."

"I hope you weren't too attached to the dress you wore today."

"Incinerated?"

"Yes."

"Thank you." I glanced around the room. "Where's my tea and toast?"

"Not here. I told you, we have to return this room to the spa."

"Your room?"

He thought of the room he shared with his brothers. Cool, dark, and quiet, it allowed them the peace they missed all day when they had to be in the light and noise. He would have liked to take her to one of the deep underground rooms, but she was human, and he would not risk frightening her.

"No, I share a room with my brothers. In fact," he said, "until recently, I never understood the desire to have a bedroom of one's own. It just seemed too lonely."

I nodded in agreement but remembered how a shared bedroom could be lonelier.

To change the subject, I touched the fabric of my robe. "Are we eating in your office? As lovely as that is, I may be a bit overdressed."

"No. I, you...we have a room. What I mean is, you have some rooms that I have designed for you, and, if it is your choice, I will stay with you...as your doctor, in case you need anything."

"Stay with me as my doctor? Is that the only reason you would stay, Grant?"

He sighed. "Caroline, I only want what is best for you. I'm not going to make any arrangements for me in your life that might stress you. It is all your choice."

It was a quiet ride in the elevator, and I wondered if he felt as nervous as I did. We had been alone in his office for a couple of weeks and together nearly every workday but going to my/our rooms was an entirely new level of intimacy. When the elevator stopped, he took my hand and led me to the end of a dimly lit hallway.

Grant paused in front of the last door.

"Do you trust me, Caroline?"

My heart in my throat, I could only nod.

He pressed three buttons on a keypad. There was a slight whirring sound and a click.

Standing to the side, he said, "I didn't know what colors you liked…so I chose them all."

I entered the room slowly. Like my gown, iridescent draperies caught and refracted pinpoints of light into every imaginable color against the pale gray walls. Enchanted by the countless misty rainbows surrounding me, I barely noticed when Grant closed the door to the world.

As my eyes adjusted to the low light, I realized he'd brought me to an apartment. With no sense of urgency, I ran my fingers over the white marble fireplace and walked around the low tables at each end of a gray velvet sofa. The fruit-filled crystal bowls cast even more color onto the counters and walls in the open kitchen. The delicate prisms of the chandelier in the small dining area swayed at my touch, and tiny lights behind sheer panels flickered like stars beyond the arched window frames.

I could not escape the feeling that I had slipped into a different dimension. I knew we had taken the elevator downward, but there was nothing familiar here that made me feel we were still in the facility.

Seeking a sense of direction, I saw a door ajar and gently pushed it open. Bathed in candlelight, I stood motionless in the doorway of the nursery. Grant took my hand, and we entered the room together. Decorated in shades of blue and white, I was immediately touched by the attention to detail and found charm in every corner of the room. I had not been able to speak since we arrived, but overcome by the beauty and, yes, love that was evident everywhere I looked, my eyes filled with tears.

"Grant," I whispered, "what did this room look like at noon today?"

He glanced down at my hand in his. "A small library," he said, "and I guess you would call it a…media room."

"And you had it arranged like this in the last two hours?"

"I asked that it be returned to the original design in the last hour and fifteen minutes."

"They must hate me," I said, smiling.

He looked at me seriously. "They adore you. If you asked them, they would demolish this entire apartment and rebuild it in half that time and think it was the best work they had ever done."

"I know. I'm sorry; I just don't want to inconvenience anyone."

"Impossible," he whispered into the palm of my hand.

His earnestness made me feel ashamed of my words. Trying to cover my embarrassment, I asked, "Is this a door?"

The recessed panel was door sized but fitted so snugly into the wall that I wasn't sure. Only the slightest shadow gave it away. It would have been invisible if the room had been brighter.

"Yes. Would you like to see what is on the other side?"

My heartbeat echoed in my ears. I knew what was behind that door. There was only one room I hadn't seen that would connect directly to the nursery.

"What is on the other side, Grant?" I asked gently.

"Dinner," he said smiling, "I thought you were hungry."

He pressed a lever beneath the wainscoting and once again stepped aside.

Nothing existent in light or color had prepared me for such beauty. I stepped cautiously into a realm of gossamer and silk feeling like a princess in a fantasy who was afraid a single breath would destroy the splendor of her world. Believing it was all an illusion, it wasn't until Grant came up behind me and held me in his arms that I knew everything I saw was real and was ours. The pain and sorrow of the day faded from my mind, and I looked up at Grant.

"This…this is the center of your labyrinth, isn't it, Grant?"

"Yes, Caroline."

He slipped on dark glasses as he walked back to the door. Moving the curtain away from the wall to expose a small panel of buttons, he demonstrated the gradient lighting system.

The sleeping area encompassing the right half of the room was the first to illuminate. Fairy lights tucked into a layered canopy of fine iridescent netting shone above an oval-shaped bed set into the curved recess. Large and small silk pillows of pale rainbow hues formed a luxurious headboard. A single opalescent sheet covered the mattress, and around the bottom was another silken rainbow of folded coverlets in different thicknesses. To the left of the bed was a pale blue bassinet covered with a square of white lace.

Pressing a second button, the lights over the bed dimmed, and the gray curtain across the room drew back. A shaded candle sconce lit the secluded alcove where a table curved in front of a low couch, and the scent of bitter honey filled the air. Silently, Grant took both of my hands in his and led me to the couch.

"Grant, I—"

"Shh, Caroline," he said. "Eat first, then we will talk."

He handed me a triangle of toast spread with the darkest honey I had ever seen. Like drinking brandy after watered wine, the taste was exquisite. I sipped the green tea slowly, letting the sweet warmth flow through my body. I thought I could live on tea and toast for the rest of my life until he lifted the cover from a dish of strawberries dipped in cream whipped with honey. Offering him a strawberry in return, he refused, saying they were just for me.

When I finished eating, he moved closer and said, "Are you cold, Caroline?"

"No. You are warm enough for both of us." I looked from Grant's face to the elegance surrounding us.

"Grant?"

"Yes."

"Who was this built for?"

"You."

"But you didn't know I would be living here until last Friday. That was only three days ago. I'm sure your construction guys are great, but they can't be miracle workers."

"Well, they can, but I had longer than that."

"How long?"

"Nearly two weeks. Plenty of time."

"You didn't know," I said slowly.

"I hoped."

"You built all this on hope?"

"And love, yes."

"Who lived here before?"

"There was no 'before.' I designed it for you."

"But why?"

"You gave yourself to me, Caroline, willingly, beautifully. I wanted to give you something that I hoped you would find almost as wondrous. So, in the tradition of my culture, I created a bower for you."

"You willingly, beautifully took me, you mean."

"Ah, Caroline, I distinctly remember hearing you say 'please,'" he said, smiling at the memory, "and 'thank you.'"

"I said 'thank you?'"

"Yes. You are very polite when you are dreaming."

"Speaking of dreaming, I'm getting sleepy."

"Yes."

"Yes?"

"That particular tea is a natural sedative. You've been through hell today, and rather than spend the night answering all the questions I see in your eyes, I wanted to make sure you and the baby would get some rest."

"You put the baby to sleep?"

"No, but when you are calmer, he is calmer. Are you able to walk to the bed, or shall I carry you?"

"Carry me, please."

"See, you are polite when you are dreaming."

"Am I still dreaming?"

"No, Caroline. Accept what I tell you now. No matter how it appears, nothing in your life has ever been as real as this moment."

Caroline put her arms around his neck. Holding her as close as possible, Grant walked to the opposite side of the room and sat down on the outer edge of the bed. Placing her gently in the center of the silken sheet, he watched as the interior of the mattress recessed, forming a shallow nest. Looking down at her, he could no longer pretend that they were not irreversibly connected. Her pain was his pain; her joy was his joy. The day that had begun as the worst nightmare of his life was ending, and the dream that had possessed him since the first moment he'd tasted the warm blush beneath her skin had finally come true. He had brought her home.

"Comfortable?"

"Oh, yes," she sighed.

"Kimono on or kimono off?"

"You decide."

Grant pulled one of the smaller pillows down for her and, leaving the robe on, loosened the sash at her back. He settled a coverlet over her and turned away.

She caught his hand.

"Where are you going?" she asked.

"To sleep on the couch."

"No. Stay with me. Please, Grant."

"Caroline, there is too much light in the room for me to sleep."

"Turn them off. Just leave a candle burning in the bathroom in case I have to find it."

"As you wish," he said.

Firmly closing the door to the nursery, he lit the candle in the bathroom as she asked and left the door slightly ajar. He pressed the buttons on the control panel until only the thinnest vertical edge of candlelight disturbed the blackness of the room.

With the anticipation of an architect finally being allowed to view his creation after a lifetime of staring at blueprints, Grant turned his back to the light and removed his glasses. A world she would never see appeared in the darkness as colors swirled and shimmered around her. It was a true bower. The white oval shape exactly replicated the smaller one growing in her body, and, just as that little heartbeat was protected by layers of delicate flesh, her sleeping form was veiled by a bioluminescent canopy that flowed like tiny stars to the carpeted floor.

As he was consistently overwhelmed by her perfection in every other way, he forgave her this little bit of human blindness. Then, picking up the lightest of the coverlets at the bottom edge of the bed for himself, he noticed her kimono neatly folded there.

Perhaps she was not so blind after all.

Touching the silk with the tips of his fingers, Grant smiled at the apparent limitless depth of her generosity and trust.

Hoping to be worthy of it someday, he moved the open jar of honey closer to the bed and began unbuttoning his shirt.

Acknowledgments

Few authors owe as much to their publisher as I do, and I would like to begin by expressing my gratitude to Liminal Books and Between the Lines Publishing and their team of wonderful, hard-working members: Abby Macenka, Deborah Alix, Liz Hurst, Jace Martell, my editor, Penny Dowden, Amber Soha, and Suzanne Johnson, as well as their marketing and design experts. Thank you for your faith, kindness, and guidance.

I also want to thank my family and friends for being so patient as I mulled over plot twists, practiced dialog, and spent hours researching human history (sorry about all the take-out). I also want to thank Dustin Boyed for keeping my computer up and running and my wonderful readers, Lindsey Hoefert, Ricki Huff, and Emilee Valken. I would never have come this far without you.

As ever, thank you, Jim, for your wisdom and unfailing insight into my writing soul. *Je t'aimerai toujours.*

When PJ isn't writing about aliens negotiating the labyrinth of human love while trying to save the planet, you will find her sipping sangria under the umbrella on the sundeck with her rescue corgi, Nymeria.

Learn more about PJ, *Finding Persephone*, and the legacy of The Fire Slayers at PJBraley.com or follow her on X (formerly known as Twitter) at @pjbraley.